The
Impetus Turn

Martin Lloyd

Queen Anne's Fan

First published in 2017 by Queen Anne's Fan
PO Box 883 • Canterbury • Kent CT1 3WJ

ISBN 9780 9573 639 5 3

A CIP record of this book can be obtained from the British Library.

Set in New Baskerville 11pt.

www.queenannesfan.com

...and the impetus turn which can be used to add grace and style to an abrupt change of direction.
(Ballroom Dancing Yearbook)

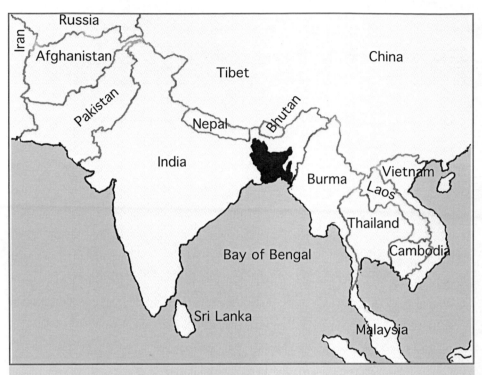

BANGLADESH marked in black.

BANGLADESH

At the partition of India in 1947, the former state of Bengal became East Pakistan. In 1971, the Awami League Party gained a majority at the Pakistan general election and declared their desire that East Pakistan should become independent. A civil war was fought and in December 1971, East Pakistan became the independent state, Bangladesh, almost entirely surrounded by India except for a short border with Burma in the south east

In the 1980s the population of Bangladesh was approximately 90m. on a surface area of 55,598 sq. miles. The UK was 56m. on 89,000 sq. miles. Topographically, Bangladesh consists of the largest river delta on earth formed by the rivers Ganges, Brahmaputra and Meghna depositing their silt on reaching the Bay of Bengal. Most of Bangladesh is less than forty feet above sea level and it is one of the poorest countries in the world.

The English call a single storey house, a 'bungalow', from the native description, *Bengali*.

1

Monday afternoon. Dhaka, Bangladesh.

Later that afternoon, Raymond Line would kill three people.
Brutally.
But just now, he was in a hurry.
His fingers tapped impatiently on the steering wheel as he forced his Land Rover into the seething traffic. Humming loudly, he sped past the sterile glass and chrome bubble of the Hotel Sonargaon. Through downtown Dhaka he drove, where bright yellow baby-taxis laid serpents of toxic blue smoke behind them as they lurched around the cycle rickshaws.

He spat through the open window. He gritted his teeth, but still the dust clawed at the back of his throat.

'Sod this for a game of soldiers!' he muttered and swerved out behind a distorted and dented lorry. He clung to its tailgate as, whistling and hooting, the truck cut a murderous swathe through the street. 'Thank Christ I don't live downtown among the bogwits!'

Banani Model Town. Gulshan Model Town. The only two addresses if you were European or rich. The white man's ghetto in Dhaka. They lay to the north of the city, linked like Siamese twins by the causeway across the swamp. His company house was in Banani.

He ignored the red light as everybody did and, with heavy tyres whining their protest, he veered off towards the roundabout called DIT 2. On the dais in the middle of the crossroads, the Bangladeshi policeman watched him impassively.

Line thought about his next appointment. He could already see the chowkidhar swinging open the gate and saluting him behind a salacious grin. Christine would be standing at the bookshelf with her back turned. She would try not to giggle as she said, 'I'm sorry Mr. Line but my husband won't be back until very late,' whilst he slipped his hands under her cotton shift. Then she would shiver and dismiss her doe-eyed Bengali maid who would be standing there with her mouth hanging open.

A lorry unloading cement blocked the road to Christine Boniface's house so Line parked in Gulshan Avenue under the meagre shade of a tree and walked down to the house. The chowkidhar was arguing noisily over the adjoining wall. Line rattled the gate to attract his attention.

'Here saheb, here saheb.' The man scuttled down and scurried to the gate, hauling his lunghi up into his crotch as he did so.

'Madam in?' Line asked. His heart was beginning to pound with anticipation. The chowkidhar rolled his eyes and grinned. 'I suppose that means yes,' Line muttered as he went into the house. 'Anybody home?' There was no noise except the rattling of the occasional rickshaw and the grunting of the day-workers unloading bags of cement out in the street. 'Christine?'

He cocked an ear to the gloomy interior. Somewhere he could hear wavering, the hissing and thrumming of running water. He poked his head around the kitchen door. No-one there. She must have sent the maid away already.

Then a slow, secret smile spread over his face. 'What's the game this time?' he wondered. 'Not hide and seek again?' Last time he had found her in the godown, wrapped in a net curtain and nothing else. What was it to be today?

He crept stealthily down the corridor until he reached the carved wooden elephant guarding the bedroom door. There, the sound of running water was loudest. She was in the shower. He stood, imagining the water falling sinuously from her hair. He squeezed off his canvas shoes and hung them on the tusks of the elephant. The thought of her made his groin stir. Christine with her face turned uppermost, her back arched, offering her breasts to the fumbling and fondling attention of the water. He pulled off his shirt, draped it over the elephant and slipped into the bedroom with a culpable familiarity.

As they rested naked on the bed, Christine suddenly asked, 'What was that?' She tried to pull herself up.

'What was what?' Line continued to nibble her ear.

She shook him off. 'No stop it. Listen, I thought I heard the...' They listened to the squeaking of the gate. 'Someone's coming in.'

'Ah, pretend you're not at home.'

An engine roared as a car pulled into the garden.

'It's Anthony!' She shook Line madly. 'He's back!'

'Shit!' Line leapt from the bed. 'I thought you said that he'd be–'

'Where are your clothes? Quick!'

'Shit!' he exclaimed again as he remembered the elephant.

'For Christ's sake hurry!'

He pulled his shirt over his head and as he yanked on his trousers, they heard the outside door bang.

'I'm home Christine,' Anthony Boniface's voice called from the corridor. 'Where are you?'

She pushed Line back into the bathroom. 'I'm in the bedroom darling,' she called out, disguising her panic as she frantically straightened out the bed and kicked the rugs flat. 'Get me a vodka and lime please darling. Vodka's in the freezer in the godown.'

'Will do!' He retreated up the corridor.

She pulled open the bathroom door and then rushed back and opened the bedroom window. 'Quick! Out of the window.'

Line stumbled halfway across the bedroom, fastening his trousers and gripping his shoes in his teeth. Then he stopped.

'There are bars on it you stupid cow!' he whispered through clenched teeth.

'Oh God! He's coming back. Back into the bathroom!' She pushed him through the doorway. 'Out through the kitchen!' She hurried to the centre of the room and composed herself.

'Good Lord, darling, are you trying to frighten the locals, standing there starkers with the window open?'

'I was just... er... letting out a chit-chat. You know I can't bear to kill them.'

Anthony Boniface handed her the glass and pulled the window shut.

'Trouble is...' he said, 'you let one chit-chat out and a hundred skeeters in.'

As soon as he heard the window bang, Line tiptoed swiftly across the corridor and into the kitchen. He pushed through the screen door into the sunlight. He roughly pulled on his shoes, ducked below the windows and ran around to the front of the house. Without waiting for the chowkidhar to open the gate, he leapt onto the boot of the parked car and from there, vaulted over the wall into the street. Thank God he had not been able to park outside. His Land Rover would have given him away!

Ignoring the stares of the natives he sprinted up to Gulshan Avenue. There he found with dismay that his Land Rover was no longer in shadow but simmering in the blazing afternoon sun.

The steering wheel was like a hot frying pan as he jiggled the van down Gulshan Avenue.

'You stupid bogwits! Get out of my way! he yelled as he forced a motor-bike and a cyclist into an involuntary embrace. 'Idiots!' He watched them in the mirror as they fell over.

He puffed the air out from his cheeks. 'Line, me ol' man, you nearly got caught red-handed there. You'd better be more careful in future. Yeah, more careful.'

With one hand he tugged at his collar to straighten it and flicked his hair into a semblance of order. He was nearly at the roundabout at DIT 2 so he blew his horn, double-declutched into third and put his foot hard down on the accelerator. He looked at his watch. Should be home in five minutes. He looked up. Wobbling across in front of him was a rickshaw carrying a Bangladeshi family. Seeing the van approaching, the rickshaw puller merely waved his hand to indicate that Line should pass behind him.

'Sod that, Ahmed! I'm bigger than you.' Line wrenched the wheel around and the rickshaw calmly turned into his path with a fatalism born of Islam. For a fleeting second he saw the horror on the faces of the Bangladeshis, then with a crunch and a lurch, the Land Rover flattened the cockleshell of painted steel and Line ducked as a surprised brown baby tumbled along the bonnet towards him.

Tuesday Morning. London, England.

'Why the hell did he stop?' Cockcroft yelled. Gibson nervously chewed his finger nail. He wasn't certain if the question required a reply. The eyes bored into him from the other side of the desk. 'Well?'

'I did say, Mr. Cockcroft, er... sir, that he hit a tricycle rickshaw.' Cockcroft's eyebrows drew together like a stage curtain at the interval. Gibson added, 'A tricycle rickshaw is like a normal rickshaw, sir – two back wheels with a seat over them and a bicycle frame bolted to the front. The puller just rides the bike.'

'I know what a tri-shaw is, Mr. Gibson.' He insisted upon the title 'Mister'. 'Didn't Line have enough sense to know that you don't stop after you've hit one? Especially if you've killed a wog!' he bellowed back.

'Three, actually sir... but the baby came through the windscreen.'

'Didn't he throw it out again?'

'Well he did sir, but he... well he had a job to find it you see sir. He'd got a bit of equipment in the back of the van and he had to climb over the seat to get it and ... er... in any case, the rickshaw was jammed under the front wheels...'

'I assume that it wasn't his fault. Not speeding or anything?'

'Oh no sir, the report from the Foreign Office exonerates him on that.

Apparently these rickshaw wallahs just shoot out of side streets straight into your path.'

'But he stopped! The imbecile! And what happened? He nearly got lynched by the crowd, he lost our surveying equipment to some light-fingered sooty and we got reps to our High Commissioner to have him removed for his own safety! When is he due back?'

'About three weeks'

'Three weeks!'

'He's coming back via Hong-Kong. Medical convalescence sir.'

'Medical convalescence, my arse!'

'Yes sir.'

'Where are the project files?'

Gibson handed to his director the two files that he had been hugging to his chest in an attempt to protect himself from the barrage.

'Shall I go sir?'

Arthur Cockcroft shot Gibson a glance that conveyed concisely and forcefully his wishes. For the pleasure of seeing the worm squirm, he added, 'Sit there Mr. Gibson until I need you.' Gibson would not have moved even if his chair had suddenly immolated itself through spontaneous combustion.

Cockcroft leafed quickly through the sheets, draft contracts, geological surveys, land-use charts, equipment estimates – everything relating to the Bangladesh Gas Pipeline contract.

'Who did this estimate?' He slid a sheet across to Gibson.

'Uh... that was Clement sir.'

'Where is he?'

'The Gambia, sir.'

Cockcroft grunted.

'Another two years to go,' Gibson added unnecessarily. They would not contemplate pulling back an engineer from the Gambia, the French were pressing them far too close for comfort in West Africa.

'Who's the fellow who did the anchors for the Chindwin bridge?'

'Marshall?'

'Yes Marshall, where the devil is he?'

'He is attached to NATO sir. Bunker technology.'

'Can't we get him back?'

'We could...' Gibson began. If they withdrew Marshall from Belgium they would lose the foot in the door of a good defence contract.

'No, he's more use where he is,' Cockcroft concluded. 'Whose is this route projection?'

Gibson glanced at it and the essence of an ironic smile danced around the corners of his thin lips.

'That's our Mr. Wrighton, the evangelist.'

Cockcroft raised his eyebrows. 'Bit of a Bible-basher is he? Well, I've known worse. What's he like as an engineer?'

'I wouldn't say he was a Bible-basher, sir. I believe his family is a bit strict. He is a non-smoking, non-drinker.'

'Does he screw?'

'Ah...um...'

'Forget it. What does he know about this contract?'

'Well, he was in at the beginning. Did quite a few of the projections. He's quite good with figures. No good with people. Not what you would call a natural leader. His progress assessments should be in the back of the file. But I wouldn't–'

'You were saying, Mr. Gibson – you wouldn't what, exactly?'

Gibson wriggled on his seat, opened his mouth, but no sound escaped. Cockcroft silently acknowledged his surrender with a wave of his hand and turned back to the file. Gibson settled back into his chair and waited. The anxiety generated by the possibility that the director might send Wrighton out to Bangladesh had brought him to the edge of his chair in mute remonstration. Cockcroft threw a teasing look over the top of the file, and then returned to his reading.

Gibson examined Cockcroft's feet under the desk. The hand-fashioned leather on his shoes contrasted strangely with the cheap socks. Presently, Cockcroft put down the file and scratched his armpit.

'Wrighton thinks we underquoted by about thirteen percent on the initial tender.'

'Err...' Gibson cleared his throat. 'Yes, that's right sir. His assessment was sent up to Finance who took it into account.'

'But didn't alter the price?'

'No sir.'

'Do engineers normally tackle the Finance Department over their tenders, Mr. Gibson?' The question was proposed rather than posed.

'No sir, they do not.' Gibson sensed victory. The sort of man who would question something outside his discipline with such assurance was obviously not the sort of engineer to be sent out to Bangladesh. Cockcroft flipped a button on his intercom.

'Sam?'

'Yes Mr. Cockcroft?' a woman's voice muffled back at him.

'Get me the personnel file on...' He turned to Gibson who was sitting rigidly in his chair, flames licking around the seat. 'Well, Mr. Gibson...? Gibson looked confused, unsure what was required of him. 'What is his full name?' Cockcroft sighed.

'Wrighton, sir, Stewart Wrighton.'

'Get me the personnel file on Stewart Wrighton, engineer. Now Sam.'

'Yes Mr. Cockcroft.'

'Go and get Wrighton.'

Gibson swallowed his saliva, got up and walked out.

Stewart Wrighton possessed only one physical characteristic of note. It was not his hair, which was a nondescript brown. It was not his figure, which was slim but without the tautness of an athlete. It was not his bearing, which tended towards the slight stoop that many tall people adopt in an attempt to make themselves inconspicuous. Nor was he endowed with a particularly striking profile – his cheeks were shallow, his nose, unremarkable and his mouth merged imperceptibly into his chin. The one notable attribute, the subtle aspect that sooner or later singled him out, was his eyes. Although partly hidden behind his spectacles, those hazel brown eyes were a perpetual danger to him because he was ignorant of their effect on others. They normally effused a calm reassurance, a warm encouragement, but if looked at too deeply, there could be discerned within them an aura which rendered tenderness more intense, and on very rare occasions, anger more violent.

Wrighton just thought of them as eyes.

He bent to his calculator again. He was finding it difficult to concentrate. Something was amiss in the office this morning. He looked around. Everybody was unaccountably busy except for that clown Chard and his side-kick. They were giggling behind their drawing boards like a couple of schoolgirls at the bus stop. Then there was Gibson asking about the files for Bangladesh and not telling him why but bolting back inside the director's office with them.

Wrighton gazed at the wooden door to Cockcroft's office and thought about Bangladesh. At that moment a gawky office junior wandered past, carrying a tray of plastic beakers.

'Liz. How did the gymkhana go on Saturday?'

Liz put down the tray and bit her top lip. She flicked her long hair away from her face and then leaned forward so that it fell back again.

'It was awful, Mr. Wrighton. I looked a right berk!' she said and then looked about her, self consciously. Wrighton took a cup from the tray and sniffed it like a cat at a hedgehog. 'I thought I would do all right in the dressage, then all them toffs turned up in their Lambourns and–'

'What's a Lambourn?'

'A big horse-box, a luxury job. Polished wood and all that. Very posh.'

'Posher than yours, then?'

The girl grinned warily. 'You taking the piss Mr. Wrighton? I haven't got a horse box. I ride Lucy to the shows. She got all muddy and–'

'Do you enter for these shows in order to win or just for a bit of fun?'

'It's good fun but I wouldn't mind winning somethink.'

'Well you must try to concentrate on something that they don't do.'

'They don't jump much. They're terrified of laming their mounts on a fence. Stops them from hunting, see?'

'Can Lucy jump?'

'Yeah, she's good at that. Pr'aps I'll have a go at the jumping next time,' she said brightly.

A plumpish middle-aged woman bustled over to them from the stairwell. 'Urgent message from Sam...' she began in a conspiratorial tone. Wrighton was puzzled. Sam was Cockcroft's secretary. He had hardly ever spoken to her except in the lift. '...the Gaffer has just asked for your personnel file and–' She stopped as the director's office door opened and Gibson announced in a clear voice, 'Mr. Wrighton! Mr. Cockcroft wishes to see you.'

Wrighton went cold inside. Gibson and Cockcroft, his personnel file and the file on Bangladesh all gathered together in the same room could only mean one thing – something had gone wrong and a scapegoat was needed. He walked across the office to the wooden door. Not a head turned. Of course, they had all known long before him, as usual. He grinned bitterly to himself. He was always the last person to know anything in this office. If he didn't drink with them at lunch time or go for a 'swift half' before catching the train in the evening, then he was excluded from the newsround as efficiently as a whiskerless crystal set.

He could count on the fingers of one hand the number of times that he had been in Cockcroft's room. When he had first started, fifteen years ago, he had been made to stand before the desk rather like a soldier at a court martial. A black-haired, thick set man had gruffly welcomed him to the firm, telling him that if he worked hard and kept his nose clean he would do well and be looked after. Three weeks after that he had been marched in and bellowed at before the open door so that the entire office could savour his reprimand.

'Mr. Wrighton!' Cockcroft had boomed, 'your qualifications say that you are an engineer and as yet you have to prove that to us. In the meantime you will dress like an engineer and not like a navvy. Go and put your tie on!'

Wrighton steeled himself as Gibson closed the door noiselessly behind them. 'At least this time it will be private,' he thought grimly. He was comforted to notice that Cockcroft had a bald patch appearing through his black hair like the area of a football pitch before the goal mouth.

'Sit down, Mr. Wrighton.' Cockcroft indicated a chair. Gibson oozed into the corner and perched on a bookcase. 'For God's sake sit down Mr. Gibson... on a chair. You surely know about unstable equilibrium.'

Wrighton grinned at the esoteric joke. Gibson blushed. Cockcroft smoothed down the papers on his desk with the palms of his hands.

'Mr. Wrighton, you did the prep. for the Bangladesh Gas Pipeline contract.'

He was right! Something had gone wrong in Bangladesh.

'Yes sir, with Mr. Clement.'

'Yes.' Cockcroft slid two sheets of paper across the table at him and without looking Wrighton knew that they would be his observations on the tender price. He had been a fool to insist that they be kept on file. What a pig-headed idiot he was, sticking his nose in where it was not wanted! Well now he was going to pay for it. 'This er.... appreciation of the initial tender price Mr. Wrighton, says that we underpriced by thirteen per cent.'

Wrighton cleared his throat but the voice still sounded clotted, 'Hm...Yes, that's correct sir.'

'Is it? Is it correct Mr. Wrighton?'

'I believed it to be correct at the time sir.'

'Did you tell Finance?'

'Oh yes sir. I circulated it to the Sub-Continent section.'

Cockcroft grinned sardonically. He could imagine what Pritchard in Finance would think of one of Cockcroft's engineers questioning their business acumen.

'Did that make you friends with the Finance Department?'

'No sir, it did not. They were very cool towards me.' He relaxed a little. 'But if you want me to withdraw it I can do so sir.'

Cockcroft theatrically raised his eyebrows. Now he would see how much Wrighton believed in himself.

'Why should you withdraw it, Mr. Wrighton? Do you believe it to be untrue or inaccurate?' What was Wrighton supposed to say? If he agreed that it was inaccurate then he had not done his job properly; if he maintained its accuracy then he would have to justify it and he quite simply did not have access to the figures now. 'Well, Mr. Wrighton, do you wish to withdraw it?' Cockcroft's eyes were twinkling. He was enjoying the manoeuvres.

'No sir, I do not.' Well, he had said it and now they could do what they liked.

'Tell me, Mr. Wrighton,' Cockroft smiled and then continued with a gentle irony hardening his voice, 'why do you, an engineer, think that you know more than the Finance Department when it comes to pricing contracts?'

'I think nothing of the sort, sir. The criticisms I made were of a slight order–'

'Thirteen percent?' interrupted Cockcroft.

'That is the figure, sir, not the criticism.'

Good point, thought Cockcroft, I fell for that one.

'I thought... I still do think that I have identified factors that they perhaps had not fully considered and so I brought them to their attention. In no way do I pretend that I could do their job because, as you said sir, I am an engineer.' Another point scored. Cockcroft was very loath to call anybody in the firm, an 'engineer' until they had proved themselves worthy of the soubriquet. This Wrighton fellow, once cornered, showed a bit of spirit and wit. A sight more than that old turtle, Gibson. 'As an engineer sir, if Finance came to me and said that I had costed an operation incorrectly I would investigate their claim. He looked Cockcroft directly in the eye. 'I do not mind admitting when I am wrong.'

Cockcroft stirred. 'And are you?'

'I don't think so sir.'

'Explain.'

'The profit on the contract will be made in dollars but it will be shown on the balance sheet in sterling. I believe that the pound is becoming stronger against the dollar which will effectively devalue our profit.'

'On what do you base your conviction that the dollar will fall?'

'It's just a feeling that I have,' he admitted lamely.

'And you think that your 'feeling' should be believed in preference to two separate independent economic forecasts that they worked from?'

'And there is the steel problem sir.'

Cockcroft sat forward slightly. He knew nothing of the steel problem. 'Go on.'

'Well sir, under the terms of the U.N. contract, the World Bank will only finance if we source our steel from outside Europe. Now Bangladesh, as you know, produces no steel at all so the obvious place for us to buy the pipe, and rod–'

'Rod?'

'We need steel rod for the pipe stays, sir, crossing culverts, under bridges and that sort of thing.' Cockcroft nodded. 'The obvious place for us to buy steel is India, but we can't.'

'Why not?' Cockcroft found himself asking.

'Political reasons sir. The Bangladesh Government will not trade with India. The customs tariffs are astronomical. The only steel goods that cross the border are contraband. No, we will have to buy the steel in Bangladesh itself.'

'But you said that they don't produce any.'

'They don't, but the Chinese are trying for the big road bridge contract over the Meghna river in Dhaka under the auspices of the Asia Development Bank. They will be providing the steel from their mills for the bridge but within that package is a commitment to provide various quotas of commercial grade and format steel for the market and that is where we will have to buy. We can't go direct to the Chinese, they will just laugh in our faces. So we will buy in taka, that's Bangladesh currency, from an uncertain source of supply. It will be fragmented, it will cost us time and money. That is why the contract will cost us more.'

Cockcroft sat silently for a moment. Wrighton seemed to know what he was talking about. Why hadn't Wrighton been sent out to Bangladesh instead of Line? Gibson would have to explain that. Wrighton watched Cockcroft closely, trying not to let his anxiety show. He had really put his neck out but if it was a matter of keeping his job, then he had been forced to do it. Deep down he did believe that he was right in his calculations however much Cockcroft could make them look spurious.

'Mr. Wrighton,' Cockcroft began, 'how long have you been with us now?' He slid open Wrighton's personnel file.

'Fourteen or fifteen years, sir.'

'Ah yes... and you resisted the proposal that you should move to the Leicester office when it opened eight years ago, I see.'

Wrighton remembered perfectly. He had wanted to go, to get away from London, a change of air but Marion had just given birth to their first child and in the confusion of post-natal depression he had been made to understand that if he went to Leicester he would rusticate in solitude. She was not leaving Wembley and her mother.

'Yes, that's right sir, er... it was a little difficult at the time, with just starting a family and all that.'

'Oh, you have children?' Cockcroft said in a tone which was intended to be solicitous but merely sounded incredulous.

'Yes sir, two boys, one, eight; one, six.'

'And let me see, what overseas postings have you done?'

Wrighton felt the coldness creeping back into his stomach. Cockcroft knew very well that Wrighton had never served abroad. They had made a sort of agreement that he would not be sent because his wife would never countenance it. Nothing had ever been written down but it was tacit and Wrighton realised belatedly, very vulnerable.

'I've never been abroad sir, but if you remember–'

'Never been abroad, Mr. Wrighton? Fifteen years in the firm and never served overseas? We must remedy that,' Cockcroft proposed with a threatening amiability. 'Sam?' he spoke into his intercom, 'have you got that other information for me?'

'Yes Mr. Cockcroft.'

'Bring it in then please.' Samantha whisped in to the office and placed a sheet of paper on the desk beside Mr. Cockcroft. 'It seems to me, Mr. Wrighton, that you are the right person to take over the assistant project engineer job in Bangladesh.'

Wrighton opened his mouth and then shut it. Surely there was someone out there already?

'What about Raymond Line? I thought he was out there.'

'He was... but not any more.'

So that was it. Ray Line had been pulled back from Bangladesh. He wondered why. 'Why has he come off the contract?'

'He killed three Banglas. Oh it was their fault of course, but the MFA – the Ministry of Foreign Affairs – got on to the British High Commission in Dhaka and had him sent home.'

'Why did he kill them?' Wrighton was flabbergasted. He had known Ray Line was a bit of a live wire but had never thought of him as homicidal.

'He ran over their rickshaw in his Land Rover. Terrible mess. Land Rover – three; rickshaw – nil, as you might say. It happens. Life is bloody cheap out there.'

Wrighton shuddered.

'But why do you want me to go out? I mean I can't... I've got a wife and family. They can't live out there.'

'Exactly. You will go out on bachelor status.'

'Bachelor status? How long for?'

'Minimum six months. Same conditions as Line.'

'That's not right sir, Line was getting a divorce. They hadn't lived together for a couple of years. It suited him to go out there on his own.

I can't leave my family for six months.'

'Well, Consolidated won't pay to take them there or house them.'

'No, I mean I can't go. Marion would never allow it.'

Cockcroft looked at Wrighton and then slowly held up a folded sheet of paper.

'You have a copy of this I believe, Mr. Wrighton?' Wrighton miserably recognised his contract. 'I asked you if you had a copy of your contract, Mr. Wrighton?'

'Yes sir, I have.'

'I would refer you to clause five which states that–'

'I know sir, it's the clause which says that I will work abroad in any country that I am contracted to.'

'You know these conditions?'

'Yes sir'

'You realise that you have been on standby allowance for fifteen years?'

'Yes sir, but that's not fair, it's just a gimmick to enhance my salary. You said so yourself sir.'

'You must have misunderstood me, Mr. Wrighton,' he referred ostentatiously to the file, 'there is nothing here to say that you were special and were to be paid to be ready to serve abroad without actually having to pack your bags.'

'No sir.'

'Of course, if you wish to renegotiate your contract on that basis... I'm sure I could get your friends,' he insisted slightly upon this word, 'in Finance to calculate how much money you owe us for the last fifteen years' allowance. With interest, of course.' He smiled again, like a crocodile at a canoe. 'Do you wish that?'

Wrighton knew he was beaten. It had been spelled out to him – either go to Bangladesh or take the consequences. He had no illusions as to his future in the company if he did not agree. With some comfort he realised that he would be given two months preparation time which would take him well into mid-December and with a bit of luck he could delay his departure until after the Christmas holidays so that at least they had Christmas together as a family. What would Marion say? He dreaded that. He had no fears for the family whilst he was away. She was capable, very capable, but she would not like it.

'No, I don't wish to renegotiate my contract, I'll go sir.'

'I thought you might,' he said and referred to the sheet of paper that Samantha had brought in. 'You can actually choose which airline you want to fly on. Now, that's a luxury with this firm.' Wrighton was not really paying attention. He would have plenty of time to think about airlines. '...Gulf Air on Wednesday, British Airways on Thursday and Bangladesh Biman on Friday or Sunday. I would go British Airways if I were you.'

Wrighton dragged his mind back to the present.

'Can we discuss that later, nearer the date sir? I'm sure you will realise that I have a lot of things to do before then.' He allowed himself a little sarcasm. He thought he could be permitted that.

'I'm not talking about the date, but about the day. You are going out next week. You can either go on Wednesday, Thursday, Friday or Sunday.'

Wrighton thought for the minute that he had not heard correctly.

'Do you mean next week?'

'Yes, unless you can manage this week.'

After fifteen years in London HQ, they suddenly wanted him in Bangladesh at eight days' notice. Wrighton's indignation quickly turned to a barely controlled anger. He stood up abruptly and leaning over the desk, pointed his finger aggressively at Cockcroft's nose.

'Thursday of next week will do me fine, Mr. Cockcroft. But you had better be ready because I will.' He turned around and strode out of the office leaving the door open.

Cockcroft recovered his composure quickly.

'Shut the door behind you Mr. Gibson.'

Wrighton came out of Cockcroft's office like a cannon-ball. Gibson flapped after him like a discarded newspaper in a windy street.

'I'm sorry Wrighton, I didn't know–'

'Thanks for your support, Gibson!' Wrighton shouted back at him. The typists stopped. They had never heard Wrighton shout. No-one had. 'You didn't even blow your nose for me.'

Wrighton zig-zagged through the patio of drawing boards to his desk. In a blur of peripheral vision he sensed that people were turning, pens were being laid down, keyboards ignored, telephones unattended. Gibson scuttled along in his wake.

'If there's anything I can do...' he proposed lamely.

Wrighton scowled at him and began to empty his desk drawers into his attache case.

'Yes, you can take over my desk for me... just in case I come back.' The last phrase rang around the office to the gentle sibilant accompaniment of the air conditioning and the distant warbling of an unanswered telephone.

'Look, Wrighton, don't take it like that. I couldn't know–'

Wrighton snapped shut his case and pulled his overcoat from the stand by the wall. A sea of faces watched as he walked to the open lift. As the doors closed, Gibson disappeared in a flurry of typists, draughtsmen and others, all demanding to know what had happened and why. Unseen, Cockcroft gazed benignly at the confusion from his doorway. Gibson's protestations floated over to him, the half-empty office magnifying their inanity,

'No, he's not been sacked... No he didn't have much choice... Well I couldn't help him... I know he is, we all do...'

'Gibson's a fool!' Cockcroft grunted to himself. 'Wrighton not a leader of men? Bollocks!' Then he quietly shut the office door on the besieged Gibson. 'I think our Mr. Wrighton might come up with the goods. He needs watching. He could be good entertainment.' He squashed a fat finger onto the intercom key.

'Sam?'

'Yes Mr. Cockcroft?'

'Lunch, ten minutes, at the grill.'

'Thank you Mr. Cockcroft.'

'You're not going!'

'Look, Marion, try and see sense–'

'Try and see sense? That's a good one, coming from you!'

'Marion. I had no choice.'

'They'll just have to send someone else. You're not going.'

'There is no one else... Anyway it's in my contract.'

'It's always been in your contract but you said that you had an agreement with Cockcroft that you would never be sent abroad. Well? Didn't you?'

'Yes but–'

'So what's happened to the agreement then? He just tears it up when he wants to?'

'Well nothing was ever written down. It was more a sort of understanding.'

'Sounds more like a misunderstanding to me. You never stick up for yourself... or us. You let people walk right over you. Well this time it's going to stop. You're not going and that's final.'

'We had better put the house on the market then,' Wrighton said quietly as he began to clear the dinner dishes from the table.

The argument had raged most of the mealtime. He had told her only after the children had gone to bed. How he had kept it within himself he did not know, but he had.

'Put the house on the market? Why?'

Wrighton laughed shortly.

'When I am unemployed, we won't be able to pay the mortgage.'

'Don't be silly.' Marion was frightened.

'Well your tuppence-halfpenny doesn't keep us rolling in caviare does it?'

'What I earn from my knitting I put into the housekeeping. It all helps. Most women in my position wouldn't have to work.'

'You don't have to.'

'And what about shoes for the children? Who pays for those? Where do you think the money comes from?'

'Look, Marion, this is getting us nowhere. It's just a waste of time. I've... we've both got to get loads of things sorted out and we only have eight days to do it in.'

Marion slapped down a plate and prowled around the table like a panther, her eyes narrowing. 'You want to go, don't you?' she accused him. 'You can't wait to get away from your wife and family for six months can you? Well...' she picked up the plate again and slammed it down onto the table, 'you might as well get to know what it's like without a wife as from now!'

She stormed past him into the hallway. Wrighton looked at the shattered crockery and then without turning, called out, 'Where are you going?'

He knew the answer.

'I'm going to see mother.'

The door slammed.

'Going to see mother.' Whenever there was a crisis she went to see mother. Then mother mediated, always on the side of her daughter and Wrighton concurred with the decisions.

He dropped into the armchair and realised that he was still wearing his shoes. He prised them off by the heels without undoing the laces. It was a crime for which he was always admonishing the boys. 'I suppose I had better get some sandals,' he thought.

Why had he said spiteful things about her knitting? Why did she push him into a corner? He cocked an ear, one of the boys was mumbling in his sleep. How would they take his absence? Tolerably well, he thought. They were young and would soon get over it. With a shock he realised that he was planning and preparing upon the basis that he would go out to

Bangladesh, despite everything.

He remembered her narrowed eyes and the accusation, 'You want to go don't you?' And he admitted to himself that he did. He wanted more than anything else in the world to see whether he could live without his family for six months, survive in the subcontinent without getting diseased and manage to do the job that he had been sent out to do. He had no fears for his family, they were safe in a semi in Wembley. They had each other. Mother was nearby. He feared for himself. He did not know whether he could do it. He was frightened but not like Marion, not frightened because of a threat to his manner of living; he was frightened by the unknown enormity of it all.

He slowly made himself a cup of tea, his body mechanical, his mind elsewhere, then he paused, teapot in hand. 'I suppose this tea could have come from Bangladesh,' he thought.

Sitting in the armchair, before the gas fire, he let his eyes rove around the room; the chocolate brown carpet with the hideous red and yellow flowers on it, the corduroy covered sofa, the knitting machine on its table in the corner under the articulating lamp, the box of children's toys sprouting arms, legs, girders and wheels in an amalgam of diverse materials and colours, his engineering text books rubbing covers with her knitting and handicrafts books, the framed photographs on the wall by the mantlepiece; her parents, father dead ten years, mother suffering from angina, their wedding photographs, the boys in their school uniform.

He would take a photo out with him, he decided.

An incoherent mumbling reached him from upstairs. One of the boys was stirring again. He climbed to the boy's bedroom and comforted him, stroking his face gently until sleep overcame the horrors of the day. He listened to their gentle sleeping rhythm. How would they develop in six months? Would they have changed that much?

As he wandered through the rooms, he languidly opened his wardrobe. Grey and brown, dull and heavy were his clothes. 'I'm going to need some cotton shirts. Yes, cotton shirts, lightweight trousers, a lightweight suit, cotton socks instead of nylon.' He rummaged amongst the racks and pulled out anything that he had bought for their holiday in Malta, two years previously. 'I can't wear that to work – it looks ghastly. I must make a list.' He returned to his chair and the tepid cup of tea. Taking a pad of paper and a pencil from the bookshelf, he began to write down everything that he would need to do or buy before he went away. He started with his wardrobe. He would need a complete lightweight kit. Where on earth would he find summer clothes in October? He should go to the dentists to ensure that nothing needed doing whilst he was away, visit the doctor and arrange any jabs, see the bank manager to arrange any overdraft facilities that might be needed in his absence. He worked on.

With a click and a sigh the central heating boiler switched off for the night. Wrighton automatically looked at his watch and wondered when Marion would return home. He hoped that he would not have to get the boys ready for school in the morning – it was so trying. He could never remember where their school clothes were kept and they seemed to derive a perverse pleasure from obstructing him in every way.

He went to bed and as he slipped into sleep, found himself both marvelling at the remarkably detached manner in which he was approaching this problem and simultaneously making a reminder for himself to sort out his thinnest pyjamas to see if they were cotton.

At breakfast next morning, Marion was tight-lipped and silent. He had not stirred when she had climbed into bed, which she had taken as a rebuttal, a pretence that his conscience was clear, and when she had set the breakfast table and cleared away his teacup from the previous evening, she had found the list in the maddeningly precise handwriting, coldly explaining what he was going to do and in what order.

'Have you told the boys?' she asked.

'Told us what, Daddy?' Richard chirped through a mouthful of cereal.

'No, not yet, I thought I would wait–'

'Why bother?' she laughed bitterly. 'You've made up your mind.'

'Is it a secret Daddy? Are we going to Granny's?' Charles asked.

Wrighton felt boxed into a corner. This was not how he wanted to tell their sons. Not blandly over the breakfast table in an atmosphere of tension and hostility.

'Your daddy's going away to work for a while.'

'Are you Daddy? Where are you going?'

'I've been sent to a country called Bangladesh. Do you know where that is?'

'South America?' suggested Richard.

'Aylesbury?' proposed Charles, a little less fancifully.

Wrighton brought the atlas to the table from the bookshelf.

'You see that country there?'

'Yes, is that Bangladesh?'

'No, that's India. You've heard of India haven't you?'

'Yes, Ranjit comes from there.'

'Well, this little country here is Bangladesh. That's where I'm going.'

'Ranjit says they have snakes in India. He saw one when it was outside his house.'

Charles' eyes bulged.

'Stop it, Richard,' Marion scolded. 'You're frightening Charles.'

'Will they have snakes where you are going, Daddy?'

'I don't think so. Snakes are usually scared of men and they keep away from the towns.' Then he added, 'I shall be away for six months.'

'Will you be here for my birthday?' Richard asked.

'No, nor Christmas, nor Easter. When I come back it will be the beginning of summer.'

'Gosh!' said Richard. He had been reading Enid Blyton and this was his favourite current ejaculation. 'Gosh!' he said again, for the pleasure of it, 'you'll miss the sledging on the common.'

The doorbell rang.

'I'll get it,' Marion said. 'It's probably the postman for me.'

A muffled discussion filtered back to the kitchen and then the door closed and Marion said as she walked back into the kitchen, 'You had better sit down there if you have to wait. Do you want a cup of coffee?'

'No thanks ma'am,' the helmetted youth declined. 'I've just had me breakfast.'

'Please excuse us whilst we have ours, won't you?' Marion threw back at him.

The boy removed his crash helmet and fiddled with it self-consciously. The boys stared at him in open-mouthed curiosity.

'Shut your mouth Richard. It's a letter for you brought by this gentleman who says that he has to wait for an answer.' Marion slid the envelope across to Wrighton and then busied herself elsewhere to show her lack of interest in the envelope that was so burningly provocative.

It was from Samantha, Cockcroft's secretary, and as Wrighton opened it, a bundle of papers fell out. One of them was unmistakably a British Airways ticket. He glanced at the letter. 'Would he fill in the enclosed application forms for Bangladesh visas, attach photos and give them to the courier with his passport?' Some other information followed regarding the amount of unaccompanied air-freight that he was allowed. The letter ended with a mysterious instruction that he had an appointment at the Foreign Office in London at ten o'clock on the following day. He was also to call in at the office on the Wednesday, the day before he left, because they had some things that needed to be taken out there with him.

'I won't be a minute,' he said to the youth. 'Make yourself at home. I've got to fill in some things and then give them to you.'

The youth smiled nervously. Wrighton filled in the forms, in triplicate and burrowed amongst the papers in the bureau until he found his passport.

'Marion, do you know where the spare passport photographs are? The ones left over from the last lot?'

'In the bureau. Come on boys, it's time for school.' She began dressing their sons and strapping them up in scarves and satchels such that they resembled desperate Mexican bandits. Wrighton found the photographs and handed all the papers to the courier.

'Do you know where you are going with that lot?' he asked.

'Yup. I've gotta take the passport, the visa forms and this cheque,' he held up an envelope, 'to the Bangladesh High Commission.'

'O.K.' Wrighton opened the door for him and presently heard the motor cycle dribble away down the road.

'That's pretty final isn't it?' Marion said.

2

Marion Wrighton clip-clopped her way down Orchard Drive, her knitting bag on one hand and a furled umbrella on the other. On Wednesday mornings she went to her knitting circle at the house of Mary Gonzales. The ladies always met there because Mrs. Gonzales' husband was something successful in the city and lived in a large detached house facing the park. Usually Marion would drive there but as soon as the boys had left for school, Stewart had asked to borrow the car to visit the doctor, the dentist and various other people in the centre.

Marion pursed her lips and circumnavigated a pile of dog mess on the pavement. She was a good wife, wasn't she? Why did he want to go to this country full of disease and natives and things? What was wrong with Wembley? They had a nice semi on a tree-lined avenue. It was a little far from the shops but it was near the school and the bus service ran along the end of the road.

She reached the corner and turned left by the newsagents shop. She watched her reflection as it rippled along the shop window; she always used this shop as a final check on her appearance if she had to walk anywhere. She was wearing her new raincoat with a tie belt, underneath she wore her plain grey knitted dress that showed off her shoulders so well. She smiled inwardly at her reflection. 'Not bad for nearly forty years old,' she thought. Her figure was beginning to fill in the curves, neutralising her silhouette. 'I suppose Angela Curnow will be there in a too-tight cocktail dress from Harvey Nichols and she will twitter on about her Desmond.' Marion was confident that in her understated dress she could outshine Angela Curnow who had gracelessly lost the fight against the onslaught of middle age. Whilst Marion still had her figure she intended to show it off to its best advantage. Was it her figure that had attracted Stewart at first? She had often wondered. He had always said that it was her wallet, laughingly.

She turned into Park Drive and automatically checked that her raincoat belt was untwisted and that her silk scarf was displayed around her shoulders. It was a real Christian Dior scarf. Stewart had paid a stupid amount of money for it in a shop in Bond Street for her birthday one year. She had perfected a style of dressing which made it appear that she had merely grabbed the first scarf in her drawer and thrown it around her shoulders. That the Christian Dior signature displayed its *griffe* nonchalantly down her back was pure chance.

The tired suburban tudor semis had given way on the other side of the road to the expanse of the park, green fading to the grey October mist, through which occasionally loomed ectoplasmic figures usually chained to an exercising dog. Away to the left a line of sentinel ghostly elms marched purposefully into obscurity. They reminded her of the potato prints that the boys did at school, where each impression, although identical to its predecessor, was slightly paler across the page until the potato had exhausted its coating of paint.

A bright red saloon flaunted itself on the gravel coach drive of Park View, Mary Gonzales' house. Marion ping ponged the door bell.

'Marion!' exclaimed Mary, as if they had stopped at the same bookstall in the Sahara. 'Come in my dear.' Her eyes swept critically up and down Marion, noting every thread and button and pricing her clothes to the nearest pound. 'Look who's here, darlings.' She propelled Marion into the front room where five pairs of eyes performed the same trick as Mary's but with less expertise.

'We thought you weren't coming,' a mousey woman said in greeting, as Marion swished her scarf from her shoulders.

'Oh my dear,' Mary pouted as she took the coat and scarf. 'Christian Dior, if you don't mind. Stewart built a bridge for the Arabs?'

Marion smiled wanly. She was grateful that Mary had reacted to the stimulus as a patella does to a doctor's hammer but was unwilling to acknowledge the score against her. Her husband was no more than a navvy. A bridge builder.

'Well actually–' Marion began.

'Oh Marion, did you knit the dress yourself? You are a clever old stick,' Angela Curnow chirped from the corner. 'It makes you look so young.' And then perhaps hoping to deflect a counter attack she added, slyly, 'But of course you have the figure for it.'

Mary carried in a tray and Marion settled herself down in an armchair.

'Coffee and naughties on the table, girls,' she said.

Knitting which had only been half-heartedly taken up, was willingly put down amidst a chatter of china and rustle of cake-shop paper as the 'girls' swooped on the 'naughties', as Mary had called them.

'...and then the shop assistant said to me, in front of the entire shop if you don't mind, "Would madam prefer the larger size for the more mature figure?" 'Young lady' I said, 'I wish to speak to your supervisor. I will not have a shop assistant commenting about my figure before the entire population of Knightsbridge'

'What happened Angela?' They hung on her every word.

Angela Curnow took a bite from her cake, which left her with a white moustache of cream as if she were about to shave.

'Well... ' she said, through the mouthful of pastry, and waved the devastated carcass of the cake in her hand. 'Well, I mean, in Roddy's one does not expect that sort of indiscretion.'

Marion had not been listening properly and was puzzled. Where the heck was this shop called 'Roddy's'? It had to be big, expensive and well known for Angela to patronise it. She leaned over to the horsey looking woman at the side of her who appeared to be knitting a purple gorilla.

'Where is Roddy's?' she hissed.

'That's what we habitués call Harrod's, surely you know that?'

'Of course, silly me.' Marion blushed and then bounced back with, 'But then it's a long time since I have been there,' which really made it look worse. She took her knitting from her bag and laid it out on her knee. The purple gorilla-knitter tried to ignore her but when the seventh ball of coloured wool came out of the bag she had to speak.

'My gosh, that must take some concentration.'

'Yes,' said Marion airily. 'It's a Fairisle sweater for my husband. Quite easy once you get the hang of it.'

'You surely don't knit all seven colours at once.'

'That is the correct way to knit Fairisle,' she replied through a tight smile. She gathered up her three needles and seven wools, spread her pattern on the arm of a chair and began to knit at twice the speed of light, dabbing the wools in and out in sequence. 'Green two, orange two, white one, black one, white two,' she muttered to herself, just loud enough for her neighbour to hear.

The woman prodded her flaccid gorilla which responded by dropping its needle into her coffee cup on the carpet.

'Tension's a bit loose,' Marion remarked without looking up. 'Dark green two, white two, light green three.'

'Let him go,' her mother had said last night when she had told her about Stewart. They had discussed it long into a third cup of cocoa, even her budgie had cocked his head, flicked his eyelids and then switched himself off to dream of equatorial rain forests and green cathedrals of hardwoods. 'Let him go.' Her mother had pinched her lips together.

You can manage without him, you know you can. I always said that he was selfish,' she had added gratuitously and quite untruthfully. 'He'll soon come back once he has realised that you won't go out there with him.'

'Mother, you've missed the point. I'm not allowed to go out with him.'

'Rubbish girl! A wife can always go with her husband.'

'The company won't allow it, or at least they won't pay for it and we can't afford all that money. And what would we do with the boys? Where would they go to school? No,' she said bitterly, 'he is going out there on what they call "bachelor status".'

'That's one thing you don't need to worry about. He hasn't got it in him to two-time you. He hasn't got the guts. Spineless, that's what he is.'

'He is not spineless, Mother,' Marion had said hotly and her mother realised that she had overstepped the mark a bit.

'Oh Marion, get me my pills,' she had gasped. 'I can feel a flutter.'

Marion had jumped to the brown medicine bottle on the sideboard and brought it to her mother, standing over her solicitously whilst she carefully picked out a pill and placed it under her tongue, sighing,

'That's better. Now what were we talking about?'

'Oh it wasn't important, Mother.' Marion had reached the frightening realisation that no matter what she said, he had made his decision already and he would go. He had decided to go and so he would go. It was an unusual stubbornness in him, almost as if it were a challenge.

'So Desmond said, "Angie, if you want the red one, then have the red one but don't blame me if you get flagged down by all the squad cars between here and Marble Arch." He's got this theory,' Angela Curnow confided to her audience, 'that the police always stop the red cars because they go faster and their owners are racier.'

'I wouldn't say you were racy, Angela, a little fast perhaps.'

Angela stuck out her tongue at her tormentor. 'Anyway, I haven't been stopped by any handsome young policemen yet.'

'How long have you had it?'

'Two days. I didn't see your car outside, Marion,' Angela added, a little contrivedly, Marion thought, since Angela had arrived before Marion and so would not have seen it in any case. Angela also knew that they had just the one car between the two of them. All the other ladies present had sporty little runabouts or Volvo estates for ferrying children and dogs around whilst their husbands drove the company saloon. But Marion and Stewart had only one, ordinary, family and paid-for saloon.

'No, Stewart's got it today to go to the doctor's and dentist's and things,' she replied without looking up from her pattern.

'Oh dear, is he ill?'

'Ill?'

'You did say that he was going to the doctor's and dentist's and things.'

She had forgotten that the earth-shattering news that she had been living with since yesterday and which had assumed such an all-consuming part of her preoccupations was still unknown to them.

'No, he's going abroad and needs some jabs and things.'

'Oh, you lucky thing! Are you going somewhere nice?'

'Bangladesh.'

'Oooh! ' said Angela. 'I've never been to Africa.'

'It's not Africa, it's India.' Marion tried desperately to resurrect the image of the breakfast table and the atlas spread out on it. 'I suppose it's what they used to call the "Far East".'

'What's this? What's this?' Mary trumpeted from the other side of the lounge. As the lady of the house she always assumed the role of honorary chairwoman, choosing and tabooing subjects like a chat-show hostess on television. 'Who's going out to the Far East?'

'Marion was saying that she was going out.'

'Marion, darling,' Mary accused. 'You never told me that you were going abroad.'

Marion tried to ignore the inference that they were such close friends that she would share her every secret with Mary. In reality, she hardly knew the woman. In fact, looking around at the well-fed faces and painted eyebrows, she realised that none of them actually knew the others. It was all a charade. It was a pantomime of strangers.

'I'm not going abroad,' Marion admitted, feeling that she had been discovered as some monumental braggart. 'It's Stewart, he's going out to Bangladesh.'

'And you're not going out with him, my poor dear,' Angela consoled her wickedly, for Angela's husband had taken her to New York on Concorde only last month, for a conference on cybernetics or something.

'No, I'm not going out with him,' Marion said firmly, as if it were her choice and not that of her husband's employers. Then she laughed. 'Have you any idea what Bangladesh is like?' She realised on the moment that she said it that she had no idea what it was like. It could be the far side of Wimbledon Common for all she knew. Luckily the others were in no mood to match their knowledge of the Far East with that of Marion's. They accepted the suggestion that nobody with the full set of functioning grey cells would want to go to Bangladesh.

'Isn't that the place where they have floods?'

'And typhoons?'

'And famine?'

'And horrible diseases?'

Marion panicked for an instant. Surely Bangladesh didn't have all those things at once?

'So I believe,' she said, as if she would be subjecting herself to the lurid list of risks.

'Coo you are brave!'

'It's not me that's going,' she reminded them. 'Although, of course, it will put an extra burden of work on me with the boys not having a father for six months.'

'Six months! He's not going for six months, surely?'

'Six months minimum, the company said.' She turned the pattern over nonchalantly. 'He's going out next Thursday.'

'What?'

'Next Thursday!'

'Now, Marion dear,' Mary began, trying to find some sense in the non-sensical account. 'Do you mean that Stewart...' she had to pause to make sure that she had got the right name, 'that Stewart is going out to this Bangladesh country for six months and he's starting next week?'

'Yes.' Marion gazed at the anguish stricken faces surrounding her, gawping as if she were a strange beast in the zoo.

'But why didn't you tell us before? How long have you known?'

They were holding their breath, waiting for her reply. She found it very amusing. She looked at her watch. 'About fifteen hours.'

They were thunderstruck. Each woman was imagining the upheaval in her own household should her husband return home from work one day and announce that he was disappearing around the curve of the earth for six months.

'But... he's never been sent abroad before has he?'

'No, he hasn't.' And then before she could stop herself she found herself saying, 'He is far too important in head office to be sent off around the world but things have gone so badly wrong that, apparently, only my Stewart can save the contract. It could cost the company millions.'

'But what about the children and that?'

'Oh, we'll manage!' She took up her wool again and the others marvelled at her martyrdom.

'I hope you will still be able to come to our little knitting mornings.'

'I don't see why not,' Marion said. 'Life must go on.'

3

The train jolted and banged across the lacework of rails, as it had done, Wrighton supposed, every day of his commuting life on this line. This morning was a luxury for him, for he was travelling after the rush.

In his carriage there sat a lady with her daughter. She was probably taking her to a museum or an exhibition, and there was an elderly man with a soft leather gladstone. When he dropped it to the floor, it clinked, and as it slowly expired, the air hissed out of it, suffocating the contents. There was a large, hairy, man accompanied by a rucksack of similar proportions and which leaned sluggishly into the corner of the seat where it nodded and rocked to itself with more life than many of the commuters that Wrighton was wont to see on this route.

Wrighton pulled the envelope from his coat pocket and slipped out the instruction from Cockcroft. He was to see a Mr. Denning at the Foreign Office at ten o'clock. He supposed it was for a briefing on the customs of the country, or the political situation. He didn't really know. He could not recall any of his globetrotting colleagues mentioning their being summoned to the Foreign Office.

After the meeting, or whatever it turned out to be, he had decided he would have lunch in a small restaurant and then look for some lightweight clothing. He had tried a foray yesterday but had given up easily. Shopping bored him to distraction and he had been intimidated by the raised eyebrows and comment of the shop assistant, 'In October sir?' when he had asked if they had any summer clothing.

He replaced the letter in his coat pocket and winced as his left arm crossed his chest. Yesterday, the doctor had gleefully given him a jab in his arm, and one in his buttock. He had then prescribed a course of malaria tablets which Wrighton should have started two weeks before departing, not seven days, and had passed on to the subject of cleanliness of the body, reminding him not to put a finger, or anything, in the mouth unless it was meant to be eaten and never to forget to filter and boil water. After that, they had chatted about the doctor's uncle who had been based in Bengal during the second world war.

The dentist had asked him a few conciliatory questions and had then stuck probes in his mouth so that he could not answer them. His opinion had been that his mouth was 'in good nick'. Not a very professional expression, Wrighton had thought.

Wrighton was a little disappointed to realise that the meeting was not taking place at the main Foreign Office building in Whitehall, but at a sort of dingy annexe in Matthew Parker Street. It was a street of towering, black, bulbous, stone-faced office buildings, which had apparently, and unforgivably, in Wrighton's opinion, escaped the blitz.

He pushed his letter under the glass partition in the window of the little wooden porter's box to a grey-haired lady, seated behind. She muttered to herself, then, getting no response, looked up at him and repeated her phrase.

Wrighton bent down to shout at her. 'I'm awfully sorry, I can't hear you, through the glass.' To add to the scenario, a particularly noisy truck decided to grind slowly past, its roaring thundering around the entrance hall. Wrighton pushed his spectacles up on his nose. 'Could you repeat that please?'

'I fed, 'bot if more mame'?'

Wrighton reflected for a second or two.

'My name's Stewart Wrighton,' he said. 'I've come to see Mr. Denning.'

'Mifta mennin,' the lady repeated. 'Ibenpipy?'

Wrighton pointed to the letter.

'There's my name there.'

'Aboo amy broo vov ibenpipy? Am office bars?'

'I don't have an office pass. I don't work for the government.'

'Ugan zee mifta mennin withower bars.'

'But I've only got this letter. This is ridiculous. Can't you phone him?'

'Igan give you a bars, if you gersho me fome form of ibenpipy.' The woman drew a pad of printed forms towards her and wrote his name on the top line and that of Mr. Denning on the second. Wrighton felt about his person for some proof of his identity.

'Look, I've got my initials on my bag.' He lifted it up to the guichet, as you would a small child at the ice cream kiosk. The lady shook her head.

'Bon't boo.'

Something with my name on, he thought. He never put his name in his diary; it was not on the collar of his coat. He tapped his pockets. Ah, his spectacles case.

'Here you are,' he said triumphantly. 'I've got my name and address in my spectacles case and look,' he took off his spectacles and fitted them in the case, 'see, they are mine, they fit in the case.'

She handed him a slip of paper marked *'day pass'* and pointed to the gloomy interior of the building.

'Uffer mog,' she said.

Wrighton nodded and tried to look as if he had understood, and then followed the direction of her pointing finger. Through the doors he found a sign announcing the proximity of the reception, and made towards it, vowing that he would show his birth mark to the next inquirer of identity.

'I have an appointment at ten o'clock with Mr. Denning,' he told the girl.

'Have you a letter?'

He didn't even stay to ask whether he could see this Mr. Denning without the letter, but directly retraced his steps to the front door where, through dint of mime and stamping foot, he managed to regain possession of his letter.

'There!' He placed the trophy, gloriously, on her desk.

'Please take a seat.' She ignored the letter.

Wrighton sat down. Sitting opposite him was a young girl, resplendent in cherry red lipstick and black stockings. Above her head a poster pinned to the wall announced with unnecessary triteness that *'Postal bombs can kill'*.

After fifteen minutes of scrutiny of the room, Wrighton knew that it was Marcia's task to make the tea this week, but Joan's to close the windows before leaving; that when the phone rang, it was an external call, and when it buzzed, it was an internal call; that the girl at reception was not a typist, but was given odd typing jobs to do to fill in time and that the lady who did the cleaning was not tall enough to reach the top ledge on the door.

Justin Denning gazed at the dour damp facade of the building across the street. Then his watery eyes swept sourly over the greying London roofs, where the city seemed to merge with the misty autumn sky. He turned back from the window, picked a hair from the cuff of his light grey suit, and meticulously dropped it into the waste paper bin.

He stood to attention before the framed photograph of his monarch, Queen Elizabeth II. Only grades higher than Second Secretary within the Foreign Office were permitted to display this print in their offices. He had chosen a dark mount and a gold frame, and had hung it beside the tall sash windows. Through the latter, the light flooded onto any perusor of the picture, and lit him so that what he saw was not a rather stiff, full length pose of a monarch, but a reflection of his own head and shoulders.

Denning edged a little to the side, and then adjusted one or two hairs across his forehead, turning his head right and then left, to ensure the symmetry of his sideburns.   He fingered the knot of his pale blue silk tie and pulled the bottom of his waistcoat downwards.

'Your Majesty,' he said to the frame, and paced slowly across to his desk. Stooping elegantly to the carpet, he rounded up a stray paper clip and dropped it with a musical tinkling, into a fine Limoges porcelain pot on his desk.   He absently ran his finger along the edge of the polished chestnut.   The desk that he had rescued from the Whitehall office; a desk across which the business of the nation had passed for decades, and upon which it had left its scars in multitudes of little scratches and stains which, he felt, added immeasurably to its worth.   It was also larger than the desk normally attributed to his grade and thus added a certain mystique and class to his office.

He resented being stuck in this annexe.   'Justin, your job is a little too sensitive to leave in Whitehall.   You can run your own show in Matthew Parker Street.'   That much was true, but nobody in the Foreign Office when on home posting, liked to work in an outstation. Out of sight, out of mind.   Once you moved away from the hub you were forgotten.

He flipped open his diary and grimaced at the entry therein. He had to try and talk to one of those confounded engineers.   He hated this part of his job. Why were they so uncouth?   So ignorant?   Give him a consular attaché any day, at least they could understand English.   You could ask the Russian Cultural attaché when the Bolshoi ballet was opening again, and you would receive two tickets for dates which just happened to coincide with your official visit.   But these engineers... you had to spell it out to them using words of one syllable.

A clerk pushed her head around the door.

'There's a Mr. Wrighton waiting downstairs to see you sir.'

'Send him up,' Denning ordered, and then slipped around his desk and sat in his leather armchair.   Then he quickly jumped up and stepping around his desk again, repositioned the chair for his visitor so that it was a little further away.

'Ah, Mr. Wrighton, pleased to meet you.' He advanced affably, hand outstretched. 'Good of you to come.'

He appraised the man rapidly.   Slightly taller than he, thinner, pasty-faced, spectacles, sports jacket and flannels, hideous tie. Age? Late thirties probably.

'Thank you,' the man replied with a strange smile.

'Please sit down, make yourself comfortable.'   But he didn't sit down, he turned around and walked back to the door. What on earth is he up to?

Denning sighed as his visitor hung his coat and scarf on the hatstand.

'A real autumn day, isn't it?' Wrighton said.

'Yes, quite... quite... Cigarette?' Denning offered a decorated marble box from Nepal.

'No thanks, I don't smoke, and you shouldn't either.'

'What?' Denning was startled.

'It's very bad for you.'

'Oh yes, well I agree,' Denning lied quickly. 'Dangerous habit of course,' he added. I shall have to work hard on this one, he thought. He turned on his most indulgent smile as he moved to a filing cabinet. 'Did you have a good journey in?'

'Reasonable, a bit different from the rush hour.'

'Where have you... where do you...?'

'Wembley.'

Denning looked ostentatiously at his wristwatch. Wrighton could see that it was an Omega. A gold Omega. 'Nearly eleven o'clock,' he said as he pulled open the top drawer and smiled conspiratorially. 'Can I tempt you to a er... small sherry?' Denning thought that the visitor was definitely not a Scotch man.

'No thank you, I don't drink alcohol, but I would like a cup of tea if you could manage that.'

'A cup of tea.'

'If you can manage it.'

Denning winced inwardly as he pressed the bell for his secretary.

'Yes sir?'

'Could you bring a cup... er two cups of tea please dear?'

From behind Wrighton's back, the girl raised her eyebrows and then pulled a face at him. 'Yes sir.'

Really, what was the world coming to! He would have to talk to that girl. She had no respect, no respect at all. He crept back to the sanctuary of his chair, the reassurance of the wood and the leather around him. Almost the same feeling, he thought, that Edwardian landowners must have experienced as they scowled down from their phaetons and landaulettes upon the waifs of their parish.

'Now, Mr. Wrighton, you are probably wondering why I wanted to see you before you went off to Bangladesh...' He looked across at Wrighton for confirmation.

'It had crossed my mind, fleetingly, during the forty five minutes I was waiting downstairs.'

'Well the fact of the matter is... Er... Did you say "forty five minutes"?'

'Yes.'

'Well I'm awfully sorry if you've had to wait long. I assure you that I wasn't told of your arrival until a few minutes ago.'

'I don't doubt it one moment,' the other replied mysteriously.

Denning consulted his diary.

'You work for Consolidated, I believe?'

'That's right.'

'Did you er... do you know Raymond Line then? We met before he went out to Dhaka,' Denning explained quickly.

'Yes, he's a colleague of mine. I'm sorry to hear about his accident. I can't help thinking that it was a funny reason to be sent home for.'

'How do you mean?' Denning enquired, his affability hiding his quiet concern.

'I don't know whether we send home foreign diplomats when they have fatal traffic accidents, but I don't remember reading anything in the papers of that sort, but of course, Line wasn't a diplomat.'

'No er... quite. This is exactly what I was going to chat to you about. After my chat, I have a colleague downstairs who can gen you up on Dhaka. We've got a sort of handbook and a bit of film footage. Just to give you an idea of what to expect.'

'That might be useful. No sugar in mine please.' Wrighton indicated the tea tray that had appeared on the desk.

'No er...? Oh certainly, certainly.' Denning poured out a dainty cup of tea and handed it to Wrighton, who sipped it. Denning pressed the tips of his fingers together and gazed at the decorative architrave as if eliciting inspiration for what he was about to say. 'The thing is, Mr. Wrighton, you businessmen, when you go abroad, you are, in a sort, privileged persons. You don't suffer the restrictions imposed on us diplomats.'

'You mean like, duty-free alcohol and official cars?'

Denning smiled crushingly.

'Of course this is the popular image of a diplomat abroad, but I assure you that the truth is far removed from this. For example, we diplomats have to get special residence visas and vast areas of the land are forbidden to us. We do this in the U.K. to the Iron Curtain countries, you know.'

'No, I didn't!' Wrighton was utterly truthful.

'Oh yes, ' Denning continued, warming to his subject, 'the Russians can only move about on certain roads and they have to let us know before-hand.'

'Why?'

'Well this is the question. Why do we and the other countries do it?

Well, it's all to do with state secrets and security. We couldn't have the Russians wandering around Cheltenham to their heart's content, now could we?'

Wrighton could see nothing wrong with Cheltenham.

'What's wrong with Cheltenham?'

'G.C.H.Q.' Wrighton looked blank. 'The Government's centre that deals with all our codes and cyphers and intelligence. It's near Cheltenham.'

'Oh.'

I don't believe this, thought Denning, then turning back to Wrighton, '...and this brings me on to what I was going to talk about. You will have freedom in Bangladesh, far more than the resident diplomats. You will be able to go into restricted areas in the pursuit of your work and you may see things that we are unable to see.'

'Yes,' said Wrighton slowly. 'I suppose that's possible.'

God! This is heavy work. He appears unusually dense, our Mr. Wrighton. 'The trouble is, you see, Mr. Wrighton, um... many foreign countries see travelling businessmen or engineers and consultants as... well... quite simply, as spies.' Wrighton laughed. 'Yes I agree, it is ridiculous Mr. Wrighton, but we must not forget that the Ministry of Foreign Affairs in Dhaka will see you as Raymond Lines' successor and thus, another spy. I mean,' he added quickly, 'not that Raymond Line was a spy, but that they might have suspected him of it. Do you see what I mean?' He dabbed at his left temple in a nervous gesture, and eyed Wrighton doubtfully, then he stepped smartly back to his desk and handed a piece of paper to him.

'This is the name of our commercial attache in Dhaka, Mr. Hardwicke. If you have any problems or anything that you want to say to him, just ring him up at the British High Commission in Dhaka.'

'Thank you.'

'You may know...' Denning continued, 'that we have two businessmen in prison in Tunisia at the moment, on charges of spying. Trumped up charges of course but we wouldn't want you, or anyone, to get into that sort of trouble, so keep in regular touch with Mr. Hardwicke and he will keep you on the straight and narrow and of course, if there is anything you want to tell him, well, he will listen to you.' I can't make it any plainer than that, Denning thought.

'What sort of thing do you think I might want to tell Mr. Hardwicke?'

Oh my God! Back to the words of one syllable. 'Just anything that might be of interest to HMG.'

'HMG?'

'Her Majesty's Government.'

'Are you asking me to spy?'

Denning choked into his tea cup, recovered quickly and then flooded Wrighton with his charming smile.

'Good Heavens, Mr. Wrighton, where do you think you are?' Without giving him any chance to speculate, he stood up and held out his hand. 'Well, it's been useful talking to you and if you need any help, you know who to contact.' Wrighton got up slowly, apparently deep in thought. 'Would you show Mr. Wrighton down to the briefing studio please?' he said haughtily to the girl. 'The chappie down there is doing a presentation on Dhaka for him.'

'Yes sir.'

'Thank you Mr. Denning, it has been most instructive.' Wrighton took his coat and scarf from the stand.

Denning watched the door close behind the engineer and then, letting out a lungful of air with a hiss, he poured himself a whisky and lit a cigarette.

'Are you the geyser for the film on Dakar?' A youth of translucid skin demanded.

'Dhaka,' Wrighton corrected him.

'Yeah, that's what I said, Dakar. In here.' He motioned him to a green baize door, whilst he disappeared into a pine-clad projection box.

Wrighton sat down in the dark of the small cinema. The screen suddenly came alive with flickering, wobbling light, which was rapidly focused into black figures in brightly coloured cotton prints, waddling across the street with babies strapped to their backs. Over the accompaniment of a jungle beat music, a nasal narrator announced,

'Dakar, Capital of Senegal, is a busy port on the coast of West Africa...'

Wrighton sighed and slowly shook his head.

'What a shower!' he said to himself, and then quietly slipped out of the room, unnoticed by the projectionist.

He walked briskly up Whitehall towards Trafalgar Square. Past General Haig, past the monolithic mundaneness of the Cenotaph, past the Horseguards, where splendid black horses stood wreathed in their own breath. It was only when the woman selling newspapers at the stand at the top of Whitehall smiled at him, that he realised that he, too, was smiling.

As he strolled gently around Trafalgar Square, he was suddenly struck by a disquieting thought, a stupid reflection, but which caught him with his defences down and literally stopped him in his tracks. Would he ever see Nelson's Column again? The Landseer Lions? The pigeons? Would he die out there in Bangladesh and never see England again? He did not feel any particular empathy for either the column, which he considered to be far too tall for the proportions of the square, or the lions, or indeed, the pigeons, which when all was said and done, were just pests, but now he understood with a profundity that disturbed him, that excrescence of chauvinism which afflicts people when separated from their homeland; the paint brush of patriotism that makes bronze lions into gold and pigeons into peacocks.

He was brought back to reality by an insistent tapping on his foot. He looked down and saw the ringleader of a bunch of pigeons. He pushed him away and turned towards the National Gallery.

He found a small restaurant-cum-cafe, near Leicester Square on the fringes of daytime Soho and ate a parsimonious roast beef and two veg. followed by a cup of tea as dessert. He then set off again towards Piccadilly, Bond Street and the specialist tailors.

'This looks the ticket,' he said to himself, as he pushed open the door above which was inscribed in gold lettering, *'Regimental tailor – tropical kit a speciality.'*

Once inside, he was not so sure. The preponderance of dummies dressed in historical military uniforms imparted a hybrid air of museum and waxworks. Along one side of the shop ran a traditional wooden counter behind the glass front of which were arranged row upon row of regimental ties in their drab blues, greens and reds, peppered with obscure emblems of profound historical significance, but with no affinity to the present day world.

One of the dummies at the darker end of the shop suddenly startled Wrighton by lurching forward to accost him.

'What would sir like?' it said, mentally measuring his shoulders, chest, hips, waist, inside leg and wallet.

'I've been sent out to Bangladesh,' Wrighton began, deferentially, 'and I need a set of clothes really.' He faltered as he calculated how much it cost the shop to keep the dummies clothed. 'Well, a few items for a hot climate.'

'Certainly, sir. Bangladesh, that would be sub-tropical kit,' the dummy informed him, unctuously and then, as if the mechanism had been suddenly engaged, he poured forth, 'cotton shirts; off-white to avoid early soiling, short sleeves, two breast pockets with flap, button collar, boxer shorts; broad elastic to avoid dhobi itch, cotton or cotton mix socks, slacks; gents, all cotton, slant side pockets and one hip pocket, fly zip, Bermuda shorts; twill cotton for heavy use, beige (we don't say "khaki" any more) lightweight jacket; half-lining, one inside pocket, unlined lapel, dinner jacket–'

'Now that sounds interesting,' Wrighton interrupted him. 'The light-weight jacket, with one inside pocket and no lining to lapel,' he added in explanation. 'Can I see that?'

The dummy stood stock still for a moment and then said, with obvious difficulty, 'Just the jacket sir?'

'Yes I think so. Just the jacket.'

'Yes sir.' He stalked away to the dark end of the shop and returned with a light coloured jacket, draped over his arm.

'This is your size sir.' He declared this as an irrefutable fact.

Wrighton removed his overcoat and jacket and slipped on the light jacket. It was almost the cut of a blazer, it was only lined over the shoulders and it indeed boasted just the one inside pocket. He stood before the mirror and pulled the jacket this way and that, lifting his arms and mimicking writing at a desk and unrolling a plan at arm's length.

'We don't have a great demand for this jacket sir. It used to be popular of course, on the cruises but nowadays, well, it does make one look rather like an ice-cream salesman,' he ended discouragingly. 'Not really Foreign Office, if I might say so.'

'I beg your pardon.'

'It's not really the Foreign Office, sir, not their style.' And then fearing that he had made a gaffe, 'You are with the Foreign Office, I trust sir?'

'No, actually, I'm not. I'll take this jacket.'

'Yes sir.' He began to refold the article. 'Do you have a tropical dinner jacket sir?'

'Ermm yes, er no, or rather, I think I'll use this one as a dinner jacket,' he pointed to his purchase which was disappearing into the cardboard box.

The dummy was scandalised into speechlessness. He eventually found the breath to utter, 'But it's not black, sir.'

'But don't they have white dinner jackets out in the Far East? I'm sure I've seen them on the films and all that.'

'A different cut, sir, quite a different cut.'

'I'll just take this jacket for now, I can always come back if I change my mind.'

Wrighton alighted from the train, laden with his purchases. It was late afternoon and the carriages were disgorging school children like peas from pods. They straggled all over the platform in groups of different sizes, laughing raucously at a prank, or arguing vociferously about football or flirting with the group behind. Every now and then, an Einstein would wander by, face downturned, lost in thought as he kicked a pebble along.

Wrighton showed his season ticket at the barrier, and then turned back to the ticket office and tapped on the counter.

'I want to cash in my season ticket please.'

The clerk silently slipped a form across to him. He filled it in and handed in his ticket with it.

'We'll send you a cheque when it has been processed. Is this the right address?'

'Yes.'

Wrighton realised that he was now no longer a commuter. It was if chains of bondage had been hewn from his limbs.

'Well the jacket is alright. Bit tight across the shoulders,' Marion remarked.

'It was all I could get. Have you any idea what the reaction is when you go into the local shops at this time of year and ask for summer clothing?'

'I can imagine. Where are the trousers?'

He held up two pairs of trousers and she looked at them.

'Where did you get them from?'

'A camping shop in Tottenham Court Road.'

'It looks like it.'

'Well they are one hundred per cent cotton, which was what I needed.'

'You'll look a clown in them.'

He unbuckled his trousers and slipped the new pair on. He turned before the mirror.

'They are a bit baggy, but I expect I'll need that in the heat. Nothing tight-fitting.'

'You don't exactly wear tight fitting trousers anyway.'

'No, I don't.'

They stood looking at each other across the bed, silently, then at last she said, 'You're going through with it then.'

It was not a question, it was a statement; an acceptance of fate. He took her in his arms and she felt the tears brimming behind her eyes. 'I won't cry,' she said to herself defiantly, as the tears zig-zagged down her cheeks.

'Oh Stewart,' she sobbed. 'I shall miss you terribly.'

'Of course you won't,' he said, awkwardly patting her hair. 'You've got good friends and neighbours here. You've got your knitting circle and your mother isn't far away. As for the children, they'll love it. I shall be back before they have had time to miss me, and you've often said that you felt that you wanted to get closer to them.'

This was true, Marion had wanted a girl. She had always found it difficult to relate to the boys. The boys, of course, thought that Stewart was God or slightly above. Everything he did was right, whether he was climbing trees with them or playing on the floor with their cars. The sum total of her involvement seemed to be feeding them and clearing up after them.

Her tears turned to bitter drops when she realised that she was jealous of Stewart and the rapport that he had with the boys. And to make it worse, he did not realise that he got on well with them, he just thought it was normal. What frightened her deep down was that he was apparently insulated from his feelings. Perhaps he didn't have any. He just did not appear upset.

She thought about their marriage. It was always she who flared up in anger or passion, Stewart merely applied his engineer's mind to it, mixed in some mathematical formula and said that 'It was silly' or 'Arguing was counter productive'. Of course it was! But it still had to be done. Stewart was cold. She had never seen him lose his temper in all the time she had known him, it was uncanny, unnatural.

'Let's try and get this suitcase finished.' She turned back to the bed and pressed down the clothes.

'Do you think I should take my swimming trunks?'

Marion pondered.

'There must be a pool out there somewhere and if you don't learn to swim in Bangladesh, you won't learn anywhere.'

She took them from his hands and pushed them down inside the suitcase with a finality that thwarted all dissent.

4

Stewart pushed his thumb nail along the groove in his brown corduroy shorts and pretended that he was ploughing a field. He ran his finger off the end of his shorts and into the top of his thigh, where it scribed a white line. The wheels of the van went thump, THUMP, thump, THUMP on the tar-ridged road and occasionally broke their beat to produce a rich churning sound. Inside the van, the heat was stifling. This was the hottest summer that he could remember. He wriggled on his box and tried to find a part of the rack which would not dig into his back so much, but failed. After a hesitant shuffle, he slouched forward, his elbows across his knees.

'Stewart! Sit up straight. Straight back.'

'Yes mum.'

He sat upright until she had turned away again and then he slumped over into clandestine comfort. Through the windscreen the ribbon of concrete stretched before, sometimes carrying a bright red lorry laden down with goods stacked under a tarpaulin, or a small black-coloured saloon into which a family had been squeezed for an outing.

Stewart screwed his eyes up at the view. It was like being at the cinema; a flickering screen with moving images, the silhouettes of the row sitting in front of him were represented by his mother and father, and he, ensconced in the mysterious darkness behind. Except for that box rack. He shifted his back again.

'Dad, can I have a cushion in the back for my head?'

'Ha ha, that's a good one! You'll be wanting an armchair next. Don't be such a cissy.'

Secure in the darkness of the van, Stewart stuck out his tongue in defiant frustration. Suddenly, the world jolted a foot sideways with a stunning crash. He glimpsed his father's arm, snaking back to the steering wheel.

'And you'll get a thick ear both sides, next time,' his father warned him.

Stewart nursed his head, biting his bottom lip, vowing that he would not cry. Thump THUMP, thump, THUMP, the wheels drummed out.

They had spent the morning at Kew Gardens, his mother and father strolling along the avenues, stopping occasionally to read a label in Latin.

'Stop dawdling, Stewart,' his mother would throw over her shoulder at him and the next minute he would be waiting for them as they stooped over a bloom. It just was not fair.

'Mum, can I have an ice cream?'

'Later.'

They had pointed out a massive oak tree to him and told him a story about it being older than Henry VIII, and they had shown him a strange wiggly tower, looking like a red Christmas tree and had said that it came from Japan, wherever that was.

'Mum. Can I have an ice cream now?

'Don't keep harruping on about ice cream.'

Albert Wrighton had slipped his arm through his wife's, and ambled slowly down the alleyway. Dorothy Wrighton secretly observed the other women's reactions to her wide-brimmed summer hat, and Albert had proudly met each man eye to eye, daring him to admire his wife. Stewart had dragged on behind, his thick shorts chafing him wherever they touched his skin. He could remember those shorts when they were still the work trousers that Uncle Daniel used to wear on the farm. He had pulled at the seat, to unstick them from his bottom, and then swung his sandal at a stone which had been sitting unconcernedly in his path. He had cringed as it had cracked his mother on the heel.

'Ouch!' She hobbled on one foot.

'What is it?' His father half-turned. 'Let me at him, I'll–'

'No Bert, don't,' Dorothy hissed and looked quickly around. 'People are looking.'

They had made him walk in front where he could not slouch, and could not dawdle, and could not kick stones.

Thump, THUMP, thump, THUMP the wheels continued to hammer monotonously. The van belonged to the shop, of course, not to his father. On rare occasions his father was allowed to use it for a weekend, and then Stewart's mother would dress up in her finery, and they would have an outing. Sometimes it was the sea-side, sometimes it was Dunstable Downs. Today, it was Kew Gardens.

He had eventually acquired an ice cream. Not just strawberry and vanilla, but green as well. Pink, yellow and green. They had discussed what flavour the green was supposed to be. The man on the tricycle had said that it was called a Neapolitan because it came from France. They decided that the green was probably lime flavour. Pink, yellow, green. That was something to tell the others at school.

Stewart looked back through the windscreen. The show. He had been recently to the cinema, or 'the pictures' as they called it. His father had taken him to see *'Twenty Thousand Leagues Under The Sea'*. Stewart had wanted to see a cowboy film, but his father had told him that this was better for him. The magic of the dimming lights and the screen suddenly becoming alive and the voices and the music coming from the walls had enthralled and frightened him in one. He was really there, the water was real, the wind was tugging at his windcheater, his hands were clasped desperately around a sodden spar, transfixed by the colour and the sound. Then the monster had come along and scared him witless, and he had spent the remainder of the film, crouched on the floor of the cinema with his head buried into the seat, whilst his father had tried to pull him back up, vowing loudly that he would never take his cissy son to the pictures again.

'Would you like to see the aeroplanes as a treat, son?'
Stewart nodded vigorously. His father changed gear and the van lurched off the road through a gateway.
'This is called, "London Airport" son. It's the biggest in the world.' The van stopped in a cloud of dust alongside other parked cars. In front, a couple in a maroon convertible were finishing a picnic. Stewart climbed down from the van and straightened his cramped limbs. He stamped his sandals and little puffs of dust sprang up like bomb bursts. 'Pow... pow...' he stamped. His parents wandered across the beaten earth between the cars towards a white fence before which, a small crowd was standing.
Stewart looked up, shielding his eyes with his hand. It was huge, and silver, and brooding, and it stared unwinkingly down at him, saying, 'As soon as they unleash me, I'll get you.' He edged around to stand near his mother.
'That's a Viscount,' a man was saying to his girl friend. 'Guess how many passengers they can carry, go on, guess.'
'I don't know Harry.'
'Well guess then. Go on. Guess.'
'I don't know how many.'
'No, but guess. Make a stab at it. How many do you think? Ten? Fifteen?'
'Thirty?'
'Over Fifty.' Harry said, relieved that she had not guessed correctly.
'Coo!'
'Just imagine. That's more than a Green Line bus, that is. And they can

fly them to Paris in an hour and a half.'

'Oooh la la!'

'That's nothing mate,' a thickset man ventured from the rail, 'they've got a prototype what holds ninety. A real airplane. That's only a Wimpy innit?'

'A what?' someone else asked.

'S'Wellington bomber innit? Worked on them in the war. Look at the wings, 'zactly the same. But this new Bristol they're bringing out can do all this can do, and carry nearly twice as many. They say's BOAC are gonna order fifty of them.'

'Blimey!' said Harry, 'that's an awful lot of Green Lines!'

Stewart peeked out at the plane. It saw him straight away. Its nose jutting up in the air like that, sniffing him out.

'Here son, get up on my shoulders so that you can have a good look. I think that one will be leaving soon, I can see people getting into it.'

Stewart squirmed, but was lifted without more ado onto his father's shoulders. He pressed his nose into the Brylcreemed hair and anxiously watched as some brightly coloured blobs pipped up the steps and disappeared into the fuselage. The door was pulled shut, and the steps wheeled away. They were in its belly. The plane was satisfied.

With a bang and a stutter, the engines started. Men in overalls moved aside and a van scurried away. The plane suddenly lunged forwards, swung around, and blew an immense cloud of dust at them. Women held onto their skirts and hunched their shoulders against the storm. By the time that they had shaken the dust from their eyes, the plane was far over the other side of the field, weaving its way around some scattered low buildings.

'Just think son,' Albert Wrighton said, 'some day, people will get on planes like that to go to work. Just like we get on the bus or train.'

'Three colours,' Stewart thought, 'pink, yellow green.'

Alan Havering would not have gone to the airport had he permitted his heart to rule his head, but the proven ability to forestall problems that had singled him out to run the Dhaka operation for Consolidated, nagged at him that this might be a wise move. He was still a little unsure of the ramifications of Raymond Line's sudden departure. Had the Ministry of Foreign Affairs overreacted? Thank goodness Line's special task had been finished before the accident.

He squinted at the sweat-stained and crumpled telex. *'LINES REPLACEMENT NAME WRIGHTON ARRIVING BA FLIGHT FRIDAY'* and then poked it back into the breast pocket of his shirt. Wrighton? The name meant nothing to him. He shrugged and blew through his lower lip. No sense in trying to read the future. He would know soon enough.

He leaned over the barrier and watched the rabble of travellers, struggling through the chicanes of officialdom on the other side of the glass screen. It was opaque with greasy handprints and other assorted, less identifiable smears. He kicked his dirty plimsoll at the base of the barrier. He had no intention of dressing up to meet this man. Today was Friday. The Moslem day of prayer and the non-believers' day of rest.

The trickle of sweat which had run down his spine and soaked through his shirt had dried now that he was inside the air-conditioned terminal. It made his back uncomfortable with its cool clamminess. He pulled at his shirt impatiently and spat the end of his cigarette onto the floor where two urchins fought over it noisily.

'Bugger off you two!' he growled and swung his foot at them.

'*Backsheesh saheb. Khana khabo, khana khabo,*' wailed a grotesque mask of a woman's face. Red-stained buck teeth and milky, useless eyes. '*Khana khabo,*' she whined, thrusting a bundle-wrapped monkey of a baby towards him.

'And you can bugger off as well.' He pushed her away with his forearm. She stood a few feet off, her bony arm stretched out towards him in the explicit upward curve of mendicancy.

'*Khana khabo, backsheesh.*'

'Oh come on, Wrighton!' he exhorted him under his breath. 'The bloody plane has been down half an hour.' He knew in all honesty that passage through customs and immigration at Dhaka airport depended, to a greater extent, upon whom you bribed, and how much. Of course Wrighton should think of that, being one of the company's globetrotting troubleshooters. He glanced at his watch. Twenty minutes to get back to Gulshan, dump Wrighton at the Transit House, say ten minutes, over to Baridhara, ten minutes. He could just fit in a game of squash with Gerry, if only Wrighton would hurry up. 'Oh sod it!' He vaulted over the barrier and walked into the baggage claim hall.

'No entry saheb, no entry,' the airport guard chanted out to him. Havering waved him away and walked up to one of the customs inspectors who was picking his teeth with his thumb nail as he surveyed the group of travellers awaiting their baggage.

'Hello Abdul Malik.'

'Mr. Havering, how do you do?'

Havering ignored the outstretched hand and waved his own hand to show that he had no baggage. 'I'm not travelling, Abdul Malik. I've come to meet a friend, a colleague, off the BA flight.

'BA flight baggage is there, saheb.' He motioned with his eyebrows.

'I don't want him to have to wait, Abdul, I'll bring him to you, OK?'

'OK. No problem.'

But Havering was watching a European untangling his hand baggage from his shoulder, and trying to slot it into the top tray of a baggage trolley. That could not be him, surely? Bespectacled, unimpressive, and inconsequential. Oh my God! Look at those trousers! Like a bloody clown, and why is he the only one to be wearing an anorak, for Christ's sake?

'Wrighton?' he called, and with sinking feeling in his stomach saw the man turn. Havering went to him. 'Wrighton?'

'That's me, Stewart Wrighton. You must be–'

'Alan Havering. Good flight?' he asked abruptly, and steered the man and his trolley over to the Customs bench.

'Yes, very impressive, only the second time I've ever flown and I–'

'Abdul, this is my colleague.' Havering ignored Wrighton, and addressed the Bengali customs officer. 'He's got nothing to declare. No stereo, no video, no camera.'

'No stereo?'

'None.'

Abdul Malik sucked on his teeth and rubbed a grimy finger in his greasy moustache.

'No video?' he enquired, in a tone of half dejection, half disbelief.

'No video,' Havering replied, stoutly shaking his head.

'No camera?' He shook his head and the whites of his eyes showed momentarily,

'No camera, Abdul Malik.' Havering looked him straight in the eye.

'Well, I have got the replacement laser sight for the theodolite that was stolen,' Wrighton suggested helpfully. 'That's a sort of optical equipment. The office asked me to bring it out for you. 'Thought you might have difficulty getting it otherwise.'

'What is 'lazy sight' please?' Abdul Malik asked, his curiosity aroused.

'For Christ's sake, Wrighton, shut up!' Havering turned away from the customs officer to hide his mouth. Wrighton swallowed hard and beat the air ineffectually with his free hand.

'Are you having import permit for lazy sight?'

Havering leaned across the bench, and drew the customs officer to him. 'Listen, Abdul. My colleague, here, thinks that he is a funny man, you know? He makes people laugh. Look at his trousers, huh? Burra pajama, huh?' He nudged Abdul Malik, "Lazy sight" Supposed to be a joke. Meant to be funny. I didn't understand it either.' He took a bundle of dirty, one hundred taka notes from his shirt pocket and pressed them into the Bengali's hand. 'You chalk the bags and we'll go, O.K.? No problem?' He grinned but a moment's hesitation stalled the negotiation.

'No video?' Abdul Malik started again from the beginning.

'Look Abdul...' Havering raised his voice, but lowered it immediately he saw that the Bengali had begun to look around for aid. 'Look Abdul,' he whispered, 'we are in a hurry. He's got nothing in his bags. O.K? Look.' He turned away again and hissed urgently at Wrighton, 'Which bag is the sight in?' Wrighton tapped his shoulder bag discreetly. 'Look Abdul.' He swung Wrighton's suitcase up to the bench, flipped up the catch and threw open the lid. Wrighton started involuntarily at the brazen invasion of his privacy. It was somehow natural in his ordered mind for a customs officer to look in his suitcase, but not for a colleague to do it. 'He's got nothing in it.'

Abdul Malik sulkily prodded the piles of clothes and pulled out Wrighton's sun glasses.

'Ah,' he said, and put them in his pocket.

'Just a minute,' Wrighton protested. 'They're my sunglasses.'

'All OK Abdul, No problem.' Havering ignored Wrighton's protests. 'Chalk the case.'

With a flourish, the customs officer scrawled on the suitcase in blue chalk.

'Come on, Wrighton,' Havering ordered.

'But they were Polaroid glasses.'

'Thanks Abdul.' Havering smiled. 'A pleasure to do business with you.'

They started off towards the door but were halted by the Bengali's hail of, 'One minute saheb.' He was pointing at Wrighton's shoulder bag and beckoning them back, all in one convoluted motion of his hand.

'Now come on Abdul, we're in a hurry.' Havering tried to sound impatient rather than worried that a ten thousand pound theodolite sight might be confiscated, but the customs officer continued to beckon, and the guard at the door had now noticed the two troublesome travellers.

'Back we go,' Havering said under his breath, with a resignation that was tinged with accusation.

'Number two bag please.' The officer pointed at Wrighton's bag again.

'Now, come on, Abdul, no problem.'

Wrighton slowly slid the bag from his shoulder and placed it gingerly onto the bench. Havering fumed. Abdul Malik looked at it for an instant, and then finding a smooth panel at one end, triumphantly chalked a pig's tail on it. 'Two piece, baggage, saheb. No problem.' He smiled and waved them away.

'Keep going!' Havering warned Wrighton under his breath as they made for the exit for the second time. 'If the guard stops you, just keep walking. I'll do the talking.'

Wrighton nodded, trying with difficulty to believe that all this was happening.

Once outside, Havering strode through the crowd to a grey Land Rover, parked under the canopy. He unlocked the back door and motioned Wrighton to put his bag in, and then get in the front. Somewhere at the back of Havering's mind was the conviction that he had missed a small but important detail. One that had caught in the gullet of his reason, like a fish bone awaiting to choke him at an embarrassing moment.

What was the lunatic up to now? Can't he even open a Land Rover door? 'Pull the handle up,' he shouted through the window at the fumbling anorak.

'Sorry,' Wrighton apologised. 'Not used to Land Rovers.'

'What do you normally–?' Havering tailed off, as the fishbone tickled him again. Got it. 'I'm sure you said back in the terminal, that you hadn't flown BA before, or it was only the second time, didn't you?' he enquired, as they rumbled off down the ramp into the afternoon sun.

Wrighton was irritatingly offhand as he looked about him, at the strange sights like a.... like a tourist, a bloody tourist!

'No, what I meant was, this was only the second time I have flown at all. It's quite a long flight for a second one.'

Havering pulled on the wheel and inserted the Land Rover between a rickshaw and a bus as he turned into Airport Road. 'Where were you before Dhaka, then?'

'London.'

'No, I know that,' he said. 'Before London?'

'London,' the man said. 'I've only ever worked in London. This is the first time they have sent me abroad. What's that place there?'

'The Barracks Railway Station.' Havering's voice seemed to leave him through the far end of a pipe. With it, went any wish to continue the conversation. He didn't want to hear any more. If he was not told of the man's inexperience, then he reasoned that he would not have to worry about it. But he knew he was not fooling himself. He was worried. Although, this bod might be quite capable after all.

No he wouldn't! If he had been any good he would have been sent out a long time ago. He stole a quick glance across the front seat of the truck. The chap was nearly as old as him, yet in engineering terms he was only a schoolboy. Look at him goggling at the traffic! Havering tried to think back to when he was like that but it seemed to him that he had always been experienced.

Was Wrighton going to try to see romance in the searing yellow globe of the sun as it sets down Airport Road, into a grey bouffant of cloud? Would he convince himself that the cloud was some distant cyclone, swirling over the Bay of Bengal? How long would it take him to realise that it was only pollution?

Would he wander through markets, as Havering had done? He remembered now, not in Bangladesh, but in some other post, Sumatra or Malawi or somewhere. Would he marvel, bright-eyed, at the displays of colourful and exotic fruits and vegetables, and not see the flies crawling over them, the excrement in the alleyways, the filth of ignorance and the corruption, bred of cupidity?

Would he look at these brown-skinned, brown-eyed people, mild-mannered and servile, and would he befriend them? Would he think that the smiles they shone on him, the bright band of white teeth, were declarations of trust and friendship? What would he feel when his cook-bearer of impeccable and punctilious honesty, stole his radio and sold it down in the bazaar, but got back home in time to, tearfully, join in the search of the house and display just the correct amount of concern and grief? When would he rumble the natives? How long would it take him to realise that they were all lying, thieving, conniving, deceitful, corrupt, cruel, unscrupulous, wogs?

Havering blasted his horn at a baby-taxi which was creeping along the wrong side of the road towards him, and forced it into the scrub. Wrighton had stopped trying to engage him in conversation after the first near-miss with a lorry loaded with sacks of jute.

What was London playing at, sending him a novice? He swung the truck into Kemal Ataturk Avenue and then tore down a side road, the exhaust bellowing between the garden walls and the tyres swirling high the piles of white building sand which were heaped outside occasional unfinished plots.

'This is Banani.' Wrighton nodded. 'All the Dips, Aid people and the like, either live in Banani or Gulshan, up the road. Mostly in Gulshan actually. You're sharing a transit house with two other chaps. Good fellows, you'll like them.' Havering tried to sound convincing.

He stopped the Land Rover at the crossroads of four, walled gardens, and blew the horn. A blue sack which had been thrown, crumpled, onto a rattan chair, suddenly leapt upwards, formed itself into the shape of a wiry native, saluted and swung open the garden gates, grinning gleefully all the while.

'Your chowkidhar,' Havering said. 'His name's Mohammed. But then, aren't they all?' he ended mysteriously.

Wrighton clambered down from the Land Rover and watched apprehensively as his suitcase was lifted from the back and carried majestically into the gloom of the interior on the thin shoulders of Mohammed.

'I'll leave you here, the other two are inside. They are expecting you. Take a day's rest to get over the flight and start work on Sunday. Don't worry, I'll send the van for you on Sunday morning. The driver knows where to go. See you Sunday,' Havering called, as he reversed the van violently out into the road. He looked at his watch. Five minutes to Baridhara, then down to the club for a game of squash.

He roared off across the causeway towards Gulshan and Baridhara, surprised that he felt vaguely settled by the safe delivery of Wrighton to his home.

'Oh shit!' he swore, as he remembered that the laser sight was still with Wrighton in his bag. 'Oh well, he'll have to bring it in to the office himself, that's all.'

He blew the horn as he turned the corner of his street and the chowkidhar had got the garden gates wide open by the time he had arrived level with his house.

'Get my things out, Raouf,' he ordered, and strode indoors. 'Mary?' he called from the corridor.

'In here,' his wife replied from the sitting room. 'I've got you a beer.'

Havering grabbed the can and, ignoring the glass on the table, he began noisily emptying its contents down his throat, as if washing away the taste of the conversation with the man from London.

'Did you find him alright?' Mary Havering asked, pushing her flame red hair back over her shoulders, and holding her magazine up towards the rays of dusty sunshine which were filtering through the mosquito screen.

'Oh yes, I found him alright!' Havering replied. 'I could hardly miss him, I tell you! He had trousers from Oxfam. No, that's an insult to Oxfam. And he was wearing an anorak. Would you believe, a fur-lined anorak?' Havering waved his arm to emphasise his point and a geyser of foaming beer ejaculated from his can and smacked on the wall. 'Oh shit!'

'Oh Alan, do be more careful,' she chided him. 'Meelong!' she called, and indicated the dripping wall to the bearer when he poked his head around the kitchen door. 'Master spilled the beer, Meelong.'

Meelong grinned a full two rows of sparkling teeth and then nodded as he began to mop the wall with the cloth that never left his hand.

'You can wipe that smile off your stupid grinning face,' Havering spat at him.

'Alan! Do sit down and calm down. Tell me about this man from London, Wilson or whatever his name is.'

Havering took a deep breath and glared at the Bengali bearer, then he let out his breath noisily and collapsed into a low chair.

'Remember Raymond Line?'

'Of course,' his wife replied, puzzled.

'Well, Wrighton's nothing like him. He's a prat. He practically handed over our laser sight to the customs at Zia Airport. 'Please Mr. Customs Officer, sir, I haven't got a camera but I have got this valuable piece of irreplaceable equipment upon which there is no doubt a hefty duty and double backsheesh payable if you would like to have a look at it, sir.' Prat!'

'He didn't!'

'He did, as good as.'

'Well, have you got the sight?'

'Yes, or rather no. He has still got it, but it is safe from the Customs in any case.' He drained his can of beer noisily. 'I'm going to get changed for a game of squash.'

'Oh I forgot,' his wife began. 'Gerry phoned whilst you were out. He said he can't make it for squash this afternoon, he's got to take Moira to Newmarket.'

'Hen-pecked twerp!'

'What do you fancy for dinner tonight darling? We could have some-thing nice, we've still got steak in the freezer. I'm sure cook could manage to grill it without doing too much wrong.'

Havering picked up his attache case and took out a sheaf of papers whilst he considered the infallibility of the cook. He was warming to a cosy evening with Mary, then his dreams were shattered by the memory of an engagement.

'We can't. We're invited to Major Haq's for dinner tonight. I'd forgotten all about it.'

'Major Haq?' Mary seemed to recall hearing that name often in connection with her husband's dealings with the Ministry of Foreign Affairs.

'Major Abdul Haq, M.P. He is somebody I have got to be nice to and so have you, I'm afraid.'

Mary Havering was quite prepared to be nice to rich and influential Bengalis, if it furthered her husband's career. Otherwise, she was not really interested in what actually occurred in the country as long as she, and her little world, were untouched. She thought of herself as the type of woman who could live on the Indian subcontinent for twenty years without it affecting her essential goodness as an Englishwoman, dedicated to her husband's success.

Havering pulled a small table towards him and began to lay out his papers.

'Do you have to work now?'

'Yes,' he replied distractedly.

'What is it?' Mary asked in a tone which Havering recognised. It indicated that she would not be fobbed off with little boy's talk.

'You remember what I was saying the other day about the pipeline, and how it behaves in a saturated subsoil?'

She frowned. 'The "holding a football under water" trick?'

'That's it. Well to hold our football down, we need to encase the pipe in a concrete jacket otherwise the bloody thing will float to the surface and rupture. I am trying to work out the optimum weight of concrete per metre that we will need. That's all.'

He bent to his work and Mary went quietly into the bedroom to lay out her clothes for the evening. Major Haq, she remembered now, liked to make love to white women.

5

As Wrighton advanced down the gloomy marble-flagged corridor, his eyes fixed anxiously on his suitcase which wobbled on the chowkidhars' shoulder, a door suddenly opened behind him and flooded the corridor with light.

Gerry Bell only ever looked plump when he was sitting down. As soon as he stood up it became obvious that he was squarely built, to which his middling height seemed to add an extra few degrees of implied strength. Indeed, the act of standing up with measured slowness was usually all that was required to encourage many an antagonist to withdraw the imprudent word or disguise the hasty deed. His shoulders were in the rugby player's mould, and his legs had meat on them that had been exercised on many a squash court. His arms hung away from his trunk, like a pair of parentheses embracing his body, and he swung them gently in his discreet swaggering walk, as if the biceps muscles were too bulky to allow them to lie flat.

His head was square, with shortish brown hair, but it was his face that had proved to be his most persuasive asset. Blue-eyed, and as freckle-nosed as a schoolboy's, it successfully promoted the uttering of statements which would have been dismissed as outlandish, impossible, untrue, fantastic, had it not been for the fervent corroboration to be read in its earnestly furrowed forehead and thin arched eyebrows. When he spoke, his voice coyly revealed vestiges of a public school education and yet, although it was rich in the modulation and timbre of that milieu, it was singularly unadorned by its vocabulary. A cello playing Cole-Porter.

Bell swung towards Wrighton, transferred his beer can to his left hand and proffered his right.

'You're Wrighton are you?' Wrighton nodded. 'I'm Gerry Bell, one of the other occupants of this luxurious residence.' He nodded to the dark end of the corridor. 'Tuppin is the other one, but he's having a siesta at the moment.' He shouted over Wrighton's shoulder to the chowkidhar, 'Mohammed! This is Mr. Wrighton.' The chowkidhar bowed his head. 'Put his case in there.' He pointed to a door at the end of the corridor. 'That will be his room. O.K.?'

'Yussup.'

'Come in here, have a sit down. We've given you Lines' old room. It seemed only fair. What do you want to drink? We've got beer, beer or beer.'

Wrighton looked around the room before sitting down on the sofa.

'I'd quite like a drink of water thanks.'

'Water!' Bell snorted. 'That'll kill you. You can have a cup of tea.'

'Yes please.'

'I'll get Moussi, that's the cook-bearer, to make some. Do you need anything to eat?'

'No thanks.' Wrighton patted his stomach. 'I seem to have been eating since I left London.'

Bell sprang to his feet. 'I'll be back in a minute. Then I can tell you how everything works.'

Wrighton sat very still for a few seconds and then said quietly to himself, 'Well, I'm here.'

He scrutinised the room. It wore a pastiche of disjointed memorabilia of such heterogeneous origins that the very diversity became a style of its own. It was like the left-overs from a jumble sale. On the wall above the dining table at the far end of the room, hung a large coloured photographic poster of a weirdly clad lady, with long tresses of black hair, doing something unspecified with a spotted snake. Next to her was pinned an ammonia print of a surveyor's map of part of Dhaka. On the low table by one of the windows was a large radio and cassette player and a native stringed instrument apparently fashioned out of a gourd. A stack of newspapers on the floor in the corner was weighed down by the bulk, and probably the mysticism, of a volume on oriental philosophy.

On the ceiling, two dust-encrusted electric fans were slowly wobbling and the windows, with their wrought iron bars outside and mosquito wire inside, seemed to have been designed to impede the passage of light. The emulsion paint was flaking from an entire wall and up in the corner sat a beige coloured lizard. With its twelve feet high ceilings and the air-conditioning unit projecting from the wall above the window, nobody could mistake this for a room in an English house.

I think I'm going to like Bell. The firm, no-nonsense hand shake, not the handful of wet fish you get in the office, and the direct look in his eyes when he speaks to you. Yes, he decided, Bell's a good chap.

'Right, where were we?' Bell strode through the doorway, beer can still welded to his fist.

'I think,' Wrighton felt almost apologetic, 'that you were going to gen me up on everything.'

'Oh yes. Well first of all, the house. You saw the garden when you were dropped off. By the way, was that your boss?'

'Yes.'

'Cheerful bugger wasn't he? Had you upset him or something?'

'Yes.' Wrighton decided that he would keep the story of the laser sight to himself. 'I couldn't open the door of the Land Rover!'

'Ah ha! You are not the first to be fooled by that. The handle goes up doesn't it? It always looks as if it should be pulled down. Is it your first overseas posting then, or have you been anywhere before?'

'No, it's my first.'

'It's my second time in Dhaka.' Bell threw a hairy leg over the arm of the chair. 'Came out six years ago as well. Just for a quick contract. It's a good set-up. Social life's good, but you have to work hard at it, know what I mean?'

Wrighton nodded. 'What job are you on?' he asked.

'The Hovercraft Project.'

'Oh. What's that?'

'You haven't heard of the Hovercraft Project?' Bell demanded, scandalised.

'Well... er...'

He grinned at Wrighton's discomfort. 'Nobody has heard of it,' he admitted. 'Some economic expert at Unesco came out and studied the situation in Bangladesh and then drew the astounding conclusion that the biggest and easiest question to solve would be the transport problem. As Bangladesh is about forty-five per cent under water, this clever chap decreed, "What they need is hovercraft." So here we are.'

'But what do you do with them?'

'We repair them, mostly. They are not very reliable.'

'How many have you got?'

'Three. Two personnel carriers and one freight. We start them up and frighten all the water buffaloes away. Then we take them for a training run across the paddy fields and ruin all the poor buggers' crops. Then we run up the river and blow a few country boats onto the banks with our prop wash. Then we try to get back to our maintenance base before anything important drops off. It's all completely pointless. When we arrived here they had prepared us an apron of beaten mud. You try jacking up a fifty ton hovercraft on beaten mud.'

'But what will they use them for?'

'They won't. You don't think that we could ever teach them how to fly a hovercraft, do you? They will always need European pilots. It's useful experience for us though.'

'Who flies their aeroplanes then? Do they have Europeans for pilots?'

'Bangladesh Biman? No they've got Banglas. They can do that.'

'Well why can't they fly hovercraft?'

Bell scratched his head, pursed his lips and then looked at the ceiling.

'I suppose they will be able to, eventually. That's a gecko.' He changed the subject by pointing at the lizard which had now crept down the wall. 'Also known as a chit chat. From the noise it makes. We leave them alone because they eat mosquitoes and as far as I am concerned, anything that eats mosquitoes must be on our side.'

'I agree with that. Is there much malaria in Dhaka?'

'Not in Dhaka. Not in the city. There's plenty of mossies though. They're quite easy to catch.' He swiped his hand in a semi-circle, snapped the fist shut, and then ground the fingers together and opened his palm for inspection. In the middle was a blood stain and a squashed black spot.

'I didn't realise that insects had blood in them.' Wrighton was quite surprised.

Bell shot him a glance. 'It's not the mossie's blood is it?' he remarked drily.

'Oh no, I suppose not.' Wrighton attempted to cover his stupidity. 'Do you take anti-malaria tablets?'

'Not always. Nobody staying in Dhaka takes them. They have shocking side effects.' He turned those blue eyes on Wrighton with sincerity. 'Some people have gone green on them.'

'My doctor said that I ought to take them all the while.'

'It's up to you. Most people start off taking them, but they always drop them, sooner or later. Here's your tea.'

A diminutive brown man, wearing a lunghi and a blue shirt, carefully settled a silver tray on the table.

'Moussi, this is Mr. Wrighton,' Bell said in a loud voice as if the man were deaf. 'He is instead of Mr. Line. O.K.?'

'Saheb.' The man looked at Wrighton and grinned.

'That's all, Moussi. No dinner tonight.'

'No dinner saheb?'

'No dinner, Moussi, Not Tuppin saheb. Not Wrighton saheb. Not Bell saheb. No dinner. O.K.?'

He acknowledged, with the native, sideways diagonal shake of the head, which so infuriates Europeans.

'We'll go out for a meal tonight. We'll treat you. Show you the sights.' He pointed to the tray. 'Drink your tea. Don't look too closely at the crockery, the Bangladesh concept of cleanliness doesn't come anywhere near ours. The milk's quite safe. It's a German aid project. They've got a dairy just outside Dhaka. Makes proper pasteurised milk.'

The tea tasted solely of sterilised milk. Wrighton took a sip and then yawned.

'Jet lag,' Bell observed. 'When you've finished your tea, get some z's in, and you'll be as right as rain later on.'

'Do what?'

'Get some z's in. Get some sleep. A couple of hours should be enough. I'll wake you at seven thirty – that'll give you time for a shit, shower and shave before we go out.'

It was not, Wrighton thought, the happiest alliterative sequence that he had encountered, but he grudgingly admitted that it conveyed its meaning.

His room was gloomy, despite the brilliant sunshine outside, for the curtains had been drawn across the window. He left them drawn, realising that this would help keep the room cool. The chowkidhar had placed his suitcase on the dressing table with his anorak laid on top. He pondered for a moment whether he wanted to unpack straight away but the bed looked too tempting, so he eased off his shoes and lay down.

He closed his eyes and listened to the street outside his window. A hawker was wandering up the street, crying 'Baaaa' at irregular intervals. The many, tinny rickshaw bells seemed to be calling to each other, one now nearby, another now down at the other corner, now one in the other lane. He puzzled at the curious slapping sound till he eventually surmised that it was the noise of native sandals or bare feet, he knew not which, as they walked along the road. Somewhere several blocks away, he could hear the uneven thick thrumming of a badly regulated diesel locomotive and the toy-like rattling of its carriages. Of course, he thought, it must be metre-gauge railway, so it would sound lighter than the trains we are used to.

Images of Dhaka drifted across his mind's eye. The airport had possessed the international characterlessness of airports worldwide. A place that you moved through. Outside, he had been unprepared for the buffeting wall of heat and humanity; the number of people everywhere, not in crowds but spaced out which made then seem even more numerous. The contact; children plucking at his sleeve and demanding

'Backsheesh,' the twisted beggars at the traffic lights, clawing at the windows of the van, and of course... the traffic.

The traffic had both frightened and awed him. The rule of the road was apparently the same as in the U.K. Drive on the left. But it seemed like a proving ground for Darwin's theory of evolution and the survival of the fittest. At the edge of the road would be found the rickshaws, or more properly, 'cycle trishaws', and the bicycles. The bicycles were all old-fashioned black upright models carrying one, two or perhaps three Bengalis, frozen into unbelievable equilibrium. Then came the private cars which were either modern saloons or jeeps of some sort. Down the middle of the road charged the trucks and buses. The trucks were yellow Bedfords, with their blue platform backs twisted and warped from years of abuse and overloading. They crabbed across the road because of their bent chasses. Rivalling them were the buses; windowless, lopsided torpedoes, lurching along with as many passengers hanging on to the outside as there were inside, wallowing from one pothole to the next.

He had been surprised by the amount of building work in progress in Banani Model Town. At every street corner could be seen a pyramid of fine, white building sand, looking uncannily like cement, and a pile of orange bricks. Enormous, unfinished private houses stood in brick and concrete skeleton, windowless, doorless, awaiting a purchaser or tenant to pay for their promotion from gaunt card-house to marble palace. Each house was surrounded by a six feet high wall with an iron gate, guarded by a chowkidhar. The manpower employed must have been phenomenal, but then, manpower was apparently a commodity of which Bangladesh appeared to have an ever-increasing supply.

Suddenly, there was a harsh and powerful banging on his door and Bell's voice boomed, 'Seven thirty, Wrighton, time to get up!'

'I must have been asleep,' was all that he could think of saying.

'...and the radar operator sat behind the captain and the first engineer. Now he always had his head over the screen. This was in the days of the old horizontal cathode displays. You know the ones I mean. Nowadays of course it's a vertical display like a television screen. Well, on the front of the binnacle, just down here,' Bell pushed his hand down to the side of his chair in demonstration, 'was the on/off switch for the scanner. You switch it off, and the scanner stops going around and just stands still.

'So there you would be, say about four miles out of Boulogne and bound for Dover with about two hundred passengers and thirty cars on board, crossing the busiest shipping lane in the world at sixty knots.

Three times faster than anything else. Tankers, coasters, fishing boats out of Folkestone and Boulogne, week-end wallies in their G.P.14's and Peter Storm waterproofs and of course, the ferries, charging all over the place.

'Anyway, we'd decide to have a bit of fun with the poor old radar op. You know. The captain would say, "Radar, ferry about two miles to starboard. Just keep an eye on it, tell me what it's doing." Then I'd switch the scanner off, and then all you got was a bloody thin bright line on the cathode, stationary. Radar would say nothing for a second or two, then the captain would ask, casually like, "What's the ferry doing?" and turn around and look at the radar officer. By this time, the poor bugger is twiddling knobs and tuning the set, like he was looking for the World Service in a thunderstorm. So the captain then says, innocently, "Anything wrong, Radar?" and Radar would come back with something like, "Just a minor fault, sir. Soon have it fixed".

'Meanwhile, we're closing five thousand tons of ferry at sixty knots and the captain is saying, 'Well is it crossing or going down-lane or what?' Radar's bent over his screen, beads of sweat breaking out on his brow, and just staring mesmerised at the bright line. I'd be looking, interestedly, out of the window and whistling to myself, then I would quietly reach down and flick the switch back on and the scanner would start up and Radar would say, in a sort of squeaky voice, "Ferry on starboard side, making way, will cross behind us on present course."'

Bell guffawed. 'You could only do that trick once, though, because as soon as Radar reported the fault on return to base, they would set him wise and then take the piss out of him something rotten. Mind you, the bastards had a go at me one day. You know those toy cars, with a battery in and the wheels that turn automatically when they reach a wall? Got a flashing light on top and a siren. Well, one of the buggers slipped this thing into an equipment locker and set it off during the crossing. Captain turns to me and says casually, "See to that alarm." Well there's so many bloody alarms on a hovercraft, there seems to be one for everything, and they all have a different sound, but I had never heard this one before. "Wee-wee-wee-wee-wee" it went.

'I looked around the cabin, I couldn't work out what it was. The captain was doing his looking-at-something-interesting-through-the-windscreen act, and Radar had got his nose stuck on his screen. Well, I looked about, down on the floor, up on the ceiling panel, "Wee-wee-wee-wee" it went. Then down by my seat I could see this sort of orange flashing light. Of course, this bloody toy car was crashing around in there, amongst the equipment, but I could see the light through the grill every now and then, when it passed. I ended up squeezed down on the floor, fishing this bloody thing out. God what a laugh they had!' Bell scooped another spoonful of rice from his plate and shovelled it into his mouth.

Tuppin took advantage of the momentary lull to observe, 'They have hostess girls on those cross-channel hovercraft, don't they?' It was an invitation, nudging Bell into a different sort of story.

Tuppin was a slight young man of about twenty five years. He had a swarthy complexion, not due entirely to his exposure to the sun, and his yellowish skin which was drawn tightly across his cheeks had started to puff and bag around his eyes, contemporary proof that he was misspending his youth and enjoying every transaction. His black hair was thick, long, and cut in the fashion of the day. He wore a bright turquoise shirt which billowed loosely about him and, Wrighton thought, made him look like a Viking sailing ship of his school-book days. His black eyes wandered restlessly about the restaurant, pausing briefly upon the few women in turn. He clearly considered himself to be the match for any woman there. His actions were somehow aimless, as if the reason or motive for making the movement had dissipated during its execution, and so it faltered to its end rather than vividly attaining its goal.

He looked back to Bell and added, as a seasoning, 'They wear uniform.'

'Oh those uniforms...' Tuppin had turned the signpost and Bell had hurtled off down the other side of the bifurcation. 'You know that they had two new uniforms each year, at one point? Silly things, always had a stupid hat with a brim or a feather, or some fine thing in it, just designed to catch the wind. You can imagine what the wind is like on three acres of clean concrete alongside the Channel, can't you? Even in the summer they always kept one hand on their hats because they weren't allowed to take them off you know. Disciplinary offence, that was.

'Someone told us that the dress designers were given the same brief each year. They had to make something with enough cloth in it to look stylish, but not enough to blow about. I don't know how they worked out the formula but every year as soon as the girls appeared in their new uniforms, there would be a race to be the first to get a new skirt up. Not only to prove the designers wrong, you understand. It never took longer than a week. There was all kinds of ways when the wind didn't oblige us.

Wrighton had pushed back his chair at the beginning of the story because he had suspected that it was going to be a little saucy. Tuppin, however, had given Bell his complete attention, his only movement being to absently fiddle with a large gold signet ring on his left hand. When Bell paused to draw on his cigarette or reflect, Tuppin encouraged him forward with a mute intensification of his attitude, willing him to elaborate or add that special fine detail that just clinched the essence of the story.

The table before them was littered with the remains of a Chinese meal: plate warmers, a multitude of oval-shaped dishes, odd pieces of cutlery and, distributed around the table, a random selection of stains and debris. Somehow, Chinese meals always seemed to end like this. They had eaten well, although, as Tuppin had warned them, 'You'll need a microscope to find the meat'.

Wrighton had drunk an iced Coca-Cola with his meal, the other two had discreetly opened cans of beer which they had brought with them. They poured them into tea cups, from which they drank with relish, and without upsetting the Muslim law. The restaurant, although it was a Chinese restaurant and not a Bengali one, was, in common with all public commerces, not permitted to serve alcohol, so the customers brought their own and since the majority of the customers were Europeans, this did not offend the natives. In fact, sometimes a trade would be established between tables as the Australians swapped their Fosters for the Americans' Budweisers, all drawn from insulated cool-boxes which could be seen lurking under the dim shade of the table cloth.

The restaurant was called 'The Pekin Duck', and was only ten minutes drive from their house. Bell had explained that in this part of the city, everything was only ten minutes away – the market, the bank, the club, the telegraph office. Only the hospital was further, it was down on Old Airport Road and the old airport was now the military air base.

'The hospital,' Bell had announced, 'is officially called something like the International Centre for Diarrhoea Disease Research, and it is very good at identifying all kinds of afflictions.' Wrighton had waited. He had only known Bell a few hours, but already he realised that some more was coming. 'But everyone calls it the "Shit Lab". Quite appropriate really. You'll get your membership card whilst you're here. Nobody, but nobody, escapes the shits in Dhaka.' His ominous warning was delivered from behind a serious grin.

A small group of Americans was now preparing to leave, moving chairs, collecting cool-boxes and threading their way towards the door. A scrubbed man in yellow bermuda shorts suddenly accosted Bell.

'Hey, Gerry! Howya doin' kiddo?' He slapped him on the back.

'Hello Don. This is a new arrival in Dhaka.' He began to introduce Wrighton, but the American, whom Wrighton realised was remarkably like a USA version of Bell, stepped around the table and thrust his hand at him.

'Don Finkelstein. U.S. Aid.'

'Stewart Wrighton. Pleased to meet you.'

'Say, do you play cricket?'

The question seemed completely incongruous in the mouth of an American.

'No I don't.'

'Gee, don't any of you Brits play cricket?' he complained.

Wrighton looked at the other two, but Tuppin was watching one of the American women adjust an eyelash, and Bell simply grinned and said, 'Don is trying to get a cricket team going. But only the Americans seem to want to play.'

'But don't you play baseball?' Wrighton asked.

'Any jerk can play baseball! But cricket, now that is something different.'

'I can't play baseball,' Wrighton admitted, wondering whether that classified him as a jerk, or not a jerk, and then wondering in the same sequitur whether the term 'jerk' was pejorative.

'Well if you want to join my team just let me know. You'll see me around. Nice meetin' yer Stooart. Come on honey.' He turned to the woman with the errant eyelash and they left.

'What's U.S. Aid doing?' Tuppin roused himself from his reverie now.

'Some project with the villagers near Tongi. Education and medicine, and things like that. They wander up in their air-conditioned Toyotas and preach to them.' Bell drew another cigarette and showed the packet to Wrighton. 'Bangladesh Tobacco,' he explained, mysteriously, 'not pukka U.K. fags. Same label but made locally. They're foul.' He grinned sheepishly. 'But I still smoke them. You don't smoke do you?'

'No, but I don't mind if you smoke.'

'Thanks,' said Bell stiffly, and he offered a cigarette to Tuppin who refused it by holding up an already lighted one. 'So you don't smoke, and you don't drink. What do you do?'

'I don't really know,' Wrighton sighed. 'Just exist, I suppose. Who pays for the rent of the house we are in?'

'That's the World Bank,' Tuppin said. 'All our projects are financed by the World Bank so they sort out the accommodation and pay the rent. We pay the servants and provide our own food, which brings me to the point where I explain the finances.'

'Oh sure,' Wrighton said, feeling in his pocket.

'Don't be silly, I'm talking about the house. We're treating you for this.' He waved his arm over the table. 'Anyway you haven't got any taka.'

'No, that's true.'

Tuppin looked across at Bell. 'Can you take him to Grindlay's tomorrow to open an account? I've got other things to do.'

'Yeah, no problem.'

'That's awfully decent of you.'

'Idiot! The quicker you get some money, the quicker you can start contributing. Right, now pay attention. We have two servants at the house, a cook-bearer called Moussi and a chowkidhar called Mohammed.'

'And a night chowkidhar, Bilbo,' Bell added.

'Three,' Tuppin amended. 'We pay them monthly, sixteen hundred taka to Moussi and a thousand each to the other two. So at the end of every month we pool our money and pay the salaries. Now, the food we pay for every day on the revered "cook book" system.' Bell snorted and Tuppin frowned at him. 'I'll show you the book when we get back. Moussi goes out marketing every day and buys the food. He writes down in the book what he has spent, or rather, what he claims to have spent. We take it in turns to put a few hundred taka in the book every morning, and then we even it out at the end of the month.'

'Moussi does the cooking, does he?'

'The cooking, washing, ironing, sweeping and stealing.'

'Not all the stealing,' Bell interjected. 'The other two help him in that.'

'Who decides what we have to eat?'

'We let Moussi do that. Neither of us can be bothered, and he is pretty good. He doesn't give us rice every day.'

'What kind of food do you have?'

'All European,' Bell said. 'All the cooks in Dhaka cook European, unless you specifically ask them for something different. We usually have a curry on Fridays. Some people... with wives,' he added darkly, 'order their meals day by day, and plan them but we can't be bothered. We are rarely there at lunchtime so apart from breakfast, dinner is the only thing to worry about and we are often dining in other people's houses. They have better cooks.'

'And better wives,' Tuppin leered.

'Are you married?' was the only remark that Wrighton could think of making at that juncture. Tuppin's attitude had made him wriggle with unease.

'Yup, I'm married. The missus will be coming out as soon as I can get organised.'

Wrighton looked across at Bell.

'Sort of,' Bell admitted, with apparent great reluctance. 'Yeah, sort of.'

He nodded his head in short, jerky movements, as if trying to convince himself, as well as Wrighton. 'Come on, it's time to go. I must get my beauty sleep.'

As they stepped outside, they were met by that waft of warm air that was soon to become so familiar to Wrighton. The 'Pekin Duck' was situated at the large roundabout called DIT 2 . At the other end of the avenue, one mile to the south, there existed its twin called DIT 1. It was explained to him that if he could quickly learn to distinguish one from the other, then the entire secret of navigating around Banani and Gulshan would have been mastered at one stroke.

Wrighton stood surveying the passing rickshaws with their hurricane lamps slung underneath, looking at the strings of naked light bulbs, hooped and looped along the front of a fruit shop, and watching the people everywhere. Some children, hardly old enough to walk, were still playing in the dust at the side of the road, tended only by their older sister of six or seven years.

Seeing Wrighton, a rickshaw diverted itself from its cruising and rattled towards him, aiming at him so that he had to jump aside.

'Hey watchit!' Wrighton called, as he stepped backwards.

'*Allo Bunder*. Rickshaw saheb?' The puller tucked his lunghi tighter around his legs and grinned an invitation as he patted the seat behind him. 'Only one taka saheb, only one taka.'

As if that were the magic key, rickshaws suddenly began converging upon Wrighton from all directions, each one aiming his transport directly at him like a battering ram.

'Rickshaw saheb.'

'Give me one taka.'

'Only one taka saheb.'

'*Allo Bunder.*'

In no time, Wrighton was surrounded by an impenetrable mesh of wheels and canopies and handlebars, as each puller vied with the others for the custom represented by one white man.

'Look, let me out. I say. Come on, be a sport.' He tried to move one of the contraptions, not realising how heavy it actually was. The puller sat astride the crossbar and said something in Bengali, and all the others laughed and jeered at Wrighton as he now began to panic, pulling and pushing at the cage, but no matter what he did, just when he had carved a passage it would close up again and he would find himself with a handlebar in his back, or a hood-spoke in his face.

'Now come on, this has gone far enough,' he said sternly. 'You must let me out, I don't want any of your rickshaws.'

'Wrighton, for Christ's sake, what are you playing at? We're waiting to go home,' Bell's voice boomed out to him.

'I can't get out. They've sort of hemmed me in.'

'Well hit them then,' came the unequivocal instruction.

Wrighton gave another despairing shove which provoked more ribald reaction from the crowd of pullers, and the tears of frustration began to prick at the back of his eyes.

At the periphery of the crowd arose a mumbling, followed by a crash and more shouting and laughing. Suddenly, rickshaws were lurching into each other in an attempt to wriggle away from the group. The cage around Wrighton began to dissolve as another rickshaw was tipped onto its side. Laughing and yelling, the remaining rickshaw pullers escaped out around the roundabout as Tuppin and Bell appeared, tipping over a third rickshaw just for good measure. Bell swung his hand lazily at a passing rickshaw and fetched the puller a stinging smack across the side of his head.

'It's the only language they understand,' he grunted. 'Come on.'

Tuppin said nothing, but just looked at Wrighton.

Bell drove frantically in the daylight, and murderously at night. His transport was a worn out Ford saloon with a stelloid crack, the size of a man's fist, in the laminated windscreen. The car bumped along noisily on its heavy duty leaf springs, and at irregular intervals the silencer thumped the floor as if a run-down pedestrian were demanding entry. He drove fast and in the middle of the road, to keep away from the rickshaws and baby taxis. Occasionally, the one, functioning yellow headlamp would pick out an unlit rickshaw travelling in the wrong direction and he would swerve roughly and shout, 'Birdbrain!' as he struggled to prevent the car from lurching into the storm drain which ran along the middle of the road.

Dark, unexpected shapes would surge out of the shadows and confront them. An unlit cow, or a Bengali carrying a bundle of palm thatch perched on his head. Neither would respond in any manner to the blasting of the horn. By the time they were winging in to their garden gate, Wrighton had consigned his fate to the gods several times over, but from Tuppin's demeanour it was obvious that this was the normal way to drive.

'Do you drive, at least?' Bell demanded as he slammed the door.

'Oh yes, I can drive.'

'That's your Land Rover around the back. It's Lines' old one, but don't go out in it till it's been resprayed. They'll kill you otherwise.'

'Who? The World Bank?'

Bell threw him a pitiful look. 'No the Banglas, of course. This little creature here, is our night chowkidhar. He takes over from Mohammed at night. We call him Bilbo.'

'As in Bilbo Baggins, from *The Hobbit,*' Bell raised his eyebrows. Wrighton continued. 'Tolkien. Sorry, but you looked surprised.'

'Didn't know you could read.' He slapped him on the shoulder. 'Beddy byes.'

6

Rubena Chowdhry had worked in the Rahman Business Centre for nearly five years. She had started on the eighth floor of the modern office block, working as a receptionist for the Aziz Brothers Trading Company and Emporium. She had spent her days sitting at a small desk, wedged onto the landing outside the main trading office of Aziz Brothers.

From her window she could see most of the Motijheel commercial area of the city and even to the stadium where, on match days, she could distinguish the ebb and flow of a straggling football game as it pounded across the brown turf, or the soporific lethargy of cricket, occasionally pinpricked by a jet of white figures running about and then lapsing into turgid inactivity for another lifetime.

She had looked out of her window for long hours, at the ceaseless heaving of rickshaws in the main street below, or at the sometimes rapid build up of cumulus cloud in the south, as if Bangladesh had suddenly acquired itself a ridge of mountains and was deciding where to put them.

She had spent so much time looking at the world from her window because, she had to be frank with herself, she had nothing to do. Absolutely nothing. The old man, Aziz (there were no brothers) had a vision. He had seen a Western film in which a great trading corporation had spiced its acres of marbled reception area with long finger-nailed women who were employed to answer telephones which were moulded in toy plastic colours, and to direct customers towards the lifts, and he had realised that this was what his company lacked.

Mr. Aziz knew Rubena's father, and so, one morning, she had tied her hair up in the tightest, neatest bun possible, and had put on her best smuggled Indian silk sari, in dark green and gold, and accompanied him to the offices of the Aziz Brothers Trading Company and Emporium. To oblige her father, was her duty. She did it willingly, but in this case, her willingness had been fired by an ulterior desire. She acknowledged, only to herself, that this senseless occupation represented for her a small, but important first step towards her secret goal.

Thus, she had found herself sitting all day long at an unvarnished desk, with an unconnected telephone, vainly fulfilling the senile, misguided fantasies of old Mr. Aziz. For four months she had sat there, arriving every morning at seven thirty, and leaving at four in the afternoon, and for four months she had seen nobody except Mr. Aziz. He would nod to her as he entered the office in the morning, and ignore her when he went home in the afternoon. He never spoke to her about his business, and she knew nothing about his activities.

At the end of the four months, she had seen the means of taking her next step. The Rahman Business Centre was, despite its pretentious name, just an office block housing several commercial concerns on different floors, and it was whilst wearily descending the stairs after work one afternoon that she had noticed a small announcement on the board of the Bangladesh Gas Power Corporation. 'Well educated persons of at least SSC level or preferably degree, required, with a good working knowledge of English, to assist in translating and interpreting on a forthcoming project.' Rubena had passed her Secondary School Certificate at the Dhaka College before going on to the University to study the humanities. Her examination marks in English had been excellent. In her unbiassed estimation, she was the ideal candidate. Next day, without warning her parents in any way, she had told Mr. Aziz that she wished to terminate her employment.

Mr. Aziz had been genuinely surprised. Here was a girl who was doing nothing and getting paid a pittance for it, and yet she wanted to go elsewhere. He had sat down at his typewriter and with one bent finger, had laboriously tapped out a reference letter for her, which glowed with the flowery literary paraphernalia, refined through generations of a race forced to be bureaucrats, in a language other than their own.

Two weeks later, Rubena started work at the Bangladesh Gas Power Corporation. It was her birthday. She was forty two years old and had been a widow for the last sixteen years.

'Rubena! Were you seeing *The Lotus* last night? Rashid discovered that the dancing girl was none other than his fiancée.'

'You know that I am not watching television, Leila, so why are you always asking me?'

'But you have a television Rubena.'

'You know I do.'

'Then why are you not watching it?'

'I am not finding it very interesting. Please let me concentrate on this letter that I am trying to translate. It is very difficult.'

'How are you knowing that it is not interesting, if you are not watching it?'

'I have watched it once upon a time, but I am not liking it. Why are you not pestering Mrs. Rosario about your "Lotus"? I am sure that she would be very pleased to discuss it with you.'

'Mrs. Rosario is upstairs, interpreting for Mr. Havering.'

'So, you have no work to do? So you keep pestering me with questions. What a trial you are. If you want some work to do, you may take a page of this letter and translate it for me.'

'You should not be short like that Rubena, it is not kind to be angry at me. Were you like that when you worked for Mr. Aziz?'

'I did not work for Mr. Aziz. He paid me, but I was never working for him.'

'But I saw your references, Rubena, they were very good. They said that you were conscientious, and accurate, and punctual, and very kind to the public.'

'That is what Mr. Aziz wrote, but I was never working for him. He paid me and I sat outside his office, at the top of the stairs. And now I work for the Bangladesh Gas Power Corporation, and I earn more taka, and do more work, but now I am sitting under the stairs. Do you realise that is a promotion? From sitting at the top of the stairs, to now sitting under the stairs. It is *ulter-pulter*. All the wrong way around.'

'Rubena, you say some funny things.'

'It is the truth I am telling you. It is not your doe-eyed, what is her name, Lily? on the television. It is not your fair-skinned Rashid, singing to a dancing girl, it is me, Rubena Chowdhry, telling you the truth, and now I want to finish this letter.'

'I have caught you red-handed there, Mrs. Chowdhry. How do you know that Rashid's fiancée is called Lily, when you are not watching television?'

'It was on last night whilst my daughter was doing her homework. I must have overheard it without realising. It really is most intrusive, the television.'

'Did you see any of it then?'

'I may have just caught a glimpse of it, as I walked past. My daughter was asking me, "Mamma, can you help me with my mathematics?" and I was saying, "Alice, you are seventeen now, you should know how to count by yourself now," but she was saying, "Mamma I can count, but it is easier when you are helping me" and so I helped her, and she was sitting in front of the television.'

'Did you see when Lily was singing of her love, and how she dreamed about him, and all the while Rashid was sitting up the tree?'

'Yes, I thought it was shocking when he jumped down and frightened her. She might have thought that he was a dacoit, and that her honour was threatened.'

'But she was surprised, isn't it? She said, "What are you doing, hiding up a tree, whilst I am singing?"'

'And he said, "What are you doing, singing around my tree, when I am trying to sleep?"'

'You have a remarkable memory, Rubena, for a person who is not watching television.'

'And now I must have a remarkable time, translating this letter, so please do not be interrupting me with your silly chatter.'

'What is the letter about?'

'It is just a chitty from a man called Askan Miah, and he is saying that the pipeline has divided his land, and taken away his livelihood, and he is wanting compensation for it.'

'But they are all saying that. Why has he not had the letter written in English?'

'You are asking me things that I cannot answer. I am not in his head. I do not know why he did not go to the letter writer.'

'Is it for Mr. Havering?'

'No, it is for Mr. Wrighton, he has been given all the compensation workings to do. Mr. Havering says that he is too busy.'

'Are you thinking that Mr. Havering is too busy, Rubena?'

'I think that Mr. Havering is a very important man. He has to speak to men in the M.F.A. sometimes. But I cannot tell if he is too busy.'

'Mr. Havering has hairs up his nose, that are fair.'

'You will be telling me next that he runs around a tree, singing to a water-buffalo. Does not your man have hairs up his nose?'

'I am not telling you where my man has hairs.'

'Leila Rose! If you cannot speak about proper things, then you must not speak at all. Now go to your work girl, I can hear the peon coming down the stairs, he is probably bringing you many difficult letters to translate and land deeds and affidavits.'

'It is not the peon, Rubena, the foot is too heavy, it is sure to be Mr. Wrighton, coming to ask one of us to interpret for him. Why is he not sending a peon, or ringing the bell for us?'

Wrighton paused at the door and then revised the names in his head. The young lively one was called Mrs. Rose, the older one, Mrs. Chowdhry and the short plump one was Mrs. Rosario. He pushed open the door and poked his head into the room, recoiling slightly at the smell which wafted out.

'Would one of you ladies please help me with some interpreting?' Why did they look at him like that? What was he doing wrong?

'I can come, Mr. Wrighton. I am doing nothing at the moment,' the younger woman said. She was the one with the saucy eyes and pouting lips. She followed him upstairs to his office and waited to be asked to sit down.

'Please, Mrs. Rose, do sit down.'

'Thank you Mr. Wrighton.'

'I've got a man outside, who is claiming compensation for five hundred yards–'

'That's a lot. He must be rich man.'

'Is it? Five hundred yards is a lot?' Wrighton had just paid out on a claim for three quarters of a mile. He wondered whether he ought to get the peon to call the man back. 'I shall have to question him, so that we can identify exactly which piece of land he is talking about. I'll call him in. No, don't get up Mrs. Rose, I can do it.' Wrighton beckoned the man in.

He was stooped and white haired. His face was a crinkled brown paper bag, shot through with two crooked teeth. His eyes flicked around the room and settled on Mrs. Rose at whom he began to frown disapproval.

'Boshen!' she shouted, and the man sat down on the chair, probably from the shock of being addressed in such a manner by a woman.

'Thank you Mrs. Rose. Could you ask this gentleman please, if he has any proof of his title to the land through which he claims our pipeline is passing?'

'Why are you calling him a gentleman, Mr. Wrighton? He is a peasant not a gentleman,' Mrs. Rose declared in a matter-of-fact tone, rather as one would say that a person was a bus conductor, not a doctor.

Wrighton sighed. Would he ever understand these people? He had been thrown straight in to the compensations as soon as he had arrived at the office, on Sunday morning. Havering had told him brusquely, that he was going to work him 'bloody hard, until he didn't know whether he was coming or going.' It was now Thursday, the last day of the working week, and Wrighton did not know which way to turn. His shirt stuck to his back, his collar chafed him in the heat. If he switched the air conditioning on, he could not hear himself think, and if he switched it off, his room heated up to boiling point in fifteen minutes. He had tried to do short bursts of work but found that the work just did not lend itself to that.

He was supposed to be evaluating the claims for compensation from the landholders along the proposed, and existing, route. He had to identify their land and calculate the compensation payable. The scale was agreed by the Ministry of the Interior. It was all set out in a chart. Wrighton had thought that it would be straightforward calculation. Some hope! The sticking points were proving the ownership of the land and identifying the land. With the Moslem practice of transferring land at marriage as a dowry on a daughter, and subdividing it amongst children, a land deed correctly signed and sealed, could be superseded twenty years later, and yet both titles would remain in existence. This allowed ample opportunity for exploitation and deceit.

To actually pinpoint the land was practically impossible. The standard of mapping and surveying was primitive and of course to complicate matters further, there was always the possibility that the land physically no longer existed. It may have been one of the many acres washed away in the annual floods, to form a mud bank in the Bay of Bengal, one hundred miles to the south.

Wearily, Wrighton pulled a roll of map from the pile on the floor behind him and began to unroll it on his desk. The man followed his action with the avid attention that a novice affords something mysterious and intriguing, yet totally incomprehensible.

'Shall we say, that it does not matter what you call him Mrs. Rose, as long as you are polite? I merely called him a gentleman because that was the figure of address that I am accustomed to use. If it upsets you, please call him a peasant. Does he have a land deed?'

The man unselfconsciously thrust his hand into the folds at the front of his lunghi and pulled out an envelope which he handed to Mrs. Rose. She gave it straight to Wrighton. Wrighton winced slightly as his hand closed around the warm, soft envelope. He gingerly drew from it, two foolscap sheets of faded Bengali script, each one bearing a superb intaglio, full-width plate engraving, in brown ink, of a five anna fee stamp, complete with head of George V. One paragraph of the deed was almost in its original condition of dark ink and clean paper. It was the innermost fold which had been protected for the last forty years. The remainder bore the dirty thumbmarks, creases and stains, with as much pride as it did the seven rubber stamps imprinted upon it. Wrighton spread the deed out on his desk. Mrs. Rose leaned over him, her loose black hair falling into Wrighton's face.

'Is this what I think it is?'

'It is land deed.'

'Could you look down it, please, and verify that it relates to this man, and then give me a description of the land as it is written?'

Mrs. Rose nodded, her eyes already working on the script, her lips moving silently in concert. Wrighton looked at the old man and then grinned. 'Soon be finished old man.'

The man grinned back and saluted.

Leila rose said, 'It is in the village of Hazapur.'

'Hazapur, Hazapur,' Wrighton chanted under his breath as he searched through a makeshift index in a notebook. 'That will be roll number two two seven.' He poked amongst his bundle of maps. 'I haven't got his map. I shall have to get the peon to bring it up.' He carefully wrote down the figures on a sheet of paper and then called the peon from his office door. The man came bowing in through the doorway, his grey cotton tunic buttoned tightly across his thin chest, perspiration showing black in the armpits.

'Ah, Abdul.'

'Yes master.'

Wrighton squirmed. How he hated that sobriquet!

'Could you get me this map roll, please?' He handed the paper to the peon and showed him the figures on it. The man grinned, and looked at them, and then at Mrs. Rose, who rattled off a harsh-sounding series of Bengali imperatives, which left the man nodding and bowing as he scuttled from the room.

'You must talk to them strongly, Mr. Wrighton. That man is not educated, he cannot understand your English. It is too polite. He is not used to it, you see.'

Wrighton opened his mouth to reply, but then merely nodded his acknowledgement. He swallowed thickly, and eased his collar from his throat. Mrs. Rose sat still, her hands clasped in her lap, awaiting her next orders. The old man looked from one to the other, not understanding.

'Could you tell him that we are just getting the correct map please, so that we can find his village on it?'

The man listened attentively to the interpretation, and then agreed his assent, with a nod. Wrighton got up from his chair, ostensibly to switch on the air conditioning, but in reality, to ease his sticking underpants from his bottom.

'Don't mind if we have the a.c. on for a while, do you?'

'You are the boss, Mr. Wrighton, you can do what you like.' Mrs. Rose pronounced the words as if delivering a lesson to a backward child, then she pulled her shawl across her shoulders to protect herself from the blast of cold air. The machine created such a rattling din that Wrighton did not hear the peon, knocking on the door, and was only aware of his existence when, on the third attempt, the door actually shook and a typed notice which was pinned to the back, fluttered at him in miniature shock waves.

'Thank you Abdul.' He took the map and immediately checked the number marked on it. 'Well done.' The man grinned again. 'Before you go Abdul,' Wrighton felt in his jacket pocket for his money, 'can I have a Pepsi Cola please?' He turned to Mrs. Rose, 'Do you want one Mrs. Rose?'

'Yes please, Mr. Wrighton.'

Wrighton held up two fingers at the peon, 'Two Pepsi Cola.' He handed the money to the peon, who repeated, *'Dui Fefsi, tikka say.'* and then crept out as if he had been given a state secret to smuggle across enemy lines.

'Right,' said Wrighton, rubbing his hands together in a businesslike manner, 'let's have a dekko at this map then.' He unrolled it on his desk, pinning the ends down with various bits of desk furniture.

'You speak Hindi then Mr. Wrighton?'

'Pardon.' Wrighton was puzzled.

'You speak Hindi? You said "dekko".'

'Yes, I'm sorry, Mrs. Rose, it's English slang. It means that I want to have a look at something.'

'It is Hindi, Mr. Wrighton. It means "look".'

'Oh, is it? Is it really? Well I never! Fancy that! All this time I have never realised that I was speaking Indian.' He mused for a second and then returned to the map. 'Could you ask him if he can read a map?' He looked at her face and said, 'No, don't bother. It's a silly question. Of course he can't. I've got to try to identify the piece of land that he is talking about.' He traced his finger along the map. 'I've got the village. Ask him if his land is in the village or outside it.'

'It is just outside it.'

'Which way? North, south, east, or west?'

'He does not know.'

'Errm. Ask him, when the sun goes down, and he is on his land, does it go down over the village or where?'

'It goes down behind him.'

'It goes down behind him. Is this when he is standing facing the village?'

'No, when he is looking towards the tank.'

'Ah, towards the tank. Towards the tank.' He scrutinised the smudgy lines, looking for a trace of the ponds that they call tanks. 'Got it.' He put his finger on the tank and then looked at the village. 'Does he get his water from the tank?'

'Which tank? There are two tanks in the village.'

'Two? Two tanks? Where? I can't see two tanks. When was this surveyed?' Wrighton looked at the date printed in the margin. 'Only three years ago... Two tanks, he says?'

'He says there are two tanks.'

'There would be,' Wrighton mumbled. 'All right then, forget the tanks. Ask him if there is a mosque in the village.'

'There is a small one, but he prays at home, or in the field.'

'Right. When he prays, and he gets down to kneel, which way does he face?'

'Towards the village.'

'Ah, now we are getting somewhere. Now, Muslims always pray towards the east, don't they?'

'No,' Mrs. Rose replied, puzzled. 'We pray towards Mecca.'

'Well yes, that's what I meant. Oh yes...' Wrighton laughed, a little embarrassed, 'of course, Mecca is west of here, isn't it? So that means that his land is east of the village.' He bent over the map, examining it. 'Just a minute...er....ask him...ask him. No don't ask him that.'

'I won't,' Mrs. Rose replied seriously. Wrighton looked up, not sure whether she was laughing at him or not.

'Ask him if he knows a man called... Farshad, who owns land out that way.'

'He doesn't know Farshad.'

'What is the name of his neighbour?'

'On his compound, or his land, do you mean?'

'Ah, good thinking, Mrs. Rose, good thinking. On his land. What is the name of the man who owns the land at the side of him?'

'Dadu.'

'Dadu? Does he have another name?'

'Dadu Miah,' Mrs. Rose interpreted and then, emboldened by Wrighton's earlier praise, suggested, 'Shall I ask him what the man's father's name is? He is more likely to know that. They would probably be of the same age.' She was surprised to find that she was becoming engrossed in this detective work. It was quite fun. More than it had been with Mr. Line.

'You're getting the hang of it,' Wrighton enthused, and he got up and switched off the air conditioning for he could see that Mrs. Rose was beginning to hold her throat.

He savoured the few minutes after the a.c. had been switched off. The office was cool and quiet. Rather like the weather after the monsoon, so people said. It was always clean and dry after the monsoon had rained itself out. People began talking to each other again, apparently, and all the social round of parties started up again. It all seemed unreal to him, but he was happy to savour his own 'après-monsoon'.

'I'm sorry, Mrs. Rose, I was dreaming, what did he say?'

'He said that the name of Dadu Miah's father, was Farshad.'

'But... Didn't he say that he knew no-one called Farshad? Ask him, tell him, that he told us that he did not know Farshad,' Wrighton said excitedly.

'No I didn't say that.'

'But he did, didn't he, Mrs. Rose? You heard him.'

'Yes, I heard him Mr. Wrighton. He says that he is a very old man and he has circles in his head.'

'Circles in his head? Oh... he's confused. Well, if he's got circles in his head, imagine what I've got in mine. Fine, so that means that his land can only be... Oh dear, it seems that a certain Askan Fawzli has already been paid compensation on this land. I've got it here, pencilled onto the plot. Ask him if he knows a man called Askan Fawzli.'

'No he doesn't. He has never heard of him.'

'How long has the land been his?'

'It was given to him by his father before the Partition of India.'

'That would be... 1947 wouldn't it? I'm afraid I'm not very good at foreign history.'

'It was British history at the time.'

'Ah yes... of course. Now, let me think... um... I know. Has he got any daughters?'

'Yes.'

'Well, how many?'

'One.'

'Is she married?'

'Yes.'

'Was any land separated out at marriage?'

'Perhaps.'

'Well was it, or wasn't it?'

'Yes it was.'

'Some of the land that he is claiming for today?'

'He is not answering that.'

'So I notice. Does that mean that it is true?'

'Usually.'

Wrighton sucked his bottom lip in deep reflection. He could not afford to spend much more time on this claim. He was behind with the work. Havering had been grumbling at him in a nasty, sniping manner about the quality of his work. As if he could be expected to suddenly leap into another man's shoes and take over, just like that! It wasn't exactly the kind of engineer's work to which he was accustomed, it was more the nature of a private detective's. He was weary, he was hot, the man was smelly, and the interpreter was bored.

'Do these people ever tell the truth?' he asked, in despair. The woman did not reply. 'What is the name of his son-in-law?'

'Askan Fawzli.'

Wrighton put his head in his hands and breathed deeply. He blew his breath out over the desk so that the map rustled, impatient to roll itself back up again.

'Did he know that we had already paid out to his son-in-law on this piece of land?'

'Yes he is knowing. But his son-in-law won't give him any of the money. That's why he came today, to claim for himself. He knows other people who are doing it. Some have claimed three times.'

'I don't want to know that, Mrs. Rose,' Wrighton remarked grimly. 'Please tell him to go away and stop wasting my time. Oh wait, he had better sign a disclaimer to the effect that he renounces his claim as fraudulent.' Wrighton scribbled hurriedly on a scrap of paper and then slid it over to Mrs. Rose. 'Read that out to him and then ask him to sign it, if he agrees to it, please.'

Mrs. Rose read the short paragraph out to the old man and then squashed his left thumb into the ink pad and impressed it on the foot of the page. The man heavily gathered up the revered pieces of paper and inserted them with the difficulty of unfamiliarity, into the envelope which, Wrighton saw, bore the legend, *'On His Majesty's Service'.*

After they had both left, Wrighton wearily pulled himself up, switched on the a.c., and stood before it, holding his shirt away from his chest so that the cooled air ran down the gap that he had made by undoing his top button and loosening his tie. He thought of Cockcroft's booming summons in his early days as an engineer, and the embarrassment he had felt for being caught not wearing a tie. Not so much for not wearing one, he reflected, but for not knowing that he should have worn one. It was a sort of snobbishness in the engineering field. If you wore a tie, then you could be distinguished from the labourers. In this country, you only had to look at the colour of the skin to distinguish the engineers from the workers.

He turned back to the chaos of his desk and began to roll up the maps. What could the surveyors know of the fate of their plans, as they trudged about in the broiling sun with a plane table and umbrella, for seventy five taka a day? As they stumbled along the line, taking bearings, registering titles 'as claimed'. What did they know, or even care, of the end product and its purpose? How much of what they did was interpolation?

Wrighton could remember his student days of surveying projects. They would survey every fifth mark, interpolate the rest by eye, and then skive off somewhere leaving the slowest, or dimmest witted student, to guard the equipment. So how could he honestly expect poorly-paid surveyors to stick unerringly and diligently at a job whose purpose was never explained to them? These large scale maps were a joke and yet, they were the best that they could produce. The small scale maps used in the office were produced to the superb quality and accuracy of the Survey of India standards, but were, inevitably, fifty years old. In the life of a developing nation, thrashing across the topography, fifty years was an aeon.

Outside in the corridor, Wrighton heard the distinctive sound of the head peon clearing his throat and then expectorating into the corner, prior to blowing the whistle. On Thursdays the office closed early, he had been told. He sighed with relief as the reedy warbling awoke slumberous peons throughout their floor, to their tasks of closing windows and generally standing in doorways with a broom in order to be in the way. He shovelled some files and papers into his brief case and with a despondent glance, recognising that this would be his first sight when he returned to work on the Sunday morning, he left his office and locked the door behind him.

'And he bought me a Fefsi Cola, Rubena.'
'He bought you a Fefsi?'
'It was just like on the films. "Would you like a drink?" he said to me, and then he ordered two Fefsi from the peon.'
'I hope you paid for your Fefsi, Leila.'
'I tried to, Rubena, but he said, "No, no Mrs. Rose, I will treat you" and he took the taka from his pocket, and gave it to the peon. That also was just like on the films.'

'You have only got the films in your empty head, Leila. You must not let him buy you drinks like that. We are not like him.'

'He is not a very strong man, Rubena.'

'What do you know about how strong he is?'

'He called a peasant "a gentleman", and he kept saying "Please Mrs. Rose, do this" and "Please Mrs. Rose do that". He is a weak man. Mr. Line would have been telling me what to do, with authority. Mr. Line would have thrown that man out of the office long ago, he would not have been listening to his lies. Mr. Line would have known that a man like that could not be owning all that land.'

'Mr. Line worked quickly, but Mr. Line was not always in the office. Sometimes he would be away for three or four days, and all the while his work would be piling up. You remember isn't it? Oh quick! There is the whistle blowing. The minibus will be waiting for us. Hurry now, we must close.'

'O.K. Sadiq, drop me here.'

'Yes saheb.'

'Here! Sadiq. No need to go in. Stop outside the gate.'

Sadiq stopped the Land Rover dead in the middle of the neat cross-roads, upon one corner of which, the Banani house was situated. Wrighton sighed with resignation. His complete inability in any foreign language, and Sadiq's fairly basic knowledge of English, combined to make any journey which involved oral directions, a work of mime and posture.

From the very first day, when Sadiq had called for him in the sparkling air-conditioned Land Rover provided by the World Bank, a good-natured battle of cultures had begun. Wrighton insisted on sitting in the front seat, next to Sadiq. Sadiq, was equally determined that Wrighton should sit in the back, like the other white men did. He would leap out when he saw Wrighton leave the office, or the house, and open the back door for him. Wrighton would greet him cordially, put his attaché case on the back seat, and then mount in the front, proudly remembering which way to pull the door handle. Sadiq would then sulk for the first ten minutes of the journey, and switch off the air conditioning until Wrighton asked for it to be switched back on again. Sadiq would continue to sulk. He did not look like a proper driver if his passenger sat next to him. What would the other drivers think?

Sadiq also nurtured some grand desire to always sweep the Land Rover into the drive at the side of the house, and in the realisation of this dream he was assisted, benignly, by the eagerness of their chowkidhar, Mohammed, who, upon sighting Wrighton's Land Rover or Bell's car, or indeed, any vehicle that looked as if it ought to visit them, would leap from his chair, energetically throw open the garden gates, and beckon the vehicle vigorously in.

Taken off-guard the first day, Wrighton had allowed Sadiq to drive straight in. It had seemed the logical thing to do, except that Sadiq had parked the van too close to the wall and Wrighton had not been able to get out without clambering over the back of the front seat and squeezing through the rear door. Whilst he was performing this manoeuvre, Bell had roared in behind them and they had had to ask him, kindly, if he would back out again so that the van could get out. He had not been pleased, and had made some remark about, 'Bloody newcomers cluttering up the place with their fancy ironmongery.'

So now, Wrighton always stopped Sadiq outside the house. It usually required three attempts and it never prevented Mohammed from swinging open the gates so that Sadiq could get a tantalising view of the inviting driveway, a sight that must have been worse torture to him, than it was possible to imagine.

Wrighton slammed the door and waved. Sadiq roared off down the road, doubtless having switched off the air-conditioning. Mohammed shuffled towards Wrighton who resigned the battle in advance, and meekly handed over his attaché case for it to be carried proudly in to the dining room and laid regally on the table. This was another of Mohammed's beliefs. Nobody was allowed to carry anything into the house. That was his job. Wrighton had tried at first not to relinquish his case, but Mohammed would tug at it insistently until he surrendered.

Wrighton now followed his case into the main room of the house, tore off his tie, and flopped onto the linen-covered rattan sofa. He winced and Tuppin looked over the top of the *Dhaka Times* to remark, 'They're not as soft as they look, these wickerwork chairs are they?'

'You are so right. Has anybody ordered tea?'

'It's just coming.'

'And toast?'

'And toast. With fish paste.'

'Fish paste? Where did Moussi get that from?'

'Bell got it from the commissary. He knows a girl there.' Tuppin winked to add meaning to the explanation.

'What's the commissary?'

'It's where the BHC staff do their shopping. It's like a miniature super-market. They import the stuff by container from U.K.'

'Oh, and what does BHC mean?'

'British High Commission. All the dips, they have to be looked after. Must be able to get their duty free booze from somewhere.'

'And are we not allowed to use it?'

'No, not unless you are a dip. on the BHC.'

'But Bell...'

Tuppin tapped the side of his nose. 'Ways and Means Act. Ask no questions, tell no lies. Naturally, it's not the best thing to brag about – that you were eating fish paste on toast at lunch time. Get it?'

'Got it,' Wrighton agreed. He liked this time of the day, when they had all three just returned from work, and sat for a while, drinking tea and eating toast. Tuppin had already changed into a pair of outrageously meagre shorts and a vivid tee shirt. Judging by the sound emanating from the room across the corridor, Bell was having a shower.

Although Moussi always served the tea in china cups on a tray with milk and sugar, the atmosphere was one of an indisputable, masculine intimacy. It did not matter that everything was dainty, the absence of anything female, by default, made the entire operation, crushingly masculine.

'Hey listen to this!' Tuppin announced above his newspaper, as Bell blundered into the room, rubbing his hair with a towel. 'Traffic incident was caused on Chittagong road on Friday, when a truck loaded with jute dashed into a Dhaka bound coaster bus. Four hapless passengers of the bus were killed and others were maimed. The killer truck was arrested but...' Tuppin stopped and looked expectantly across at Bell, and they finished in unison. 'The driver is absconding. A case has been registered in this regard.'

'What a bloody country! Every time one of those killer trucks has an accident they manage to arrest the truck but not the driver.'

'How can you arrest a truck?' Wrighton enquired ingenuously.

'They do in Bangladesh. Have you noticed the two smashed up trucks outside the police station in Gulshan Avenue? They've been arrested. So there! That'll teach them not to do it again!' he finished sarcastically.

'Most of the drivers are Pathans, from Pakistan. Mad buggers,' Bell explained as he poured out the tea. 'So they know they'll get short shrift if the Banglas get hold of them. That's why they never hang around. Mind you, the same goes for you. If you ever have an accident, get away quick. If you can, don't stop. If you do stop, don't get out. You have to move before they realise what has happened. Banglas turn very nasty when they are excited and in fifteen seconds you'll probably have fifty people around you.'

'Is that what happened to Line?'

'Line was unlucky. He had to get over the back seat to throw out the baby.' Bell slipped two sugar lumps into his cup. 'Do you take sugar?'

'No thanks.' Wrighton shuddered.

'I'll tell you what,' Tuppin continued reading the paper that he had thrown onto the carpet, 'you know all that fuss with the rickshaws down in Motijheel? Well it was a 'government drive against unlicensed rickshaws plying on the thoroughfare,' it says here. One hundred and twenty rickshaw pullers were fined and eight hundred and fifty taka in fines was collected.'

'But that means they were fined about eight taka each. That's about fifteen pence!' Wrighton was incredulous.

'Exactly. It's quite remunerative, being a policeman in Bangladesh.'

'Not nearly as good as being a customs officer,' Bell added.

'Quite a good photo of my new traffic lights though.' Tuppin held up a page of the paper for their inspection.

'Are these the ones you said that you were going to install vertically like we do, instead of horizontally?'

'Them's the ones. Work beautifully. Nobody takes any notice of them of course, that's why they always have a policeman there.'

'But nobody seems to take any notice of them, either.' said Wrighton.

'No, but at least they are there,' Tuppin insisted obscurely. 'The whole point about designing a traffic system for Dhaka is that it is pointless. It is unworkable. We tried to build a computer model of the traffic flow, putting in the tolly-garis at two miles per hour, rickshaws at eight and so on up to the killer trucks and staff cars but it would not work out. They are doing things in Bangladesh on the roads that defy the logic of integrated circuitry. They should not be able to move the amount of traffic that they do on the space that they do in the time that they do, but they do. Any improvement I suggest will only slow it down. You see, we are not dealing with a finite quantity here. Every person in Bangladesh can become a road user when needed. You only have to build a brand new avenue and it will be choked the day it is opened and nowhere else in the city will you see a diminution in density of traffic. It's unfathomable. Chuck us a bit of toast.'

Bell obliged and in catching it, Tuppin kicked over his cup of tea.

'Shit! Moussi! Moussi! Where is that lazy sod?'

Moussi scurried in and mopped up the mess on the carpet. 'No problem, saheb, no problem,' he said, then disappeared into the kitchen and reappeared a split second later with another cup and saucer. Whenever Wrighton saw Moussi he was always wearing a grin on his face which was a mixture of indulgence and worship; the type of expression one would expect to see glowing on the face of the proud mother of a spoilt but charming child. It was as if Moussi were convinced that these three men were always up to something naughty or mischievous and his job was to clear up after them and in doing so some of the notoriety rubbed off onto him.

'I know what I was going to say,' Wrighton began, 'why do they call Pepsi Cola "Fefsi"?'

'Its the Bangla way of pronouncing the "p". They transpose the "p" and the "f" so that "Pepsi" becomes "Fefsi".'

'And "party" becomes "farty",' Tuppin sniggered.

'You're pulling my leg, aren't you?' Wrighton accused.

'I'm not am I?' Tuppin looked across at Bell for corroboration.

'Absolutely true,' Bell confirmed. 'Do you know what we have got for dinner tonight?' Wrighton shook his head. 'Pish and Sifs'

'Piss and what?' Wrighton laughed.

'Not "piss", well I hope not anyway, Pish and sifs. Oh look, now you've made me drop my toast into my tea.' Bell was beginning to giggle.

'If you don't believe him, call in Moussi and ask him,' Tuppin suggested as he choked on his tea.

'I will.' Wrighton pulled a straight face. 'Moussi, could you come in here for a minute please?'

'That won't work,' Bell scoffed. 'He doesn't know you are talking to him. Moussi!' he roared. The door creaked open and Moussi appeared. Bell looked across at Wrighton.

'Um... er Moussi.'

'Saheb?'

Tuppin and Bell snorted in their chairs, Tuppin wiping from his eyes the tears which had been the fertile product of his choking.

'Errm....' Wrighton endeavoured to make his voice sound natural although he was not accustomed either to ask what was for dinner since he normally took no interest but merely ate what was put before him, or to speaking to servants. 'What do we have for dinner tonight, Moussi?'

'Dinner?'

'Yes Moussi.'

'Tonight?'

Wrighton nodded.

'Pish and sifs,' Moussi declared seriously and then looked startled as Bell fell off his chair howling with laughter and Tuppin started choking again.

'And for dessert?'

'Oh No! I don't think I could stand the dessert! Aaargh!' Bell knelt in his saucer and catapulted the remains of his tea onto his bare knee.

'Affle fudding,' Moussi grinned indulgently, having understood merely that the mad English sahebs were having another of their turns about which he would be able to gossip down at the market. He collected the debris of the conflict and returned to the kitchen.

Tuppin asked where the apples came from and then explained to Wrighton, 'There aren't any apples in Bangladesh.'

'Whatshisname from Vickers – Benny, brought them back from Bhutan.'

'Where?' Wrighton said.

'Bhutan. It's a country up north of Bangladesh. You know that Bangladesh is the second poorest country in the world? Well Bhutan is number one.'

'But at least they grow apples.'

'Not very good ones but beggars can't be choosers.'

'I'm gonna get some shuteye,' Bell announced. 'You coming up the club after dinner? Thursday night is TGIT night.'

'Go on then,' Wrighton prompted, 'what is TGIT?'

'Thank God It's Thursday. It's a good evening. Some of the boys from up country manage to get back by Thursday and tonight is the first time they will have seen cold beer for five days.'

He knew that he would have to go to the British Club at some stage but a mixture of fatigue, apathy and fright had prevented him up to now. Perhaps this would be his best opportunity. 'Yes,' he smiled, 'maybe I will.'

'Good man. Good man.' Bell grabbed his towel. 'Dinner six o'clock,' he shouted over his shoulder as he crossed the corridor to his bedroom.

'I think I'll get my head down as well,' Tuppin said. 'Give a bang on my door if I'm not up by half five.'

Wrighton nodded and then he was alone in the room.

Bhutan? He had never heard of the place yet here were two ordinary chaps who had. He supposed that it was true that travel broadens the mind. He got up and as he wandered down the corridor to his bedroom, he muttered to himself, 'Pish and sifs, affle fudding,' in the best imitation of a Bengali accent that he could manage, wobbling his head from side to side as he did so.

The British Club was a rambling whitewashed house. It stood in a quiet residential road, in a rather rundown area of Gulshan. It provided a neutral focal point where diplomats and expatriates could chat, drink, argue, beat a ball about the tennis or squash court, swim, play billiards or simply get quietly and discreetly drunk. The most popular facility of the club was the bar. It was not an especially impressive bar, it was not spectacularly well-stocked, but in a country which forbade the selling of alcohol to its natives, a bar was a rare and cherished possession.

The designer, if such a locale had indeed been designed, by using local materials had striven to recreate the atmosphere of that mythical establishment, the typical British pub. So the shelves were backed with mirrors, albeit with the silvering peeling from them; the bar top was a polished wood which had warped in the humidity and heat; the glasses were suspended over the customers' heads on a specially made cane glass-rack and the clientele could either lounge in the ubiquitous rattan chairs or perch bravely on twisted, insecure Bangladeshi interpretations of bar stools.

Wrighton slowly sipped his Coca-Cola under the mosquito screen on the verandah. He could hear the hubbub of conversation coming from within. On his lap lay the yellowing edition of some long-forgotten English daily newspaper which he had taken from the rack as his habitual defence against social contact. He had not bothered to open it . He was peacefully happy in the muggy warmth of the night and the gloom of the faintly lit verandah. He realised that the strain and the worry of the previous days' work were slowly slipping away from him and he was relaxing. It had not occurred to him until now, just how tense and tired he must have become.

He hearkened to a sudden upsurge in the ribaldry emanating from the Vickers engineers inside. They were playing darts in the corner of the bar and Wrighton had to accept that they, too, in their own way, were relaxing. The only difference being that they required alcohol and he did not. 'You pious humbug, Wrighton!' he said aloud, and added solely for the pleasure of hearing it again, 'Pish and sifs and affle fudding.'

'I beg your pardon.' A woman's voice came softly to him from the darkness of the far end of the verandah.

Wrighton started and the newspaper slid from his lap onto the tiled floor.

'I'm sorry, I didn't know anybody was there,' he gabbled, attempting to attribute some form or outline to his clandestine interlocutor.

'So you didn't want to talk to me?' the voice teased.

'Well, no or rather, perhaps I would have done had I known that you were there,' he flustered.

'So you were talking to yourself then?'

'I suppose I was,' he admitted, 'but you were eavesdropping.' He shifted his position to try to see into the dark corner. He heard a gentle swishing noise followed by a discreet thud. He stood up warily and addressed the corner. 'May I introduce myself?' The words were corny and opportunist. He stopped and listened. The corner sounded empty. Before, it had been vibrant with the modulations of the voice, but now it was stuffy with emptiness. Then he heard the outside door bang and in a trice he had confirmed his suspicion, as his hand closed around the handle of the door which had been invisible to him in the corner, and which presumably led to the gardens. Whoever it was, had escaped. He rubbed his palm down the back of his neck and tried to convince himself that the clamminess there was due to the humidity.

He looked at his watch, it was nearly ten o'clock. He had been at the club three hours, the longest time that he had spent in any pub since he had been married.

When he re-entered the bar, he had to pause on the threshold so that his eyes could become accustomed to the light. It was from this position that he was hailed by Bell.

'Hey, Wrighton, come over here. Where have you been hiding?'

Wrighton started glumly forward, but hadn't progressed more than two steps before a hairy hand gripped his arm and arrested him.

'Oi, watchit tosh! Go around the back or Dave'll use yer 'ead for a pin cushion.' And in confirmation, a dart whizzed past his nose on its journey to the board.

'Sorry,' Wrighton mumbled and rubbed his arm where it had been grasped. He grinned stupidly at Bell. 'Went the wrong way across the dart field. Didn't hear them yell "fore" or whatever it is they shout.'

'That's golf, you prat! Hey you must meet this chap,' Bell insisted with the bonhomie of tipsiness and pushed him towards a thin, bearded man dressed in shorts and tee shirt, who was standing at the bar with him. 'He's on the club committee, aren't yer Geoff?'

'That is so,' the bearded man replied. 'I'm Geoff.' He held out his hand.

'Stewart Wrighton.'

'Well, Stewart, how are you liking Bangladesh? First time that you've been out here is it?' The enquiry was innocent and professional.

'Oh, it's quite a change from Wembley,' Wrighton said diffidently. 'The buses are a different colour for a start.'

'Buses are a different colour! Rather! Very good! Do you do any sport? We've got a football team–' The man winced as the Vickers engineers exploded in another bout of arguing. He regarded them ruefully. 'And a darts team as you can see. Practising hard.'

'I'm afraid I don't do any sport at all. Not even tiddley winks.'

'You might get terribly bored here you know.' He stirred his drink thoughtfully with a swizzle stick. 'You're with Consolidated aren't you?' Again the endearing voice of an interviewer, coaxing him onward. 'Did you know Raymond Line?'

'By reputation.'

'Only?'

'And I worked with him in London on some project or other.' Wrighton felt in his shirt pocket for his chit book, 'Another drink?'

'Ermm.' He gazed into his glass as if the answer lay inscribed therein. 'No thanks, not this time, but soon.' The man smiled broadly, placed his glass on the bar and made his way out to the verandah.

Wrighton was left gazing at a brown-skinned European with a pot belly. He had a few whisps of white hair on his head and he was wedged into the corner by the ice bucket.

'New, are you?'

'I beg your pardon?' The man's remark had coincided with another outburst from the darts players, amongst whose numbers Wrighton could just distinguish the flushed face of Bell. The man beckoned him with a curiously vague movement of his finger and tapped the stool at the side of him. Wrighton glanced discreetly around him for a lifeline. Tuppin was talking ardently with a dark-haired woman in the corner and did not want to be disturbed. He knew no-one else. With a sinking heart he slid off his stool and wandered over to the man.

'Bring your glass,' the man instructed. Wrighton had left it as an anchor, but he had now been outmanoeuvred by a captain of greater experience, inviting him to share his mooring buoy. 'You're new.'

'Yes, been here a week, nearly. How long have you been here?'

'My name's Harry. What's yours?'

'Wrighton.'

The man picked, fumblingly, at something in his mouth and on his tongue but failing to dislodge it, spat onto the bar. The Bengali bartender, a sleek, suave, groomed man, quite unlike any Bengali that Wrighton had seen up to now, swiped the bar with his cloth and then continued stacking empty bottles into a crate under the counter. With the horror that the ensnared fly must regard the spider, Wrighton realised that the man was drunk, maudlin drunk.

'Damn stupid things, round tables,' Harry commented and without awaiting for Wrighton to react, launched into a dissertation. 'Look at those two there.' He nodded at a couple who were seated at a round table. 'See what I mean? Look! Nowhere to put your elbows. When you're sitting at a round table, all the table is getting away from you isn't it? I mean, it's curving away from you. To be really useful it should curve around you so that whichever way you turn you've got table. Ever tried eating at a round table?' Wrighton shook his head. 'Your elbows keep falling off it. Whatever possessed man to make a round table? Eh? You tell me that.'

'Wasn't it King Arthur and his knights?'

'Poppycock! Fairy tales! Mind you,' Harry conceded generously, 'coffee tables can be round. Coffee tables should be round, otherwise you bang your shins on the corners. I think there ought to be an international standard to ensure the roundness of coffee tables.'

'Where do oval tables fit in to your scheme of things then?' Wrighton was relieved that this drunk had turned out to be harmless.

Harry peered at Wrighton as if seeing him for the first time in his life. He scrutinised him through freckled eyelids and watery, vague eyes, then he pushed back onto his crown the few whisps of white hair that had fallen forward, cascading down his face like a mountain rill.

'Well now, that's interesting you should ask that because er...' he scratched the back of his neck where his tanned skin was drawn taut, then he leaned forward confidentially, 'ever heard of the Piltdown Man?'

'Yes,' Wrighton said slowly to hide the frantic racing of his mind.

'Well what was he?' Harry demanded.

'A fraud.'

'I know that. Forget that. What was he supposed to be?'

'He was the missing link between monkeys and humans or something like that.'

'Exactly.' Harry sat back smugly, having proved his point to his own satisfaction, but completely unaware that the explanation retained its clogging obscurity for Wrighton.

'Oh yes,' Wrighton said politely but something in his tone betrayed his ignorance for Harry raised his eyebrows and shook his head.

'The oval table is the Piltdown Man isn't it?'

'The Piltdown Man. Right.'

'There never was an oval table was there? It was invented to explain man's transition from making round tables to rectangular tables. It's the missing link – a rectangular circle. A rectangular circle. It's what everyone would have expected to have happened but it didn't. It's a fraud. Man made round tables and he made rectangular tables. He didn't make oval tables till some philosopher came along and asked the question, "How did we get from round to rectangular?"'

Wrighton laughed in spite of himself.

'I can't fault your argument,' he generously told him and then ducked as a dark shadow swooped over his head. An ironic cheer sounded throughout the club as the lights dimmed and brightened alternately.

'Dhaka Power have just lost a phase,' Harry explained. 'What did Hardwicke want with you?'

Hardwicke? Hardwicke? The name rang a bell somewhere in his memory but he could not place it.

'Who?'

'Geoff Hardwicke, the rake with the beard. What was he conning you into?'

'Oh him. He wanted me to play football, or anything I think. He was worried that I might get bored.'

'Well he would,' Harry said, darkly. 'Smooth as Irish sandpaper, he is. A diplomat from the BHC. Great man in a struggle. As far as he is concerned, the reason why his arse has got a crack in it, is so that he can sit on the fence without falling off.'

'What does he do at the BHC?'

'He's the spy.' Wrighton choked into his lime and soda. 'Of course they don't call him a spy, he's a commercial attaché or some fine thing. But everyone knows he is the spy.'

'Geoff Hardwicke, commercial attaché. I remember.'

'Do you?' Harry's vague eyes had a disconcerting sudden propensity to focus.

Wrighton thought back to the comic turn that the Foreign Office had put on for him before he had left London, and the insistence by that grey-suited mandarin that he should get in touch with 'our man Hardwicke'.

'I must have heard his name from somebody at work.' Wrighton convinced himself that he was not actually telling an untruth.

Harry nodded and then cocked an ear to the room.

'Brigadier Wha-Wha is in fine form tonight.'

Wrighton listened to the droning and bubbling of conversations, accusations, arguments and teasings and fought back a smile as he identified one particular noise emanating from a neat little man sitting by the piano. His face was the proof of years of good restaurant meals – bloated eyes, poached cheeks and from his drooling mouth came a clapping sound, 'Wha wha aha ha fa sasa fa wha wha.'

'What's his real name?'

'Don't know, don't care. He's Brigadier Wha Wha as far as I'm concerned. Ah Goody! We're going for the tower tonight.' Wrighton followed Harry's gaze to the table near the dart board, where a pile of empty beer cans was slowly being built into the shape of a cylindrical tower. 'Come on, we've got to drink it up to the ceiling.' Harry shifted himself ponderously from the stool.

'But I don't drink beer...' Wrighton began to excuse himself but stopped, perplexed, as Harry continued his descent from the stool to a graceful collapse on the floor. He sat looking up at Wrighton, eyes vague again.

'Must have missed my footing.' He made no attempt to rise but pushed back his head and yelled, 'Rickshaw!' at the top of his stentorian voice.

Wrighton tried to edge away from him as everybody stared in their direction, then, guffawing and leering, some of the darts players staggered over and with little ceremony and even less compassion, they half-dragged, half-walked the almost insensible mound of Harry out towards the street door.

'Having a good time?' Bell's voice was loud in his ear and before he could reply, "Having a good time?" I said.'

'I heard you the first time, Bell,' Wrighton said quietly. He tried to shrug off the brawny arm that Bell had draped around his shoulder.

'Come and meet the lads,' he insisted, swaying gently and upsetting Wrighton's balance so that he had to adopt a staccato staggering stance to avoid being pushed over. 'You're pissed.' Bell stabbed his finger into Wrighton's chest. 'You're pissed on Coca Cola.'

'I am not pi... drunk,' Wrighton retorted angrily. 'But you most certainly are. Don't you think we ought to be going home?'

'Going home? Going home? Where's home? This is home.' He waved his free arm and they both staggered.

'For Pete's sake, Bell, straighten up. People are looking at you.'

'Here's looking at you kid.' Bell slurred out his Humphrey Bogart impression, drained the can in his hand and tossed it over to the barman. 'There y'are Abdul, present for the missis. The bibi. No problem. Ha? No problem.'

Wrighton looked for Tuppin but the corner was bare. He would just have to manage this by himself. He had had very little experience of drunks and this irrationality in Bell's behaviour was difficult to cope with. He could feel the hot flush of embarrassment creeping up his neck to his ears as he began to steer him towards the door.

'Come on Bell, time to go home. Where are the keys?'

'You're my mate,' Bell confided in him, as Wrighton managed to pick the car keys from his shirt pocket without him noticing. 'You're my mate. He's my mate he is!' Bell shouted to the assembly. 'He's my mate!'

Wrighton was mortified and disaster was not far away, for just as he was congratulating himself on getting Bell as far as the street door, a commotion outside announced the return of the dart players who had sent Harry off homewards in a rickshaw. They crashed through the doorway, separating Bell from Wrighton who was knocked sprawling into the lap of a large middle aged dame in a flowered teeshirt.

'Excuse me, I'm most awfully sorry. Please excuse me. I was pushed, caught off balance.'

Removing the slice of lemon from her bosom she observed, frostily, that 'He ought to take his friend home and not get drunk with him again'.

Wrighton bounded up in anger and grabbed Bell by the arm with such ferocity that he allowed himself to be pushed through the doorway without any further fuss. The Club chowkidhar helped to prop Bell up in the back seat of the car and Wrighton tipped him with some taka that he took from Bell's pocket.

'This car is a confounded wreck,' Wrighton mumbled angrily as he eased a precocious seat spring out of his buttocks. After much lazy whirring, the engine sluggishly fired and turned over like a concrete mixer with a cannon ball in it. He selected what he assumed to be a forward gear, let in the clutch and they lurched off down the road, Wrighton peering ardently through the cracked windscreen. 'Lights!' he thought. 'Lights. Where are the confounded lights?' He pulled a switch and a skeletal windscreen wiper scratched an arc across the screen and then stopped to admire the view.

'Me limousine! Don't bust me–' Bell's plaint was interrupted as the back wheels clipped a storm drain. The car banged down onto the suspension stops and the breath was knocked out of both of them. As he grabbed at the wheel, Wrighton must have unknowingly hit the headlight switch, because a pool of lemon curd spilled out from the bonnet onto the road ahead.

'Oh brilliant!' Wrighton said and then swerved tensely around a brown mass of ambling cow. A rickshaw hurtled past him, the spokes of the rear wheel catching the sticky headlight glow like some ghostly, stylised sun. Before he could recover his surprise, a man's face materialised before him. He stabbed at the brakes and spun the wheel. The brake pedal had no effect. He pumped it once, twice. At the third pump, the brakes jammed fully on, the rear wheels locked and the back of the car slid towards the central island upon which a goat was sitting serenely.

Bell crashed forward from the rear straight into the back of Wrighton's seat, which lifted from its rack and threw him onto the wheel, jamming his foot harder upon the pedal. As the car described a shrieking semicircle, Bell fell back. Suddenly, the interior of the car was lit as bright as day as the night bus which had been trundling along in the darkness behind them, turned on all its lights.

Wrighton remembered the inconsequential manner in which he had remarked to himself as he waited for the crash, that it must have been one of the newer, Japanese buses because the headlights on the old Bedfords were not as bright as that. With a hideous, death-shrieking whistle, like a murderous banshee, the bus swerved off the road to avoid the immobile car, raising a cloud of choking dust behind it. Wrighton madly rammed the lever into reverse, booted the accelerator, took his foot from the clutch and performed a spinning turn, worthy of the more popular American police series which were even showing on Bangladesh television. Before the car had finished turning it was in first gear and, wheels still spinning, it snaked off into the cloud of dust behind the bus.

Wrighton was as angry as he was afraid. The car bounced and banged over the potholes. When he reached the roundabout at DIT 2, he blasted his horn, put his headlight onto main beam and screeched around the curve with his tyres scrabbling along the kerbside edge of the drain. To the left of a rickshaw, across its nose to the right of the next rickshaw, around a bicycle and off down the causeway towards Banani. Wrighton gritted his teeth and then grinned to himself as he caught sight in the mirror of a very sobre-looking, white-faced Bell, holding on to the seat.

'Ha.' Wrighton thought with bravado. 'That will teach them that they are not the only ones who can drive like racing drivers.' Even as he thought it, his hands began to shake.

7

The papaya grinned up from the plate at him like a gondola. The slice of glistening lime – the parasol of a Venetian debutante. As Wrighton ate his breakfast he found himself slowly shaking his head in amazement at the recollection of the previous evening. The mysterious woman speaking from the shadowy gloom of the verandah, teasing him. His neck tingled again as he remembered it. The wasting, drunken sop with the theory about oval tables; the coarse brute behaviour of the dart-playing engineers; the infuriating, patronising drunkenness of Bell and his own mortifying humiliation when he had sprawled into the tee-shirted beldam's lap . And what about the terrifying ride home in the car? He smiled as he remembered the pasty image of Bell's face in the rear-view mirror.

He heard the gate open and a rickshaw bell jangled uncertainly. Who could be visiting them at this time of the morning? Wrighton's surprise was compounded when Tuppin breezed in to the dining room. The thought of Tuppin taking an early morning rickshaw ride before breakfast was one which did not bear close examination.

'Watcha Wrighton, having breakfast?'

Wrighton nodded. He could not take his eyes from the apparition before him. At length he said, 'Have you only just come home?'

Tuppin swung his leg over a chair and pulled it to the table.

'Yeah. Stayed out all night like a naughty boy. Didn't sleep much though.' He winked grotesquely. 'She wouldn't let me.'

'Who?'

Tuppin tapped the side of his nose with his forefinger and snatched a piece of toast from the plate that Moussi had just brought in.

Wrighton said, 'Help yourself to my breakfast.'

'Just a snack. Had breakfast already. Where's Bell?'

'I last saw him tucked up in bed at about one o' clock this morning.'

Wrighton felt sour. He had never had to put an adult to bed before. Bell had been an octopus, limbs everywhere, draped around his neck, knocking the framed picture of a dark-haired woman from the chest of drawers. With great difficulty, for Bell was a well-built man, Wrighton had stripped him down to his underpants and rolled him into his bed. He had glanced around the room before switching off the light and had noticed how much larger it was than his room, then he had thrown the switch on the air conditioning and shut the door behind him.

'Mustn't leave him to sleep on his day off,' Tuppin said. He skipped out of the room and a few seconds later, a thunderous drumming resounded around the hallway. Wrighton winced as he imagined Bell being summoned back to consciousness by that reveille. Tuppin reappeared, grinning. 'He'll be in for breakfast soon.'

Hardly had the last word left his lips than the hallway echoed with a crash followed by a multi-barrelled oath whose ingenuity was outshone only by its crudity. The door burst open and there stood Bell, resplendent in his underpants. Behind him, Wrighton could see the grovelling form of Moussi, silently sweeping the remains of the tea service back onto the tray.

'Tea's OFF!' Bell boomed and then held his head. 'Me bloody head. Good binge last night wasn't it?' He addressed the last remark to Wrighton.

'I understand you enjoyed it. Wrighton's coolness soon melted as he warmed up his offended dignity. 'But next time you want to go out and make an ass of yourself, and expect a taxi service and nursemaid, you can find someone else. I am not interested. I have far more important ways of spending my time.'

'Name one!' Bell sat down opposite Wrighton and took his other piece of toast. 'Breakfast goes quick in these parts. Listen, Lord Snooty, it's not my fault that you are a stuck up git with a chip on your shoulder. I don't mind people knowing that I'm sharing with a milksop, but get this straight, boy'o; we stick together. You need me as much as I, God forbid, need you. When you are out in a place like this, the Whites stick together. They have to. You never know when you might need someone. It could be someone to change your wheel or to take you to hospital, anything, but we have to stick together.'

Wrighton looked at Bell with what he hoped was a withering gaze and said steadily, 'I don't need you Bell.'

Tuppin had been following the exchange, weasel-like, from the end of the table and decided that this was a propitious moment to yell for more tea.

'Moussi! Moussi!' Moussi appeared. 'Tea for Mr. Bell and me.'

'And me,' Wrighton added.

'Toast, two piece,' Tuppin continued.

'Four piece,' Wrighton corrected.

'Six piece,' Bell interjected, 'and one piece fried egg. Did you get your leg over last night then?' he asked Tuppin.

Tuppin smirked. 'She was a bit frantic.'

'Where's hubby then?'

'Up country. Not back till Sunday night.'

'You'll get caught one day.'

'Pah, no chance! He's up in Sylhet with the BHC roving commission or something. Even if he started out now, he wouldn't get here before Sunday. Three ferry crossings and that road through Amiriganj would soon see to that. He wouldn't do above twenty m.p.h.'

'He would if he drove like Wrighton. Christ! I nearly shit myself last night. Where did you learn to drive then Wrighton? On the Monte Carlo?'

'Wembley.'

'Bloody hell! If everybody drives like that in Wembley I'm staying out here.'

'Is he bad?' Tuppin nodded towards Wrighton.

'I'd swear we went around DIT 2 on two wheels.'

'As many as that?' Wrighton said. 'You should see me when I'm in a hurry.'

'I'll bear that in mind. What are we doing today?'

Tuppin ran his fingers through his lank hair. 'I'm going to have a shower and a bit of shuteye. We've got to do the cook book.' He slid a school exercise book across the table. 'Are you going down to the Sonargaon?'

'Yeah, might do. Do you want to come, Wrighton?'

'What do you do there?' Wrighton could see no reason to go to the international hotel in Dhaka other than to drink expensive western drinks in sumptuous air-conditioned surroundings.

'A bit of shopping. Get an English paper, if they've come in.'

'O.K.' Wrighton acquiesced. After all, he reasoned, he had nothing else to do today. There was no lawn to mow, shelves to put up or gables to paint. He was not even allowed to wash the dishes.

'You see,' Bell remarked heavily, 'you do need me.' Wrighton squirmed a little but Bell was quite without malice. 'Pompous git!' he added.

'Come on, the cook book,' Tuppin insisted.

'Barret, twelve taka. That sounds all right to me,' Bell said.

'Barret?' Wrighton repeated.

'What you make toast with.'

'Oh.'

'Melk, that's a fixed price, they can't fiddle that.'

'Melk?'

'To put in tea.'

'Ah.'

'He's put in some cile pudar again. They must be using it on their own meals, we only have curry on Fridays.'

'When did we have pumking?' Tuppin asked.

They scratched their heads. When did they last have pumpkin? Wrighton found this sort of exercise impossible. He took no interest in cooking and ate what was put in front of him, he always had. He thought no more of it than a train driver wondered why people were going to their destinations.

'Got it!' Bell said, jabbing his finger at another entry in the book. 'It was stuffed wasn't it? Look, there's the garan vif.'

'Garan vif?'

'Ground beef.'

'Of course.'

'We can't have used all the zely!'

'We must have done – they don't eat it.'

'Zely?'

'I do wish you would pay attention,' Tuppin scolded. 'Zely is what you eat at a farty with ice cream. Ice cream and zely.'

'Oh yes, silly me!'

Well that seems all right,' Bell concluded. 'Hundred taka each. You stick mine in Wrighton, I've got none on me.'

'If you will eat breakfast clad only in your underwear, what do you expect?'

Wrighton and Tuppin threw floppy rectangles of filthy paper money across the table and Bell marked the float down into the right hand column.

'I'm going to get my head down.' Tuppin stood up, yawned and then tottered off to his room. Moussi waited deferentially until he had cleared the doorway, then he bowed in.

'Madam visit,' he announced.

'Christ yeah!' Bell snapped his fingers. 'Friday. Hey Wrighton, do you want a massage?'

Wrighton was astonished. There could have hardly been a thought further from his mind. Of course he didn't want a massage. He wasn't a sportsman. Massage? That smacked of Turkish baths and saunas and strange rituals with twigs and hosepipes. Ha! You wouldn't catch him doing that, which was why he was so surprised when he heard himself saying, 'I've never had a massage, I may as well try.'

'Good man. It's only a hundred and twenty taka for an hour. Bloody cheap. Have you got any baby oil?'

Wrighton could only shake his head.

'You can use mine today but get your own for next week.'

'She comes every week does she?'

'Every Friday. Her name is Mina. She's a Hindu woman. Ugly as sin but with enormous tits.'

'Is that relevant to what she has to do?' Wrighton was becoming worried that perhaps he had misinterpreted the nature of the massage.

Bell looked at him sideways. 'You dirty old man! She won't do anything like that. She's a married woman, got a baby of her own.'

'No, I didn't mean... Anyway, how do you know she doesn't?' Wrighton returned to the attack."

'I asked her. Pointed to me John Thomas and said "Do a trick on him" but she just said that she didn't do that,' Bell admitted brazenly. 'I'll go and have a shower. Give her a pepsi and then you can have your massage whilst I'm shaving and making meself beautiful.'

Rather like a Whitehall farce, as Bell left, another door opened and into the room swayed a heavily built, Indian woman in a yellow sari.

With grudging admiration, Wrighton had to acknowledge that Bell's description was of a stunning accuracy. A pair of enormous, rounded, firm breasts, tightly bound into the Indian blouse of thin cotton, so that the dark nipples showed through even the patterned silk of the sari, were surmounted by a pointed jaw, a large mouth, a gargantuan nose and furry caterpillar eyebrows, crawling across the forehead towards the black, greasy hair which had been drawn back into a tight bun and staked onto the back of the head with a wooden billet of native carving.

'My word, she's ugly!' Wrighton found himself thinking and then hating himself for being so uncharitable. 'Hello. You have come to give Mr. Bell a massage have you?'

'Good Marning. Mr. Bell wants massage?'

'Yes, Mr. Bell wants massage. He wondered if I could have a massage as well.'

'You want massage too?'

'Yes please. Can it be done this morning?'

The woman gave the sideways nod which Wrighton had learned meant assent.

'My name is Mr. Wrighton.'

'I am Mina. Mr. Line not here?' Mina looked around as if she expected him to materialise from the bookcase.

'Er... no.'

'But his car is outside.'

Wrighton remembered the damaged Land Rover which was half hidden behind the house. 'Yes, that's... broken down. Actually...' he could see no reason to blacken Line's name if Mina had heard nothing about the accident, '...he's gone back to the U.K. I am his replacement.'

'You are replacing Mr. Line?' Mina remarked with such genuine and evident surprise that Wrighton felt bound to ask,

'Am I not good enough to replace Mr. Line then?'

'I don't know,' she replied, unaware of the great gaffe that she had committed. Somehow, Wrighton felt a warmth to this culture that allowed you to express your true opinion and just let it stand for what it was – an opinion.

The door opened suddenly and Bell's torso appeared with a bottle of baby oil in his hand. 'Catch!' he shouted as he tossed the plastic bottle to Wrighton.

Wrighton had never been a sportsman. The intricacies of the plotted trajectory of a sphere through the atmosphere had remained for him an enigma throughout his childhood, and disregarded in adulthood. He dropped the bottle. It was oily and slippery. It was like trying to catch a bar of wet soap.

'Butterfingers!'

Mina led the way to his bedroom and locked the door behind them with a naturalness that forestalled any allusions. The curtains had remained closed to prevent the morning sun from heating the room.

Wrighton did not know what to do next. He handed the bottle of oil to Mina and waited. She took it and, likewise, waited. Wrighton wished ardently that he had questioned Bell a little more closely about the format of these massages.

'Do I pay you now?'

'If you like or you pay me afterwards.'

'What should I do? Should I lie on the bed? I've never had a massage before.'

'First time? Lie on the bed please. Are you wearing underpants?'

'Yes'

'Leave your underpants on.'

'And take everything else off?'

'Yes please. Lie on your tummy please.'

The coolness of the oil caught him off guard for an instant and he jumped. He was immediately admonished in the flat, matter-of-fact tones of the masseuse.

'You must relax. Just lie there. Put your head as you feel comfortable.'

The large, strong hands began to rub the oil into his leg, up from the calf to the back of his knee then downwards, fingertips dragging along the front of his shins and back to the calf. Then up from the knee to the back of the thighs pushing hard, upwards towards the buttocks, round and then down to the knee again. The same movement repeated ten, fifteen times, Wrighton lost count. He became a sack, an inert lump being moulded and kneaded into the contours of the mattress. Up and down, up and down, round and down, round and down, his legs began to tingle but he did not want to move them, he could not, he had no volition – it was being teased out through his feet as Mina drew her hands down from his buttocks to the tips of his toes, pulling each one in turn, draining the tension from his body, expunging the fear. He closed his eyes and could feel himself floating outside of his body.

'Turn on your back now.'

'Mmmph?' Wrighton was aware of someone speaking.

'Turn on your back now please. I do your front.'

Wrighton turned over. He could not remember when he had been so indulged. His limbs were glowing yet somehow they seemed... contented, if limbs could be that. He especially liked the stretching of his arms from the shoulders all the way down to the fingertips. The sensation was one of having the aches and pains drawn out of you, like squeezing the sausage meat from a skin. He opened his eyes and squinted up at the impassive face of Mina. She was a little frightening in the detached, impersonal way that she rubbed and pummelled his body as if it were just a body and not an adult male, nearly naked. He could almost imagine her as one of the original thugs, cold-bloodedly strangling her travelling companions with the same impassive face.

'You have very long legs, Mr. Wrighton. It is difficult for me to reach to the top. I will have to kneel on the bed.' She apologised as if some damage would accrue to the bed. She stood back and in three or four circular motions of her arms and with a grace characteristic of the Orient, she unwound her sari and dropped it to the tiled floor. Hitching up her long cotton petticoat to her knees, she knelt on the bed and resumed her work.

'I must... I must write to Marion,' he thought in a detached moment.

'They've got three servants,' Marion announced to her fellow knitters with grim humour showing in her voice. 'He will have to forget any of those ideas when he comes back, ha!'

The others tittered. Angela Curnow said, 'Three servants does sound rather excessive. There are only three people living in the house, you said. Is it like having a batman? Do they have their own personal servant to polish their shoes and run their baths and things?'

Marion laid down her knitting and glanced at the glittering gilt and glass chandelier as she tried to recall the phrases from his letter.

'No, it's not that,' she began unsurely. 'I remember he said that they have what they call a cook-bearer. They share him. He does all the cleaning, the housework and washing and ironing and cooks the meals. Then they have what they call a... now what was that funny name? Just a minute, I've got his letter here.' She rummaged in her bag and pulled out the sheets of neat handwriting. 'Ah yes, a choke... er a chow... no I think it is pronounced "chowkidar". Anyway, he is the chap who guards their gate for them.'

'Why do they need a guard? Is it dangerous?'

Marion realised with a stab of doubt that she had not considered that aspect. She had merely accepted that they had a day gate-keeper and a night gate-keeper.

'No, I think it's just tradition.'

'What else does he say, Marion dear? What is the weather like? Is it the monsoon?'

'Just a minute... It's very hot. It gets very hot from about seven in the morning.... the... er... the monsoon is practically finished and the tanks are all full, whatever that means. I suppose he means water tanks. He has a lizard in his room, called a gecko and it lives behind the air conditioning unit and comes out every now and then and eats mosquitos.'

'Err, how disgusting!' Angela Curnow shuddered. 'I hope he is being paid lots of money for this.'

'I don't know, actually,' Marion admitted. She did not know how much he earned normally. It never occurred to her to ask him.

'Oh Marion dear, what do you mean, "you don't know"? Surely you know how much bonus or allowance or whatever they call it he is earning whilst he is out there.' Mary Gonzales wanted figures. She wanted to be able to then compare them, in an off-hand manner to the fabulous sums of money that her husband was no doubt earning. She was looking for a point to score and Marion could feel herself under pressure.

'And he's had a massage with an Indian woman,' Marion quickly changed the subject.

'*With* an Indian woman?' Angela Curnow giggled.

'Well, not *with* her, except in the sense that she did it to him.'

'Oh a good massage can be heaven...' another woman said. 'You feel so... so... loose afterwards.'

'You mean you felt like a loose woman?' Mary teased. The others laughed.

'No, I didn't mean that, you know I didn't. It's just that, when I was at Champneys, the masseur–'

'Why were you at Champneys dear?' Angela Curnow pinpointed the weak spot and needled her stiletto into it. 'Did you have a problem with your weight?'

'No dear, no,' the other replied, sweetly. 'I was invited there by some friends who... who knew the owners.'

'Stewart certainly seems to have enjoyed his massage. He says that he is going to have another one next week.'

'Well I'm sure you can trust him, Marion.'

'Yes, so am I,' Marion said shortly.

Fish fingers. That's what she would do for supper. The boys always liked fish fingers. It would be a treat for them. They deserved a treat. She winced as something crashed to the bedroom floor above her and the boys began to shout again. She wrenched open the living room door.

'Will you stop arguing?!' she shouted up the stairs.

'Richard's got my gun, Mum. Make him give it back.'

'S'not your gun. It's my gun.'

'Tis not.'

'Tis so! I got it for Christmas from Aunty Beryl.'

She threw down her tea cloth and stamped up the stairs.

'Right! Give the gun to me.'

'Oh mum.'

'Come on. I'm waiting. Give it to me if you can't play properly.'

'Mum!'

She took the gun from Richard who immediately burst into tears.

'Serves you right!' his brother shrieked at him. 'It serves you right.'

Richard screwed up his face, gritted his teeth and with all the energy he could muster shouted, 'Bugger!'

'Richard!' Marion was horrified.

'Bugger, bugger, bugger, bugger!' He stuck out his tongue at her. 'Bugger, bugger, bugger, bugger, bugger!'

Her arm snaked out and cuffed him on the head. He fell into a gulping heap in the corner of the bedroom.

'Don't smack me Mum, don't smack me Mum! I didn't say it.' Charles hastily moved to protect himself but he need not have worried for if Marion had been shocked by Richard's language, it was nothing to the revulsion she felt at having hit the child. She knelt down and put her arms around the sobbing, shaking lump.

'Come on, come on. Mummy didn't mean it but you mustn't say things like that.'

'I...uh...want...uh...my...uh...Da...Dad-dy,' the little one gulped.

Emboldened by his relative impunity, Charles voiced a doubt which had been rattling in his uncluttered mind. 'Mummy, is Daddy coming back?' Richard wailed even louder. 'Warren says that his daddy went to Saudi Arabia and stayed there. He didn't come back.'

Marion hugged both the boys to her and they became one sodden bundle on the bedroom floor. She buried her face in the smell of Richard's damp hair as her strangled voice assured them hoarsely, 'Of course he's coming back. Your Daddy loves you.'

Until then, she had never known the absolute desolation of despair.

'Come on, let's get a newspaper,' Bell insisted, 'that's what we came here for.'

Bell had given this as the reason why they had gone to the Hotel Sonargaon but, somehow, once inside the air-conditioned oasis, it had lost its importance.

They had ambled through the spacious marbled corridors lined with display cases of silks and carved woods. Occasionally they had met another European to whom they had nodded. It seemed the correct sort of thing to do, as if acknowledging membership of the same club.

But now they were at the hotel shop. It could have been a small western newsagents, yet on closer view the range of goods sat uncomfortably together: a selection of popular paperbacks in various languages, several of them had been patently read from cover to cover; some bottles of after shave; a pile of maps which Wrighton looked through without finding a map of Dhaka but discovering a street plan of Rio de Janeiro; some jute bags bearing the motto, 'I leov Bangladesh'; a teetering tower of rope sandals; some boxes of chocolates and a rack full of newspapers.

'Oi Abdul! Have you got any English newspapers?' Bell demanded.

The man, whose name was obviously not Abdul, sorted in a cardboard box and proudly flourished an *International Herald Tribune*.

'That's American, you peabrain. Have you got a *Telegraph* or a *Times?*'
He looked into his box and drew out a *Paris Match.*

'Oh come on, we're wasting our time.' Bell turned away in disgust.

'Goodbye,' Wrighton said to the man who saluted him respectfully.
Bell shot him a pitiful look.

'It's no good being polite to the Banglas, they won't understand you.
You know, there is no word for "please" or "thank you" in Bengali. They
had to be invented when the English came here. They don't know what
politeness is.'

'Possibly,' Wrighton said noncommittally, 'but it can't hurt them and it
makes me feel better.'

'You great girl's blouse! I don't suppose you have met many people
yet, have you?' Bell said as they ambled across the broiling car park
towards his car.

'No I suppose not.' Wrighton was thinking to himself that he had met
socially more people in the last week than he had met in the previous year.

'Have you had any invites? Parties and things?'

'Well... I don't really go to parties. I'm a bit of a spoilsport.' Wrighton
laughed, embarrassed at the desert which was his social life.

'Everybody goes to parties here, Wrighton, everybody. And of course at
Christmas there is the British High Commission New Year's Eve Ball.
You'll have to go to that. It's the highlight of the season. I'll see if I can
get you a ticket.'

'Already?'

'No, you idiot, when they come out. But not everybody gets one. You
have to know someone. I've got contacts. I'll see what I can do.'

Wrighton settled on the scorching hot plastic seats of the car.

'Ouch!'

'We'll go down to the club,' Bell shouted as they swerved out into the
avenue. 'You can get some lunch there if you like. Got your swimming
togs with you?' Wrighton shook his head. 'We can stop off at the house on
the way back. Do you do much swimming?'

Wrighton thought of the brand new swimming trunks, purchased two
years ago, resting at the bottom of his suitcase in his bedroom.

'Not much.'

'I do.'

'You would,' Wrighton mumbled.

'Whassat? Yeah I'm a pretty good swimmer. Best swimmer in the
school I was. Used to do the big stuff. Long distance swimming, you know,
five miles, ten miles, that sort of thing. I used to do three miles every day

before breakfast when I was a kid.'

Wrighton gawped. Such distances he would shirk at covering on foot. To do them lying on your belly with your mouth shut was beyond his imagination.

The club in daylight appeared singularly theatrical. The overhead sun lighted the garden, the pool, the tennis courts, the gucha porchway and the scattered chairs and tables with a bland flat light, shadows falling vertically, adding nothing poetical to the forms that spawned them. Like a theatre stage with all the stage lights full on. On the patchy lawn people were eating and drinking. Children were running around shrieking with a hamburger or a sausage in their hands. One jumped into the pool to escape his pursuer, forgetting that he was holding a bread roll. It was the children that amused Wrighton the most. They were all as brown as berries and dived in and out of the pool with a facility and familiarity that Wrighton could only marvel at. Somewhere in the garden, without bothering to look, Wrighton knew that Brigadier Wha Wha was seated. His see-saw vowels rising above and then dropping below the general drone of the conversations.

Bell pulled up one of the cane chairs to a rickety table and sat down, expansively. 'Mine's a beer, Wrighton, have one yourself.'

'Er...right. You'd like a drink would you?'

'You're quick, I'll say that of you.'

Wrighton padded through the verandah into the bar, conscious of his sandals slapping on the tile floor. Taking his chit book from his shirt pocket he began tearing off the necessary chits as he ordered a beer for Bell and a lime and soda for himself.

'Still not drinking then, Wrighton?' Harry's thick voice slurred across the bar to him. Wrighton glanced across at the figure slumped on the very same stool that he had last seen him fall from. He waved a dismissive hand vaguely in Harry's direction, hoping that the gesture would shipwreck any development of the conversation but Harry was either too drunk to notice or had decided that he would not conform to the social niceties.

'I pity people who don't drink,' he pronounced loudly.

'I don't ask for your pity.'

'Do you know why I pity people who don't drink?'

'I can guess.'

'Go on then.'

'Well–'

'No that's not it,' Harry interrupted him. 'Listen. I pity people who don't drink because when they get up in the morning, that's the best they are going to feel all day long, but if I've had a drink or two the night before, when I get up, I feel better and better as the day goes on and that's a much nicer idea.'

'You may be right.'

He returned to the garden and whilst Bell sipped his beer, Wrighton surreptitiously surveyed the pool. It was rectangular and blue. It appeared to have a deep end because there was installed at one end, a short diving board from which the children were launching themselves like the train that crashed over the central span of the *Bridge on the River Kwai*. Despite the noise and movement, there were very few people actually in the pool. Most of the adults were stretched out on sun beds around it. Wrighton decided that he would wait until most of the children had settled down to eat and then he would quietly clamber down the steps and paddle about a bit as if he were just cooling off.

'Why are there so many American kids here?' he asked Bell.

Bell made a face at him through his glass.

'Where?'

'Well those two there, for a start and that girl with the black hair... and the boy with the football.'

'They're all English. Those two are the kids of one of the ECO's at the BHC.'

'ECO's?'

'Entry... er something Officers. They are out here to give visas to the Bengalis, or rather, they are here to *not* give visas to them. But the kids are English.'

'They can't be, listen to them,' Wrighton insisted as the children providentially broke out in a cacophony of Americanese.

'Oh that's only an accent,' Bell dismissed it. 'They get it from the school. The only school that they can go to is the American School, so they all end up speaking American.'

'How horrific!' Wrighton remarked. 'Are you going for a swim later?'

'No, I don't think I will bother, I'm playing squash. I don't want to tire myself out. Are you?'

'I might drop in for a paddle,' Wrighton replied deferentially. 'When the population has thinned out a bit.'

'That's the problem that I have, of course, you can hardly do a length without having to get out of someone's way. When I want to get some miles in I generally swim in the evenings.' He looked across the garden.

'Isn't that your boss?'

Wrighton looked across to see Havering in shorts and a tee shirt striding towards them. In his left hand he was gripping a tennis racket by the neck as if he were strangling a cat.

'I wonder what he wants.'

'Wrighton!' Havering pointed the racquet at him. 'I want you in the office tomorrow morning.'

'But I don't work Saturdays!'

'You do as you are told Wrighton. In the office. Nine o clock tomorrow morning.'

'My name's Bell, pleased to meet you.' Bell half rose from his chair and proffered his hand.

Havering turned his head. 'Do you mind? Listen Wrighton. Those figures that Armri brought back from up country–'

'The alignment?'

'Yeah, based on Lines' calculations. They don't work. They are all to cock. You've got to go through them and check them all out. He's got the Mirsharai valve station a kilometre out.'

'But there must be over two hundred datum points on that survey.'

'There are, that's why you've got to start early. I've got to see the minister on Sunday morning and I must have those coordinates. And whatever you do, don't let the Banglas touch any of your calculations. Give them tea to make or something but keep them away from the work. I don't want them buggering it up any more. Call themselves surveyors!' He turned and stalked away, still strangling the cat.

Bell nodded his head. 'Charming fellow. If I had to work with him I think I'd lay one on him.'

'He can be a bit abrupt sometimes.' Wrighton was already thinking of his work for tomorrow.

'Still, he's got the right idea about the Banglas. A useless shower they are.'

'Oh I don't know. Our problem is that we have a one-for-one match on the project so I have an engineer to match me. He's called Armri or something like that. He is supposed to be the same calibre of engineer as me but quite frankly, without any false modesty, he cannot really cope with the tasks we set him so I have to go around behind him checking everything. It's a confounded nuisance, of course. I would rather do a job from the beginning than have to check and correct somebody else's work. But we can't be choosers.'

'Yeah,' Bell said absently. 'Are you eating back at the house tonight?'

'Yes, I thought I might.'

'O.K. I'll see you there. You can walk back can't you?' He grinned and strode away.

Stewart cowed as the hand snaked around into his shade behind the deck chair. It took him several moments to recover and realise that it was not searching for a target but it was proffering something – a threepenny bit.

'Here you are son, go and get yourself an ice cream.'

Stewart took the coin dumbly and gazed anxiously up at the crowded promenade.

'Will you come with me Mum?'

'Leave your mum alone. You're eight years old. You can get one on your own.'

Stewart looked up at the promenade again. The rail was crowded with people, mostly young men, loafing, joking, perusing. Behind them a constant throng of colour and bare legs moved like a kaleidoscope as families strolled first down the promenade and then back up again. He gripped his threepenny bit firmly in his hand and ran his finger nail over the flat edges as he staggered across the yielding sand towards the stone steps. The bottom few steps were half buried by the sand and rounded like logs. As they were, it appeared that some subterranean machine was forming these sausages of stone and spewing them upwards, volcano-like and as they climbed higher they cooled and formed themselves into harder, more rectangular shapes until by the time that Stewart had reached the top all the steps were crystal-cut, hard-edged granite.

'Don't stop there sonny, you're in the way,' a jovial man in braces said to him as he pushed past.

Stewart found himself moved with the crowd, hemmed in. His legs working mechanically, he caught occasional glimpses of the railings and balustrades moving past him like the telegraph poles along the railway line. Where was he going? Where was the ice cream man? Bright lime green and cream coach with gold writing on the side; dark blue and light blue with sun glinting on the top; maroon and grey, sun shining orange through the perspex roof light; rich chocolate brown with a swirling custard stripe. Hot sand powdery crunchy on paving stone, wasps swirling around the wastepaper basket.

The ice cream man.

Stewart stood in awe at the length of the queue. It disappeared off in the opposite direction and even as Stewart watched, more people were joining it. He stumbled along and self consciously stood at the end. A big woman nudged behind him. Every time the queue moved forward she edged him forward with her midriff. The sun beat from a cloudless sky, another nudge in the back and he stumbled forward trying not to shunt into the greasy back of the man in front.

'Watcha topsy!' a boy in green swimming trunks addressed him. He ignored him and two other boys joined the first, sneeringly. Another nudge in the back. The queue moved on, the sun beat down.

'Wotcha doin?' The boy poked him in the shoulder. Stewart flinched.

'I'm waiting to buy an ice-cream.'

'He's waiting to buy an ice cream,' the green swimming trunks said to his cohorts. 'Where's yer mum and dad then?'

Stewart decided he did not want to continue this conversation. The boys had a roughish, wily air about them.

'This yer dad?' The boy pointed at the man in front.

Stewart shook his head, his fear having deprived him of speech.

'This yer mum?'

Stewart did not reply.

'You're not waiting to buy an ice cream. You're just taking up space in the queue for someone else.'

Here was an accusation, something at last that Stewart could refute.

'I'm not! I am buying an ice cream.'

'You won't get one with a ha'pence.'

'I've got a threepence.'

'Oh he's got a thruppence,' the boy repeated for his mates. 'Aren't we rich? He's got a thruppence. You haven't got no thruppence. You haven't got no money at all.'

Hot tears began to brim behind his eyes. With the disinterested impermeability of rank, the adults in the queue ignored the vile, insidious intimidation. It was kid's stuff. Nothing to do with them.

'I have got threepence,' Stewart almost shouted. 'I have too, look!'

As the three boys ran away, one shouted to the other two, 'That's two we' got. Nar we' gotta get one for Billy Boy.'

Stewart could not see his empty palm for the tears of frustration and rage and disappointment and fear that were pearling down his face. Another nudge in the back, he turned to the woman,

'Those boys stole my threepence!' he shouted. She ignored him, looking over his head and staring stolidly at the back of the man in front. 'Those boys stole my threepence!' he shouted louder at her.

'They was yer mates playin' a game wiv yer,' she assured him.

'They're not my mates. I never saw them before.'

'Then wotcha give 'em your thruppence for then?'

'I didn't!' Stewart screamed in frustration. Why couldn't the woman understand? Perhaps she didn't want to. 'They stole it.'

'What's 'e 'ollerin' about?' the man in front asked.

'Some of his mates nicked his thruppence. He'll get it back.'

Stewart watched in horrorstruck wonderment as the conversation continued over his head, taking on a life of its own, ignoring him, creating its own folklore and mythology,

'I saw 'im chattin' to 'em.'

'Yeah, I 'eard 'em.'

'He 'eld it out on the palm of 'is 'and, just like that.'

'They must ave been 'is mates.'

'Then they all ran off, giggling.'

'But they're thieves...' Stewart whimpered to himself.

'Got any more money?' the lady enquired.

'No, that's all my dad gave me,' Stewart answered meekly, sensing the generous, better soul, beneath the woman's harder exterior.

'There don't seem no sense in stayin' in the queue then, does there? Takin' up a place.'

Dumbly, Stewart allowed himself to be evicted. The woman moved up to fill the space.

'Ere wotchit missis, quit shovin will yer?'

Stewart listened through benumbed ears as he wandered away. He would have to pretend to his father that he had eaten the ice cream. He dared not tell him that he had been robbed. He knew that he could get away with it since he had spent so long futilely standing in the queue that his father would not know when he had bought his ice cream.

He clomped heavily down the steps to the beach and wandered over to his parents' deck chairs. But his parents were not in them, another couple were sitting in them. Astonished, he looked about him and saw his parents further on; he had mistaken the deck chairs. But when he got closer he saw that these too were not his parents. He stared at them in disbelief which was surely turning to panic. They stared back at him.

'Don't you know it's rude to stare?' The man could see an insolent urchin standing before him. Actually it was a lost little boy, unaware that he was in the middle of a three mile long beach hosting the recumbent or sessile forms of over ten thousand people but only knowing with a poignant certainty that he was lost and nobody seemed to care.

'Mum!' he tried to shout, but his voice, only a croak, was lost in the hubbub of shrieking voices and crashing waves. He didn't try to shout again for the sound of his lonely voice had scared him more than his predicament. He turned around and ran back to the sea wall and scampered up the steps, with the intention of trying to spot them from the promenade, but once the promenade gained, he could not approach the railings for the press of youths leering at the sunbathers or the holiday-makers with handkerchiefs stretched across their faces and feet propped proprietorially up on the railings. He ran along, darting in and out, pecking at the gaps. Then he came to another set of steps. Were these the steps that he had climbed with the threepenny bit held so expectantly in his hand? He thought that they might be but then again, he could not remember having repassed by the coaches and surely he would not forget such a colourful array? Where were the coaches? He strained around. He thought that he could see the sun glinting on coach roofs a little further on. He ran on. Another set of steps. He ran on down them and fell head-long into the sand at the bottom.

'Get up you blithering idiot. I suppose you've dropped your ice cream in the sand?' his father's voice bellowed out at him from a few feet away.

He looked up. Solid as a rock his parents sat splendidly permanent in their deck chairs. They had never moved.

'I've finished it,' Stewart lied. It was not challenged.

'Why don't you go down and have a paddle?' his father suggested, swatting a fly from his arm.

'Oh yes, that would be nice, Stewart,' his mother agreed. 'Go and have a splash with the other children there.'

Stewart wandered down to the water's edge. Pink bodies, red bodies, brown bodies ran past him and threw themselves into the water, shrieking and yelling. He walked into the surf. It was cold. He kept walking out towards a belt of children who were tumbling over each other. He stood a little way off, watching them. The water was almost at his chest when suddenly his heart stopped with fright for his feet were no longer touching sand. Terrified, he just managed to scream as the wave which had lifted him from the sand hurled him backwards, tumbling headlong back to the margin. A mass of green swirled over him and then he was up, spluttering, pink-faced and shrieking like the others, running back to do it again.

Then his father was at the side of him, holding his hand.

'Come further out,' he entreated.

Stewart looked back at the strident strand and then out behind his father to where it was all bluey-green and nothing else. He shook his head.

'Come on, I'm waiting. I'm going to teach you how to swim.'

Stewart shook his head and began to back away.

'Don't be such a baby.' His father walked out, dragging the reluctant Stewart behind him. The water reached his neck. Here the waves were gentle rhythmic movements, not crashing cacophonies of foam. Here, the wave gently lifted your feet from the bottom so that you did not realise and when you struggled you went under and you still could not touch bottom. Stewart fought.

'You're nothing but a baby. When I was your age my father threw me into the river, I soon learned to swim. You great baby, you're no good at anything.' His father released his hand in disgust.

Stewart madly clawed at the water, but it didn't care. He frantically thrashed and scooped with his arms but it ignored him. He kicked and screamed but the syrupy water dragged his kicks downwards, his screams became gurgles and splutters. Water roared in his ears then all his hearing became muffled by the weight of water. He closed his eyes in fright. He was slowly spinning in a black, sound-deadened universe, suffocating, stultified by fear. He didn't want to struggle anymore, he had no strength, he gave in. He didn't care, he couldn't breath, someone would save him, someone would come.

The noises became sharper, light filtered across his eyelids. Wrighton burst back up through the surface and grabbed the side of the pool to which he clung, coughing and spluttering in the Dhaka sun. He hung there for a while, to regain his breath and his composure. Neither seemed to come easily. Then he discreetly looked around him. Nobody had noticed his plunge into the deep end. At the far side of the pool a young woman in pointed sun spectacles could have been looking in his direction but it was difficult to tell.

'When you want a drink you go to the bar not jump in the pool,' one of the Vickers engineers said as he walked past.

Wrighton raised a hand in salute. He was shaking with black fear. Ever since he could remember, he had been afraid of water. Not water for drinking, or washing in, but dark water between walls, canals, mill races, powerful surges, even dank ponds held a foreboding for him. Jumping into the deep end had been an act of bravado on his part, precipitated by the rationalising in his engineer's mind that there was no logical reason why he should not learn to swim. It could be proven by elementary hydraulics that if he took a deep breath and jumped in, he could not actually sink. He would go under on initial impact of course, but he would not stay down, not for ever. It had been long enough though. The blackness and the roaring in the ears; the disorientation had been enough to decide him to put off the rest of his lesson until another day. He teetered along towards the shallow end and pulled himself up the steps to dry out on his sun lounge.

His heart was still thumping madly but he nevertheless felt a small reassurance. At least he had started. There was no going back now.

8

Wrighton arrived at the office just as Mac Macleod was alighting from his Land Rover in the yard.

'I'm sorry I had to call on you Mac, it's darn good of you to come in on your day off.'

'It's your day off as well Stew,' Mac replied. 'The old man is kicking up a shindig is he?' He spoke with a discreet Irish lilt.

Wrighton grimaced.

'He collared me at the club yesterday.' They walked up the steps together. 'You should have seen the way he spoke to Bell.' Wrighton laughed. 'Do you know Bell?'

Mac squinted up at the ceiling.

'Stocky fellow, on the Hovercraft project? Plays squash?'

'That's the one.'

'What are you doing with him? Not really your type, I would have thought.'

'Sharing a house with him. I've got no choice really. He's alright. I don't know what my type is, anyway.'

'Well I meant he's a bit brutal. Bit of a tough.'

'And I'm a softie... a bit of a wet.'

Mac looked at him seriously.

'Yeah, that's what I think. Didn't old Bell used to hang around with the Vickers boys?'

'He still does.' Wrighton unlocked the office door.

'That's what I meant.' Mac followed him inside.

Two cockroaches caught in the middle of the floor by the surprised intrusion on a rest day, scuttled away with a scratching noise to a dark corner somewhere.

'I hate those things,' Mac admitted shyly. 'I picked up a crate of beer at home the other day and one of the bloody insects ran up my arm. Mother of Mary! Dropped the crate and broke about four bottles. Now... what's the problem?'

Wrighton spoke over his shoulder as he searched through the top drawer of a filing cabinet. 'You know the route projections that Line did before he left?'

'For the Chittagong extension?'

'That's the ones. Havering reckons that they are all to cock – as he so put it.'

'Quite possibly,' Mac remarked calmly, 'but that's not your pigeon.'

'Well it is now. And I have strict instructions to keep Armri out of it. Havering does not want any Bengalis to touch the calculations.'

'So what does he expect you to do, check them all out?' Mac laughed at the preposterous suggestion.

'That's exactly it. I thought that it might be easier on that number cruncher of yours.'

'But there must be over two hundred co-ordinates on that plot.'

'Three hundred and nine,' Wrighton read from the end of a list that he had just withdrawn from the folder. 'So the sooner we get started....' He looked at Mac. 'Look Mac, this is nothing to do with you. It's not your work. You're not even in my section. I can't ask you to do this work, so if you want to clear off home then go ahead. I honestly won't feel bad about it and I mean that. Havering doesn't know a thing about me asking you so he won't know if you don't want to do it. I shan't tell him.'

'And if I don't do it?'

'I've got a calculator and a slide rule.'

'I've never liked Havering,' Mac replied. 'Stick that plug in the voltage stabiliser will you?' He pointed to a red box in the corner. 'But you're all right Stew, and it's a typical trick of Havering's. Have you done anything to upset him?'

Wrighton stopped short.

'I don't think so. I've not really had time. Do you mean that he's a bit vindictive?'

'Just a bit,' Mac replied laconically. 'Now what are we doing?' He studied his monitor screen, flicking menus with a tap of a key. 'Pass me that brown book can you?'

'A French dictionary?' He handed the book over to Mac. 'I thought so. That screen is all in French.'

'A great thing, international aid co-operation isn't it?'

'Do you mean that the program we want is in French?'

'Not just the program, the entire software package is in French.'

'Why? Why?' Wrighton insisted.

'It was bought from a French company.'

'You're joking.'

'Would I joke about such a thing? The World Bank sub committee which was dealing with the floating of the gas project decided that it would put out a tender within the European Community for the software package, and they chose a French company. So what language would you think the software would be in?'

'Well didn't they realise that?'

'You can see that. I can see that. But don't forget, these people are Experts. They can't be expected to have to worry about a little thing like human language compatibility. So I have to use my dictionary. It's not too difficult but every now and then I come across a word that I can't make sense of.'

'But do you speak French then?'

'Do me a favour. I went to a comprehensive. The trouble with this project is that it's too fragmented. We are all kept separate for budget purposes and this dismembers any sort of cross contact. I mean, what is the point of the whole project?'

'Well, in a nutshell, I suppose it is to lay a pipeline where it is needed.'

'Right. And how many pipelayers have you met?'

'None.'

'No and you won't either. Just because we don't actually need to see them, we never do. For all I know the pipelayers could be Russians!'

'That's a prospect to be played with.'

'O.K. I'm ready. What is my job going to be, checking the maths?'

'Yes, and I can do the triangulations over here, then we can replot the co-ordinates onto the grid.'

'Sounds O.K. to me. Off we go then.'

They worked solidly. Not talking unless the work demanded it. A professional communion of silence. At midday, Mac sent his driver out for some shingara and iced coke and they continued to tap keys and plot angles whilst bludgeoning their taste buds with ice cold drink and searing hot shingara. Wrighton was not particularly fond of shingara but they fulfilled a purpose and he abided by the dictum imparted to him upon his first making acquaintance with the batter-fried delicacy – 'Never look inside it and if anything crunches in your mouth, spit it out because it will be a dead cockroach.'

From time to time, bits of conversations and negotiations from other business inhabitants of the block drifted into their office and out again. On Saturdays, not all the companies took a day off. Everybody did on Friday as it was the Muslim day of rest. Although being European Christian absolved one from Muslim restrictions and thus, in theory, one could work on a Friday, in practice it was impossible since the Bengalis necessary to run the infrastructure just would not be there. There would be nobody to sweep the stairs, park the vans, open the doors, make the tea, file the letters, interpret, deal with their own countrymen and the hundred other tasks that went towards the running of an office building of this scale.

At half past three, when Wrighton was finishing the final triangulations on the charts, Mac appeared with two cups of tea.

'Chi, saheb!' he announced.

Wrighton pushed back his chair and pulled at the collar of his shirt. His back was aching from bending over the charts. Mac placed the cup silently on his desk. Wrighton smiled wearily up at him.

Mac said, 'So, what have we got?'

Wrighton rubbed his chin and then studied his written comments, scratched contemporaneously on a sheet of paper. The handwriting was blurring before his eyes.

'I think I'm seeing double,' he complained lightly.

'Only double? Lucky you!' Mac retorted. They were both aware of an unspoken bond which had arisen between them from having arduously applied themselves to the joint realisation of a difficult task. But now Mac wanted to know the result. 'So what's the secret?'

'Well,' Wrighton began slowly, 'the pipe has a twelve degree bend in it just east of kilometre fifty two. If you are going to end up with your valve station almost a kilometre out then that is the obvious place to look for a fault. Raymond Line only needed to be a few metres out there, or a degree or two in the angle and that would be the result...'

Mac sensed that this was not the answer.

'But he's not is he?'

'Not as far as I can calculate. It's all spot on.'

'So what is it then?'

'Well he appears to have made one mistake. Not a very big one but inexcusable. He's forgotten to allow for the curvature of the earth.'

'How does that affect it?'

'Putting it simply, the maps we use are flat but the earth they represent is curved so the distances are not exactly correct.'

'Is that important?'

'Oh it's important. A fundamental mistake that someone of his experience should not have made. But at that distance it still only produces a divergence of a matter of metres not kilometres.'

'But Havering says that the Mirasharai valve station site is a kilometre out?' Wrighton nodded, not taking his eyes from his sheets of calculations. 'How was the fixing done?'

'Line would have gone up country with the surveyors and fixed the key points himself and then would have left the others to fill in.'

'So Mirasharai could be between two of Line's fixes, and been misfixed by one of the Banglas?'

'Well... unlikely. You see Line would have fixed the site of the valve station himself. It would have been one of his key points. He would not have got that wrong. I don't think that he would have let one of the locals do it.'

'But he didn't allow for the curvature of the earth? Something that you declared was a "fundamental mistake"?'

'Yes,' Wrighton said slowly, 'I think you've got something there. It certainly points to a gross error on the survey. In any case, all the triangulations tie up. You can see for yourself.'

'Well I hope Havering is pleased with the discovery. He loves to exploit other people's weaknesses and mistakes. Makes him feel powerful,' Mac said grimly as he pulled out the plug. 'I'm going home. We've finished.'

'You're dead right. I'll tell Havering what I think tomorrow. He can do the worrying. Come down to the club and let me buy you a drink at least.'

Mac looked at his watch.

'No can do, I'm afraid. Got an appointment with Memsaheb. Bit late already.'

'Oh Mac! You should have said–'

'No matter. Can I drop you anywhere? By the way,' he interrupted himself, 'how did you get here?'

'Baby taxi.'

'You've got guts.'

'And no transport... You can drop me off in Banani if that is on your way please, Mac.'

'Sure.'

The Land Rover crept out of the yard and began forcing its way through the traffic like a homebound ice breaker on a Friday night. Neither man spoke on the journey. Presently Mac poked his driver between the shoulder blades and said, 'This is where you alight. Kemal Ataturk Avenue good enough for you?'

'Perfect. Thanks Mac. What's your driver's name?'

'Driver.'

'Thank you Driver.'

The Bengali split a white grin and saluted as he let in the clutch and bounded out into the traffic, aiming at the dorsal line of a killer bus. Wrighton hummed as he strolled down their lane. He was quite pleased with himself.   Not only had he risen to what he could now see was a back-breaking test set by Havering as part of the attrition, but he had found a good sturdy assistant in Mac.

The first object to meet Wrighton's gaze on reaching the murky hall of the Banani house was a pair of plimsolls, encrusted with foul-smelling slime and mud which had dried on in a redolent rime.   They had been deposited on the floor in the middle of the hallway, their cracked carapace giving them the appearance of a pair of ancient turtles fossilised in the act of copulation.   A few feet further into the hall, a filthy teeshirt had been sloughed off; through the grime he could read the legend *'Dhaka Hashers do it on Saturdays'*.

Wrighton turned aside, leaving the articles where they lay.   The servants could see to them.   In the living room, the only main common room of the house, Bell was standing by the low table, a can of beer in one hand and a cassette tape in the other.   He was wearing what was obviously the missing portion of the wardrobe which Wrighton had already inspected. It was coloured in the same pattern of splattered and streaky mud.   Bell half-turned and raised his can in salute then crashed the cassette into the machine and stabbed at one of the buttons.   'Keith Jarrett!' he yelled. 'The King. Magic. World's best jazz keyboard, yeah!' He was glowing with health. His hair was plastered down onto his head by the sweat which had then run down his face, carving rivulets in the dust and dried mud.

'So, judging by the detritus in the hall and the state of yourself I assume that you have just run on the Hash.'

'Bloody marvellous!' He gulped another mouthful of beer. 'It was up by Tongi, round by the shoe factory. Bloody marvellous. Old Benji got the Hashit.'

'Who got the what?'

'Benji, the big Dutch fellow, works for the Dutch equivalent of Oxfam. He got the Hashit 'cos he fell into a tank.' Bell laughed as he recalled the image to his mind. 'It was a tank the whole village used as a bog as well. Ha!'

'And what does the Hashit consist of?'

'You get two gallons of cold water poured over you, from the cool box.'

'And this is a reward or a punishment?'

'A tradition.'

'I suppose if one had fallen into such a septic tank then one would be grateful for a dousing in relatively clean water although at the tempera-ture we have been enjoying today, I would hope that the victim would have a strong heart.'

'Doesn't do any harm. The Hash has never killed anybody yet. Nearly did last year though. The hares set the course over a brick wall and across a big field. They set the course in the late morning, just before the "off",' Bell explained. 'It wasn't until about eighty runners had got to the middle of the field that they realised that they were running across Zia Airport from the far side. The Air India 707 didn't like it either. There was a bit of a stink about that one.'

'I'm surprised that they could tell the runners from the goats, although... I suppose the goats don't smell as much.'

Bell sniffed at his armpits in grotesque pantomime.

'Lovely! Are you coming down the club this evening?'

'I hadn't really thought about it.'

'Well I'll take you, if you are ready in time. Oh, and by the way, your boss, whatsisname...'

'Havering?'

'Yeah, he wanted to know if you had gone into the office today.'

'He came around then did he?'

'No... He was running on the hash. Quite a nice bloke when you get to know him.'

'Oh,' said Wrighton.

Mrs. Rosario caught Rubena Chowdhry's eye. They both looked across to the door which separated their little cubbyhole from the stairs. The raised voice of Alan Havering could be heard indistinctly booming down the stairwell. Rubena pursed her lips and made a gesture of futility with her hand, like the opening and closing of a bloom. They both returned to their work.

'Havering Saheb is not in a good mood today.' Leila Rose remarked. 'You can hear him shouting better if you open the door.' And to demonstrate this obvious claim she leaned backwards on her rickety chair and pulled open the door. 'He even shouted at the peon this morning for spilling water on the step.'

'Mr. Havering always is shouting at the peon,' Mrs. Rosario observed.

'Yes but this morning the peon was not being stupid.' Leila explained the important nuance in her observation.

'The peon is always being stupid,' Mrs. Rosario replied. 'That is why he is a peon.'

Up on the landing, the office door had obviously been opened because Havering's voice could now be heard more distinctly.

'I did not give you the authority to call on other staff to help you with this work, least of all from another section. Is that clear?' A mumbled assent could just be heard. 'You don't understand... you cannot understand the political implications of this job. We are working to international aid budgets and their rules. Everything must be accounted for. You're not in a sloppy London office now. Here, everyone must pull their weight and the sooner you get that into your head the better. Now go and get on with your work.'

Rubena Chowdhry did not possess that almost ghoulish curiosity that kept Leila with one ear turned towards the shouting and the other reluctantly tuned in to the rest of the world. She did not enjoy other people's misfortune. Rubena did not know whether Leila enjoyed it either, but she knew she was certainly intrigued by it.

'I don't think we are needing to hear this,' Rubena said quietly and got up and walked across to the door. As she closed it she saw the new man, Mr. Wrighton, walking heavily down the stairs, his face downturned as if unsure of his footing.

'Good Morning Mr. Wrighton,' she greeted him, correctly.

He looked up smartly as if his head had been attached to a string on the top banister rail and he had just reached its limit. He was very red in the face.

'Good morning Mrs. Chowdhry.' He smiled but it was not the smile of a lion. It was the thin bravado grin of a lamb.

'Was it Mr. Wrighton who was being shouted at, Rubena?'

'Do not concern yourself with that, Leila, continue your work.'

'I think it was Mr. Wrighton. Do you think it was, Mrs. Rosario?'

'You have ears as the rest of us, Leila, why are you not using them?' Mrs. Rosario replied, shifting her weight impatiently at the table.

'Why do you not go and ask him?' Rubena suggested tartly, 'I'm sure he would be very pleased.'

Before Leila could respond, a buzzer sounded harshly above the door.

'Quick, that is Mr. Havering. Is it you Mrs. Rosario?'

'No. It is me.' Leila jumped up, tucking her saree around her and gathering up her notebook and ballpoint pen.

'Leila, Leila!' Rubena hissed at her urgently. 'Your shoes!'

Leila Rose made a face and scrabbled under the table for her flip-flops which she slid onto her dusty feet and then she was gone, slapping up the stairs to Havering's office. When, a few minutes later, the tinny bell above the door hauled itself into life and teetered on the brink of a tintinnabu-lation it was such an unexpected sound that Rubena merely gazed up at it in bemusement. Then she slowly realised that it was Mr. Wrighton ringing his bell. He had not rung his bell before. He always came and asked the interpreters to come and assist him, or at the most he would send a peon for them but he did not seem to like the summoning authority that the bell push gave him. Decidedly a weak character, unable to accept the responsibility of management.

'Well, that must be Mr. Wrighton ringing for me,' Rubena said in surprise. As she left the cubby hole, Mrs. Rosario was still gazing at the bell.

'Are you ill, Rubena?' Leila enquired cheekily. 'Are you indisposed?'

Rubena jerked herself out of her reverie to face up to the banter of the girls in the minibus.

'Why should I be ill?'

'You are not saying something. Normally when we are driving home you are talking and chattering isn't it?'

'You will learn, Leila Rose, that with the wisdom of age comes the power of restraint.'

The bus lurched roughly as the driver swerved around a tolligari and plunged into a hole in the road. The ladies all screamed.

'Are you trying to kill us, Mouse?' Leila teased him.

She always called him Mouse. He was a small man and appeared to be perpetually in awe of something or other. At first, when they had given him the air-conditioned minibus to drive instead of the small saloon to which he had become accustomed, he had been intimidated by the big wheels and the bulk of the body and the weight of it as determined through the steering wheel. Now that his acquaintance with the minibus had established itself on a firm footing, he had time and opportunity to be scared of his passengers. Every morning he collected the female workers for the Project from their various homes and brought them to the Rahman Business Centre. Every afternoon, at the close of work, he performed the reverse operation. The job was done in accordance with the official directions for the protection of office personnel but he did not know that. He did it for the money which to him, was very good. The women appreciated the transport that was provided because it saved them money, it was comfortable and convenient. In a country where many of the men still did not believe that the woman should leave the home, it was the safer way to travel and it added some mystique to their job to have a minibus call for them every morning for the neighbours to see.

'Leila, do not distract him. It must be terrible, trying to drive a minibus in this traffic with a person like you sitting next to you.'

'I'm sorry Mrs. Chowdhry,' Leila began in a respectful tone as she always did when she was intending to be cheeky, 'did I take your favourite seat next to Mouse?'

The other women giggled.

'One day Leila Rose... one day...' Rubena began but lost the interest and thus the impetus of her threat. Leila Rose was just a silly, young housewife still trying to come to terms with the paradisical new-found freedom of employment outside the home. She meant no harm, Rubena realised, she just knew no better. She lapsed back into silence and the chatter washed over her. She was feeling tired. Perhaps she was getting old. No! that was ridiculous. She was only forty two years old and her father waiting for her at the home was to be eighty two years old this year. She was not old, just tired.

She had been very happy to hear the whistle blowing to summon all the peons to the closing of the offices. Today had been a drab day. Some days were like that. Irrespective of the climatic weather, some were sunny and some were dull. Today had been dull, despite the glaring sun at ninety degrees. Even Mr. Wrighton had been subdued. Normally he was quite chatty, not that he knew much, but he was often asking her questions about how she lived and what her house was like and she in turn, found that he could settle some of her beliefs about life in the west, but today... well.

She sucked her lips in meditation. Perhaps it had been that silly little incident with Mr. Wrighton. The sort of misunderstanding that was inevitable when a mix of cultures had to work together in proximity. Perhaps she had overreacted but after all, she had been shocked; he had touched her, quite deliberately. Wrighton had wanted to pass behind her chair whilst she was sitting at the end of his desk working at a document. The space had been limited but he had said, 'Don't move, I can squeeze past' or something like that and he had put a hand on each of her shoulders, she realised now, to emphasise what he was saying. Quite naturally she had squirmed free from such an outrage and would have reacted quite angrily had she not seen the look of absolute shock on Mr. Wrighton's mild face. She had merely said,

'Mr. Wrighton, in Bangladesh, you must not touch a lady. It is very rude.'

He had blabbed out an apology and had been mortified. And now Rubena had discovered that this demeaned him in her eyes and the realisation that this was so, annoyed her irrationally.

'It was his fault,' she kept saying to herself. 'What could he expect? You cannot go around touching women on their shoulders like that.' It confirmed for Rubena the debauchery of the Christian West that she could see on the television in the American programmes where people were getting married and divorced just as quickly and all the women drove cars and kissed men in the street and drank alcoholic drinks and even walked up and down the sea-shore in nothing more than their underclothes for everyone to see. It was disgraceful and Mr. Wrighton was merely a part of it.

The minibus had stopped. The road was blocked by people: students, young men and some girls. They were chanting and waving their arms in the air. One young man, presuming leadership, a task, Rubena realised, quite easy in the circumstances, had jumped onto a tolligari to lead the chant. Rubena strained her ears and could just define the outlines of the chant, 'Revise the Joint Matriculation Committee' as it rolled out in a peculiar arhythmic wave over the shimmering heads of the crowd.

'Why are we not going on?' somebody asked.

'The road is blocked, the students are demonstrating,' Leila Rose replied. 'Mouse, why are you bringing us by the university, you must be knowing that there would be demonstrations.'

The driver looked at her in surprise as if something that he had regarded as a vase of flowers had suddenly bitten his ankle.

'Don't be silly, Leila. Mouse is not knowing that they will demonstrate today and in any case, we are always coming this way, you know we are.'

Rubena looked from the bus window to see figures moving into the alley alongside them, between the typewriter repair shop and the travel agency.

'I think we should turn around, driver,' she said.

Picking out the one concrete suggestion from the mish-mash of accusations and criticisms that were now being bandied about in the bus, Mouse began the tortuous manoeuvre of turning the minibus in the street. He had to alight twice to push the rickshaws backwards to allow himself room to turn. When at last they accelerated away back up the street they could hear the thudding of the first bricks as they bounced off the steel shutters that the shopkeepers were frantically pulling down to protect their stock.

'If you turn right here, down the Great Elephant Road, you can let me alight at the other end and I can walk down to my block,' Rubena said. 'It will not then be necessary for you to be coming back towards the University.'

The driver nodded and a few minutes later Rubena was picking her way down a muddy alleyway, her saree bunched in her hand before her to avoid dragging it in the mud.

Her father was still sitting in a chair pulled up squarely to the table. His head was thrown back and his entire face was pinched as if the object that he was grasping at arm's length were a decomposing rat and not a hardback book. His thin, silvery hair was falling long and straggly down one side of his face as he tilted his head to see better through the lower part of his bifocal-lensed spectacles. He did not greet his daughter as she entered but turning his head stiffly in her direction he remarked,

'You know, Lord Curzon was a sly old fox really. You have to admire him.'

Rubena peered over his shoulder at the volume that he was reading and kissed him on the forehead. He pulled away irritably, and Rubena could ironically see a repetition of her recoil from Wrighton earlier in the day.

'I have told you before, Rubena, it is not fitting for a daughter to kiss her father on the forehead, it is disrespectful.'

Rubena ignored his protest as she always did.

'You have nearly finished that one, father. I can get you another one on Thursday. I shall go to the British Council again directly from work.' She glanced through the open doorway to the inner room. 'Have you eaten already, father?'

'No, I have not. Didi has not told me that food was ready. Didi is becoming very lazy. I don't think that we should keep her. She is a drain on our resources.'

Ever since Rubena had brought the homeless woman whom they called 'Didi' to the house to act as servant, her father had, with morbid glee, expected them to be poisoned by fish or smothered in their beds. Why should they have the homeless woman there? The country was full of homeless people and Rubena's placid response, 'Well where will she go then?' did not even scratch the granite of the majestic plinth of prejudices that her father had erected for himself.

'Father I don't believe that you can be so cruel. If it is a question of money, really, as you claim, then I can pay her from my army pension.' Rubena knew that this was only a pretext since they were comfortably well off as a result of judicious property purchases in the aftermath of the War of Independence, which now yielded them a monthly income more than sufficient for their needs.

Her father looked sharply across at her and glared through watery eyes.

Her reaction was grossly unfair. He had commenced hostilities with a little amiable sniping and she had replied by detonating an enormous mine beneath him. All the family knew what Rubena's military pension meant to her. It was the only tangible reminder that she possessed of her dead husband. She had not seen his body after it had happened. She had not even been told but had had to ask. The news had been given to her dispassionately by his best friend. It had been the subsequent fight for the military pension that had fired Rubena's determination to do something.

'We will not touch your late husband's pension Rubena. We will keep Didi if you wish it.' The old man sighed so that she could understand that he was making a great concession. 'But I am wanting my food now.'

At that moment the woman, Didi, entered the inner room bearing a tray of steaming food which she began to lay out on the table.

They all ate together at the same table. The custom that the man should eat first had been gradually eroded as her father had aged. The extra attentions that he required, Rubena had subtly but ruthlessly traded for little concessions although, for his own peace of mind, he refused to recognise them.

'Did you do your lessons well today, Alice?' Rubena enquired of her daughter.

'Yes Mamma,' the girl replied respectfully and then added in a whining tone, 'But Mamma I am too tired to eat, you will have to feed me.'

'If you are too tired then I will give the food to the beggars they will eat it for you.'

'I am hungry but I am too tired. Please Mamma feed me,' she implored, dropping her cheek to her shoulder.

'You must eat or you will have no strength to eat,' Rubena explained with a parent's logic.

'If I have to feed myself then I will not eat because I am too tired and I will get thinner and be indisposed.'

Silently Rubena moved around the table, collecting a spoon on her journey and began to spoon feed her seventeen year old daughter. She had been prey to this kind of emotional blackmail for many years, indeed from the moment that Alice had realised that she was the most precious being in her mother's life, then she had contrived to make that life a tool for her own designs. Rubena's father remained aloof, looking without seeing. It was no concern of his. Only Rubena's minute, sparrow-like mother remarked acidly,

'Feed sweetmeats to the ox and he will starve on hay.'

'By the way,' her father jerked himself in recollection, 'Ali said that he saw your Mr. Havering's wife with your arch enemy, Major Abdul Haq M.P. in the bar at the Sonargaon Hotel. I wonder what intrigue he is dreaming up now.'

The name of Major Haq twisted Rubena's stomach into pangs of anger and sadness at her husband's death which seemed to be with her every day. She realised that her father was merely firing the last shot in today's engagement, knowing that the target was sure and immovable.

9

'Major Abdul Haq M.P. will be back very shortly Mr. Havering.'

Havering nodded. The clerk cleared his throat and spat into the corner of the office. Havering watched him with a mixture of disdain and disgust. The man was the epitome of all that was wrong with Bangladesh. An ignorant peasant dressed up in sham western clothes and stuck behind a desk. He probably could not even write his own name but that would not prevent him from taking an almost childish delight in obstructing a foreigner at every twist and turn just to prove that the Banglas were running their own country.

Havering let out a long regulated sigh to control his anger. It had been like this the last time that he had come to visit Major Abdul Haq M.P. at the Ministry. He was always 'temporarily indisposed' or 'at a business meeting' despite the appointment having been made for a specific time on a specific day. Havering knew that Haq was purposefully absent or late just to make him wait. It proved power to your subordinates if you could make a Westerner wait outside your office for you for thirty minutes.

'Well,' thought Havering, 'he won't do this again. If he isn't here next time when I arrive I shall go back to the office and he can bloody well sing for me.' But he knew that he would have to come to the Ministry sooner or later to beg some favour or demand some right.

He drummed his fingers on the table top and then stood up and walked to the window. Looking out, he did not see the dusty streets and ignorant loafers but the image of Wrighton gleefully explaining how he had checked the survey points. He had watched Wrighton's excited face as he had opined that the work would have to be resurveyed however unpleasant a job it might be at this time of year. He had hated those brown eyes sparkling with boyish excitement and he had immediately known whom he would send.

The corridor door banged and the clerk stood stiffly to attention behind his desk. Abdul Haq came in and was immediately full of smiles and pleasantness. He always wore Western dress in the office as it was considered smart and authoritarian. He was wearing a light coloured suit of a nondescript material and a Bangkok copy Lanvin tie. He pulled up his sleeve to ostentatiously consult his Rolex watch which Havering also knew was certainly a Bangkok forgery purchased at a hundredth of the real price.

'Ah... Mr. Havering, how nice to see you. I am sorry I am late. The meeting went on for some time. You know how it is.'

Havering looked at the paper bag that he was carrying with his brief case.

'At the Sonargaon?'

Haq stumbled imperceptibly but quickly found a sure footing again. He held up the bag and laughed easily.

'We all like our luxuries Mr. Havering. I have to buy something for the wife every now and then on the way home. To pacify her.'

Abdul Haq had been educated at Oxford. He had failed his degree but this was no shame in Bangladesh. The fact that he had attended an Oxford university college was sufficient to raise him shoulder high above the ranks. He had a good command of English with an excruciatingly correct accent which riled Havering for it provided too good a contrast to his own, nondescript accent.

But no matter how much Abdul Haq spoke English and dressed as a Westerner, Havering had no doubts about his way of life and it was a preposterous lie that the man was bringing something home for his wife. He was certain that Mrs. Haq if she were in Dhaka, which was not proven, would never leave the house and would certainly not have the control over Haq that he had so theatrically implied. No Muslim woman could exact a levy from her husband for a day's amusement, in the manner that a Western woman could blackmail her spouse. Haq was merely playing the game to make Havering feel at home. To make him think that he was amongst friends, people like him.

'Well I hope she likes it,' Havering said. He might as well play the game.

'Mr. Havering, come into my office,' Haq directed him, expansively and then turning to his clerk, 'I have an important meeting now. I must not be disturbed, even for the President.'

Haq could not see Havering smiling at the cinema that was being presented to him. Haq was not in the rank within the government where he could expect the President of Bangladesh to turn up to talk to him, but it sounded good and implied that he thought Havering was very important. But that was not why Havering was smiling. He was imagining the scenario in which, through some mischance, the President did actually call for Haq. He was smiling because he knew that the bird-brain clerk would take Haq at his word and not let the man in. He could imagine the protestations, 'But I'm your president!' And the response from the clerk, 'No one allowed in sir, Major Abdul Haq M.P. is in a meeting with very important man, Mr. Havering.'

'A drink, Mr. Havering? A whisky?' Haq crossed the office to the refrigerator. 'Please sit down.'

'Whisky and water,' Havering replied, knowing that he should not really drink alcohol so early in the afternoon.

'Whisky and water it is.' Haq returned to the desk with a tumbler for Havering and a tea cup and saucer for himself. It was a useless stratagem within his office. All his staff knew that he was not drinking tea. Had he been in a restaurant then the tea-cup trick was acceptable, but here in his office, it was merely ridiculous.

'I do look forward to our little chats, Mr. Havering, they are so useful and as you know, I have a great interest in what Consolidated is doing in our country.' He emphasised the 'our' to ensure that Havering did not forget that he was only there as a guest whose stay could be terminated at any time. 'How are we doing then?'

Havering knew the form, he knew the conventions, but he was still fuming from the snub he had received by having to wait, so he dived straight in. This put him at an immediate disadvantage because he was already asking for something.

'The maps are a problem still.'

'The maps?'

'Yes, the maps that we need for the Chittagong proposed extension. I spent nearly all of one day last week down at the Army Survey office being shunted from pillar to post but at the end of the day I still had no maps.'

Havering had been referred from one man to another, upstairs and downstairs, explaining each time his request, showing the letter from the MFA. He was listened to courteously, always courteously, the letter was fingered and then the response was given. 'Well this isn't my department Mr. Havering, it is Mr. Sunnee that you need to see.' Or it would be Mr. Lal, anybody but the person in front of him. By the end of the day he was as sweat-stained and dirty as the letter. His temper was frayed and he still had no maps and no promise of any.

'Did I not give you a letter, Mr. Havering?' Abdul Haq showed shocked surprise.

'Oh yes. ' He pulled it from his shirt pocket. 'I have it here. Everybody at the Army Survey office has read it. I think some have even wiped their... noses on it. But the arrangement that we made obviously did not work. Perhaps it is not getting through to the right person,' Havering suggested with an innocence that thinly covered the accusation.

He had paid ten thousand taka to Haq as baksheesh for Haq's contact in the Army Survey office, to ensure that he got the maps. Havering knew very well that the first negotiation in a baksheesh deal was for the person taking the baksheesh to try to achieve the desired result without parting with the money. This always failed because the other party always knew that promises of promotion or reward were never realisable and, in any case, there had to be baksheesh in the deal somewhere and if he was being asked to do something then he was entitled to some of it. So Haq had kept the ten thousand taka and had tried to persuade his contact in the Army Survey Office to issue the maps. The contact, whoever he was, was presumably holding out for as much baksheesh as he could extort. If he held out long enough, he might even get a quarter of it, the other three quarters would never leave Haq's office. The sum of money although small by Western standards, was equivalent to ten times the average annual per head income of Bangladesh. Havering could see nothing immoral in what he was doing. It was the way the Bengalis did business. They wanted a pipeline didn't they?

Haq fiddled with the ends of his moustache, feigning embarrassment. Havering was obviously annoyed and it looked as if Haq was going to lose some of the baksheesh.

'Leave it to me, Mr. Havering, I will see to it.'

'I left it to you last time,' Havering remarked abruptly. He had to get Haq on the defensive. 'And I left you something.' Custom forbade that he mention the baksheesh by name but Haq knew very well what he was talking about.

'Yes, yes... I remember. I cannot think what has gone wrong.'

'Well I could hazard a guess...' Havering threatened.

Haq loosened his collar with his finger. Havering grinned inwardly. If the stupid gorilla wanted to ape the West then so be it. But he only had himself to blame if he was hot in a collar and tie. Havering was wearing an open-necked short sleeved shirt as he always did.

'I don't think conjecture will help Mr. Havering,' Haq said awkwardly. 'Leave it with me and I will see what I can find out. It certainly is a mystery.'

Havering paused for a few moments as if considering the offer but in reality to make Haq stew a little longer before he made another request for a favour. If he had manoeuvred correctly he should get the favour for free. He showed reluctance.

'Well... O.K. I'll tell you one thing. You know my new assistant,

Wrighton? Well no, you don't know him but you know that I have one?'

'Yes,' admitted Haq, in a neutral voice.

'He has not had his residence permit through yet.' Haq raised his eyebrows. 'And that,' Havering observed, 'is your department. I am sure that you do not want to hold up this project.' Havering knew that if there was any Bengali anywhere who thought he could make a taka or two by holding up the project in any way whatsoever then he would do it, but he continued in the fiction. 'Without a residence permit, as you know, he cannot go up country at all.'

Haq sat back in his chair thoughtfully. Would it serve his purpose to make Havering aware that he knew...? Not yet. Not this time. So with a measured, detached interest he enquired, 'Does he need to go up country then?'

Alarm bells began to ring in Havering's brain. Why had he asked that question? Did he know about the survey points? He thought rapidly. No, it was not possible. He had not met Wrighton, he was not a member of the British Club and so would not have been there when he had told Wrighton that he would have to work an extra day. The only other person that Havering had told had been Mary, his wife. Haq must be bluffing.

'It is always a useful capacity to have, I am sure you can see that. I can never predict when I will need to send somebody up country, you know how it is. And on a higher plane, if a flood or some other natural disaster should overtake us, then it would be an unfortunate situation if we had to await the MFA's decision before we went up country to assist.'

'But, at the moment, he is not needed up country?' Haq confirmed, quietly.

Havering felt uneasy. Haq was confident about something. He would just have to use his ultimate weapon.

'It might be useful to have another engineer whom I could use occasionally on our project.'

'You have surely not told him about our own little project.'

Havering laughed easily to dispel Haq's anxiety.

'No I haven't and even if I spelled it out to him and drew him diagrams he is so thick he would not know about it. That is why I could occasionally use him on our work. He wouldn't know the difference. And in any case, he won't be in Bangladesh for long. He's only here for a few months.'

Abdul Haq contented himself to leave it at that for the moment. These Europeans were so convinced of their superiority that this very conceit prevented them from realising just how childish and patent they were.

'All right Mr. Havering. I will get his application hurried through this week if I can find it.' He pushed back his chair and stood up in the traditional Western discreet notification of the termination of an interview.

'I knew I could rely upon you.' Havering shook his hand firmly across the desk. He noticed that Haq was sweating. 'He's probably wearing a nylon shirt,' he thought to himself.

'And give my regards to your wife,' Haq added.

'I'm in here,' Mary Havering called a reply to her husband's greeting. 'In the bedroom.'

She heard a crash as he threw his attaché case onto the table followed by the noise of his shoes being kicked off.

'Bearer!' he shouted and grumbled as he entered the bedroom. 'Where the hell is everybody?' And then stopped short at the sight of his wife. She was standing stark naked to face him.

'I've sent the servants away for a couple of hours. They won't be back till seven.' She kissed him, pushing her hips into his and then held him to her. 'We're all alone,' she explained, 'to do what we want to.'

Before he had even started to speak she knew what he was going to say and he could feel her body growing tenser next to his. It was always the same, she thought bitterly, either too hot, or he was too tired or not enough time.

'O.K. That's all right,' she said. 'I'll get dressed.'

'Oh Mary, you know how it is... I've got a load of stuff from the office to do.'

'It's a pity your assistant doesn't do any.' She could not hear the response, he was in the kitchen looking in the fridge for a beer. She wanted her husband to make love to her today, now. She wanted to know what it would be like. Would it be like it had been at the Hotel Sonargaon...?

'Really Mrs. Havering, you haven't seen the roof of the National Assembly Building? Well I think we should remedy that immediately.'

'Oh but Major Haq,' she had protested.

'Oh it is no bother, sweet lady, I have a room up here on the eighth floor which I use as an office. It has a beautiful view. You can see the roof of the National Assembly building from there. Come I will show you.'

The perfect gentleman. Attentive, courteous, holding back the lift doors whilst she entered, unlocking the office door with the key from his pocket.

'Here, come to the window. You see it goes from ceiling to floor but you cannot fall through it. It is so strong. Look, look along my arm there, no come closer.'

Then the brown hands were everywhere. Caressing her, stroking her, teasing her, in her shirt, through her skirt and the moustache was tickling her and nibbling her in all parts of her body at once. She wanted to go, she wanted to run away but she was pinned against that window. That picture window. She didn't want to go anywhere. She liked it. She knew that it was going to happen. It had been apparent even before they had entered the lift. She knew what he wanted and she knew that she was going to give it to him. His hands were ubiquitous, flitting from button to zipper. As quick as she refastened one button her clothing went loose somewhere else. Licking her navel, her belly. She shivered with a mixture of delight and horror. Her pants came down, they had gone. No! Not standing up, she couldn't. She dug her nails into his shoulder and bit his neck.

'Well, Mrs. Havering,' he grunted between thrusts, 'do you like the view?'

'Oh my God!' She suddenly realised that she was pinned with her back against a plate glass window, eight storeys above the street. 'Not here, not here!' she protested. 'On the bed.'

'Here, Mrs. Havering. You know, there's quite a crowd forming down-stairs in the street.'

'No, let me out, let me out! Not here!' she panted.

'And now the policeman is trying to move the traffic but they are all looking up.'

'No, no!' she shrieked, struggling against him.

'And they can see your naked legs and your bottom being squashed against the glass. They can see it all do you hear?' he whispered into her ear.

'Yes, I can hear,' she answered, her voice dry, her hands kneading the small of his brown back. 'I can hear... what can they see?'

'They are looking up. Up to the eighth floor. They can see a white woman...'

'Yes... what is she doing, the white woman?'

'She is leaning against the window. Her bare bottom is squashed against the glass for all to see.'

'Yes and what else? What else?'

'There is a man there. Between her legs. And now the policeman is looking up as well.

'What's the man... what's the man doing?'

'He has got his member in her.'

She felt her hips moving involuntarily. She was afraid, she could not stop it, it had never happened like this before. Faster and faster, harder and harder, banging, banging against the glass...

She heard the faltering tapping of her husband's old mechanical typewriter as it rattled on the table top. She found that she was leaning against the cool wall of their bedroom, her hand lying languidly between her legs. She picked her clothes from the bed where she had lain them. She slowly wandered through to the shower.

10

'So how long have you been in Dhaka now, Stooart?' The woman peered up at him through thick-lensed spectacles. She spoke with a New York accent and like all the Americans that Wrighton had met so far, pronounced Dhaka as 'Darker'.

He shifted the paper serviette from under his glass but condensation was still dripping from it so he let it be. He was still unaccustomed to absolute strangers addressing him by his Christian name as soon as they were introduced. The Americans certainly did not stand upon ceremony.

'It must be just over four weeks now,' he replied, thinking to himself that given what he had done in the time, it seemed like four years. 'What er... who do you er... Are you working in Dhaka?'

'Well I'm not here on vacation!' she screamed and coughed a rasping, smoker's cough which was so similar to her voice that it was difficult to distinguish her coughing from her talking. Wrighton looked about the party-goers but nobody seemed to have noticed her outburst. 'I'm sorry Stooart, that was out of order. I'm with the U.S. Embassy. The Welfare Section.' She thumped her roll-top bureau of a bosom and explained, 'I'm their little mamma upon whose shoulder they cry when they can't stand it any longer.'

'Oh, that sounds er–'

'Stooart, it's exhausting but I love it.'

'Have they, I mean have you got many Americans working at the Embassy?'

'About two hundred and fifty. Excluding the marines.'

'The Marines? You mean you have got warships in Dhaka?'

'Haa!' she began to laugh again and doubled up in a fit of coughing, pointing an accusing finger at him whenever she could straighten herself sufficiently. 'Ha, that's a good one! You Brits really are a scream. Jeesus I gotta get me a drink.'

She staggered away, her cherry red flowered dress billowing like a half-inflated montgolfière.

He felt conspicuous on his own. He had never liked parties. He started to polish his spectacles with his handkerchief. It was something to do. And as he mused upon the coincidental manner in which he had been invited to this party, his gaze drifted lazily to a framed print on the wall of this magnificent residence.

He had been in the general store at D.I.T. 1, trying to buy a piece of equipment that he had omitted to bring from the U.K. – a vacuum flask. If he had been asked before leaving what would be the most useful object to take to Bangladesh he calculated that a vacuum flask would figure on the list somewhere between the snow-shoes and the hot water bottle. But this was to admit the narrowed view of an inhabitant of a temperate climate wherein the vacuum flask was regarded almost exclusively as a container of hot liquids. After a few days at the office he had realised that he needed some way to bring drinking water with him since he could not stomach an ice cold pepsi cola every time his throat dried up and he dared not drink the tap water for he had no guarantee that it had been filtered and boiled for twenty minutes as had the drinking water at Banani house.

'Not that one!' an American voice had instructed him. 'Give it back to him, don't take it.'

He had turned to see a vaguely familiar face but try as he might he could not place it.

'Oh hello. What's wrong with that flask then?'

'It's Chinese. Don't buy Chinese vacuum flasks.'

Wrighton was dumbfounded that anyone could take their political beliefs into a general store.

'It doesn't matter to me about the politics of the country,' he had replied shortly. 'Whether they are made in Taiwan or China or... Viet Nam,' he had added unkindly, 'doesn't matter a jot to me. My country doesn't tell me how to think.'

'Mine neither. But if you buy the Chinese vacuum flask then you'll regret it within a week.'

The man's smugness riled Wrighton.

'Of course,' he remarked sarcastically, 'I would normally buy a good British Thermos flask but for some reason they are unobtainable in this far-flung bastion of our empire.' He had worked out who the man was. It was the one whom he had met in the Chinese restaurant. The one who wanted to play cricket.

'He's got Thermos flasks but he wants to unload these Chinese flasks. If you want a Thermos flask then you shall have one.' He addressed the shopkeeper. 'This man is my friend. Would you please get him a British Thermos flask from that cardboard box under your counter, and would you please take back this Chinese flask since his political beliefs prevent him from buying it.'

'I never said–' Wrighton was incensed but the other just laughed it off and handed him the flask.

'He'll want another hundred taka for a good old British Thermos flask.' The man mimicked Wrighton's accent and laughed at him again.

Wrighton handed over the note and turned away from the merchant.

'Your name's Stooart and you've forgotten mine haven't you?'

This outright frontal approach left Wrighton completely disarmed and defenceless. He nodded.

'Don.'

'Finkelstein,' Wrighton added. He had remembered now.

'S'kinda funny how everyone remembers my surname.'

'Well it's–'

'Yeah I know. It's stupid. Well I don't think it's stupid.' Before Wrighton could comment he added, 'You know, you would have really regretted buying that flask.' Then he waited for Wrighton to ask why.

Wrighton was still coping with the humiliation of having been shown up as a forgetter of names, except stupid ones and a layer-down of foreign policy. Eventually he surrendered.

'All right. Go on then. Why would I regret buying the Chinese vacuum flask?'

'Because they all leak, you dope!' Finkelstein slapped him on the back. It was a contact that Wrighton had not been expecting and once executed, he still could not see the justification for it. He winced. 'My Government does not tell me how to think!' the man mimicked him again and then laughed at his discomfort. He opened his mouth to protest that the joke had gone far enough but was pre-empted by Finkelstein who continued. 'You saw that Chinese writing down the side of the flask?'

'Well... yes.'

'You know what it said?'

'"Thermos flask" in Chinese?' Wrighton guessed.

'Nope! It said, "Reject" or I think the accurate translation was something like "unsellable".'

'How do you know?' Wrighton demanded suspiciously. 'Can you read Chinese?'

'No but I bought one. It leaked,' he replied in a flat voice. 'It leaked in the Chinese restaurant and the cook there told me what the chopstick writing said. Easy. They were all a bum batch from the factory but rather than trash them they must have figured that the Banglas wouldn't know Chinese and wouldn't know that they were no good. They are smart little cookies, the Chinese!'

Wrighton felt mortified at his pompous self righteous reaction to what was after all, a piece of friendly advice.

'Look... I apologise. I was very silly and unfair to mention all that about politics and being told what to think.'

Finkelstein looked at him as if he had just produced a water melon from his navel then he burst out laughing again.

'Ah... you guys! Say, you really crease me up! Forget all that crap! It don't matter.'

'Well, that's very good–'

'What are you doing tomorrow night?' The question was unexpected and Wrighton had to think hard. 'Ah don't say you're booked up. Look see I got an invite to the party at the Cultural Section tomorrow night and I've gotta give it to someone and you're the only one I've seen today,' he ended frankly.

'A party?'

'Yeah, you know, drinks and eats. A lot of talking and joking and horsing around. Ah! You know what a party is!'

'Yes I do, I do,' Wrighton assured him. 'But I'm not usually invited to parties. I mean I don't usually go.'

'Well you're going to this one baby.' He tucked the invitation into Wrighton's shirt pocket. 'Grab that, you'll need it to get past the guards. Party starts at twenty hundred hours p.m. in the evening. Dress casual.'

'But where is it? Who'll be there?'

'Bottom of Gulshan Avenue, Residence of the Head of the Cultural Section. You can't miss it.' He began to move out into the sunshine towards an enormous chrome and smoked-glass delivery van surmounted by an equally vulgar air conditioning unit. 'Be there,' he ordered and then he drove away.

Wrighton smiled as he recalled the incongruous sight of the van weaving its route through the prehistoric Dhaka traffic. His eyes had just focused lazily back on the framed picture when a woman's soft voice said,

'Do you like it?'

He turned to a neat, attractively dressed woman of about thirty years who was holding a cocktail glass in one hand and an intricate fan in the other.

'You've been scrutinising it intently for the past two minutes,' she accused him.

'Oh Gosh! Have I?' She nodded. 'Well... er... well then, I suppose I must like it then.'

'You are Stewart Wrighton aren't you?'

'Yes, yes I am. But how do you..? Have we met? Look...' he began quickly, hoping to repel another incident like that of forgetting Don Finkelstein's name. 'Look I have a terrible memory for faces and names and things and so it is quite possible that we have met but I have forgotten your name but please don't be upset because I do it with everyone so even if you are special you still get the same treatment. I'm sorry.'

'Well,' she smiled indulgently, 'that was some explanation! But it was quite uncalled for you see, we haven't met, not really. We have spoken. In a manner of speaking.'

The voice sounded familiar but Wrighton despaired of ever identifying it.

'Well you have me at a disadvantage then because, and I apologise once again, I'm afraid that I don't know who you are.'

'I am Sandra Hardwicke. My husband Geoff is the commercial attache here.'

'Ah yes, I think I met him once at the club.'

'Yes you could have done. He's on the committee. He's always down there on some pretext or other. So you like this picture do you?'

'Um.'

'You said that you did.'

'Yes I did.'

'That's very interesting you see it is a novice's copy of a Hindu temple frieze of bas relief.'

Wrighton had not the slightest idea what she was talking about. He had not been looking at the picture and seeing it, it had been an amalgam of gold, salmon pink, royal blue and pale turquoise which had formed the backdrop to his recollection of the conversation with Don Finkelstein. She was still talking, he must pay attention...

'...And you can see that the figure at the back, under the canopy is the temple virgin and she has the man's phallus in her mouth, look, you can just see...'

'His hi... his... what?' Wrighton stuttered, aghast.

'His phallus,' she repeated in a matter-of-fact voice then noticing Wrighton's lower jaw becoming slack and the colour rising into his face she added in mock excuse. 'Oh I do believe you are embarrassed! Surely you knew that it was a Hindu orgy scene!'

'No!' Wrighton's voice had unaccountably become very squeaky. He looked around the room, frantically. 'Please excuse me Mrs...'

'Hardwicke,' she prompted.

'Mrs. Hardwicke... I must get some more lime and soda. Excuse me, please.'

He hurried away, mopping his brow with his handkerchief as he crossed the room. What was the word she had used so sweetly? Phallus. That was it. Oh Gosh! He took a large mouthful of the soda whilst it was still fizzing and choked on the effervescence. 'The man's phallus was in her mouth' she had said. Oh crikey! If any woman had said that in his father's presence she would have been knocked across the room and told to wash her mouth out with soap and water. What a subject for discussion! And she had said it quite normally as if... as if she were saying that the cat was sitting on the mat.

He swung at his glass again and nearly knocked in his front teeth on the ice cubes. Perhaps Bell was right.

When Bell had seen his invitation he had warned him that he would not be able to 'handle it'. Bell explained that this was the reason why he had turned down his invitation: because he knew the place would be full of high falluting posers talking about culture and statues. Of course Wrighton could go if he really felt he wanted to, but it was not really his scene, in fact, he could not understand how Wrighton had come to be invited in the first place. When Wrighton had sketched out the outline of his meeting with Don Finkelstein, editing it heavily for the sake of Anglo-American understanding, Bell had exclaimed in a flash of enlightenment that Don must have offered the invitation to Wrighton after Bell had just turned it down that very morning.

Well... Wrighton would be able to tell Bell that the first bit of culture that he had met was a charmingly sweet lady talking about a man's phallus in her mouth. That would please him!

'Apparently,' Marion announced as she scratched her head with the end of her knitting needle, 'in order to get into this party, he had to show an invitation to an armed guard. You know, a soldier.'

The girls ooed and aahed and well-I-never'd.

'Why did he have to go to this party, Marion?' Angela Curnow enquired. She seemed to find it difficult to accept that an engineer should be invited to a party at which there should be people who were not engineers. It was as if she suspected, deep down that he had been invited rather as one would invite a plumber and then ask him to fix a dripping tap.

'Well you know how it is,' Marion explained genially.' They work with all different kinds of nationalities and get invited to different 'do's'. It's quite normal.' Marion herself was not convinced of the validity of this argument so she added quickly, 'He met the American Ambassador there.'

She had been impressed and a little overawed by the thought of her husband meeting the American Ambassador. In Wembley they knew no Americans at all yet Stewart goes half way around the world to shake hands with an ambassador. She hoped that his shoes were shiny. He was always forgetting to polish them.

'I met the Chilean Ambassador once. He was a charming gentleman.'

'Oh Deirdre, you never told us that you moved amongst the royalty,' Mary Gonzales remarked with a warm smile that almost outshone the soupcon of sarcasm.

'Hardly royalty, Mary, hardly royalty. He was a "His Grace the most honourable something or other plenipotentiary". He was a very polite man. He kissed my hand. It was quite thrilling.'

'He didn't have a moustache did he?' somebody asked suspiciously. 'I can't abide men with moustaches kissing my hand. It's like feeding a horse.'

'Not that I remember.'

Mary Gonzales decided that the story about meeting the Chilean Ambassador hid some facets that perhaps the teller had not wanted to turn to the light.

'Deirdre, darling,' she began softly. She was at her most dangerous when she was soft. 'Where were you when you met this foreign gentleman?'

'The Chilean Ambassador?'

'Yes,' she replied in a syrupy voice. The patent reluctance to give an immediate reply only served to gleefully confirm her suspicions. Once again she was certain that she had pinpointed the weakness.

'It was on Tyneside, I think they called the place,' Deirdre admitted.

'Tyneside!' Mary repeated loudly in case anybody had not heard. 'Tyneside, my poor dear! Just imagine!'

'Tyneside is not all that bad,' Deirdre remarked in a calm, almost flat manner. 'It has its good points!'

'But my dear... Tyneside!' Mary Gonzales looked meaningfully around her little circle to ensure that they had understood that the significance of meeting the Chilean Ambassador had been besmirched by the meeting's geographical location. Deirdre appeared strangely unmoved, a hidden strength apparently maintaining her discreet buoyancy above the morass of snide inference that Mary was creating.

'My dear, you must tell us... why were you and the Chilean ambassador in Tyneside? Why Tyneside of all places?'

'Because that was where they had built the ship,' she explained, 'and you have to launch it where it is. You can't shift it about to some other, prettier place and launch it from there.'

'Oh... it was a Chilean ship was it and the Ambassador was there to launch it?' Mary made a great show of understanding the situation.

'Well yes and no. It was a ship for the Chilean Merchant Marine, a bulk carrier, one hundred and ten thousand tons. *"The Pacific D"* it was called but the ambassador wasn't actually there to launch it, he had been invited to attend the ceremony. A point of protocol I believe.'

'Oh yes and you were also invited...' Mary suggested with dread.

'Yes,' replied Deirdre with a beautiful sunny smile 'Yes, I was invited to launch it. That's why it was called *The Pacific D* you see. "D" for "Deirdre". That's what they said anyway.'

After his encounter with the red portmanteau of a woman who worked in the Welfare Section and his nerve-racking brush with Sandra Hardwicke, Wrighton made of himself a slowly moving, erratic target, grinning to people whom he did not know whilst trying to work out how to get away from the place.

At one moment he had been inadvertently included in a conversation when someone turned to him and said, 'But you see, I don't believe we will ever make a discovery in Bangladesh to rival the importance of those of say, Mohen-jo-Daro or even, Taxila, because, quite frankly, I don't believe that the civilisation has been here that long, don't you agree?'

'Well I don't really know...' Wrighton had replied with unintentional honesty.

'Say, you're British. Are you with that unit digging up in Sylhet? Now what's its name? "Archaeology Foundation" or something like that?'

'No I'm with Consolidated,' Wrighton had replied unhelpfully. 'We do some digging but rather than dig things up, we bury things for future generations to ponder over.'

'So you're not with Munro's outfit then...?'

'Not as far as I know.' Wrighton had sidled away.

A hand descended onto his shoulder and turned him around.

'Hiyah Stoo! Glad you could make it.'

'Hello Don.'

'How's the Thermos Flask?' he pronounced very carefully.

'You won't let that die will you?' Wrighton laughed. 'Did you manage to get rid of all your invitations?'

'I only had one,' Finkelstein replied in mock hurt, 'and you were the most important person I could find. And the only one.'

Following a hunch, Wrighton remarked casually,

'Why didn't you try Gerry Bell?' I'm sure he would love this set up. Genteel cocktails, Myocenian hieroglyphs or whatever.'

Finkelstein laughed.

'How is the old trooper? I haven't seen him for weeks. Has he been up country?'

'No, he's been about,' Wrighton replied, eyeing the bobbing blonde head of Sandra Hardwicke as it approached through the throng. 'Don!' he said urgently, 'Quick! Introduce me to somebody over that way,' he directed with his eyes.

'Someone you want to avoid eh?' Finkelstein understood quickly.

'Hurry!'

Wrighton found himself propelled gently by the arm towards the broad squat back of a grey suit. As Finkelstein spoke, the man turned to show a grey face to match the suit and a pair of enormous brown-rimmed spectacles welded to an aquiline nose which looked as if some philistine aggressor had pushed half a pyramid into a face of putty.

'Mr. Murray sir, I'd like you to meet Stooart Wrighton here. He's over in Bangladesh as a consultant on ethnic affairs to the World Bank.' He squeezed Wrighton's arm and winked at him.

'Pleased to meet you Stooart.' Mr. Murray welcomed him with a professional handshake. 'That sounds like a mighty interestin' job you have there.'

'Well I–' Wrighton gulped.

'Do the World Bank send you to many countries or are you only specialised in the Sub Continent?'

'I've only been sent to the Sub Continent so far,' Wrighton stalled carefully, making a silent vow to puncture all the tyres of Finkelstein's hideous delivery van.

'Kinda tryin' you out are they, son?' he enquired.

'I suppose that would be a fair way of putting it. We all learn from our jobs I'm sure, as we go along,' he finished lamely.

The grey face pondered this dogma and then observed, with what Wrighton considered to be a beautiful compound of precision and ambivalence, 'Yessir!'

Wrighton knew that he had to gain the initiative in the conversation.

The best form of defence was to attack so he said, 'Do you get about the world much?'

'You could say that,' the man conceded with a twinkle lurking behind the drooping eyelids. 'Yup, I suppose I've been to a fair few countries in my job. Yessir!'

'And you work in the U.S. Embassy as well do you... or the Cultural Section?' This was going swimmingly.

'Well a bit of both, yessir, a bit of both.'

'Like a general Dogsbody,' Wrighton laughed. The grey face also crumbled into a laugh which seemed to creep up on the owner and surprise him.

'Well, I've never heard my job described like that before, but it's a fair observation.' He laughed again. 'I'll let you into a little secret, son...' He leaned closer. 'I'm the ambassador.' And then he laughed again.

Wrighton felt that as a bluff it was a fairly unnerving one since this man had the age and bearing and even the suit of an ambassador.

'Go on!' Wrighton nudged him good humouredly in the ribs and as he did so, at the margins of his vision he caught a look of horror on Finkelstein's face. It was genuine horror. He laughed nervously.

'Ha. ha. You are the ambassador aren't you?' he nodded in a black dread.

'Yessir, that's me,' the man grinned back at him. Wrighton decided that he would puncture Finkelstein's spare wheel as well. 'It's been most enjoyable talking to you Stooart but I'm afraid I can see my aide waving at me over there. I expect he wants me to do something that I don't want to. Please excuse me.'

This brought Wrighton three steps nearer to the door which he had belatedly realised should have been his single-minded goal. He frowned. The wife of the Head of the Cultural Section to whom he had been introduced on entry, was standing sentinel over the door, affably turning back those trying to escape.

Try the verandah. All these houses have verandahs. He slipped behind a tall and voluptuous potted rubber plant and to his surprise found himself in a little alcove. A haven of peace occupied by two chairs and a man in a check shirt. Wrighton recoiled slightly at the sight of human occupation but something in the man's demeanour jogged his sensitivities. He was staring at Wrighton with widened anxious eyes. Slowly the man raised his finger to his lips and nodded to the empty chair. He was a kindred spirit.

'Just drift down slowly out of view. Gentle does it,' the man instructed.

'That's it. You're O.K. now. You're out of sight.' He held out his hand. 'My name's Lee and I am not a culture vulture.'

Wrighton shook his hand.

'My name's Stewart and I'm an engineer.'

'Great! Now if we keep a low profile here, that old dragon by the door won't see us and drag us out to pontificate about batik prints. Engineer? What kind of engineer?'

'Pipeline engineer, gas.'

'Gasoline?'

'No, natural gas – methane.'

'Oh right. Say do you get problems crossing people's land with your pipelines?'

'My entire job at the moment consists of settling disputes of some sort or another due to that. What do you do?'

'Deep Tubewell Project.'

'What's that?'

'It's a U.N. project to bring drinking water to the villages. Most of them draw their water from the tanks and then die of cholera and typhoid. You know they shit in the same tanks that they drink from? Jeesus!'

'So what do you do?'

'Well we do a seismic prospect to locate the underground water and then we sink a tube well. It's just a five inch tube. We keep drilling down till we hit lucky.'

'How far down do you go?'

'Well in some places the sweet water is over sixty feet down. Above that it's all contaminated of course, but it ain't no bother. There's no bedrock. This whole Godammed place is just one heap of mud. We don't even wear out the drill bit.'

'How do you get the water up? Artesian pressure?'

'Partly. Mostly we put a motor at the top to pump it up. That's where the problems start. We call a meeting with the village. They all sit around on their butts and we tell 'em about the tube well and how it works and then they vote upon it and usually agree to have one. Let's face it, it don't cost 'em nothing.

'Then the trouble really begins. The headman always wants the well sunk on his land so that he will have control of the pump and the water distribution. It's power you see. Trouble is, the well has to go where we can distribute from, that is, the highest tract of land and that never, in my experience, belongs to the Godammed headman. So they all fight amongst themselves and either the headman simply evicts the man on whose land the well is to be dug, or if he is too strong, then the headman refuses to allow the distribution across his land.

'Sometimes the headman gets the well built on his land and has control of the water, but it can only reach a third of the lands because we can't get it to flow uphill in a gully. But he doesn't care. As long as he's got his water and control of the distribution, that's all that matters. To hell with the rest of the village.'

'They don't seem to help themselves much do they?' Wrighton responded. He was appalled at the picture that the man had painted. 'So how do you overcome these problems?'

He sucked on his teeth. 'Well we don't. The wells get dug in the wrong places. The water don't flow to the fields. The headman still has his stranglehold on the village and they steal the motors from the well heads and put them in their country boats and ply up and down the river with them. That's the trouble with this country. Every man for himself. If he can make a quick buck he'll do it and to hell with the rest.

'Now take the duty on imports,' he changed the subject, 'There's a hundred per cent import duty on automobiles.'

'I didn't know that.'

'Well there is. You want to import an automobile you have to pay the purchase price again to the government of Bangladesh. And you have to import automobiles 'cos they don't make 'em here.'

'Yes I knew that.'

'Right. About five years ago the Canadians had an agricultural aid project going on. A sort of mechanisation of the paddies and they brought over fifty tractors. What are those Canadian tractors called?'

'Massey Ferguson?'

'Yeah that sounds like it. Well they were allowed to bring them in on Aid plates. You know, licence plates. Pay no tax on 'em.' Wrighton nodded. 'At the end of three years they pulled out to let the Banglas run the project as was always their intention. It had been agreed. It's always the best idea anyhow, you can't keep helping them.

'So they decided that they would give the tractors to the project centres. One tractor to a village or some such thing. "Fine," says the government, "but you'll have to pay a hundred per cent import duty on them". "But we're givin' the tractors to you", say the Canadians. "Don't make no difference", says the President, "Hundred per cent." "But they're a present!" "A hundred per cent duty," says the President. "Well stuff you!" says the Canadians and they take them back and put 'em on a ship in Chittagong.

'Next problem. What to do with them? Like who in hell wants fifty tractors which have spent three years in Bangladesh? So the boat puts to sea. Fifty miles out in the Bay of Bengal they push them over the side, one at a time. Splash, splash, splash.'

'That's terrible.' Wrighton was shocked.

'T.I.B.'

'T.I.B.?'

'This is Bangladesh.'

'Oops!' Wrighton exclaimed, 'I think we've been spotted.'

The American peered lazily through the foliage of the rubber plant.

'Aah she's a doll! That's Sandy. One of the leading lights of Dhaka Stage.'

Sandra Hardwicke had, indeed, been discussing Dhaka Stage with a short bubbly American woman who wore bright red lipstick, dresses one size too small for her and her hair in a bun. She had the unforgettable name of Belinda Clynch and was an avid thespian. Her husband did something at the U.S. Embassy and she did nothing, which allowed her the time to attend all the meetings of the Dhaka Stage and thus get elected to the board. If she didn't pass the audition for the production then she would be found backstage doing make-up or prompter; if she wasn't backstage then she would be front of house, selling programmes, taking tickets, arranging chairs; if she wasn't front of house then she would be in the audience for every performance, leading the applause. She loved the whole razzmatazz. She breathed in the dust swept up from the stage floor, she lived on greasepaint cocktails, she recharged her energy from the glow of the lights but most of all, she liked the young men who played. Preferably ten to fifteen years younger than her so that they still had some energy to which she could add her experience and imagination. She was an indiscreet lover but somehow her romances had never reached the attention of her husband. This was surprising since she did not appear to have either the wit or the inclination to hide them.

Sandra was quite content to be seen in her company because when placed next to the bubbling bombshell of Belinda, the juxtaposition provided a happy and rewarding contrast.

'So what's wrong with *"The Price"?*' Belinda was asking.

Sandra thought that she knew damn well what was wrong with *'The Price'*. It was Arthur Miller. Sandra resented the wholesale takeover of the Dhaka Stage by the Americans. It was supposed to be multinational but somehow the Yanks always got in there with *'The Matchmaker'* or *'The Wizard of Oz'*. Why not try some George Bernard Shaw?'

'It's quite a small cast as I remember,' she replied truthfully and took another glass from the white-tunicked bearer.

'Yeah, four or five, I don't remember exactly, but think how easy it will be to rehearse.'

'But it won't be any easier with a smaller cast. You will still get people not turning up and when they do, because of the tightness of the action you will be worse off than in a big production. One actor missing from four is a lot worse than two from twelve.'

Belinda eyed her shrewdly.

'It's because he's Jewish isn't it?' she accused her.

'Oh for Heaven's sake, Belinda, don't be so outrageous! I don't care if he's a Martian! I just think that Arthur Miller is a little too intense for the kind of audience we have in Bangladesh. It's not a standard theatre-going audience. It's too cosmopolitan.'

And it will be one more play that English actors will not be able to audition for successfully because the Americans will only jeer at their approximations of New York Jewish American accents. She would have to convince some of the lethargic British or Dutch members of Dhaka Stage to voice their protest or, better still, suggest a different play. 'Anyhow, bring it up at the meeting on Wednesday.'

'You bet!' Belinda vowed. 'Now you go and round up another dozen people to come to our poetry reading, we are still short.'

'Yes,' Sandra was distracted. She had just noticed that funny engineer fellow partly concealed behind a potted plant with Lee from the Tubewells. 'I know just the person,' she said.

What was he doing in that little alcove? It almost looked as if they two were hiding. They were probably talking shop. It was always the same. Get two engineers at a party and they would go off into a corner and decide how to flood the Sahara or melt the North Pole or some such fantastic idea... He had been sweet about that Hindu erotic print. She had been idly watching him and he was obviously miles away, dreaming, not looking at the print at all. It was most unfair. When she had made him admit that he had been looking at it and then pointed out to him what it was all about he had been really shocked. She felt a little mean for that. She had not met such a prudish person for a long time. Fancy being upset by a picture! Although, she had rather insisted upon certain details in her interpretation of it. It had not been really necessary but something in his comportment seemed to challenge her. He was so sure and confident in some respects but in others he was like a fish out of water.

'Now then you two!' she rounded the rubber plant. 'Caught smoking behind the bicycle shed again!'

They looked up guiltily as if the accusation had had an unintentional grain of truth in it.

'Hiyah Sandy! Say, don't give us away. If you just slip down slowly behind the plant no-one will notice.'

'Shame upon you! What a suggestion and you a married man!' She automatically glanced at the other engineer's hands. He wore no rings of any sort.

'Sandy, this is Stewart Wrighton.' he began the introductions.

'We have met already,' the man explained succinctly. It was a fact. Nothing more. He was apparently still upset.

'More than once, actually,' she added mischievously and was rewarded by a sprinkle of nervousness showering behind those brown eyes like a Hollywood snowfall. He was frantically trying to either remember the occasion or, she laughed to herself, her name.

'Say, pardon me, pardon me! I didn't know you two was buddies...'

The man cleared his throat. 'Well I wouldn't say–'

'Lee, why don't you just push off? I want to talk to Mr. Wrighton about something.'

'O.K. sister.' He turned to Wrighton. 'Fine buddy you turned out to be, selling me out to the enemy.'

'You don't appear to be suffering too much from the betrayal,' Wrighton observed lightly but whilst he was saying it, Sandra could feel his nervous glance flick across to her and back. He was trying to work out where she was going to sit. In fact, he had just realised that she was going to sit cosily next to him and this threatened proximity was already worrying him. Silly man.

'So it's state secrets we're discussing is it?' Lee addressed Sandra. 'I'm not worthy of you?'

'Lee, if I said to you "Dhaka Stage" would you–?'

'O.K. sister, don't threaten me no more!' He held up his hands in horror. 'I'm off!' He launched himself back into the mainstream of the party.

I am going to sit next to him whether he likes it or not, Sandra decided. 'Now, can I call you Stewart?' she asked as she squeezed into the chair that Lee had vacated, moving a little closer to him than was strictly necessary. He politely eased himself away.

'Um yes.' He cleared his throat.

'And you must call me Sandy.'

'Oh. I think that I would rather call you Sandra.'

'All my friends call me Sandy. Don't you want to be my friend?' she leaned over to him and asked mockingly. It was tittle tattle, it was rubbish talk, it was softening up, it was teasing. Men and women did this to each other at parties but this great idiot pushed his spectacles up on his nose and considered the question with gravity.

'Well, I don't ever want to alienate someone on purpose and so I would not respond by saying that I did not want to be your friend but I am sure that you can see that the state of being your friend is an unknown quantity to me. It has no doubt, advantages and commitments and I, at this stage, have no experience of either so I don't really feel that I can answer that question truthfully.'

She did not believe this. People didn't talk like this. Although he was undeniably nervous there was, underlying what he was saying, a vibrant strain of confidence in a belief that she could not identify. It unnerved her.

'As for calling you "Sandy",' he continued, 'if you feel that you prefer me to then I will, but for me "Sandy" is a description of a porous subsoil whereas "Sandra" is a pretty woman's name.'

'Aha... Did you mean that the name was pretty or the woman?' she teased him.

'Ah!' Again he adjusted his spectacles on his nose. When he grinned she noticed how the worry lines engraved in his forehead were magically metamorphosed into lines of laughter, how his brown eyes crinkled up with happiness. Here was a face that once had liked to be happy and laughing but was now surprised when the rare occasion arrived. 'I will have to concede, Sandra, that you are much better at this than I am. Perhaps you have had more practise. Now what did you wish to see me about?' He had become professional. It was a work relationship he was adopting to put himself back onto firm and recognisable ground with known hurdles and beaten paths.

'Poetry reading. I want you to come to a poetry reading.'

'Me! Whatever for?'

She echoed his question in her mind. Whyever did she want him to come to the poetry reading? She knew that Lee was a lost cause, there would have been no point in broaching the subject with him, but why did she want this man to come? She candidly divulged the truth.

'Well nobody else will. Scraping the barrel really.'

'Thank you very much.'

'You asked. I thought that you were the kind of person who would appreciate the truth.'

'Yes, I am, and truthfully, poetry is not really my line.'

'Rubbish!'

'How can–?'

'When did you last read a poem? Go on, when was it?'

'At school.'

'Exactly. At school. Have you based your entire critical appreciation of life upon how you reacted at school? God forbid! Life goes on, you know. People grow up, their tastes change.' This man's complacency annoyed her. She handed him the card, 'That's the address, it's our house, and that's the date. You're not doing anything else that evening, you can't kid me, and if you're not there I shall send a rickshaw around to your house and drag you out.'

She smiled triumphantly, she had won. He put the card meekly in his pocket and then looked about him.

'I've been trying to get out of here for the last half hour but I'm frightened of that woman at the door. Could you get me past her?'

She looked at him and then burst out laughing.

'Get up. Come on, you can take me home.'

He followed her towards the door.

'But isn't your husband–?'

'Geoff is in Calcutta on business.' She turned to the hostess and whispered, 'A convert to Dhaka Stage,' as they slipped past. It worked like a password.

Outside in the muggy heat, Wrighton was confused as to how he was supposed to be taking her home.

'I haven't got a car,' he apologised.

'I have, but I left it at home. We only live down there.' She pointed at two orange gate lamps, the eyes of a drowsy dragon, glowing further down the avenue.

A rickshaw rattled up alongside them.

'Rickshaw saheb, rickshaw. Only five taka.'

Wrighton was about to explain that his services were not needed when Sandra said shortly,

'No. Push off!' The puller grinned uncomprehendingly and continued to slowly follow them in case they changed their mind.

As they ambled slowly down the road with the rickshaw creaking and groaning hopefully behind them, Wrighton was suddenly struck by the immense blackness of the sky.

'Isn't the sky dark?' he exclaimed.

She stopped and looked up.

'It's always like that near the equator. I think it's something to do with the curvature of the earth and things.'

'Yes and the stars are different here as well. All in different places. It's funny.'

They resumed their walk. Behind them the brown lean body of the rickshaw puller arched like a seahorse as he slowly pressed on the pedal and strained his muscles to overcome the inertia of his machine. Each house gateway was lighted by a lamp on either side. Some bore the house number etched into the glass or crudely painted on in dark blue paint. In the soft yellow circle that these lamps cast onto the road, the night chowkidhars sat in groups of two or three or four. Gossipping about their masters whilst keeping an eye on their gates they would look up as the two strolled by, always interested to look at anything. Down at the end of the road a baby taxi burbled by on Gulshan Avenue, bound for the taxi rank at D.I.T. 1 where it would await the revellers leaving the Chinese restaurant. There was not a breath of wind, the air hung hot and heavy.

'What's that scent?' Wrighton sniffed.

'That's a frangipane tree. That one there.' She designated a tree behind a garden wall. 'It always smells in the evening. It's quite heavy isn't it?'

'It's almost like an anaesthetic. One sniff of that and you could take my appendix out!'

'Could I?'

'Well no, you couldn't actually. It's already been taken out.'

Suddenly a small dark shadow detached itself from the storm drain at the base of the garden wall on one side of the road and scurried across their feet to the other drain opposite. Sandra screamed and grabbed Wrighton's arm in fright. He jumped, startled by her reaction.

'It's only a rat. It's gone now. I think you must have scared it away!'

She gripped his arm harder.

'It frightened me.' She looked about her carefully. The chowkidhars were chattering volubly and laughing. It was cabaret time for them.

'You frightened me. Scared me out of my wits. It's gone now.' He put his hand on hers for comfort.

Presently she said, 'This is where we live. Will you come in for a nightcap?'

'Um...' he hesitated. 'I don't drink, not alcohol anyway. I know it's terribly boring.'

There he goes again, taking me literally. Doesn't he understand the conventions? 'Cocoa ! I've got some cocoa. Got it from the Comm.'

'Fine! Cocoa it shall be.'

'So why don't you drink then Stewart?' She asked him as she brought in the tray from the kitchen. She had made the cocoa herself because she did not want to waken the bearer and, in any case, she could not trust him with the cocoa. Anything sweet or alcoholic and the Banglas could not keep their hands out of it.

'Oh well...' Wrighton began, wondering if he really knew why he did not drink alcohol, 'I think it was all due to my father.'

'Oh was he a drunkard? A Victorian scoundrel who would beat the wife and starve the kids?' Wrighton was shocked by the suggestion but managed to conceal it.

'No, it wasn't that. I suppose that I just never got the opportunity to drink alcohol. My father never went to the pub and would have beaten me black and blue had I gone. He was a strict Baptist. Not that you have to be an abstainer but somehow he considered it Godly to be like that. And he had got a point. When I look around and see what people do when they are drunk. Stupid, silly, ridiculous things. And all the while they think they are so clever and witty and they are not, they are ridiculous and nasty.'

'Do you mean that you have never been drunk?' Sandra exclaimed as she tucked up her legs underneath her on the sofa.

'I should say not! Never.'

'Have you never drunk anything alcoholic?'

Wrighton thought back to the few occasions when he had crossed tastebuds with alcohol.

'Don't laugh.'

'I won't.'

'I had some sherry trifle at my aunt's house at Christmas one year and it was hideous. Horribly, stinging hot. Ugh! Completely spoiled the taste of it. And I once tried a friend's beer when I was at university. He had brought a bottle home. It was horrible. Gassy and bitter. I didn't like it at all so I thought to myself, 'What is the point in trying to get accustomed to liking a disgusting drink that weakens your moral fibre and deadens your sensitivities?' I haven't tried any since.'

Sandra sipped her cocoa thoughtfully. This man was a boy. She felt a hundred years old next to him.

'So you don't go into pubs?'

'Rarely.'

'Can you play darts?'

'No.'

'Shovehalfpenny?'

'No.'

'What can you do?'

'I am an engineer.'

Suddenly she pointed at a painting of a colourful pair of figures on the wall opposite.

'What do you think of that painting?'

'You're not catching me like that again!' He was surprised that he could now laugh at his discomfiture.

'No, seriously,' she insisted, 'it isn't rude, I promise you.'

He stood up and crossed to the wall to inspect it more closely. She switched another light on.

'It's supposed to be–'

'Rudolph Valentino dancing the tango,' he interrupted her.

'Yes. How did you know?'

'I think it has been copied from a black and white cine still hasn't it?'

'Probably. My brother did it.' She looked away. 'What do you think of it?'

'Oh that's very nice! You tell me that you know the artist and then ask my opinion. I'm an engineer not an intellectual arty.'

'Alright then. As an engineer, what do you think of it?'

'I could not paint such a painting. I have not the technical skill.'

'What do you think of it?' she insisted.

'It is as cold and lifeless as the blueprint of a stopcock.'

'Go on.'

'It is technically correct. The people are the right shape, the feet are in the correct positions, the body is in almost perfect alignment for the step they are doing but it has no verve,' he said strongly. 'It has no excitement. It has not captured in any way the thrill, the speed, the sheer devilment of a tango being danced. Don't forget that this dance was practically banned in the dance halls of England at the time because it was considered indecent. These two could be down at the supermarket buying potatoes for all we can see.' He stopped. She was looking at him, very red in the face.

'You don't pull your punches do you?'

'I'm sorry, perhaps I went a bit far. Looking at it I must admit it has–'

'Don't!' she almost screamed. 'Leave it as it is.'

'I think I had better go.' He collected his cocoa cup.

'Stay where you are. Sit down.' He sat down abruptly. 'You have got some questions to answer. Firstly, how did you know that it was me who had painted it?'

If a feather had happened to stroke Wrighton's cheek with the softest of caresses he would have tumbled like a pyramid of oranges.

'I... you...? Oh dear...'

'I didn't think you knew,' she admitted obscurely. 'You are absolutely correct. It is lifeless. It's bland.'

'Well I didn't say all that,' Wrighton protested.

'You are the only person who has said it... ever.'

'Well... well...' Wrighton was at a loss for words. He really did not know where he stood in this conversation. It appeared that his gross rudeness and horrific gaffe had been interpreted as devout politeness. 'I only said what I thought. You did ask me,' he reminded her.

'I ask everybody.'

'You didn't tell me that it was a sort of trial. I'm no good at party games.'

'Something you said earlier...' Sandra searched her memory.

'I really think I ought to go. I'm sorry if I upset you.'

'You haven't upset me,' she replied brightly. 'You've taken a great weight from my mind. Just let me think... I've got it. You said all about the body being the right shape and the feet and that.'

'Did I?' Wrighton said warily.

'Yes, you did.' She looked him directly in the brown eyes. 'How did you know?'

'Well, I had a few dance lessons when I was a boy. Ballroom dancing.'

'Show me.'

'Show you what?' he was alarmed at the turn of the conversation.

'Show me why my painting is correct but lifeless.' She stood up, feeling a little light-headed from the vodkas that she had been drinking at the party. 'Can you do that step?' She pointed at the painting with a degree of recklessness and defiance. Wrighton rose and brushed down his trousers nervously. 'Show me!' she demanded, holding out her arms.

'Alright then. Stand here. Now hold my hand. No! like this. That's right. No don't grip it. It's not a trial of strength.' She pouted. 'My right hand goes right round here. No you have to turn your body more. No, come closer, no, closer.' Exasperated at her slowness he forced her into the tango hold. 'Left foot slightly in front of right. That's it. Now our hips should be twisted like this to bring us into body contact.' He put both hands on her hips and squeezed them into staggered contact with his own. He did it as an engineer.

She was wounded to discover how coldly and methodically he could grind their bodies into a searingly intimate contact and ignore the existence of any secondary inferences. 'Now take my hand again.' His hands left her hips. She could feel where their heat had stuck the thin cotton of her skirt to her body. 'No, like this, remember?' She bit her lip. 'Now relax your shoulders. Let them droop.'

'I can't, twisted up like this!' she complained. She was beginning to doubt his opinion of the painting. This did not seem a breath-takingly sensuous position to her; it was just bloody uncomfortable.

'You must relax before you can attempt the sweep that they are doing. For Pete's sake, this is no good! Go soft, you're all tense,' he accused her.

She stood there aware of his body, of his arms around her, surprisingly strong arms, of his head near to hers, of his heart beating, of his 'body contact' as he had called it. He began to hum softly a tango and gently sway her to the music.

'Dum dum dum dum dum, der dum dum dum dum, dum dum dum dum.'

She closed her eyes. Her knuckles lost their whiteness, her hand rested in his, her shoulders softened despite their preposterous position. He was moving his body gently now, half a step forwards half a step backwards and she found that she had to follow him, she had no choice. She began to hum under her breath the same tune. Softly, gently, soothingly.

Her world suddenly fell about her in a blur as she tried to open her eyes. The force of the movement welled up behind her eyes like on a fun-fair ride as she was thrown backwards over his left knee, her breasts surging upwards to her neck, trying to break from her shirt. For a mad fluttering instant her eyes opened and she registered the image of the room upside down, the fan lazily turning on the floor, the sofa hanging above the window. Before she could collect her breath she was hauled strongly upwards, her sense of balance engulfed in a whorl of vertigo and then she was shaken left and right and returned to her position, panting and flushed. He looked at her dispassionately.

'That was quite good,' he conceded. 'Do you see the difference when you relax? Your body marries itself to the curves more easily.'

She stared at him wide-eyed and teetering. Her heart was thumping somewhere up in her throat and yet he was standing there as cool as a cucumber. A bloody engineer. This bloody engineer could dance and he was telling no-one.

'Do you think we might sit down?' she managed to say at last. 'I feel a little giddy.'

'I'm most awfully sorry. Please forgive me, I didn't think.' He led her to the chair and stood over her whilst she sat back and closed her eyes. She could feel his presence before her. His warmth lingered in her crotch. How dare he? He had held her more intimately than almost anyone and yet there he was, cold and unmoved. At length she opened her eyes. He was sitting anxiously on the edge of the sofa opposite.

'Did I give you a bit of a fright? But I had to do it when you were fully relaxed. You can't do it properly otherwise. It's not the same feeling...' His voice tailed away.

'You know, you are absolutely right about my painting. It hasn't got that sensuousness in it at all.' She chose the word purposefully, 'My!' she gasped again as she relived the breathtaking lunge.

'That was only a little one.'

'So you can dance then, Stewart?'

'Well no... I used to, when I was a boy. A long time ago.'

'But you can still remember it?'

'Oh yes. You don't forget it. It's like riding a bicycle. You never forget the essentials.'

'Well I can't dance.'

'You must be able to!' He didn't believe her. 'You're–'

'The wife of a diplomat?'

'Well... yes.'

'I can't dance. I was never taught. Would you teach me Stewart?'

'What now?' He looked at his watch. 'It's a quarter to two in the morning.'

'No, not now,' she laughed, 'but would you teach me? I would be very grateful.'

'But I'm not a teacher,' he protested, 'I'm an–'

'You're an engineer. Yes, I know that, but you have got the gift. You can teach. I know you can.'

'Don't talk daft! What about your husband? It's no use learning to dance if he can't dance with you. I could teach him as well.'

My God this fellow was either naive or stupid!

'Geoff can already dance. This would be a nice surprise for him.'

'I suppose it would,' Wrighton replied.

'So what time did you get in then, last night?' Bell shovelled a fried egg into his mouth and grabbed the piece of toast that Wrighton had earmarked. 'Moussi!' he yelled. 'Three piece toast for Wrighton Saheb.'

Tuppin looked over the top of the motoring magazine that he had received from the U.K.

'It was gone two o'clock. I heard you.'

'Little boys like you should be in bed and asleep at that time,' Wrighton admonished them. 'I hope you weren't reading under the bedclothes.'

'No, nor anything else,' Tuppin added.

'Party was good was it?' Bell enquired and then explained, 'I had to go out with the boys otherwise I would have gone.'

'The party was lousy,' Wrighton admitted. 'Finkelstein parked me on the ambassador and didn't tell me who he was so I ended up asking him what he did for a living.'

'You asked the U.S. ambassador what he did for a living?' Bell pointed a mangled piece of toast at him. 'Ha ha! You pratt!'

'Well I didn't know,' Wrighton said. 'He hadn't got "*ambassador*" written on his jacket or a big neon sign on his head.'

'No, but you must have seen him about at functions.'

'No, I hadn't. Have you?'

'Loads of times. Me and him are like that.' He held up two fingers rudely diverging in parody. 'Oi Tuppin. Your green coconut's arrived.'

Tuppin eased himself out of the low chair as if he were carrying a fragile parcel on his lap.

'What's the green coconut for?' Wrighton asked.

'The shits,' Bell said. 'So who else was there at the party?'

'Loads of people I don't know. I met a bloke from the Tubewell project and he and I found a corner to hide in till we got winkled out by Sandra Hardwicke.'

'Oh, Randy Sandy. What did she want? To sign you up for *'Macbeth'* or something?'

'Well almost. She wanted me to go to a poetry reading.'

Tuppin choked on a piece of coconut and sprayed Bell with milk.

'Watchit!' Bell warned him, 'or you'll be wearing that coconut. Did she offer you her body? Cor what I would do to get inside that!'

Wrighton always felt uneasy at such allusions.

'I don't think so. She offered me cocoa instead.'

'Cocoa? Real Cadbury's cocoa? You lucky blighter! I trust you took the cocoa and left her body for another day.'

'Something like that.'

'So you and Randy Sandy were sipping cocoa till the early hours of the morning. What! Boy-o, you've got it made! Her husband's away isn't he?' Bell added.

'I understand that he is in Calcutta on business.' Wrighton replied in as normal a voice as he could muster. He suddenly realised that his performance the previous evening could be open to misinterpretation. He decided that he would maintain a discreet silence on the dancing lessons. 'It always surprises me how everybody knows everybody else's business in this place. How did you know that he was in Calcutta? I didn't, until she told me.'

'Oh I heard it somewhere, you know how it is...'

'Madam visit.' Moussi poked his head around the door and as he withdrew it Mina glided in for their massages.

'Good morning Mr. Wrighton, good morning Mr. Bell, good morning Mr. Tuppin,' she greeted them with Victorian correctness.

Bell got up from the table, scratching his nose and took Wrighton aside in an embarrassed manner.

'Lend us two hundred taka, there's a good chap. I haven't been able to get down to the bank.'

11

Alan Havering angrily flicked the butt of his cigarette into the corner of his office and lit another one. His eyes never left the paper on his desk which had been absorbing his gaze for the previous five minutes. What had the fellow been doing in Dhaka? Why hadn't he been told? It was courtesy, after all, if someone concerned with your project was passing through your area. He drew heavily upon his fresh cigarette and frowned at a commotion in the stairwell outside.

'Silence!' he shouted.

Immediately the door opened and the tousled head of the peon poked through.

'You are wanting me saheb?'

'Get out you idiot!'

The man went. Havering returned to the papers, his temper not diminished one iota. He knew of course, that he had brought a part of the trouble upon himself. He had seen the report of a passing survey commissioner of the U.N. who had happened to notice the state of some crumbling concrete piers on the pipeline near the Gas Station, a few miles outside Dhaka.

But it wasn't his fault if he had put the report in his tray and had then overlooked it. He had been busy. At the time he had dismissed it as unimportant. It was the impression that a superannuated surveyor had gained from a fleeting glimpse through an air-conditioned car window as he roared past, busy on some unrelated matter. That section of the line had been built almost three years ago. It was carrying gas. He had forgotten about it but its construction had been his responsibility. How was he to know that the International High Flying Mr. Civil Bloody Servant for Brussels or Washington or wherever had been actually involved at the planning stage of the project and would have more than a passing interest in a line of concrete piers supporting a pipeline? He had not meant to ignore the letter but he had enough on his plate without having to answer obtuse, fiddley queries from meddling do-nothing clerks.

Unfortunately the meddling do-nothing clerk had taken exception to his rude lack of response and upon his return to the U.K. had written directly to Consolidated. Havering fingered the telex from Cockcroft.

Cockcroft was not pleased. He hated to have to kow-tow to civil servants and Havering had let him down by not dealing with this thing locally and now that Cockcroft was involved, there could be no half measures. Cockcroft wanted an investigation of the state of the piers and a recommended course of action, reply by telex in forty eight hours.

What could have caused the concrete to fail if indeed it had begun to fail? A long time had passed since Havering had left university. Malaya, Indonesia, all those places had taught him things impossible to learn in academia but he realised now that he had forgotten a lot of unused knowledge.

Concrete. Properties of concrete? What were they? What did they used to say? 'Strong in compression, weak in tensile strength.' Yes that was it. That was why it had to be reinforced with steel which is high in tensile strength and low in compression, wasn't it? He took a pencil from his drawer and began to scratch down the snippets of his knowledge. Then he stopped and blew away a swiss roll of cigarette ash that had fallen to the paper and his pencil would not return. He knew that he couldn't do it on his own. His melancholy discovery was interrupted by a brisk knock on the door.

'In!' he shouted. It was Wrighton. That was all he needed this morning. 'What is it Wrighton? I'm busy.'

'Good morning.'

I'll give him 'good morning'.

'What do you want? No, just a minute, before you start...' If it's going to hit the fan he didn't see why Wrighton should duck. 'What do you know about concrete?'

'Concrete? You want a bit more than the old "strong in compression and weak in tensile" adage do you?'

Havering quietly covered his pencilled notes. 'Sit down.' He pointed to the chair which was aligned so that the occupier could read the notice pinned to his desk which announced, *'Assume that I have said good morning'*. 'Take a look at this, Wrighton.' He handed the telex to him and watched the man's eyebrows frown in concentration. At length Wrighton remarked,

'Someone out to make trouble?' Havering shrugged non committally. 'Political reasons perhaps? The Gaffer doesn't sound very pleased.'

'He is bloody furious.'

'Well, we shall have to go and have a look at these piers then. Are they far from here?'

'You're right!' Havering had made the admission before he had realised what he had said. 'Get a driver and a truck and meet me by the front gate. I'll get the spec. file and local contracts on this job.'

'Right.'

Havering snatched up a town plan of Dhaka. It was the sort that the petrol company had produced several years ago and it was now worth its weight in gold. It actually had the streets correctly marked with their names.

'Peon!' he yelled as he burst from his office, 'get me my bag.' He dictated to the little man who trotted dutifully beside him in the corridor. 'Take it down to the front gate.' He crashed into the plan office. 'Out of my way bird-brain.' He pushed the Bengali clerk away and delved into the drawers, pulling out what he did not want and discarding it. 'Well don't stand there, bogwit, put it all back!' he snapped at the man when he had found the roll he wanted. 'Now where's that bloody spec file? Armri!' He wanted Wrighton's tandem Bangladeshi engineer. 'Armri!'

The man appeared sedately from the other end of the office carrying a spotless briefcase under his arm.

'Mr. Havering, please to not call me like this. It is most unbefitting a person of my status to be called like an oxen.'

Havering checked himself. He knew that he had to be careful to not upset the Bangla engineers. Although they were worthless, they were still powerful in a negative way. They couldn't help them to complete the contract but they could do their damnedest to slow them down.

'Alright Armri...' he began in a conciliatory manner then his anger got the better of him. 'Don't you tell me how to talk to you!' he roared, 'If you could do a hundredth of the job that you are paid to do then I wouldn't need to be here at all.'

'Mr. Havering, I must protest–'

'Stuff it! Who did the piers for the Gas Station length? Was it you?' The man hesitated, fearing having to admit if it were he. 'God help you if it was you!' Havering pointed a vicious finger at him and turned away to a door leading into a filing room. As he exploded into the tiny room a minuscule Bengali man rose from his squatting position on the floor and saluted prior to opening a conversation.

'No!' Havering cut him short and strode straight across to the lines of filing cabinets and began to scan the labels on the drawers. After several false starts he snatched the relevant files from the drawer, inspecting the contents briefly and then swirled out like a typhoon. Racing down the stairs two at a time he caught up the peon on the ground floor, shuffling along with his bag under his arm and he swung a hefty kick at his buttocks.

'Juldi!' he shouted at the terrified man who scurried out into the daylight and over to the Land Rover waiting by the gate. Wrighton was already there, talking to the driver. The interpreter, Mrs. Chowdhry was standing a little apart.

'Ready?' Havering asked and then jerking his head towards Rubena Chowdhry, 'What's she ...?' He left the question open. He could not think what she was doing there.

'Thought we could take her along. Never know when an interpreter might be useful.'

'Hell's bells. Get in Wrighton. It's concrete we're looking at. It doesn't talk.' Now what is he doing? Oh my God he's getting in with the driver, and he's opening the door for Mrs. Chowdhry.

Havering did not enjoy the ten mile drive across Dhaka and out into the country. Once Mrs. Chowdhry had self-consciously settled in the seat at the side of him and said 'Good Morning' he had ignored her brutally so that she would know that she was an intruder. If she had to come, she should be next to the driver. But Wrighton was up there. 'And how is the bibi?' he was saying and 'Is the boy getting bigger?' And the bloody driver was grinning and nodding and loving every minute of the attention.

'For Christ's sake Wrighton, don't distract him or he'll have us all in the ditch.' His warning had little effect.

So they sat there. Wrighton gabbling like a cracked water main and the driver lurching and swaying through the traffic. Havering tightlipped and tense, staring out of the side window and Rubena Chowdhry, presumably occupying herself with whatever these interpreters had in their little lives. From time to time Havering would glance at his map and issue a directive to the driver, following it invariably with, 'For the love of Allah you don't have to turn around to listen to me, look where you're bloody going.'

When they reached the Gas Station they drove slowly alongside the road, inspecting the pipeline in silence. This was what that meddling busybody had seen and Wrighton now understood why he had been interested. At this point the pipeline was carried on concrete piers approximately four feet high. Havering could not remember the exact reason but he thought that it had something to do with the shifting subsoil at this point because of the seepage erosion or something of that nature. The fourteen inch pipe sat there, strapped to the concrete piers where they ran for about three miles before diverging from the road and entering the Gas Station. Havering poked the driver in the back and he pulled the Land Rover in to the side of the road. He and Wrighton gazed pensively at a pier which had crumbled so much that the daylight could be seen underneath the pipe where the pier was supposed to be supporting it. They silently got out of the van and walked over to it.

'It's not good,' Wrighton remarked.

'Three bloody miles!' Havering grumbled. 'Three bloody miles and then the pipeline leaves the road. I've looked on the map. It only follows the road for three miles. Why the hell did he have to come this way?'

'That's not really the point is it?'

'No it bloody isn't,' Havering agreed. 'Somebody hasn't done their work and somebody's head is gonna roll for this.'

They returned to the van where the interpreter and the driver were talking in muted tones. They had correctly measured the importance of the journey although they had not understood the ramifications. Havering was searching his brain for a reason for the failure. Was there such a thing as 'concrete rot'? Had he heard the expression somewhere or was it only in jest?

'Probably a duff bag of cement...' he suggested, half seriously but more to draw some response from Wrighton.

'For three miles? Who supplied the cement, do we know?'

Havering silently passed him the file. The clever dick could find out for himself. Havering wanted to look at the pier.

He studied the concrete. It was brittle and crumbling. He pushed the sole of his sandals onto it and brought away a coating of dust. If he didn't know that it was impossible, he would have said that it was frost damage. He grunted. Frost damage! He could see Cockcroft swallowing that.

'Well who was it?' Havering called.

'Our usual supplier, according to the file. We've even got a copy of the invoice and bill of lading.'

'Indian?'

'Yes.'

'Not Chinese?'

'Not according to the invoice,' Wrighton replied. 'I wonder... they wouldn't have used high alumina for this would they? I mean that could degenerate quickly if it were allowed to set too quickly and was not covered for curing.'

'Yes... I was thinking along the same lines,' Havering lied boldly as he frantically tried to recall what he knew about high alumina cement. High alumina... quick-setting so it probably gives off a lot of heat in the curing... 'The old high alumina gives off a lot of heat in curing,' he chanced.

'That's right, and if they didn't cover it... The only trouble is, it wasn't high alumina cement, look, there's the chemical analysis taken at the output silo of the production plant. There's your A L two Oh three at seven per cent. Your lime clocks in at sixty five, the silica at twenty two and the F E two Oh three at four point three. That's a slow-setting mix. No doubt about it.'

They ambled slowly over to the pier and stood, heads bowed in inspection. From a distance they could have been mistaken for mourners in mute supplication before a tomb. At last Havering muttered almost inaudibly,

'Well I don't know, I'm sure...'

'I'll just have a look inside,' Wrighton remarked and returned to the van. He opened the back and pulled out a small cloth bag that clanked in a heavy, metallic manner. Unwillingly intrigued, Havering glanced into the bag as Wrighton withdrew a cold chisel and a five pound hammer. With one blow he chipped a chunk of concrete approximately the size of his fist, from the pier. Havering started forward.

'For Christ's sake Wrighton, don't make it any worse!'

'No difference. It will have to be replaced in any case, and this,' he weighed up the chunk, 'might provide us with some clues.' He paused and then enquired as an afterthought, 'Did they do a slump test on the mix?'

Havering was stumped. He opened the files again.

'Slump test,' he muttered to himself, 'Slump test.' Miraculously as he repeated it his eyes fell across the very title. He coolly replied, 'Yes, two slump tests on two mixes. Both gave a one inch deflection on a four, eight, twelve mould.'

'Who did them?'

'Would you believe, Armri?'

'Well it's not that then...' Wrighton's voice tailed off as he inspected the broken crust of concrete. 'Oh no, I don't believe this.' He was silent for a moment, then he asked, 'What was the aggregate spec?'

Havering did not want to be Wrighton's clerk.

'One inch max. river gravel, washed.'

'Where did they get that from?' Wrighton looked up.

Havering delved into the file again and then came up with a start.

'I remember getting the aggregate. We had a hell of a job.'

'I'm not surprised, ' Wrighton retorted, 'all the rivers seem to be mud here,'

'No, it wasn't that. We were going to import from India in any case but the MFA wouldn't give us a licence. Yes I remember it now. Five hundred tons, we had to bring in, through Chittagong and then trucked up here in killer trucks.'

Havering had cause to remember it because he had had to grovel in a particularly unpleasant and abject manner in order to get the connivance of Major Abdul Haq M.P. in the issue of the necessary licences. Abdul Haq had taken quite an interest in the supply of aggregate, possibly because it had served as his first confrontation with Havering. It had been instructive. Havering had learned since then and had not grovelled so overtly since that first occasion. The memory of it was still painful to him, however, and he had no intention of mentioning it to Wrighton.

'Five hundred tons?' Wrighton was surprised. It was obviously well in excess of the requirements for the piers.

'Shipping five hundred tons is no more expensive than fifty tons if the ship has no other cargo. There's so much competition in these coasters you can practically name your tariff. We got rid of the surplus... the MFA disposed of it.'

'You got rid of all of it.' Wrighton viciously smashed the lump of concrete into sugar. 'Look!' Havering had heard what Wrighton had said without understanding its meaning. He bent closer to study the shattered concrete. 'Brick! Smashed brick!' Wrighton said. 'Not a pea of gravel to be seen.'

'The bastards,' Havering muttered.

'With that brick in the mix, soaking up the water like a sponge, no wonder it failed.'

'The bastards,' Havering repeated, louder. 'The double-dealing, back-stabbing bastards. And it's for their own bloody country we're doing this! The bastards!'

Wrighton walked along to the next pier, his hammer and cold chisel dangling from each arm, heavy in the heat. Dimly, Havering heard the single sharp, professional blow and then the slow footfalls trudging back towards him along the edge of the road. He looked around him and all he saw was the dumb driver, the stupid interpreter and forty Bangla bogwits standing around and grinning at the antics of these white monkeys in their country.

'Well?'

Wrighton slowly shook his head and walked on to the pier nearest in the opposite direction.

Wrighton tested thirty piers. There was not a speck of the aggregate in them. They had all been made with treacherous crushed brick. The men stood at the back of the truck, sweat dribbling down their cheeks, the interpreter nervously adjusting the scarf on her sari and flicking it over her shoulder.

Just on a whim, Wrighton said,

'Mrs. Chowdhry, would you do something for me please?' She nodded. 'You see that man over there in the crowd? The tall one with the rag on his head?' She nodded again. 'Would you ask him to come over and talk to me please?' Wrighton could see that she did not relish the job but she boldly hitched up her sari and scrambled over to the group.

'Come on Wrighton, we haven't time for party games.' Havering was feeling testy again now that the cause had been discovered. He wanted to get back to the office and beat that Armri into a little brown pulp for faking the slump tests and cheating on the spec.

'This won't take a minute,' Wrighton replied as the Bengali man stood before him and saluted. Wrighton turned to Rubena . 'Ask him if he is a day worker.'

'He says "yes".'

'Ask him if he worked on this pipeline. Making these er... you had better call them "walls".' He indicated the piers.

'He says that he and many men worked on them.'

'What did they do?'

'Some men were cutting reinforcing bars with snippers. His job was smashing bricks because he is only having one hand.'

'Yes, that's why I chose him. What did they use the brick for?'

The man pointed at the piers with his chin.

'Fairly conclusive,' Havering muttered as he clambered into the back seat of the van, smacking the seat at the side of him so that Wrighton would not mistake his place this time for the return journey.

'Just before we go,' Wrighton added, as Mrs. Chowdhry clambered in next to the driver, 'ask him if he can remember the name of the boss here?'

'He says it was Ishak.'

'Does he know Armri?'

'Armri was there but he wasn't the boss.'

'Ishak?' repeated Havering. 'Ishak? Don't know no Ishak. Who's he talking about?'

'Search me.' Wrighton's mind was working on another aspect of the problem as the van rumbled back towards Dhaka town centre.

Alongside the road at irregular intervals, huge, crudely drawn hoardings were advertising washing machines of twenty years vintage, proudly owned by salmon-faced Bengali women; or grey swirling ceiling fans reputedly manufactured by some obscure subsidiary of the General Electric Company. Wrighton gazed at a shopping precinct which had been built on the Bangladesh lines. It looked like three storeys of private garages, each floor connected to a balcony. In each alcove nestled some commerce or other. The sign board proclaimed that this modern shopping centre was being built by the 'A.H.T.Co. of Dhaka' and it gave the date, now passed, for its completion. 'Stop!' Wrighton shouted so sharply that the driver stamped on the brake and the Land Rover skidded sideways across the dusty tarmac.

'What the bloody hell are you...?' Havering protested as he picked himself from the sweaty back of the driver's shirt. Mrs. Chowdhry twisted her wrist on the dashboard but Wrighton was already out of the van and opening the back door.

'Wrighton, what are you doing?' Havering dodged across the road behind the flitting figure carrying the tool bag. He caught him up in the shopping precinct. 'For Christ's sake Wrighton, we haven't got time for your shopping.'

But Wrighton was not hearing. He was looking at a concrete shopping centre which, according to the faded board propped up outside, would have been finished about six months after the pipeline piers. Wrighton smashed his hammer into the plinth of the stair pillar.

'Wrighton! Listen to me!' he grabbed the man's shoulder, 'You can't go demolishing...'

Wrighton stood up. In his hand he held the crushed concrete from the pillar. Havering looked at it, nervously, as if it were pepper dust to be thrown in his face.

Wrighton said, 'That looks to me, very much like one inch max. river gravel aggregate. Our aggregate.'

Havering looked about him, surrounded as he was by the enterprise, and felt an unease stealing over him.

Melissa Fox-Crowe screwed up her dark eyes to read the face of her wristwatch which was propped up on her towel. Another five minutes for her back, then ten minutes for her left side. She closed her eyes again and allowed the heat to soak into her body. She found that if she relaxed perfectly she could relegate into obscurity the cries of the children, splashing in the pool, the nerve-jangling rickshaw bells, the hawking beggars and even the airliners straining to lower themselves through the hot air to land gingerly on Zia airport a few miles beyond the walls of the British Club.

She took her suntanning seriously. She used the best barrier creams and adhered to a thoughtfully constructed timetable designed to cover her body with a uniform golden glow. Not for her the impulsive lounging by the pool at midday followed by three days of agony and burnt shoulders then two weeks of peeling skin. No sir! At midday she was indoors, eating cool sandwiches and reading a book. Once the sun had passed the zenith, then she repaired to the British Club, discreetly, in the small Rover and without the pennant, where the only sunbed which evaded the afternoon shade from the trees or the verandah, was reserved for her. Not, of course, in so many words, but the manageress of the club always ensured that the empty crates were left upon that spot until she arrived. Not many people sunbathed at the club in the afternoons for they were either engaged in some sport or other or, poor lambs, having to work.

Being the wife of the British High Commissioner, it was considered unfitting for her to take gainful employment. The implication would be that her husband's salary was not sufficient for their needs – an undiplomatic slur on Her Majesty's Government, so any pastimes that she engaged in leaned towards benevolent or voluntary work: rolling bandages for the Red Crescent or teaching a clean Bangla woman how to read English.

Melissa Fox-Crowe tried to arrange her day so that any engagements did not encroach upon her sunbathing time, but sadly, this was not always possible. Today, however, she had arisen at the ungodly hour of nine fifteen in order to receive four visiting lady missionaries at the Residence, this being the only time that they could manage before boarding a plane to another God-forsaken part of the world. She had dressed herself soberly in long flowered cotton which served to set the good ladies at ease and to hide the fact that she was already wearing her bikini.

She had passed a gruelling hour and a half trying vainly to find a subject in common with them but had been painfully aware that the contrast between her sensual flowing black hair, lithesome body and dark flashing eyes and their tight lips, angular elbows and freckles seem to underline the fundamental justification for their work. If only she could have been, well... meeker. Oh well, it was all over now. They were up there in the burning sky in an aeroplane. 'Nearer my God to thee...' she thought. Time to turn over. She looked for her sun tan oil.

'Babs,' she addressed the woman on the nearest sun bed. The woman looked over her sunglasses at her and raised her eyebrows. 'Have you finished with my sun tan oil?'

'Oh my dear, I quite forgot.' She bustled over and sat on the foot of

Melissa's bed. 'To tell you the truth,' she admitted, 'I was watching that gorgeous man in the pool.'

Melissa's heart flipped slightly.

'Oh? Which one was that?'

'Why, that one in the blue trunks by the diving board. He's often in the pool in the afternoon Must be an aid worker or something.'

Melissa hauled herself up onto one elbow and began to apply her oil in gentle, caressing strokes to her flanks. It was a movement that she found quite soothing.

'I doubt if he's Aid. They don't have the time or the money to come here poor dears.' She peered at the head bobbing at the edge of the pool. 'He doesn't seem to be doing anything.' This was intriguing.

'You should see his body!' Her companion nestled up to her and giggled. 'Long, shapely legs, heavenly! If the rest of him is in the same proportions, well....'

Melissa Fox-Crowe, sucked in the corner of her lip to avoid smirking at the suggestive remark.

'Can't you see when he gets out, my dear?' she enquired, wide eyed and innocent.

'I think he's rather shy. He just comes out of the changing room and gets straight into the pool, messes about a bit and then gets straight out again. I mean... he doesn't flaunt himself.'

'Babs I'm surprised that you don't bring a tape measure with you sometimes, you know, you could swim down and measure it.' They giggled together.

'Are you going down to the Comm?' Babs asked.

'Um... no... Not today. No, I don't need anything.'

Melissa had intended going down to the Commissariat to buy a few odds and bobs that she needed. They had put some back bacon aside for her and she had been meaning to go and collect it. She would have to go soon because there was none left on the shelves and the other customers would not be pleased to see her wheeling away a trolley load of frozen bacon for the freezer. However, bacon could wait. She had worked hard this morning with those missionaries and she deserved a bit of fun now.

Babs was collecting her towel and bag from the sun bed and hobbling over the hot bricks to the verandah. Melissa lay back slowly on her side, she was two minutes behind on her timetable. She arranged a towel under her armpit and pulled her dark glasses down from her forehead to the bridge of her nose. It was completely undesigned that she could see into the swimming pool from this position.

Wrighton gazed up at the cloudless, boring blue sky and let the water take his weight. He had rested the back of his skull on the tiled edge of the pool which was level with the water. He concentrated upon breathing regularly and maintaining buoyancy.

Since his first venture into the pool he had tried to take a dip every day. It had been none too difficult, with the perfect weather, just a little too hot perhaps, and the servants doing everything at the house. He could come and go as he pleased. Fitting in a half hour in the pool per day was no problem. It was his fear of the water that was the problem. It was silly. Adults can swim. They have no need to be frightened of water. But Wrighton had never learned to swim. He was determined now, though, that whatever else he did in Bangladesh; the grinding work, the bowing down to the insults, whatever, he would learn to swim. 'Even if it kills me.'

That first dip had been all his fears rolled into one. In the coolness of the bar afterwards he had clinically analysed them and decided to tackle them one by one.

To start with, it had been his fear of the darkness, for every time his head went under water he shut his eyes. He assumed that this was normal, that everybody did it but then by observation and reasoning he came to the conclusion that you couldn't swim about in a pool with your eyes shut without doing yourself a nasty injury. So he had lowered himself into the shallow end, amongst the children and had sat down. The water came up to his chin in this position. Then he had taken a deep breath and plunged his face downwards as if searching for something on the pool floor. Then he had opened his eyes.

The first time that he had done it he had shut them immediately, feeling the water on his eyeballs and remembering the shampoo and soap that had trickled into his eyes when a child in the bath. On the second occasion he had forced himself to stare, ignoring the tight pressure on the sockets and to his amazement, after fifteen seconds, he was able to distinguish a wavy, wispy, form of his hand on the blue bottom of the pool. Turning to one side, he could see little feet paddling about.

During the next few dips he made the acquaintance of the underwater world of vision, the distorting amoebic shapes of well-known objects assailed him. A pair of goggles, a flipper. He also observed, with distaste that many children piddled in the pool as they swam.

He next decided to tackle breathing under water and very quickly found that he could not. He sat on a chair and watched the others. Either they had enormous lungs or there was some trick to it because he could not see them breathing. This was something that he resolved to review at a later date and turn to another aspect – that of horizontal displacement through the medium of water. His engineer's brain told him that a smooth line, presenting as small a resistance to the water as possible would be the most efficient manner of travelling. This meant that he had to put his head under water but as he could now look about him, he did not panic until his breath expired and then it was a mad spluttering choking panic-driven thrash to the edge where he would cling to the tiles and cough up gallons of water as discreetly as he could.

One successful day, when for reasons unknown to him, there appeared to be fewer people in the pool, he had measured up the dimension with his eye and estimated that he could get across the pool by combining one huge thrust of his legs with a water-friendly profile, as he liked to think of it. He had bunched himself up as tightly as a coiled spring and, forcing his head down between his outstretched arms he had launched himself across the pool. The opposite wall had lurched up ,to him so fast that he had cracked his knuckles in stopping. In his own quiet way he was elated. He had crossed a pool under his own steam, as it were. By the end of the practice he had managed to cross, recross and cross again all on one breath. It was a rewarding feeling but he knew in his heart of hearts that this was only the bottom rung on the ladder.

He could see that the natural progression to gliding across the pool was to make a few lazy alternate strokes with his arms to pull himself through the water but to render this really valuable he would have to uncover the trick about the breathing and learn a bit more about his buoyancy. When he learned some new trick in moving about in the water he was often humiliated to realise that he was merely practically applying grammar school level physics. It had taken him six weeks to realise that he was markedly more buoyant with a lungful of air than without. Had the problem been put to him on paper he would have come to the conclusion immediately.

He was now working on the buoyancy theory. Allowing his body to float and controlling the volume of air in his lungs to alter his displacement in the water. Occasionally he would misjudge it and his head would slide under, he would swallow water and thrash with his legs until he had reached the side. He knew it was wrong. He knew that if he went slowly he would still have enough air in his lungs to gracefully glide to the edge, in consort with the water not in conflict with it, but the panic grasped him quickly when he faltered and it was hard to beat.

Lying in the water was a most relaxing pastime. He could almost feel the pressure of work being washed from him. He thought of Havering and the concrete. The great man had patently not known what he was talking about. He had been waffling. Out of his depth. He smiled to himself at the pertinence of the idiom. No doubt Havering was now burning the telex circuits along the Empire Link, if they still called it that, to ensure that Wrighton's concise and accurate report got to the Gaffer on time. Wrighton had been proud of the little bit of detective work. He had found it exciting and it would do him no harm in London for Cockcroft to know that it was he who had done the work. He didn't believe that Cockcroft thought very highly of him. He wondered what Cockcroft would think of Havering's proposal for the recasting of the piers and charging it to 'Sundry works'. He mused on, an asinine grin bedecking his face.

She was certain now. She had been watching him since Babs had waddled off to the Comm. Something stilted in his movements and his unwillingness to take a position far from the edge of the pool shouted out to any experienced swimmer such as Melissa, that the man could not swim. Even worse, by the way that he had panicked a few minutes ago when his head went under, the little weed was even afraid of the water. Cheltenham Girl's School had taught Melissa to swim strongly and fearlessly, in complete and utter union with the water. Her finishing school in Lausanne had introduced her to such refinements as high-board diving and long distance lake swimming. Melissa Fox-Crowe was an accomplished and confident swimmer and despised any adult who claimed to be afraid of water. 'Cluttering up our pool! ' she muttered to herself as she snapped the lid back onto her suntan lotion bottle, 'I'll show him what a pool is for.' She stood up at the side of her bed, and stretched languidly, aware that the eyes of the two or three men who were drinking pots of beer on the verandah, were burning through the mosquito screen. But she was the wife of the High Commissioner. She was untouchable. With one lazy sweep of her arm she peeled her sunglasses from her face and allowed them to drop to the towel on the bed, then, taking a measured pace, she approached the pool like an Australian fast bowler.

This was it. Wrighton had decided. He was going to put his theories to the test. He looked down the pool towards the shallow end. It looked an awfully long way. How far would he have to go before he would be able to put his feet down? Halfway? Two thirds? He was not certain. He would try looking down, he would surely see the shelving floor rise towards him. He gripped the edge of the pool firmly. Not just yet. Wait a while perhaps.

But he knew that it had to be now or never. There was nobody else in the pool to distract him, they had all drifted away to other tasks. The pool was his.

He looked back down to the shallow end and the brick hut containing the filtration plant. He could have sworn that the hut had retreated by six feet. He knew what was required – graceful strokes with his arms, over his head and in front of him, pulling the water towards him and then down by the side of his legs. It was easy. He could wiggle his legs a little if he wanted also. He had been watching, now he knew. This was the way it was done. All that was needed was to do it.

Now! He launched himself from the wall. Keep your head down, down, let the water flow over your back. Arms out straight in front of you. Keep them there, straight. Don't paddle, wait, wait till you float to the surface then you will have lost your forward momentum. He could feel the water rushing over his ears and then the beginning of the buoyancy in his legs which told him that his forward displacement was almost finished. How far to the end? No! Don't look up, it will slow you down, look down. The deep blue of the pool merged into a vague carpet below him. He could be lying on a glass topped table or the bottom could be fifty fathoms below for all he could see. Oh no! Not fifty fathoms. Not that deep please, and then he was sinking. Pull with the arms, one at a time you idiot! Right, left, right, left. Not too quickly, don't forget, conserve your breath, adopt the smoothest profile, make every stroke count. Where was the bottom of the pool? Where was the lightening blue to tell him that it was shelving upwards to within toe tip reach? That tightness in my chest is only worry, I have plenty of air I know I have. I can cross the width of this pool three times on one breath. I'm not getting anywhere. I'm standing still.

He ducked involuntarily as a shadow passed close over his head and then suddenly the water before him was boiling, bubbles, black hair and bikini. He swerved violently to the left to avoid her but she was gone, nowhere to be seen. Just the boiling water. Make for the edge! Forget the end, make for the side! Agh! What was that on my foot? She's under me and around my side. He swerved again to the right, writhing out of her way but again she had vanished, a glimpse of a navel and a foot and that was all. The water closed over his head as he slipped under the surface, legs downward. His chest was bursting. He gave a mad kick to force his head above water and gasped a mouthful of air and a lungful of water before he went under again, disorientated, rolling, thrashing with his arms and legs, teeth gritting, tendons in his face straining to hold back the underwater choke that would draw more water into his lungs. Where was the light? Where was the top? Above him the perfect silhouette of a woman's body passed between him and the light then his foot touched the bottom. He held back his reflex. Wait, wait! This will be your last kick, it has got to be right.

The moment the toes of his other foot touched the bottom he launched himself upwards with all the energy that the teabag full of oxygen that was his lungs could supply. His head broke daylight, he gasped down a lungful of air on top of the water, kicked himself into a horizontal position and thrashed out for the nearest side of the pool. His eyes were shut tight, he was blind, he was dying. His outstretched hand closed around something, it was flesh. Another hand took his wrist and drew it to the side of the pool. He hung there, like a limpet, eyes staring, coughing and heaving water and air from his lungs, choking downwards into the pool like an outboard motor, his lungs in knots.

A woman's face was near his, laughing, perfect white teeth, long black hair, dark, bubbly, spiteful eyes.

'It's easy when you know how!' She laughed again and hauled herself lightly from the pool and left him there like a discarded rag in a canal.

12

Alan Havering glanced at his wife when she entered the dining room and then put down his coffee cup in surprise.

'Yeah! That looks good. That green always suits you.'

Mary Havering stood away from the breakfast table and performed a small pirouette, fanning the skirt of her dress outwards as she did so.

'I had it copied from one that Moira brought out last time. I think it's only Marks and Sparks but in this material it looks really something doesn't it?' She lifted the hem and studied the cloth, hiding her face. Did he suspect anything, she wondered?

'I wouldn't have thought that dress would suit Moira.'

Mary pulled up a chair to the table and began to cut herself a slice of pineapple.

'It didn't,' she smiled. 'But you can't tell Moira anything.'

'She'll kill you if she sees you in it.'

'Oh it doesn't matter. She knew I wanted it for copying.'

'I didn't mean that,' Havering explained. 'I meant that she would be jealous.' He reached across the table and felt her breast through the material of the bodice. She squirmed away playfully. 'She hasn't got the tits that you have.'

'Oh Alan! You know I don't like you talking like a navvy.' Mary's stomach began to flutter inside. She was always excited by her husband's rough side and he knew it.

'Your nipple's sticking out.' He pointed at her bosom with his coffee cup.

'Stop it!' she snapped and crossed her arms. But it didn't stop the sensual itching.

'What's the occasion today then? Coffee with Melissa?' he suggested fatuously. He used the Christian name of the wife of the British High Commissioner in a derogatory sense as most of the pretenders to her company did.

'No, it's just one of these women's things, you know.' She was confident that this explanation would suffice. Her husband had never lost the impression that women did trifling things whilst men worked.

Havering paused in his mastication and looked at her pensively. For a moment she thought that she had been discovered but when he did speak, what he said was as unexpected as it was welcome, although for different reasons.

'You know... I'm glad you've decided to get about a bit. Since you started going to these coffee mornings and whist drives and meetings and things, you've perked up a bit. Yeah you have.' He looked out of the window in response to the horn of his Land Rover. 'Gotta go!' He kissed her fully on the mouth and ran his hand around her buttocks before she wriggled free.

'Not in front of the servants!' she complained, without conviction.

For a reply, Havering smacked her bottom and followed his bearer out to the car. 'Expect me when you see me!' he shouted over his shoulder.

She watched from the window as his van rumbled down the road and out into the rush hour stream in the avenue. She could feel her pulse rising with excitement and the fluttering returning.

She would have to wait for an hour before leaving, just to be safe, then... then... It was the way he used his hands that really excited her. He seemed to get them everywhere at once, but then, she supposed, Bengalis were accustomed to using their hands more than their brains. She thought of the window on the eighth floor of the Hotel Sonargaon. Doing it there, whether anybody could see them or not, had really excited him. It was the thought that they might be seen, she supposed. She did not want to admit to herself that it had excited her just as much.

The severed chicken's head was thrown onto the pile of rubbish that the black and grey crows were poking and prodding. The knife sliced again in quick, economical, downward strokes, chopping the carcase into component parts. Several more crows dropped down like black paper bags to fight over the garbage in the yard. The boy continued chopping, before the bright beady eyes of the next candidate, sitting contentedly on the warm earth, its feet hobbled with a short length of twine.

'Bloody heathens!' Havering grunted and turned away from his office window. 'Even the ruddy chickens are Moslems, waiting calmly to be disembowelled.'

He sat on the corner of his desk and lit a cigarette, flicking away the spent match, then he turned again to the chart that he had unrolled. It was the site of the Mirsharai valve station on the proposed Chittagong extension. He drummed his fingers impatiently on the table top.

Since sending the report on those faulty piers everything seemed to have proceeded without a hitch. This was an occurrence practically unknown in Bangladesh where asking your bearer to wash your socks could easily result in a blown up washing machine. Even Mary seemed to have relaxed a bit lately and made fewer demands upon him. But this resurvey would be the next hurdle to clear in order to get them back onto target.

He was impatient to get on with the job but he couldn't send Wrighton until his residence permit came through from the MFA. They were now five weeks behind but he could do nothing to expedite the processes. It was like trying to run in treacle.

Should he ring Abdul Haq? He didn't particularly want to go and see him, it was such a palaver. He thought of Abdul Haq. They were in this thing together but Havering cultured no illusions as to the politician's loyalty. The man was corrupt but then, weren't they all? How else did you become a politician?

The resurvey should only take three days. If they could get it done this week, then they might be able to start on trench digging after Christmas, which would give them four months before the start of any appreciable rains. If...

His reflection was interrupted by the telephone bell. It was Major Abdul Haq M.P. informing Havering that Wrighton's residence permit was on its way around to their office with a peon. Oh joy! At last Havering could see the perspective lengthening before him as his mind raced through the plans. He was paying only scant attention to Haq's pleasantries on the phone and responding with the correct sounding noises or interjections. The important thing was that Wrighton could do the resurvey and they could.... He stopped suddenly. Something had jolted in his mind. The telephone line was quiet. Relatively speaking that is, for any telephone line in Dhaka came with resident whistles, echoes and growls.

'Hallo, are you still there Mr. Havering?' Abdul Haq's voice was tinny in his ear.

'Yes, I'm still here.'

'I could not hear you,' Abdul Haq explained. 'What I asked was, 'Have you solved the problem of those concrete piers at the Gas Station yet?''

'Yes I heard you,' Havering replied mechanically. The bastard! How had he found out about that? Someone had talked, Havering reasoned. 'Yes, no problem,' Havering shouted down the phone with as much confidence as he could convey. 'Just a little local erosion. Nothing to worry about.'

'Oh is that all?' Haq remarked. 'I am glad. I was worried that it might be serious enough to delay the entire project.'

Havering understood perfectly what Haq meant. Haq was telling him that he knew the extent of the problem to a nicety.

The summons to Havering's office was unwelcome. Wrighton did not really want to go. He knew now that he was afraid of Havering and what he could do. He didn't like his temper, his shouting and his bullying.

'Mr. Havering in a bad mood?' he asked the peon who had brought the message. For an answer the man rolled his eyes like marbles in a saucer.

Wrighton sighed heavily and knocked on Havering's door.

'In!' came the barked command.

He went in. Mrs. Chowdhry was standing meekly before the desk. Havering was sitting behind it like a headmaster. His eyebrows were practically flat – always a bad sign. Wrighton looked around and, noticing a chair by the wall, brought it forward.

'I didn't tell you to sit down!' Havering snapped.

Wrighton paused for a minute, then calmly and with a little irony, he greeted Mrs. Chowdhry,

'Would you like a seat Mrs. Chowdhry?' She glanced fearfully across at the smouldering Havering, not knowing what to do. 'Oh I'm sure Mr. Havering had not intended you to stand when there was a chair available,' he assured her. She sat down as if the chair were made of glass.

'Finished?' Havering asked. Wrighton nodded, not daring himself to speak. 'Shut the door.' Wrighton leaned backwards and with as much negligent insolence as he dared, pushed the door carelessly with his finger tips. 'Now listen you two. Half the world knows about those bloody piers at the Gas Station. I haven't told anyone. You were the only two others there. Who have you been talking to?'

So that was it. The cat was out and rather than chase after it with the empty bag and a bowl of cream, Havering was trying to find out who had slit the strings. Wrighton could feel his hands beginning to tremble and his voice sounded a little shaky when he remarked.

'That's not strictly true is it?'

'Are you calling me a liar, Wrighton?'

'No, what I am saying is, that we were not the only people there, were we? There was also the driver.'

'He doesn't understand English.'

'But we talked to a chap in Bengali, Rube... Mrs. Chowdhry interpreted for us.'

'You talked to a bogwit in Bengali, I didn't. Stupid idea!' he muttered under his breath. 'Mrs. Chowdhry, have you told anybody about the piers?'

With a dignified serenity that could have been concealing either pent-up fury or barely-restrained laughter, Rubena Chowdhry said, 'I am not talking to anybody about my work, Mr. Havering, I am not knowing anybody who is interested in it.'

The validity of the argument was not lost on Havering who could see that he risked making himself look ridiculous. Fancy asking a bird-brain Bangla if she had been gossiping about the theory of reinforced concrete construction! No, it must have been an engineer and Wrighton was the only other engineer present, apart from himself and he had told no-one except Mary and she was his wife, damnit!

'Alright Mrs. Chowdhry, you can go.' Wrighton moved to the door. 'I didn't say that you could go, Wrighton.'

With pointed courtesy, Wrighton opened the door for Mrs. Chowdhry who sailed through it like a galleon. He knew that his action would only anger Havering all the more but he could not help himself, he did not know why he did it. Perhaps it was a false bravado.

'Who did you tell then Wrighton?'

Wrighton thought carefully and let Havering see that he was thinking. A silence developed in the office and again the image of the headmaster's study came back to Wrighton. It was the kind of silence that immediately succeeded the asking of the question which if answered truthfully, would result in a beating and so it denoted the silent weighing-up of the pros and cons of lying. But Wrighton did not have to lie. Only when he was certain did he say, 'I don't think I told anybody.'

'Think! You don't think!'

'Well I don't know anybody who is interested in my work either.' He re-used Mrs. Chowdhry's defence partly to discomfort Havering. 'Other people would have been privy to the information surely?'

'Name one.'

'Well, you sent a report didn't you? To London? By telex?'

'Mac Macleod sent that telex and he is utterly reliable.'

'But anybody could have seen the telex before or during transmission.'

'For God's sake, Wrighton, we're talking about somebody gossiping and gossiping in the wrong places.'

'Well it isn't me.'

Havering looked him in the eyes and faltered. Damn the man and damn his brown eyes! There was something about them, something intangible but threatening. He could feel it.

'All right.' He turned away. 'Your residence permit is on its way from the MFA. Haq has just phoned up to tell me.' Havering continued quickly but was unable to avoid Wrighton drawing the obvious conclusion that it was Haq who had found out about the piers and had embarrassed Havering. 'You can go up country and get those survey points realigned. Take my driver and van, he has done it all before. He knows the ropes.' He stopped at a knock on the door. 'In!' The peon crept in and gingerly held out an envelope to him. 'Well give it to me then! I haven't got the arms of a bloody gorilla.' The man relinquished the envelope and scurried out. Havering peered inside it and then threw it over the desk to Wrighton. 'There it is, get on with it. Don't start today, it's too late. You'll need to leave at about five tomorrow morning to get to the river crossings before the rush.'

'Oh, I'd got something on tomorrow night–'

'Well you haven't now. You'll be up country till the end of the week.'

The first thing that Wrighton had to do upon his return to his office was to telephone Sandra Hardwicke to explain that he would not be able to give her the first dance lesson on the following evening as arranged. She solved the problem by utilising the infinite elasticity of the social scene in Dhaka and invited him around for dinner with her and her husband that very evening, after which he could give her the lesson.

Next, he went to collect his charts and ask Mrs. Chowdhry to telephone up country to ensure that their local surveyor would meet them at the rendezvous point. This was the Bangladeshi man who had overseen the survey. As far as Wrighton could tell from Dhaka, the man was blameless, he had been working to faulty data supplied by Line.

On the way through the chart room he had accosted Mac Macleod on the subject of the telex. Yes, he had remembered it, did Stewart want to see the duplicate? There was no reason for him to do so but just out of curiosity, to satisfy himself that it was still there, he said 'yes'.

The duplicate was safe, in the file, locked in the drawer of Mac's desk. Neither of them could now see how it could have been compromised. Mac always locked his office when he left it, even to go across the corridor, ever since the day he had lost five thousand taka from his case whilst absent for two minutes. It was wicked. The theft had obviously been perpetrated by one of the Bengalis who worked in the office, they must have watched him like a hawk and had worked out where he kept the money and how long he would be absent. It was trying on relationships to

know that the people in your outer office were working with you on everything but considered it fair game to steal at the first opportunity.

Wrighton had handed the telex copy back to Mac, feeling a little
subdued. It was the first time that he had seen the text of it and he had
assumed that in the greater part, it would be his report. Yet, his name was
not mentioned on it anywhere and Havering had reworked it to make it
his own piece of work. It was his prerogative, of course, after all, he was
the boss in Dhaka and reports had to go out in his name but Wrighton
would have liked a little recognition for what he had done. Then he
dismissed his thoughts as being childish and packed up and went home.

'You'll need a gun of course, or a knife,' Bell remarked as he casually
lounged on the sofa and heaved his feet onto the coffee table top.
Wrighton laughed.

'I've always got a knife with me.' He pulled out a pocket knife.

'I'm serious.' Bell's blue eyes bored into him. 'If you're going up
country you need to be able to defend yourself.'

Wrighton stopped packing his grip for an instant and looked at him.
He realised that the man believed what he was saying.

'Have you got a gun then?'

'Yeah. In the Land Rover. Bought it in Hong Kong. Just a little pistol,
but enough.'

'Have you ever had to use it?'

'Come close to it a couple of times.'

'In Bangladesh?'

'Yup. It's the dacoit season. The warm weather brings them out. When
it rains they are all fighting for their lives, they are too busy to rob each
other but as soon as the winter comes, out come the dacoits.'

'I can't see what use a small pistol would be against a dacoit armed with
a rifle.' Wrighton had a fear of firearms. 'There is no point in me taking
a gun because firstly, I wouldn't know how to use it, secondly, if I did know
how to use it I could never fire on a fellow human being and thirdly, it is
merely one more thing to be stolen from me and it could cause damage
in the wrong hands.'

'Making a big mistake,' Bell warned him, and then shouted out into the
corridor, 'Tuppin! Are you ready yet?'

'Oh, you're running on the Hash aren't you?'

'Yeah.'

'Why is it called 'The Hash'?'

'Oh it all started out in... er... Hong Kong I think it was. Some fellow decided to have a paper chase, just to keep in trim. An expat. of course. And where they finished each week, you know, where they parked the cars, was outside a Chinese restaurant called the Hash House. That's what '3H' means. Hash House Harriers.' He pulled his tee shirt straight so that Wrighton could read the motif on it.

'And is this fellow in Bangladesh now then?'

'No, it has just spread world wide. They have hashes everywhere. Even in Surrey.'

'Really? I didn't know that.'

'I reckon you ought to come on the Hash with us. It would be a good introduction to going up country. Don't you think so Tuppin?'

Tuppin nodded as he counted tins of beer into the cool box.

It was such a preposterous idea that Wrighton agreed.

'I wish your firm would get some seats put in the back of their van,' Wrighton yelled at the sweaty back of Bell's neck as it wrinkled and stretched with the effort of keeping the bouncing Land Rover within the parameters of a controlled trajectory.

'Shut up you great cissy! It's better than me Ford!' Bell shouted back over his shoulder just as Tuppin barked out a warning from the seat at the side of him.

'Look out!'

'Shit!' Bell swore as the van bounced over a railway sleeper that was stretched across the carriageway. Wrighton was hurled off the wheel arch where he had been perched and cracked his head painfully on the roof. At the same time he saw the sleeper rearing upright behind and spinning like a top as it crossed the road into the path of an empty killer truck. 'Bloody hell!' Bell wrestled with the swaying Land Rover till it stopped oscillating. Behind them the killer truck was ploughing into the brush at the edge of the road, scattering people and raising a hideous cloud of dust that was already obscuring the highway.

Bell flashed his headlights at another European in a car travelling towards them and waved his arm from the window to slow him down but the man was already braking and taking the dusty verge as an escape route.

'We're well out of that lot!' Tuppin remarked. 'It might make two lines in the paper tomorrow. Isn't this where we turn off?' he asked, looking at Bell.

For a reply, Bell braked hard in cadence, depositing Wrighton back on the floor again, where he decided to stay, and then swerved across the oncoming traffic to hurtle down an earth track. About a hundred yards further down, the track was crossed by the railway embankment which made no concession for a level crossing. The track climbed straight up one side of the nine foot high mound and down the other.

'Do you reckon we'll beat him?' Bell enquired dispassionately as the Land Rover scrabbled up the loose earth.

Tuppin looked out of the passenger window at the huge filthy brown diesel locomotive which was trundling towards them. He ignored the question, considering that his observation on the state of tune of the locomotive's power plant was more pertinent.

'Look at the bloody flames belching out of the roof of that engine. They must be about eight feet high.'

Bell stopped the Land Rover on the rails and leaned across to have a look. The van vibrated with the weight of the oncoming locomotive. Wrighton was speechless with fear as the engine moaned out a warning to them on its horn. Bell let in the clutch harshly.

'Ha!' he laughed as he reached for the ignition key. 'Stalled it!' He started the engine in a leisurely fashion and allowed the van to roll down the other side of the line. Before they had reached the bottom of the bank the locomotive was already grumbling its train of trundling trucks across behind them. At last Wrighton found his tongue.

'You confounded idiot, you nearly killed us all!'

Bell turned around and guffawed.

'You feeling all right Wrighton? You look a bit pale.'

Tuppin looked across at Bell and they sniggered. Wrighton shut his mouth in anger. They had frightened him, which had been their intention.

They pulled into a rough field in which were already scattered cars and vans of various nationalities. Several of the participants had brought along their chowkidhars who would patrol the vehicles whilst the owners were off running.

This was Wrighton's first look at the country and he was surprised by how green it was. Everywhere that he looked, sprouted trees and bushes, all fully leaved. Fields of obscure and exotic crops were intersticed with drained paddies, the rice straw lying white and crackling on the earth.

Wrighton had pounded down paths of beaten dust, the impact of each footfall leaving a minute puff in the air; he had milled around in a group of twenty or more searching the ground for the paper shreds until someone had called 'on paper' from over to their right and they had all charged off again on the correct track; he had skittered along the top of a broken brick wall providing as it did, the only dry passage between two ponds of a hideously obscure brown water; he had slipped off the slimy mud boundary wall of a paddy field and along with four other runners had slithered into the tacky, smelly mud at the bottom, much to the amusement of the fleet-footed natives who had stood around in groups and jeered and cheered at the antics of their European Masters. It was free entertainment for them. He had recognised other runners usually as they trotted past him. The chaps from Vickers were out at the front with the men. Don Finkelstein had run alongside him for a while and they had swapped accusations over Wrighton's treatment of the U.S. Ambassador and Finkelstein had unsuccessfully tried to enrol Wrighton in his projected game of cricket. He had recognised some of the children from the British Club pool as they too had playfully swerved and jumped down the tracks, their limbs a beautiful uniform brown, their joints displaying the suppleness of youth. A complete Swedish family, statuesque, typical and healthy had run past him in line astern, the youngest child being about eight. In fact, the only person he seemed to have overtaken was a rather overweight Negro American lady wearing a sparkling white tee shirt which dazzled in the hot afternoon sun and reminded Wrighton of the effect of ultra violet lights he had seen at some obscure local scout 'Gang Show' back in his childhood where the costumes had fluoresced with an unreal luminescence and the faces and hands of the dancers had merged into a uniform chocolate colour.

As they had run through one village, winding their way around the wattle houses, ducking under the washing hanging out to dry, scattering the chickens and children, he had felt a small sting in his back and then another on the back of his head. He had turned around to find that the children were throwing the husks of some fruit or nut at him with an accomplished accuracy. He had stopped and playfully thrown a few back whereupon the children had screeched delightedly and run back inside their houses.

It was only supposed to be about a five mile run but already his limbs were leaden. His tee shirt was stuck to his body like a second skin, his shorts caked with the vile-smelling mud which had now dried to the consistency of cake icing. Only his plimsolls were still wet, squelching regularly into concealed holes of mud or inescapable quagmires that the hares had sadistically discovered when they had set the course earlier in the afternoon.

By the time that he and the few stragglers had returned to the departure point, his hair was wringing wet and the perspiration was dripping into his eyes and out again to dribble down his cheeks and gather upon his top lip where he could blow it away with each pant. They staggered up to the group of runners who were drinking beer from tubs of ice which had been brought out in the vans.

Something was going on. Somebody was reading aloud from a book but he could hear nothing of this. The sun was rapidly approaching the horizon, the shadows were lengthening by the minute and the mosquitos were beginning to feast on the ankles, elbows and ear lobes of the steaming, stale, grubby runners.

Wrighton had come back from the run feeling physically purged. He had sweated more in that hour than he had ever done since he had left school, his pores were wide open, his limbs were throbbing from the physical effort; an effort far beyond that which had been demanded of them for years. But now they were stiffening, the sweat was drying. Despite the heat he began to feel chilly, the mosquitos were becoming more persistent. He didn't want to stand here listening to all this boloney, what he wanted was to go straight home and have a good, cleansing shower.

Not before time the ceremonies appeared to be over, people began to drift away from the group. One of the children had offered him a Coca Cola from their tub and it had gone down his throat without wetting it.

Out of the throng appeared Bell and Tuppin, covered in mud, their eyes gleaming triumph and masculinity through the grime. They smelled of ponds and beer.

'What-ho Wrighton, you got back then!' Bell threw a brawny arm around his shoulders and hugged him. They were both clammy, it was uncomfortable. Wrighton was impatient to free himself.

'Yes,' he joked. 'I took the bus in the end.'

'You see old Juno over there?' Bell nodded at a large man swishing at the ground with a hefty switch. 'He cracked three of those little buggers on the head with his cosh. They were chucking something at him.'

'Yes I had that trouble,' Wrighton admitted. 'I just threw back at them.'

'Juno doesn't believe in half measures.' Bell was obviously proud of knowing Juno. At that moment the man in question turned and Wrighton realised that he had not beaten the children with the switch in his hand but indeed, with a cosh whose stubby handle he could see protruding from the belt of the man's shorts.

'Are you coming to the On On?' Bell asked.

'What's that?'

'The On On,' Bell repeated obscurely, as if its meaning were patent. 'It's at the Chinky at D.I.T.2 at eight o'clock.'

'Oh, What? To eat?' Wrighton finally understood.

'Well we don't go there for the cabaret!' Tuppin interjected sourly.

'Oh I can't.' Wrighton had just remembered. 'I'm dining out tonight, with the Hardwickes.'

'Oh, get you! Dining with the Hardwickes eh? Mixing with the swells. Our company not good enough for you eh?'

'That's just about it, yeah.'

'You did say the "Hardwickes" didn't you?' Tuppin enquired slyly. 'In the plural?'

'Yes, Geoff and Sandra Hardwicke have invited me around for dinner tonight.' Wrighton declared as they climbed into the Land Rover and so that there could be no misunderstanding in that corrupt, perverted little mind of Tuppin's he added, 'Both of them.'

The warm water sluiced down Wrighton's face to join the turgid muddy river sluggishly draining from the bath tub. It was an indescribably sensuous luxury, cleaning out the grime, the filth, the muck. To feel the real body emerging from its coating. He pushed the shower head into his scalp, revelling in the impression of a swelling head that the water imparted as it sought out and rinsed each individual hair on his scalp from follicle to tip. He tipped his head back, open-mouthed to allow the stream to trickle down his spine and drop between his buttocks, then he fumbled for his scrubbing brush and vigorously scrubbed himself from eyebrows to toe nails.

Glowing with well-being, he turned off the smooth-worn brass tap. On the bath were two taps, hot and cold. The choice of water was warm or scalding. The warm water came from the hot water tank which was fitted indoors. Luckily the immersion heater in this tank did not work so that the water was at ambient house temperature. The scalding water came from the cold water tank which was the galvanised mound perched on the flat roof under the full rays of the sun. The water spat and bubbled from the cold water tap, so whenever he washed, he used the coolest source of water available – the hot tap.

As he stood there drying, he could hear a mixture of wailing and thumping coming from the tape recorder in the dining room and he wondered if he also should have brought a similar machine out with him but he knew that he lacked the guts and authority to impose his choice of music on the other two occupants of the house and if they had wanted to listen to their music he did not doubt for one instant that his would have been turned off and discarded without the courtesy of eliciting either his opinion or permission.

He wandered through to the bedroom with his wet feet slapping on the tiled floor and switched on his small short-wave radio by the bed. He scooped up the latest copy of *'London Calling'* and lay on the bed to try to decipher the bar chart on the back cover to discover when he could next pick up the World Service in English. Its complexity defeated him and he threw it to the floor.

Something tickled his ankle and then horror grabbed him as he felt a light, coordinated touch covering the width of his ankle. He peered down the bed towards his feet, moving his head stiffly, his jaw tense with revulsion. Across his foot was moving a large, hairy-legged spider. It easily measured the span of his hand and his hands were not small. His breath became shallow and fast as he tried to simultaneously watch the spider, praying that it would not bite or sting him and cast about for some ultimate weapon with which he could sweep the repulsive thing from his ankle. The *'London Calling'* was too flimsy and in any case was out of easy reach on the floor. He gritted his teeth as the spider now encroached upon his left ankle, eye stalks waving, legs wriggling up and down with a finesse of mechanical coordination. By his right ear the radio was muttering something inconsequential to itself in Hindi.

As the last electric contact was broken and the spider stalked slowly across the remainder of the bed, Wrighton slowly let his breath out and turned his head to track the thing's progress across the room. When he considered that it had reached a sufficient distance he leaped from the bed by the far side and followed it at a safe distance. It unconcernedly ambled across to its hole behind the wardrobe. He stood looking at the hole wondering what to do. At length he decided that it was pointless doing anything since he could not keep such creatures from penetrating his room, he merely had to learn to live with them. He set his mind to dressing for dinner and tried to ignore the nagging possibility that encounters such as these would certainly be more frequent, once he was 'up country'.

At Wrighton's request the night chowkidhar, Bilbo, shuffled up to Kemal Ataturk Avenue and came back slouched in a rickshaw which settled down to wait for him at the gate. As Wrighton passed down the corridor, Bell's voice hailed him from the dining room.

'Oi, Wrighton, are you off now?'

Wrighton poked his head around the door to address Bell who was sprawled across the sofa, feet on the table again, smoking a cigarette. It struck Wrighton as odd that someone could make an activity out of smoking a cigarette yet that was exactly what Bell was doing, for he was doing nothing else.

'Yes, I'm off now. Don't wait up for me, mother.'

'Tuppin's gone out with some tart he met on the hash,' Bell stated. 'What's this 'do' that you're going to at the Hardwicke's? Could you get me in on it?'

Wrighton was flabbergasted at the directness of the request.

'Well it's not really a 'do' you see—'

'Well who else will be there then? Is it a party?'

'No, it's just dinner. For me, as far as I know.'

'That's weird, What do they want a boring old fart like you for dinner for?' Bell drew heavily upon his cigarette. Wrighton noticed that his hand was shaking.

'I'm as mystified as you are,' Wrighton lied and shut the door.

It was a strange encounter, Wrighton thought as he jogged along the causeway in the rickshaw, ever ready to throw himself onto the grass to avoid sudden death. Poor old Bell! Despite his rudeness, he had wanted something. He had wanted company. He was lonely. It was somehow humiliating to Wrighton to realise that Bell was a human being under-neath it all. He wondered whether he ought to turn around and collect him but soon realised that he could never excuse himself to the Hardwicke's for such a blunder. The invitation to dinner was plainly just for him.

He paid off the rickshaw puller at the end of their street. He paid him too much, he knew, but it was only Monopoly money. As he walked down their road, passing from one pool of yellow light to the next, the various chowkidhars wished him 'good evening saheb' as if he were one of their neighbours. He was surprised for they had seen him only once and surely the maxim that to the Europeans, all the Banglas looked the same, surely applied reciprocally to the Bengalis and their perception of the Europeans? He responded with a 'Good evening to you,' which seemed to please them for it never failed to set off a grin.

'Stewart! Come in, come in.' Geoff Hardwicke opened the door. 'Sandy, Stewart's here!' he called to his wife.

'Coming.' The reply wafted back, tinged with the echo of a room with no curtains.

'Sit down.' Geoff Hardwicke pointed to the sofa. 'You know,' he became theatrically confidential, 'Sandy thinks a lot of you. She's really looking forward to learning to dance.'

'I don't know what to say to that,' Wrighton laughed with an uneasy truth.

Hardwicke slumped into an armchair and almost as soon as he had stopped moving he leaned forward again and addressed him. 'So how's business?'

'Oh so so. We'll get there eventually. Despite the assistance from the Bangladeshis and the MFA,' Wrighton replied laconically.

'Problem with the MFA then?'

'Well not really. I don't think so. No more so than we would have, were we to deal with anybody else. I don't think that the MFA is particularly problematical.'

'The old T.I.B. factor eh?'

'Oh yes,' Wrighton remembered. 'This Is Bangladesh. Yes, I think that sums it up.'

Sandra Hardwicke strode into the room and walked straight over to Wrighton, giving him no time to stand up respectfully.

'Shove up!' she said, pointing to the sofa.

Wrighton, caught by surprise, did as he was told and she curled up beside him. He could feel the warmth of the soles of her bare feet against his thigh. She was wearing a garishly flowered pair of baggy trousers and a cotton shirt.

Geoff Hardwicke grinned across at them both.

'We'll have to get a bigger sofa,' he laughed.

'Don't you dare! Spoilsport!' Sandra pouted. 'It's nice and cosy, isn't it Stewart?'

'Well er–'

'You don't look very comfortable,' Hardwicke observed with a twinkle in his eye.

'No, no. I'm, er...fine.'

'We're going to have dinner almost immediately,' Sandra leaned over to him as she explained, 'because boring old Geoff has got some boring old work to do for the boring old High Commission. Then that will give us lots of time for a dancing lesson.'

'Yes, I shall leave you to it Stewart after dinner. I'm afraid you'll have to amuse yourselves.'

Wrighton looked up and down the room, quickly measuring the space available for dancing once the furniture had been pushed to the side. It was considerable.

'Yes that's fine, fine,' he said, as a white-coated servant appeared in the doorway.

'Come on then.' Sandra slapped his knee which jerked involuntarily. 'Dinner's ready.'

'Bring your drink if you like, Stewart.' Hardwicke apologised, 'I'm afraid we haven't got much choice for teetotallers in this house. You're the only one I know.'

'So what sport do you do?' Hardwicke asked.

'Well...none. I didn't realise it was compulsory.'

'Don't you play cricket, or football or tennis or squash?'

'No.'

'How do you keep in trim then?'

'I don't. I am probably the most out of condition person in Dhaka. No. Tell a lie, the second most out of condition. I overtook an enormous Negro woman on the Hash today, so there is one person in Dhaka who is slower than me.'

'There you are then. You run on the Hash, that's sport.'

'Ah... I don't run on the Hash in the present continuous or whatever the tense is. I ran on the Hash today in the definite past historic.'

'It was too tough for you was it?' Hardwicke teased him. 'In your decrepit condition?'

'Now come along boys, stop squabbling. It's becoming tedious.'

'Yes dear,' Hardwicke simpered.

'Actually I liked the running part of the Hash,' Wrighton admitted. 'I hadn't run so hard since I left school. The sweat was pouring off me – it must be healthy. But there were some things that I didn't like.'

'Such as?' Sandra asked.

'I thought that all the paraphernalia at the end was a bit childish. Correction. I thought it was very childish. All the chanting and the mock ritual.'

'Yes I found that a bit tedious. That's why I gave it up.'

Sandra snorted.

'You gave it up because it was too much like hard work! You're a fine one to talk about the tedium of ritual. Your whole work is constructed about obscure and pointless ritual!'

'Now now dear! Don't knock the Dip. Service. It pays our rent and provides all your beautiful frocks.' He nodded at her baggy cotton trousers. She stuck out her tongue at him.

'Another thing I didn't like,' Wrighton continued, 'was the way that the

Banglas were treated by some of the runners. There was one there, a great big bloke, I can't remember his name, who was armed with a stick and a cosh which he was using on the children.' Wrighton caught Hardwicke and his wife exchanging glances across the room, but he continued. 'I can't understand the mentality of a person like that. Why go out armed for an afternoon run?'

'Well...' Hardwicke was uneasy, 'there have been incidents of Hashers being attacked by groups of children and beaten or stoned.'

'I'm not surprised,' Wrighton exclaimed. 'We were running through the middle of people's villages, through their compounds, sometimes through their crops and their gardens! Of course they are going to react to our presence.'

'But there is no excuse for stoning,' Hardwicke protested. 'We have to be able to protect ourselves.'

'All right then. Get a couple of Bangladeshis from Oldham, let them run through the stockbroker belt in Weybridge or somewhere, throwing paper all over the place and then get them followed by two hundred scantily-clad compatriots, jumping over garden fences and running down residential streets, trampling on their lawns and allotments. What do you think the reaction would be in Weybridge?'

'Well it's hardly–'

'And what if one of the Bengalis playfully clubs some of the middle-class children around the head with a wooden cosh as he runs past? How do you think that would go down?'

'But it's not the same is it? You can't make the comparison. You weren't running through the stockbroker belt of Dhaka. They were mud-scratchers. They were peasants.'

'And that makes it alright does it?'

Hardwicke took a deep breath and let it out noisily. He had been argued into a paper bag. A career diplomat had been made to see that his opinions were untenable by an engineer unskilled in oratory but strong in a disproportionate sense of humanity. Time for him to use his skills of diplomacy. He tugged at his beard.

'Why didn't you join the Foreign Office instead of becoming an engineer? We could have done with you.'

'All right,' Wrighton laughed. 'I'll leave it alone.'

'Geoff, don't you think you've had enough of Stewart's time? Isn't it time for you to leave us alone? Together. To do what we have to do.' Sandra joked.

'Ah yes.'

Wrighton addressed Hardwicke, 'You had better tell me what you want me to teach to Sandra. '

'All the usual stuff. Waltz, foxtrot, quickstep. You know.'

'What about the tango?' Sandra enquired.

'I never learned the tango,' Hardwicke scoffed. 'It's just a show-off dance.'

'I want to learn the tango.' Sandra stamped her foot and pouted like a spoilt child. Hardwicke turned to Wrighton and sighed indulgently.

'I suppose you can teach her the tango?'

'If you wish. It is possible. But if you can't dance it I will have to teach you as well.'

'I am not going to dance the tango. Never in my life.' Hardwicke exclaimed, horrified.

'Well what is the point then? Sandra won't have anyone to dance with.'

'I can dance it with you,' she said.

Wrighton looked at Hardwicke and raised his eyebrows inquiringly.

'Oh it's alright as far as I'm concerned. She can do what she likes.'

'Fine. If you make sufficient progress on the waltz, quickstep and foxtrot, then I shall teach you the tango.'

'Oh goody!' She leapt forward and kissed him on the cheek. Wrighton pulled back with embarrassment. 'Where do we begin?'

'I can clear a dance area here by moving the furniture back whilst you get ready if you like.'

'I am ready.'

'Oh but...' Wrighton looked down at her trousers and then stopped in confusion. She followed his glance.

'What's the matter? My trousers? What's wrong with my trousers?'

'N...Nothing, nothing at all,' Wrighton stuttered. 'No, they're fine.'

'But they're not for dancing in? What should I wear then? A ballgown?'

'No, look. er... You misunderstand me. I didn't say anything.'

'You didn't have to, the way that you looked at my trousers.'

'Oh dear, we have got off to rather a bad start haven't we? Let me explain what I mean then you tell me what you mean. For me, dancing is not just putting our feet in the right place in time to music. There is a purpose to it. Why do you think formalised ballroom dancing developed?'

'Well, amusement—'

'It was the only way, when you think about it, that a man could be alone with a woman and hold her without transgressing the rules of correct conduct. It's a means of expression, a way of communicating between a man and a woman; it has a language which you can learn and yet still be surprised by its nuances; it has a grace and fluidity; an elegance a–'

'What you mean is...' interrupted Sandra, 'if you dance with me in trousers you could be dancing with a man?'

'Well....' Wrighton felt very awkward. 'It's just that, when you perform a beautiful impetus turn in the waltz or a quick open reverse or some such similar step for example, part of the beauty of the execution of the step lies not only in the position of the feet relative to each other but also in the line of the body, the shape of the shoulders, the tilt of the head and the sweep of the skirt. If you can only see four trousered legs it might just as well be a pantomime horse dancing.'

As Sandra had been watching him, a slow, indulgent smile had crept over her neat little face. She flicked back her blonde hair.

'I'll go and put a skirt on,' she said. 'You only have to say, you know.' She skipped out and Wrighton began to lug the furniture to the edges of the room. The bearer came in as soon as he heard the movement and between them they carried the enormous potted plants to safety and rolled up the carpet to reveal the tiled floor.

'Is that better?' Sandra swirled in, some minutes later. She was wearing a long, red, pleated skirt and a matching blouse.

'Yes, that's er...fine. Actually, it's very pretty,' he conceded. She smiled. 'Can you move in it?'

'What do you mean?'

'Is it a fullish skirt? Can you take large steps?'

'I want to learn to dance not do the triple jump.' She paced out a grotesquely long step with ease.

'That is great,' Wrighton said. 'Now come here and I will show you how to stand.' She came into his arms. She smelt warm and delicate. He glanced over her shoulder to the wall behind. 'You've taken down old Rudolf,' he observed.

The conifers in the front garden of Park View were black and dripping with persistent winter rain as Marion scrunched up the drive to the front door. Mary Gonzales took her wet raincoat from her and hurried it into the cloakroom on a hanger.

'Go on into the sitting room Marion dear, and dry out,' she called, her voice muffled by the folds of wet coats hanging on pegs. 'I've lit a fire to make it nice and cosy. I think a real fire makes all the difference don't you?' she said as she re-emerged.

Marion mumbled something vague and pushed open the sitting room door. She greeted her knitting friends and picked her way across the no man's land tangle of bags and balls of wool and patterns.

'This is welcoming.' She nodded at the flickering yellow flames in the grate.

'Yes isn't it?'

'You know...' began a woman who was not known for her alacrity of thought or the percipience of her observation, 'I had never really noticed the fireplace in this room in all the time that we have been meeting here, but a real fire in it certainly makes a difference. It's a sort of focal point isn't it?'

Marion nodded with the others and idly gazed at the condensation misting over the windows, blotting out the herbaceous borders. It was hot in Bangladesh. Hot and dry and sunny. And in Wembley the condensation was misting over the windows like the numbness misting over her life. Women were talking...

'I suppose Mary has got central heating hasn't she?'

'Yes, look, there's a radiator over there.'

But they were saying nothing. They would still be talking this claptrap a decade from now. She looked through the remaining clear pane. That stupid little croquet lawn really was quite pretentious.

'I wonder whether the gas board has cut her off.'

'Perhaps she's burning her gas bills to keep herself warm.'

'What has old Stewart been up to lately then Marion, we haven't heard about him for a while?'

Why should she tell them? What business was it of theirs? Why did they want to know? – so that they could gossip about it at some other coffee morning? 'Well, my dear, I know a woman whose husband has gone off to Bangladesh. It's a terrible country. She says he's very important but we can't help thinking that important people are sent to Washington or Paris or places like that, do you see what I mean?'

Marion said, 'Well I told you that he went to a party and met the U.S. Ambassador didn't I?'

'Oh yes, that's old hat,' someone complained. 'He doesn't seem to do any work at all. All play.'

And that's another thing. Stewart's letters. I won't have them pulling them apart and criticising and making comments. Just because he doesn't write about his work it doesn't mean that he isn't doing any does it? Does it?

'Actually, he has started teaching ballroom dancing to one of the diplomat's wives.'

'Fancy that. You'd think that the Foreign Office or whatever would teach them, wouldn't you?'

'Well it doesn't and she needed to learn so my Stewart is teaching her.' Put that in your pipe and smoke it. 'I think she's the wife of the Commercial Attache.' Marion was certain that this snippet of information would impress her friends as it had done her.

'But can Stewart dance?'

'Of course he can.'

'I've never seen him.'

'Stewart was a champion dancer when we first met. He's got cups and medals and things.'

'But he doesn't dance now does he?'

'Well, he found with his job and that, when we got married he just didn't have the time to do it anymore.' I am not stupid. I wasn't having my husband gallivanting about the place with other men's wives. And yet... there he is, in that despicable country, dancing with women I've never even seen.

'Is that where you met him, at a dance hall?'

'No it is not! I don't dance. We were properly introduced – at church.'

'The boys don't visit me as often as they used to, Marion. I'm sure you could manage to bring them.'

Marion sighed silently and carried the teapot from the table to the kitchen sink.

'It's not always easy, Mother, there's such a lot to do with Stewart being away.'

'You should never have let him go. I told you so at the time.'

She knew that her mother had said the opposite. She suspected that her mother also knew, but they both understood that Marion was not to question the lie. It would stand in the archives of their family as a concrete truth.

'I didn't have the option, Mother. Do you want the tea leaves on the compost?'

'You should have kept a closer rein on him. He's weak, Marion, he needs your guidance. Your father was just the same. He did have his crackpot ideas. If I had listened to him we would all have lived among the pigs and cows in some hovel in the country.' Marion could remember her father dozing in his armchair by the fire, a dog-eared copy of *Farmer and Stockbreeder* on his lap and peace on his London-grey face. 'It was me that kept him in the City. Regular hours, that was what he needed. But he didn't know it, poor soul, I had to keep telling him.'

'I suppose you're right Mother.'

'Of course I am.' She pinched her lips together and raised her eyebrows. 'I can't imagine what you thought you were doing.... and what is he up to out there? Hmm?'

'He does write, mother. I have read you his letters.'

'Why doesn't he phone?'

'It's something to do with not having a phone in the house and not being able to phone abroad from the office.' And even as she said it, Marion could feel her mother's rancid disbelief.

And why not! What was he doing out there without Marion? Without his wife to tell him what decisions to take? Away from the subtle pressures which she employed to guide him as her own mother had guided her father.

'Don't forget you've got Brandon blood in you, Marion. Brandon women have always been strong.'

'Oh I know that, mother.'

This Bangladesh thing was unsettling the balance. And of course, the longer he stayed out there, outside Marion's influence, the more he would discover about himself.

13

Something had awoken Wrighton. He turned towards the window. It was still dark outside. Then he heard the knock on the door and realised that an earlier summons must have drawn him from his heavy slumber. It was a quarter past four in the morning. Why on earth was he being woken up at that time?

'Come in!' he shouted at the shuffling form of Moussi, bearing a cup of tea. 'Just put it on the table please.'

'Saheb.'

Wrighton remembered. He was going up country today. He had to start at five. He shook himself and sat up to drink the sweet tea. Moussi always made the tea sweet no matter what instruction he was given. Bell reckoned that it was to hide the appropriation of half of the sugar that went into the house. If the masters always had sweet tea they would be convinced that all the sugar was being used on them.

It really was ironic, Wrighton thought, as he swallowed the liquid, that you could not get a decent cup of tea in a country where they grew the confounded stuff! The flavour was not improved in any way by the skimmed, homogenised milk that they had to use.

He switched on the light and swung himself out of bed, scanning the floor carefully for insect life before placing his bare feet on the tiles. In a yawning, scratching, stupor, he staggered around the bedroom and bathroom, switching on and off lights and turning on taps until his toilet was over.

He had finished his papaya and was crunching through his toast when he heard the squealing of Land Rover brakes and the squeak of the gate being reluctantly opened by a somnolent Bilbo. Moussi flew to the front door to deny Bilbo entry to the house. He heard a mumbling of voices in the hallway and then a sharp interjection by Moussi followed by an insolent riposte as Bilbo admitted defeat. The door opened.

'Car here, Saheb.'

'Thank you Moussi. Could you put that bag and the small case into the van please?'

Moussi left the room and shortly afterwards Wrighton could hear him calling Bilbo in the garden. Bilbo was night chowkidhar – he could carry the bags to the car. With his trousers flapping like elephant's ears, Bilbo waddled in and shouldered the bags. He and Moussi were on the most cordial of terms now that they had recognised the traditional spheres of influence. The previous disagreement must have been because Bilbo had wanted to enter the house to announce the arrival of the car. This was patently the cook-bearer's job.

'Sandwiches Saheb.' Moussi handed a soggy package to Wrighton who regarded it suspiciously.

'What's in them, Moussi?'

'Barled egg, feanut batter.'

'Aha. Boiled egg and peanut butter eh? Well that should stick me to the ground.'

'Saheb?'

'Thank you Moussi. See you tomorrow night.'

Havering's driver was standing by the Land Rover, waiting in the gloom. White teeth and glinting eyes. Wrighton had carefully wrapped his sandwiches in a polythene bag and he now placed them gingerly in his case which was lying on the back seat.

'I'll sit in the front. What's your name, driver? I can't keep calling you 'driver'.'

'My name Oggi but Havering Saheb call me Shit'ed.'

'He calls you what?'

'Shit'ed.'

It was some moments before Wrighton realised what the man was saying.

'Well I shall call you Oggi. Is that alright?'

'Like you want.' The man was disappointed. He considered it a great honour to be called 'Shit'ed'.

They drove without speaking, down the wide avenue through the Tejgaon Industrial Estate, by the biscuit factory, past the college towards the university. Down through Mogh Bazar they drove, the tyres whining on the tarmacadam.

Along the pavements at irregular intervals, Wrighton could see ragged bundles of people, sleeping as best they could. A cigarette vendor curled around his suitcase full of stock. A beggar, asleep on his back, mouth drawn open in mute mimicry of the begging bowl alongside him. Already, at five in the morning the children were out at the traffic lights. Pickings were thin at this hour.

The bulk of the stadium loomed dirty white on their left as they turned down towards Old Dhaka and the road to Chittagong.

'Oggi, have you got the headlights on?'

'No saheb. Headlights not good.'

'Do you mean that they don't work?'

'Headlights working saheb. Headlights not good.'

'Well, put them on just the same please. I would feel safer.'

Oggi twisted a switch and the road ahead was flooded with revealing light. Immediately a killer bus which had been pounding towards them, turned on yellow lamps and swerved across the road at them, blowing its whistle furiously. Wrighton grabbed the dashboard in fright just as Oggi killed the lamps. The bus rumbled past, avoiding a collision by at least a foot.

'O.K. Oggi. You've made your point. Headlights upset other people. I would prefer to have them on but if you are satisfied that you can see without them...'

'Oggi very good see, saheb, very good see,' he said as he swerved around a cow which was wandering across the road.

The Demra police station junction was a well-known landmark and by the time that they reached it, the sun had risen. The rising was not violent and sudden, it was nevertheless quick, but subtle, disguised by the heavy mist that was lying down by the paddies along the Burra Ganga. All at once Wrighton realised that he could see the greyness in the mist and, looking up through the windscreen, he could detect a lightening of the heavens.

They had to stop at the police station for Wrighton to have his residence permit inspected. It was returned to him covered with dirty finger marks. He tried not to wince as he slid it back into his pocket.

Oggi turned the Land Rover around an enormous yellow earth-moving machine which bore a metal plaque along the side in English: '*A Present of the Government of the People's Republic of China*'. Next, Wrighton found himself clutching the dashboard as the nose of the van lurched skywards and they climbed a mound of earth. He kept his own counsel, resolving only to jump out if the river were on the other side of the hillock. The car slithered over the bank and before them lay a dual carriageway stretching off into the distance. To be precise, it was the foundation for a dual carriageway, because, clearly, the road had not yet been built. The characteristic orange Dhaka bricks had been laid edgeways on, zigzag across the road from one kerb to the other. Thousands of bricks. The pattern gave the impression of driving along an enormous tweed belt.

'New road, sir,' Oggi announced, proudly.

'Well yes... but... it's not finished, Oggi. Where does it go?' At either side of the road he could see rollers and other bits of machinery skulking under tarpaulins. Wrighton knew that he was reacting like a hide-bound Western engineer but he could not help it.

'Shittagong road sir.'

A quarter of a mile further up, the foundation turned back to soft earth for a stretch and then the brick began again and more traffic joined them from a nearby bus stand. Soon the mist was heavy with diesel fumes and dust and Wrighton could neither see nor get his bearings. Buses churned past them in the opposite direction, three-wheeled baby taxis buzzed around like wasps, sometimes bouncing a wheel from the ground when they encountered a portion of surface not yet furnished with bricks. Wrighton decided that he would be philosophical about it all and sit back and just let it happen. Perhaps he could try to catch up on his sleep.

He had enjoyed little sleep that night. He had left the Hardwicke's at about one o'clock and jostled home, perched upon the back of a rickshaw. He had purposefully chosen one sporting the regulation hurricane lamp swinging from the back axle. He merely hoped that it was not filled with petrol as they sometimes were. The knowledge that you were trundling along with a Molotov cocktail suspended directly beneath your bottom and only a few inches above the road surface, assisted greatly in concentrating all your faculties on self-preservation.

He thought back to the Hardwickes. An unusual couple. Geoff was obviously bent on struggling up through the Diplomatic Service as far as he could go and although Wrighton could have no real idea of what his job consisted, he knew, somehow, that he was good at it. He had that air about him.

And Sandra? Well he wasn't quite sure what she did with her daytimes. Did she do any more painting? He could certainly not broach the subject after the last embarrassing discussion. Apart from that, she obviously wanted to learn to dance because she had paid rapt and intense attention to what Wrighton had taught her and had wanted to practise it until she was sure that she had got it right.

That was why he had been so late away from the house. Geoff had gone to bed at about midnight, leaving them to sort out the quarter turn in the foxtrot. It had been funny feeling a woman moving against him after so many years. He never thought of it in a sexual way, dancing wasn't like that. He derived his pleasure partly from arranging the sequence of steps to fit the shape of the floor, partly from the thrill of attempting something and finally getting it right. It was a straightforward, common-sense, working relationship. Somebody had to lead and decide which steps to do otherwise the whole idea was unworkable. It fell neatly into his nice, tidy, engineer's mind.

He thought it a little immodest to admit even to himself that he had been pleased with his performance on the previous evening but in the secrecy of his own mind he allowed himself that little luxury. Despite not having danced since... well, since he'd got married, really, he found that he had not lost the control of his body, the balance, the poise and the rhythm. Obviously he was a little rusty on the more complicated steps but they would not be attempting those for some while, if ever. He felt that he had acquitted himself quite adequately considering that he was having to teach the woman's steps, which were, of course, different from the man's. He smiled to himself in contentment, then stopped quickly, feeling guilty. Guilty of smugness and pride.

He suddenly jerked upright as the car squeaked to a halt. He had been dozing. He peered through the grey, dusty, throng, milling in front of them.

'What is it Oggi?'

'Ferry ghat saheb.'

'How long will we have to wait, do you know?'

'Ferry unloading now saheb.'

Hooting and whistling up the gravelly slip came a killer bus covered inside and out with passengers like flies on a sticky bun. The object of its anger was a rickshaw whose puller had dismounted in order to push his rickshaw up the slope. In the back sat the largest Bengali man that Wrighton had ever seen. He sat serenely unaware of the tumult as his scrawny puller's bare feet skidded and scraped on the loose surface, fighting vainly for a purchase. Around the bus crowded men carrying on their heads shallow baskets piled high with bunches of bananas, wrapped in green sacking. Wrighton was certain that he would never know the answer but it amused him to speculate as to why there seemed to be as many men waiting to board the ferry with bananas as had just disembarked with bananas. It seemed a funny way to do trade.

Eventually the buses, lorries, rickshaws, jeeps and beggars no longer straggled up from the river and Oggi let off the handbrake and rolled down to the water's edge. The ferry was of a style to be found throughout the world – a simple pontoon with a ramp at both ends and machinery accommodation set into the sides. Wrighton's Land Rover was pulled out of the queue by an oily man in an oily lunghi who appeared to be in charge, and pushed to the point of the bows so that it would be the first to disembark. Wrighton was pleased although he did not really like jumping the queue but as soon as the real reason became apparent, he felt mollified. The greasy man banged the bonnet and tapped the headlights. Without a word, Oggi turned them on. Wrighton's Land Rover was being used as fog lights to avoid colliding with the ferry which they would cross upstream. The greasy man had obviously realised that a World Bank Land Rover would be sure to have good strong working headlamps and not the Halloween lanterns of a killer bus.

Roughly two thirds of the way across the river, a rusting brown hulk loomed up dead ahead. With a clanking of machinery and a screeching of metal the two ferries veered off and slid past each other, ghostlike in the wispy grey light. Then they were alone again on the water and Wrighton could feel a slight unease creeping over him. He looked over the bonnet of the van at the grey-green mirror that they were rippling as they slid across like a phantom barge on a lake in some Camelot legend. Occasional knots of bladder-floating river weed drifted slowly past, giving them the impression of sailing across the top of a drowned forest. Wrighton began to count the screws on the dashboard. Deep green water. One, two, another one down there by the steering column. Bottomless, dark, smothering, all-pervading, deep water. There was no apparent current. Still waters run deep.

Suddenly Oggi blasted his horn and flashed his lights up and down on a pile standing up out of the water. More clanking of machinery and screeching of metal and then they were grinding ashore.

At the side of the slip sat a forlorn killer bus, windowless and streaked with the stains of dried mud. It was curious to see an empty bus and curious to see dried mud up to the roof line. Oggi glanced at it briefly as he let in the clutch and sent the back wheels spinning gravel. He stopped and banged the car into four wheel drive and they lurched sure-footedly up the slip.

There had been something in the newspaper.... Wrighton searched his memory. One of those afternoons when Tuppin had been reading aloud snippets of the newspaper to them as they sat about drinking tea. He remembered. A killer bus had missed the ferry. That was what Tuppin and Bell had laughed about, missing the ferry. In England when you missed the ferry it meant that you arrived after it had left. In Bangladesh when you missed the ferry it meant just that, you aimed at it and missed and fell into the river. Most of the passengers had been trapped and drowned and this had been an occasion not of 'driver is absconding' but 'driver is drowning'. Wrighton shuddered as they left the ferry ghat and the salvaged bus behind them.

The afternoon that Tuppin had read about the drowned bus they had also exposed the scandal of the light bulbs which had so infuriated Bell and Tuppin but which, to their intense annoyance, Wrighton had merely found amusing.

It had started quietly several days before, when the light bulb in Bell's bathroom had expired. He threw it away and told Moussi to nip up the road to the bazaar and get another one. Moussi had asked for the eight taka, Bell was very insistent that the others should know that he had paid something out for the running of the house. At that time, Bell still owed Wrighton five hundred taka but he had a remarkable facility to make his eight taka, which was in reality, Wrighton's, sound far more important than the five hundred. So the light bulb had been replaced and all was fine and dandy, till the following afternoon when, on turning on the wall lamps in the communal room, Tuppin had discovered that another one of the bulbs was unlit. Moussi was sent on the same errand. Over the next few days, several more bulbs expired and each time, Moussi was sent up to the bazaar to buy a replacement. The phenomenon of the sequential failing of the light bulbs had intrigued Wrighton enough for him to mention it to Mac Macleod at the office. Mac had laughed.

'Give them one dead bulb and they'll re-equip the entire house,' he had exclaimed obliquely.

'I don't follow that.'

'Old Mossy, or whatever his name is, is ringing the changes. He's pulling the wool over your eyes. He just wants a bit of pocket money that's all.'

'What do you mean? What's that got to do with the bulbs?'

'Well you pay him for them don't you?'

'Yes, but he has to buy them.'

'Not "them" – "it",' Mac laughed. 'There's only one bulb.'

'There can't be, we've had four... no, five bulbs go in as many days.'

'No you haven't, but you've certainly paid for five. Look, this is how it works. You're sitting at home and plop! the light bulb expires. In comes Mossy–'

'Moussi.'

'Right. In comes Moussi and removes dead bulb, takes the proffered eight taka and beetles off to the bazaar to buy a new bulb which he installs. O.K.?'

'Yes.'

'What does he do with the old bulb?'

'Well he throws it away, of course.'

'Wrong! He keeps it. Whilst master is out at work, he removes a functioning bulb and replaces it with the dead one. Master comes home and sends him out to buy another bulb. Moussi pockets the eight taka and goes for a stroll around the block returning with the bulb he removed earlier in the day but wrapped in the carton from yesterday's new bulb. He replaces the bulb and, magic, the light works. Then he carefully stores away the dead bulb till the morrow.'

'But that means that we are paying him eight taka a day to remove and replace the same bulb!' Wrighton exclaimed indignantly and then, seeing the funny side of it, started to laugh.

'The only way around it is to smash the dead bulb,' Mac explained.

'Or mark it so that you can count how many times it has been used.'

And that was what he did. Without consulting the others, next time that a bulb had apparently failed he had scribed his initials on the brass. Two days later, when Bell and Tuppin were still scratching their heads over this epidemic of bulb failure, trying to blame the current surges or the humidity, Wrighton had shown them the bulb and explained the principle. The effect had been theatrical. Bell had stormed out after Moussi, his face contorted with red rage and Tuppin had sat down to calculate how much they had been swindled.

'Oh come on!' Wrighton had cajoled them both. 'It's all a bit of fun. We've been had and it's only cost us eight taka a day.'

'You could have told us before,' Tuppin grumbled.

'I didn't know before.'

He found that he was smiling to himself again and looked about the car surreptitiously to make sure that Oggi had not seen him.

'How much further to Laksham?' This was where they were going to meet their local surveyor, Abra Huda.

'Two, maybe three hours saheb.'

Wrighton nodded and settled down to the jolting of the car as it bounded along the patchy tarmac. He felt very, very tired. Soon he was dozing fitfully despite the rough road.

They bowled into Laksham at about eleven o'clock. The bright yellow sun lit up the clouds of dust which billowed from their wheels and engulfed the shanty shops lining the street. Laksham was an important railway junction, this was where the lines from Noakhali and Hajigonj met the main line from Dhaka to Chittagong. The station yard was scattered with black, hissing, snorting steam locomotives and black and brown goats. There were more goats than locomotives.

Standing under the shade of a fig tree by the station buildings, Abra Huda awaited them. He was dressed in the baggy white pajama of a civil servant of the last century. In his hand he flourished a rolled up chart, to prove his profession to the passers-by and his servant carried his brief case and the black umbrella.

Wrighton had written the man's name down in his notebook to ensure that he made no mistake. Abra Huda. He wanted to call him Abracadabra and expected him to suddenly pull a rabbit from the furled umbrella.

He climbed stiffly from the car, easing the numbness of his buttocks with the palms of his hands. Abra Huda stood under the tree and waited for him. Wrighton realised in retrospect that this was, in a way, a rather cheeky demonstration of Huda's belief in his own importance and he could feel Oggi scowling at him behind his back as he walked over to the surveyor. By that one gesture, he had lowered himself in his driver's eyes. The man would still display the outward signs of respect but deep inside him he would despise Wrighton's weakness. Abra Huda, however, beamed at him from his fig tree.

'Good Morning,' he exclaimed. 'You are being Mr. Wrighton.'

'That's right. You must be–'

Abra Huda fumbled in the recesses of his cotton and drew out a pasteboard card.

'My card.'

Wrighton sucked in his cheeks viciously and took the proffered card. It read, *'Mr. Abra Huda. BSc. Chittagong (failed), Chattered Sruveyor'*.

'Ah yes, Mr. Huda. Pleased to meet you.'

They shook hands, Huda beaming about him at the crowd as he demonstrated how well he could communicate with these white people even down to the custom of shaking hands. Wrighton thanked providence that he was wearing dusty grey trousers as he secretly rubbed the grease from the palm of his hand. They walked out into the violent sun and Huda spread out his chart onto the bonnet of the Land Rover.

'Now,' said Wrighton. 'I want to check the survey points from here,' he tapped a point just outside the town, 'out to Mirasharai.'

'Impossible.'

'Why do you say that?'

'From here to here?'

'That's right.'

'Impossible. That is fifty miles distant.'

Wrighton glanced quickly at the scale of the chart and made a rapid calculation.

'Well then, we had better get started.'

Abra Huda motioned to his servant to climb in beside the driver and then pointed his stomach at the Land Rover and squeezed his greasy bulk into the back. Wrighton slipped in alongside him. Oggi started the motor and turned around awaiting instruction.

'Let's start at your control point at Laksham, shall we?'

'If you wish.' He gabbled some directions to Oggi who sullenly let in the clutch and drove off.

'Tell me, Mr. Huda, how many surveyors have you used on this stretch?'

'I have a team of four. One on plane table, one on tape and one on pole.'

'And the fourth?'

'Umbrella.'

'Of course.'

'How is Mr. Havering? Well, I hope?'

'Yes, I believe so. He certainly looks well.'

'He is being your boss isn't it?'

'Yes, in a sense he is my boss. He tells me what to do.' Wrighton laughed. 'Who is your boss?'

'Mr. Abra Huda has no boss.'

'That's nice. How long have you been working on these surveys for the pipeline?' Wrighton knew the answer to this because he had read the file quickly before departing from the office. He had not understood why the surveying had had to be subcontracted and fragmented so much. It was almost as if Havering did not want any one person to obtain the overall view. Havering had explained, however, that it was all to do with the policy of the World Bank and the employment of indigenous experts.

'This is our second section, Mr. Wrighton. We finished it just before the rains this year. Right on target.'

If that claim was correct, it would have been the only thing to have achieved its target this year, Wrighton thought to himself.

'Aah. Here we are, Mr. Wrighton. We started from the Laksham valve station.'

The car squeezed through a wire gateway into a compound of bare earth and patchy scrub. At the top end of the compound, Wrighton could see shining, the pipes and valves of the gas pipeline which represented the furthermost reach of actual pipe. From here onwards they had about eighty miles of line to survey and lay. The car grumbled up the gentle slope between two sentry-like lines of the most antiquated and bizarre ironmongery. Cable-lifting bulldozers nestled alongside diabolical tar boilers mounted on cast iron wheels. There was a chain-steered scarifier, its blades chipped and pitted, an Aveling and Porter steam roller with several of its vital portions missing and a huge Chevrolet truck of pre-war vintage, its chassis broken by its amateurish conversion to a tank lorry, was leaning against a small green crawler-tractor.

'This is Highways Depot,' Abra Huda said.

Wrighton nodded in acknowledgement. Back in the U.K. it would have been called a scrap yard.

They clambered out towards where the red and silver pipes were glowering at them from behind their sturdy protection of angle iron and galvanised chain link fencing.

'Do you have any trouble keeping this in condition?' Wrighton rattled the fence with his finger.

'Nobody is wanting this type of fence,' Abra Huda explained. 'So it is quite safe.'

Wrighton looked at the tangle of pipes. It was a long time since he had seen an actual valve station in the metal rather than as a symbol on his drawing board. Two eight-inch pipes arching over in parallel and disappearing into the mass. They must be the bypass valves and they would indicate the direction of the pipeline. He looked across the compound. Yes, they were pointing vaguely south east, so that was basically correct. He studied the tangle of metal again. It didn't look like this on paper. So, there were two pipes, fourteen inch, two bypass valves, and two 'T's ready for pressure reducers to be fitted for the domestic distribution of the gas. So what was that great U bend of pipe ending in a pressure joint and hinged door? It didn't lead anywhere. It was not pointing in the correct direction. He searched his memory about pipeline procedure. It must be something to do with the laying of the pipe. Then he remembered. After laying and welding a length of pipe it was pressure-tested and then the swarf and burr was cleaned off the inside by sending down a plug of metal called a 'pig'. This thing would hurtle along the pipe, cleaning it as it went and then bang into the dead end of pipe here to be unloaded. This was what they called a 'pig trap'. So that pipe from the top of the trap lead back to the downward side of the valve to allow the gas trapped by the pig to escape. He nodded confirmation of this theory to himself.

'Right then, Abra Huda, where is your control point–' He glanced at the chart. '–number thirty two?'

'All very correct, Mr. Wrighton. Tickety boo.'

He waddled across the compound and stood, examining a piece of ground at his feet.

'It is here, Mr. Wrighton. Number L 32. L is for Laksham.'

Wrighton carefully lifted his theodolite from the back of the van and set it up over the miniature concrete monument, taking more time than was strictly necessary to centre the plumb and settle the bubble. He wanted them to see that he was serious and did things meticulously. If they saw him working shoddily then they would also. He squinted down the sight.

'Where is L thirty three then?'

The surveyor pointed to a discreet hummock.

'Send out the tape and pole please then and I'll just get a sighting on this one.'

Abra Huda gave out his orders and one man shouldered the pole and began to lollop off across the scrub, the other unrolled the tape.

'You are not doing this to all the points?' Abra Huda enquired. His anxiety showed considerably. Wrighton wondered whether it was because he had something to hide or whether just the thought of such a task frightened him.

'Are they all correct then, Abra Huda?' he asked casually as he bent over the sight again.

'All absolutely correct and tickety boo.'

'You sight-fixed them all did you?'

'Every one.'

'You, not someone else.'

'Every one done by Abra Huda, chartered surveyor.'

'None interpolated?'

'My word no!' he exclaimed at such a sacrilegious suggestion.

'Not even the difficult ones?'

'No sir.'

Wrighton sighed gently and straightened up.

'You know, Abra Huda, I'd rather you tell me if you have interpolated any. After all, it's a long and complicated survey to do with a team of four.'

'I swear to you upon the Koran–'

'That's not necessary,' Wrighton assured him quickly and then bent to the task of taking a sight. He stood carefully braced, feet apart, careful not to lean on the theodolite, many a good reading had been distorted by a tired surveyor leaning on the theodolite, he was not going to commit any such mistake. He looked through the sight again. The pole had been replaced by a greyish blue furry blob. He looked up.

'Could you get that gawping villager out of the way please?' Abra Huda sent his umbrella bearer to shoo the man away. Wrighton bent back to the sight and then straightened up almost immediately. 'And his confounded goat!' he shouted. 'Of all the places to stand!' he mumbled to himself in disgust.

He made the final adjustment, took the reading and then compared the two sets of co-ordinates, his and Abra Huda's.

'Nothing to worry about Abra Huda. They are slightly different but well within the margin of error. Good Man. Let's get on to...' He looked at the chart. '... what about L forty six?'

'Yes sir, good idea sir.' Abra Huda agreed enthusiastically, patently relieved that Wrighton did not intend to attempt to resurvey the entire fifty miles in a day and a half. He was never certain what these *burra sahebs* thought themselves capable of.

They packed up, Wrighton not allowing anybody to dismantle the theodolite but himself and then they bumped out of the compound and off up the hot dusty road to their next stop.

It was a long, tiring day for Wrighton. One sighting succeeded another. The bumpy ride in the car next to the greasy Abra Huda; Oggi bristling with indignation at the curt directions he was given and Wrighton, power-less to change the situation since he did not know the area. Then the arrival at the next point and the stamping around in the grass and brush, looking for the miniature concrete monument over which to set up; the calibration of the theodolite becoming more and more difficult as the day wore on, sweat dripping into his eyes, fingers slipping on the screw; the occasional pair of buzzards circling high in the blue sky; the ubiquitous villagers popping up out of the ditches to stand and gawp with dreary, unfocussed eyes and the slack jaws of ignorance; the comparison of the two sightings; Abra Huda's anxious glance at Wrighton's calculations and his nervous declining of the offer to check them over and always, infallibly, consistently, persistently at the back of Wrighton's mind was the weight of Sandra Hardwicke in his arms and the perfume in her hair.

Wrighton looked down at his figures again, puffed out his cheeks and expelled the air noisily. His head was aching, his eyes were dry with the glare and dust and now his mind was wandering off the job. Oggi was squatting in the shade of the van, smoking a K2 through his bunched fist, Abra Huda was magnificent under the shade of his umbrella but a little soiled, like some cracked Indian god in a country temple.

Wrighton scratched his head with his pencil and looked across the dry gully to the red and white pole. The man tending it had propped it up and was squatting at the side of it, awaiting a signal to show that he was needed in position again.

Clink, clink,clink, down the track came the unmistakable sound of Coca Cola bottles rattling together. Wrighton rubbed the dust from the corner of his eyes. Clink, clink, clink. The urchin approached them surely, limping grotesquely from the weight of the galvanised pail that he was hauling along. Wrighton beckoned the boy over to him, he believed that enterprise should be rewarded as far as was possible and this poor mite must have walked about three miles with that bucket of ice and Coca Cola. It was a mystery how the boy had known that they were there for it was not coincidence that he should have come along that road.

'Come on, let's all have a drink. Take this one out to the pole and have this one yourself,' he addressed the tape man. 'Here you are Abra Huda, sink that.' He pushed a bottle into the surveyor's podgy paw and gave another to his umbrella man. 'How much taka little man?' he said to the urchin.

The boy looked into the bucket and then up at Wrighton whilst his thumb counted rapidly up the joints of his fingers and his bottom lip moved in calculation.

'Twenty four taka boss.'

Abra Huda immediately directed a torrent of Bengali at the lad who despite his ten years, stood firm by Wrighton.

'Hey, hey! What's going on, Abra Huda? What's all this about?'

'This boy is a teeth. Proper price for Coca Cola is tree taka fifty. He say four taka. I will beat him.'

'Just a minute, Abra Huda, don't worry, I'm paying, see.' He took out a bundle of small taka notes.

'The boy is a teeth. It is shocking!' Abra Huda asserted and erupted again in a bundle of Bengali invective.

The boy looked nervously from Wrighton to Abra Huda.

'I think that four taka is a fair price, Abra Huda. Where does he come from? Could you ask him please?'

'He comes from the town three miles up the road.'

'Well don't you think that for walking three miles with a bucket full of ice and bottles, he could be permitted to raise his prices a little? I do.'

'He is a bad boy.'

'I don't care, he's brought us cold drinks.'

Wrighton gave the boy twenty five taka and sent him on his way, then he flopped down at the side of Oggi in the shade of the van and finished his final boiled egg and peanut butter sandwich, rinsing down the last mouthful with a sense of tremendous achievement. He never wanted to have to eat that concoction again.

The sun was already beginning to adopt an orangey hue prior to its dive towards the dusty horizon when Wrighton discovered the fault. They were about sixteen kilometres from the projected site of the Mirasharai valve station, the one which had been carelessly misplaced by a kilometre and he was taking a sighting. His back and shoulders were aching with the repetitive bending and his left eye, the one he used to sight with, was beginning to twitch.

'Send out the pole,' he had commanded wearily and straightened up to await the positioning. After more fussing about than usual the pole was still not fixed. He turned to Abra Huda, irritably.

'Where is the point they are looking for, do you know?'

'Well it's out there... somewhere...' He waved his arm towards a drained paddy, along the edge of which ran a curious thicket of dried sticks.

Wrighton bit his lip to control himself.

'Could you possibly go and show them please or we shall still be doing this at nightfall and that pole isn't luminous,' he added sarcastically. 'After all, you did fix these points didn't you?'

He realised that this was not a fair comment since no surveyor could hope to remember the position of all his little concrete bench marks but Wrighton was tired and irritated by this man's pompous uselessness and was tried almost beyond measure by the heat and dust.

He also knew that he should have slept more on the previous evening and he was a little worried that Sandra Hardwicke kept creeping into his thoughts. There was obviously nothing untowards in this, he assured himself but it was a little distracting to be thinking of her when one should have been thinking about co-ordinates.

Abra Huda looked as if he was going to argue but the sight of Wrighton frowning at the chart decided him not to tempt the gods and he waddled off across the paddy, venting his feelings on his servant whom he cuffed for not keeping him completely shaded by the umbrella.

Wrighton watched the sun slowly turn three quarters orange whilst the Bengalis in the paddy wandered around apparently unable to find the monument.

'Oggi!' The driver looked up. 'Don't let anybody touch this,' he ordered, pointing at the theodolite.

Oggi stood up importantly and nodded.

Wrighton started off across the field, the dry rice stubble crackling under his sandals. He was just plain angry now. The sun was orange, it would start to plunge any minute now. He stamped towards the Bengalis who were now chatting heatedly.

'Well?' he demanded. 'We can't stay here all night.'

'It should be here,' Abra Huda explained.

Wrighton took the chart from his hands.

'That line there is the five metre contour.' He looked up at the terrain. 'Which comes about half way up that bank over there, doesn't it?'

Abra Huda nodded sideways and for the first time, it riled Wrighton.

'Do you mean "yes"?'

'Yes.'

'O.K. Well it's quite simple.' He looked at the chart again. 'The point is... over there, behind those sticks.' He began walking towards them and immediately a babble broke out behind him. He stopped and looked around.

'Not to go there sir.'

'Not to go there? Why not?'

'Sacred burial ground sir.'

Wrighton looked again at the straggle of sticks stuck into the ground.

'What? That?' he demanded incredulously, 'but you put the survey point in the middle of it. How did you do that if you couldn't go in there?'

Abra Huda gabbled off at the other two for some seconds and then one of them pointed to the side of the burial ground.

'We have remembered. It is here,' Abra Huda said and followed the pole bearer across the paddy.

They stood looking at the monument that had been so hard to find. Wrighton, Abra Huda, his umbrella man, the tape man and the pole man. Wrighton was thinking very carefully. The others were fidgeting. At last he formulated his questions, calmly.

'Abra Huda, as the surveyor...'

'Yes Mr. Wrighton?'

'Could you explain to me why this point is positioned approximately one hundred and twenty metres to the north of its plotted location on the chart?'

'You see Mr. Wrighton, it is sacred burial ground, must not be disturbed.'

Wrighton decided not to ask why, then, he had not plotted short and sighted across.

'Abra Huda, you say that you are a trained surveyor...'

'Bsc. Shittagong sir.'

'You must know that to put your bench mark a hundred and twenty metres from its plot is an absolute nonsense. No wonder Mirasharai is a kilometre off plot. With the compounded error over the remaining fifteen kilometres or so, we're lucky it is still in Bangladesh,' he shouted angrily.

'Not Abra Huda's fault Mr. Wrighton,' he announced sensationally. 'This is Babu's plot.'

'Which one is Babu?' Wrighton turned to look at Huda's assistants but as he did so he knew that none of them was Babu. 'Abra Huda, you didn't do this plot did you? That's why you didn't know where it was.'

'It was raining.' He grinned sycophantically.

'But you told me that you had finished before the rains,' Wrighton retorted. It made no sense to him. 'Did you or did you not do this plot?'

'Babu wanted to try.'

'Who is Babu?'

'My assistant.'

'What? One of these here?' Wrighton examined the entourage.

Abra Huda laughed easily at what was obviously a joke.

'Oh no Mr. Wrighton! You know he is not here.'

'Well where....' Wrighton stopped to collect his thoughts and realised that he was being led inexorably away from the truth that he was searching. 'Did you do this plot?'

'It was good practise for Babu.'

'Did you do this plot?'

'It was raining, I cannot be everywhere.'

'Did you do this plot?'

'Babu is very assiduous student. Works very hard.'

'Did you do this plot?'

Wrighton could feel his fists clenching and he very much feared that if his question was not soon answered he would smack the grotesque, self-satisfied, smug face of Mr. Abra Huda.

'Mr. Wrighton, you must have some discretion.'

Before he knew what was happening, Wrighton felt his hand snake out towards Abra Huda and grab his shirt lapels in one fist. He dragged the startled gargoyle of a face close to his, bulging eyeball to eyeball and hissed through his teeth.

'Mr. Abra Huda, you must answer my question. NOW!' He shouted the last word and twisted the man's shirt so that it tightened across his throat. He could hear the servants muttering and shuffling their feet but he was not worried. In his present state he felt that if they wanted to start anything he could make mincemeat out of all of them. The more the merrier. 'Did you do that plot?'

'Mr. Wrighton you are hurting me,' Huda protested. Wrighton twisted the shirt tighter. The Bengali's eyes stared ludicrously. Wrighton raised his right fist. 'No, no!' the man shrieked. 'I did not do it. I was not there that day. I sent Babu,' he gabbled. 'Babu did it, not Abra Huda. Babu made mistake.'

Wrighton released the man, disgusted with him.

'You could have told me that five minutes ago.'

Now that he had regained his distance, Abra Huda began to re-establish his position with the vigour of an eternal survivor.

'I protest against you man-handling me. I have three witnesses here and I shall–'

'I asked you earlier...' Wrighton ignored the blustering but was glad of the distraction so that he could hide his shaking hands, '...if you had done all the plots yourself and you said that you had. You were even going to swear on your Koran weren't you? It wasn't true was it?'

'I didn't do this plot, Babu did this one.' Abra Huda repeated the hard-won truth as if hoping that its repetition would placate this mad Englishman.

'Is that all you have got to say? Not even, "Sorry Mr. Wrighton for wasting fifteen miles of survey time"?'

Wrighton gazed with simmering anger at the corpulent Bengali standing brazenly before him and he realised that the man was untouchable, unless...

'Have you been paid for this survey yet?' he shot at the man. Anxiety shadowed Abra Huda's face. Wrighton grunted with the satisfaction of seeing his chance shot hit the powder magazine. 'I'll make sure that you don't get paid for the last fifteen kilometres of this survey, Abra Huda, and if I can do it I'll make sure that Consolidated unilaterally renegotiates the fee for the first part of the survey based on a taka for taka reduction to cover the cost of checking your work. You are a liar and a rogue.' He pointed his finger menacingly at the fat, contorted face of the surveyor. 'Call yourself a surveyor? You won't work for us again.' He turned to his driver. 'Oggi! Take me to Fraser's Rest House!'

Wrighton sat in the quickening gloom of the verandah watching the moths beat themselves stupid against the mosquito screen. He had been thirsty when he had arrived at the rest house but when the servant had brought the tea he had found that his hands were shaking so much that the tea cup had rattled annoyingly on the saucer and although he was alone in the house, the tinkling noise had served only to fuel his irritation. He had left the tea. He glanced down at it now. Nearly an hour had passed and it would be tepid but he reached out for the cup, relieved that he could now grasp it steadily. An hour had passed in reflection, in amazed self-analysis mixed with disbelief. He had not done those things! Grabbed a man by the shirt? Threatened him with a clenched fist? It was all a mistake. It had been someone else He had never hit anybody in his life. He wouldn't know how to.

He took a small sip of his tea. He swallowed the first mouthful as delicately as he could but it still plummeted down his gullet like a slug down a plastic drainpipe.

What had happened to him? He had never known himself to become so uncontrollably angry. In his professional life he had from time to time encountered worthless colleagues who had buried their inefficiency beneath a crust of provocative insolence and yet he had always managed to deal with them. But the sight of that fat, greasy, smug....

He shook himself again. This was a most uncharitable perspective to take of a fellow human creature. He could almost hear his father talking. It was most uncharitable. They may not be Baptists like us, or even Christians, but they were all made in God's image and they all worshipped him in their own ways, peculiar to themselves. It was not done to look down on them. 'But even so ...' he could hear himself half protesting to his conscience...

The Rest House at Fraser's was planted on a good tarmac road which led up from the gate office, through the corner of the tea garden to a small compound of administrative bungalows dotted along just below the crest of the rise. Most of the European-run estates maintained a guest house of some sorts to entertain travellers or visiting staff. It meant that accommodation was readily available when needed and enabled the Europeans on the staff to occasionally see some different faces. They rarely had time to drive or train down to Dhaka so they enticed people working in the area to stay with them. Wrighton was not the first and would not be the last person to be thankful to discover the proximity of a tea garden at the end of a difficult day. The alternative was a Bengali hotel which would be filthy dirty and bug-ridden. The certainty of a probably clean bath, followed by an almost palatable meal and then perhaps a game of whist or a quiet smoke or tipple had prolonged well into the twentieth century a system of hospitality that should have died out with the last visiting magistrate.

He had seen a couple of estate workers in the gate office. They had looked at him with interest, a new white face was always worth a diversion, but by the time the clerk had sorted out the Rest House accommodation and he had paid and signed the register, ordered dinner, ordered breakfast, given instructions to Oggi as to the time he was to be picked up in the morning, the two estate workers had grabbed a roll of paper from a teleprinter and banged out through the back screen door to a battered Land Rover and driven away. In retrospect, this sympathised with his mood. He did not want others around, he wanted time to reflect, to think and to sleep. Especially sleep. They were missing nothing by not enjoying his company tonight.

From the verandah he could see the lights of the office at the bottom of the drive and the occasional headlight flick by on the main road. Across, opposite on the gentle rise which was the twin of his, he could see a cluster of lights, greenish in hue, probably propane lamps amongst the trees. There must be a little village up there somewhere or perhaps it was accommodation for the native workers. He was not sure. As he watched, a vivid blue electric arc flashed amongst the lamps as some enterprise plugged in to the overhead mains electricity by using the illicit bent-wire-on-a-bamboo-pole technique that was widespread throughout the country and sapped half the nations's electricity for no revenue. He drained his cup and looked at his watch. It was nearly a quarter to seven.

Flickering up the drive came a propane lamp. 'That must be my omelette,' he said as he got up and went in to the dining room, sending a pair of geckos scuttling boggle-eyed up the wall in fright. 'That's alright lads,' he addressed them, 'you help yourself to my mossies. Have as many as you like, I shan't be needing them.'

The silent servant bobbed in with the tray of food and set it out wordlessly on the table before him. As Wrighton began his meal the man quite unconcernedly took Wrighton's grip into the bedroom and laid out his pyjamas and turned back the sheet. Wrighton started in surprise at the man's boldness and thought that he should be worried for the man's honesty but then he realised that if the man intended to rob him, he would do it some time during the night, when Wrighton was really asleep and when it could never be traced back to him except circumstantially.

The next morning Wrighton awoke late, at about seven, with a thick head. At some time during the night the air conditioning unit had tripped out but in his exhausted state he had slept on and now he was wringing wet. He staggered into the shower and sluiced himself down in cold water and then cut himself as he shaved.

As he drank his tea out on the verandah he felt drained. He should have felt invigorated, full of zest, recharged but now he was just stale.

'Anyone home?' a voice called out in the bungalow.

'On the verandah!' Wrighton shouted back in surprise. It did not occur to Wrighton as it apparently had not to his visitor, that perhaps he wanted to be left alone.

A short squat man in khaki Bermuda shorts and a check shirt rolled in. Wrighton immediately put him down as a seaman. He just looked like one.

'Mornin',' he said. 'My name's Sandy.' He held out his hand. 'I saw you come in last night so I thought I would look you up.'

'Thanks, I'm Wrighton. I was only here overnight. Do you want some tea?' Wrighton pointed to the pot.

'Can't abide the stuff.'

'But... don't you... I mean, you work in a tea garden? I suppose it's like people in chocolate factories not liking chocolate.'

The visitor pulled out a chair with a horny hand and installed himself comfortably.

'I'm not a tea worker. Good God no!' He laughed easily. 'I'm a sparky. I'm rewiring the three phase.' He jerked his head in the direction of a line pole from which Wrighton could now see dangling a black cable. 'Been out here three months. You work out here?'

'I've only been sent out temporarily, for about six months. I work for... a gas engineering company.' The man would not recognise the name of Consolidated. 'We're laying, or trying to lay a pipeline. Do you do a lot of this sort of work abroad?'

'First time I've been out of England. Practically the first time I've left Durham,' the man admitted proudly. 'The missus was a bit miffed when I left, but all the kids have grown up and left home so, what the hell?'

'Yes, mine was a bit... er miffed as well.' Wrighton sipped his tea.

'Another month and I reckon I'll be finished, then it will be bye-bye Bangladesh and back on the big silver bird.'

'How many are you doing this job then?'

'Only me. On me todd. I did have a lad. You know, a wog lad.' The man used the term without nastiness. 'They gave him to me, you know. A sort of gopher but I booted him out. Caught him nicking cable. Can't have that. It's naughty.'

'It's pretty widespread though. A sort of national pastime.'

'Not off the bloody pole during the night after I've spent all day putting it up. The bugger knew that the power was off.'

'Yes, I suppose that is a bit greedy.' Wrighton tried to hide a smile.

'I'd be here for the rest of me life running the lines if I let him carry on.'

'Yes I suppose you would. Aren't you worried that they'll turn on the juice whilst you are up there knitting?'

'You don't get as old as me without worrying about things like that before they happen.' He fished in a leather satchel and pulled out two ceramic fuses, each one the size of a paperback book. 'And I've padlocked the switchbox in case they try to stick a bolt across the terminals instead of these.'

Wrighton could only marvel at the man's wisdom but then, he admitted, if your life depended on it, you made doubly and triply sure.

If your life depended on it. Perhaps that was where he had gone wrong. It was just that. He had never done anything upon which his life depended. It had always been so safe. So sure. So predictable. If your life depended on it.... What would he do if he were up a pole holding two bared cables when somebody switched the power back on? No, that wasn't really a possibility. It wasn't relevant. What was he ever going to do so that his whole life depended upon its outcome? Was he ever going to see his existence hanging by a thread? He doubted it.

'That's your truck isn't it?' Sandy interrupted his thoughts. 'A World Bank project, eh?'

'How do you know?'

'The colour. The only Land Rovers in Bangladesh that are that colour are World Bank vehicles. Someone told me that. I forget who.'

'Oh.'

They ambled outside into the sun.

'Bloody weather,' the electrician said. 'Too hot for pole work. That's why I get out at five. Get some work in before me napper gets fried.'

'My sainted aunt!' Wrighton exclaimed. 'What's that?' Sandy looked at him, bemused. 'Well I mean I know it's a swimming pool but, well, that's a surprise. I didn't know it was there.'

The electrician scratched his head to hide his embarrassment. It was quite a feature of the guest house that it had a pool outside it. How could this twerp have not seen it?

'Well I suppose it would be a surprise if you fell in it,' he remarked charitably.

'I could have done, quite easily if I had gone out for a stroll last night.

Well I never.'

The electrician from Durham shouldered his satchel in a workmanlike manner. 'Been nice meeting yer, Wrighton.' He nodded towards a pole as he held out his hand, 'I've gotta get on with me monkey work . See you again sometime.' He rolled away with that curious gait that Wrighton now realised was the result of years of walking carefully to prevent his satchel from banging on his hip.

The return journey Wrighton found interesting despite the heat and the dust. Although it was practically the same route as they had taken the day before, he was now seeing more of it in broad daylight. This also meant that they were on the road at its busiest time. Wrighton had guessed that this would be the case but he had been dog tired the night before and had been willing to pay this price. Unfortunately in the heat and dust of the morn, with his unaccountably thick head added to the lassitude which assailed him, the dividend did not seem so attractive to him.

After a particularly vicious series of transverse corrugations had shaken the contents of their van and set the roof drumming, Wrighton persuaded Oggi to stop at the side whilst he stepped out to stretch his legs. He walked stiffly around to the front of the truck whilst Oggi patiently waited. Oggi did not try to understand what was going on. He just obeyed. That was all he had to do.

The driver of a bullock cart, lumbering past on creaking wooden wheels, decided that here was a spectacle and so he stopped to watch. The pair of bullocks stood flicking their ears at the sound of horns and impatient whistles but otherwise paying no heed to the blockage they were creating. A killer truck drove off the track, two wheels on dry paddy, to circumnavigate the blockage and his tailgate clipped the corner pole of the thatched roof of a wattle hut which collapsed like an empty paper bag. The truck continued, shaking off a few palm leaves as it bounced over a dry gully and then lurched back onto the road, forcing a rickshaw into the ditch. A baby taxi which had tried to follow the truck was surrounded by the crowd and harangued. From under the mound of thatch and wattle crawled a wizened woman, one hand holding the shawl to her hair. Wrighton stood there in appalled bemusement at the consequences of his wanting to restore feeling to his cramped limbs.

'Come on Oggi. Shove up, I want to drive for a bit.' He motioned to him to move across into the passenger seat and the Bengali grinned. 'I'm not joking, Oggi, I'm serious. Move over. I want to drive.'

'Master drive?'

'That's right Oggi. Master drive. Move over.'

The driver moved across the front seat without attempting to hide his reluctance.

'Master drive?'

'That's right Oggi. It can't be that difficult.'

Wrighton pushed the gear lever home and they lurched away. It took some time for him to become accustomed to the enormous steering wheel with which he seemed to need to wind up the slack before the directional effect made itself manifest on the orientation of the van but once he had steered around a few potholes and learned to give the brakes the three days' written warning that they needed to arrest the car's progress, then he began to enjoy himself.

'Are we in two wheel drive or four wheel drive?'

'Two wheel,' the man replied, glancing down at the lever to make sure.

'Right then,' Wrighton said, 'let's find some mud.' And to the obvious consternation of the Bengali who clearly thought that Wrighton had lost his mind, he drove the car carefully off the road onto a track across which a drainage ditch ran.

'How do I get through this then Oggi?'

'Master drive through?' Oggi showed the whites of his eyes as he enquired.

'That's right Oggi. It's not deep, it doesn't come up to that child's knees,' Wrighton assured him.

Oggi explained the levers.

'Four wheel drive, two wheel drive. High, low.'

'High low?'

'High low,' Oggi repeated.

Wrighton reflected for a second and then decided that it was high and low ratio for the gearbox.

'Off we go then.'

Wrighton drove under Oggi's direction, through the muddy gulley. Churning slowly and smoothly. They went through it twice in each direction until Wrighton was satisfied that he had acquired sufficient basic skill upon which he could build at a later date, should the need arise.

'Now what about climbing banks?'

'Not understanding.'

Wrighton pointed to a five foot high levee at the side of a paddy.

'How do we get up there?'

'Master go up there?' Oggi was crestfallen.

They slipped and slithered, scrabbling and tramping up the bank, turned on the top and then plummeted back down again. Wrighton's heart rose into his mouth on the descent, he was convinced that the car was going to bury its nose into the ground but it lurched up just in time.

'Well that was fun wasn't it?'

Oggi regarded his truck upon which the slimy mud was already drying crusty white and said nothing.

14

Just after a make-shift spicy lunch at a roadside food stall, there occurred an incident which though of minor interest at the time was to assume a dreadful, ponderable importance at a later date. It was something which not just Wrighton would have ample cause to remember.

Oggi was driving and Wrighton was sitting next to him, one hand on a map spread across his knees and the other twisted through the grab strap. The pipeline that Wrighton had been surveying had branched from the Sylhet-Dhaka line at Ashuganj, southwards towards Chittagong. The southern part of the Sylhet-Dhaka line was under pressure and had been in use for several years. It ran parallel to the road about a hundred yards away at this point. Sometimes it was buried, sometimes supported on concrete piers depending upon the topography. Merely from professional interest, Wrighton was following it on his chart.

'Oggi, in a couple of miles, there should be a valve station on the left here. We'll have a look at it.'

Oggi nodded but Wrighton had no way of knowing whether or not he had understood.

A few minutes later Wrighton declared helpfully,

'It should be coming up soon.'

Oggi pointed at a clump of bamboo a few hundred yards to their left and turned off the road onto a path.

'Walve station,' he said, confidently.

Wrighton raised his eyebrows in surprise but then remembered that Oggi was Havering's driver and had certainly been along the line before. Sure enough, at the end of the path he could see the chain link fencing surrounding that part of the valves and piping which protruded above ground. On the map his finger traced the inked line that represented the pipeline.

'This should be station DS 13.'

Oggi remained in the car whilst Wrighton walked slowly around the perimeter fence. A Bengali stood in the bushes watching him as if he had just alighted from a space ship. Wrighton ignored him. He was accustomed to this reaction.

The tin plate which was wired to the padlocked gate confirmed that this was DS 13. Wrighton stood for a few moments, his hands in his pockets, just perusing the pipes and valves. A boy appeared at the other side of the enclosure shielding his eyes with his forearm. These people seem to rise from the earth itself, Wrighton thought. Wherever you stopped there would always be someone within hailing distance. He looked at the pipes again. What did they think this thing was? This tangle of twisted tubes momentarily leaving the obscurity of the ground to plunge back into it again. Did they know that it was natural gas? That it was drilled in their country? He turned back.

'O.K. Oggi. Off we go.'

The car ground back onto the patchy tarred road and picked up speed again. They had not travelled but ten miles when Oggi began to slow down again. Wrighton opened his eyes, he had been dozing fitfully now that the thickness in his head had at last deserted him.

'Walve station sir?' Oggi enquired.

'Oh no, no thanks Oggi. I was only being curious. Once you've seen one, you've seen them all.'

He shut his eyes again but as the car accelerated he opened them suddenly and sat up. Valve station? He turned to Oggi.

'Stop a minute Oggi I want to look at the chart.'

Oggi pulled the car up on the verge, disturbing a cloud of white dust that slowly drifted past them as they came to rest.

'Are you sure that there is a valve station here?' Wrighton asked.

Oggi pointed across a paddy to a spinney.

'Walve station.'

Wrighton bent over the chart again. There would not be another valve station so close, not within ten miles of the other one. The next station marked on the chart, DS 12, was not for another thirty miles. He checked again. Yes, there it was. The two stations were a good forty miles apart at a quick calculation. He looked up.

'Where did you say the valve station was?'

Oggi pointed through the windscreen at the spinney.

'Master want to see walve station?'

'Yes, why not?' Wrighton's curiosity was aroused. It probably was not a valve station at all but some other works, although he could not think what at the moment. But Oggi had been out many times before with Havering who had supervised this pipeline, so he should know.

Oggi's interest did not extend as far as alighting from the car once they had reached the parsimonious shade of the copse. Wrighton went on alone. There was indeed a valve station there amongst the spindly trees.

It was quite a big one as well. It had a pig trap and a couple of gauges linked to pressure reducers that were hissing busily as the gas passed through them. It was quite an installation. Wrighton checked the gate. It was padlocked but the plate that would have divulged the station number was missing.

'I suppose one of the locals found a use for it,' Wrighton muttered. He circumambulated the fence but could find no plate at all. He returned to the car and spread the chart out on the bonnet. With his pencil he carefully marked the position of the valve station and added a question mark to it. *'Baderpur'* he wrote at the side of it, being the name of the nearest village.

'Come on Oggi, you had better take me to the next one just to be certain.'

An hour later, Wrighton was standing by another chain link fenced gate which bore the plaque 'DS 12'.

'Oh blast! They've obviously missed one out on the plan. ' It was an easy mistake to make under Havering's insistence upon fragmenting the surveying of the line. And it was an easy one to overlook, once committed. Oh well, nobody could accuse Wrighton of not giving money's worth. In two days he had discovered that the surveyor was as straight as a French horn and that someone had omitted to mark an entire valve station on the chart. He smiled grimly as he predicted whose responsibility it would be to come back up country and relabel the stations.

They rolled in to fume-laden Dhaka in the late afternoon, meticulously timed to benefit from the crippling, hooting, snarling rush hour. In fits and starts they crawled along the Saddarghat, by the rows of overladen river boats and rotting paddle ferries, by the stacks of Dhaka bricks being unloaded by hand from creaking wooden barges onto canary and blue Bedford trucks. They squeezed their way up rickshaw-jammed alleyways to rejoin the pulsing artery of the main street. Begrimed and weary, Wrighton noted the landmarks as they slipped slowly by; Kamalpur Railway station, the Stadium, the Survey of Bangladesh offices, the biscuit factory.

Not before time he saw the grinning black face of Mohammed as he opened the gate to entice Oggi into the garden.

Indoors, the thumping cacophony of one of his cohabitants' favourite music was spurting around the gaps in the warped dining room door. Mohammed carried his bag through into his bedroom.

'Thanks Mohammed. Ask Moussi for tea in the dining room for me.'

'One cup tea?'

'One cup tea.'

Wearily, but with a warm sense of achievement, he began to wash off the grime of the journey. Something was amiss. Something different. He straightened up and looked around his bathroom. Hanging on the door handle was a pair of black briefs. A woman's briefs. He picked them up and inspected them curiously. They appeared to have been hung there to dry. But who would be washing ladies' underclothes in his bathroom? Drying himself with his towel he braved the music. Bell was slouched on the sofa, eyes shut, one hand beating time upon the arm of the furniture.

'Sorry to disturb you,' Wrighton raised his voice above the noise, 'but do you know anything about these?' He held the garment aloft. Bell opened his eyes and focused on his hand. 'I found them hanging in my bathroom. And they are nothing to do with me.'

'Oh yes....I bet they belong to... whatsit... Maisie or some such thing. Some bit of fluff that Tuppin brought back last night. They used your room cos it is bigger.'

'Did they indeed?' Wrighton was angry. He marched off down the corridor, nearly knocking the cup of tea from Moussi's hands. 'Are you in there Tuppin?' He banged on Tuppin's bedroom door. There was no response. He delicately hung the garment on the outside door handle and then returned to his bedroom.

'What cheek!' was all he could trust himself to say, 'What cheek. Using my room as a... as a...' He sat down on the bed. Plop! One of his light bulbs expired.

'Home sweet home,' he sighed.

'Mr. Wrighton just said "Good Morning" to me,' Leila said as she bounced into the interpreters' cubby hole, her body still betraying the spring of a girl.

Mrs. Rosario adjusted her dark-framed spectacles on her nose and peered at Leila, expectantly. Rubena Chowdhry finished writing her sentence and then looked up.

'Mr. Wrighton said "Good Morning" to you,' she repeated flatly, unable to divine its news content. 'Is he not saying "Good Morning" to you every morning?'

'Yes.'

'So why are you coming in here...' she paused to inspect a minute gold watch on her wrist, '...late, and telling us this juicy morsel of gossip?'

'You are not in a good mood today Mrs. Chowdhry. I can see that.

Mr. Wrighton is in a good mood. He was grinning and he said to me, "Good morning Leila.." He called me Leila. "How are you today?'"

Mrs. Rosario looked from Leila across to Rubena and then back to Leila as if spectating at a tennis tournament.

'Well that is very important news,' Rubena observed emptily and bent over her work. Leila Rose made a face at her and Mrs. Rosario scowled at Leila but said nothing.

Rubena Chowdhry was thinking of Mr. Wrighton and how he had changed since he had arrived at their office. He was still meek and he was still scared of Mr. Havering but from time to time he managed to do extraordinary things. She thought of the way that he had discovered the cause of the crumbling piers. It was not Mr. Havering who had worked it out but Mr. Wrighton. She was still thinking about Mr. Wrighton when the door opened and he poked his head around into their room.

'Good morning ladies. Who is with me today?'

Leila leaned dangerously far back on her chair and consulted a timetable pinned onto the board behind her. It was quite unnecessary because their life was not so complicated that they could not remember the allocation of one week's duties.

'It is me, Mr. Wrighton,' Rubena Chowdhry replied. 'Do you want–'

'Look out!' Wrighton yelled and lunged into the room. At the same moment, Leila, who had overbalanced on her chair, shrieked and flung out her arm desperately seeking a stabilising purchase. Wrighton caught the chair, arresting her fall abruptly. Leila's legs flew upwards in a most unladylike manner showing her calves, then Wrighton lowered her gently to the ground.

'Oh. Thank you Mr. Wrighton. You are saving my life isn't it?' Leila laughed when she had recovered from her transient fright. 'Was I hurting you?' Wrighton was blotting his lower lip on the back of his hand. 'I was not meaning to hit you,' Leila explained.

'No harm done,' Wrighton said. 'I'll duck next time you aim at me.'

Mrs. Rosario touched Leila's arm and nodded her nose at the girl's sari. She pouted and pulled it down to her ankles.

'Are you wanting me?' Mr. Wrighton?' Rubena asked.

'You're not going to hit me as well are you?'

'No I am not!'

'I was joking, Mrs. Chowdhry, I was joking. If you could come up when you have finished whatever you are doing, I am in no hurry, it's just a bit of correspondence.'

She nodded and he closed the door.

Rubena did not know whether to ask him now, today, the thing that she was going to ask him or whether she would put it off for another day. She had been thinking about it for some time but lacked the courage. What would he say? Would he be offended? She paused outside his office door and knocked loudly in case he had the a.c. switched on.

'Come in.'

He looked up and smiled at her from his desk as she went in and he was humming something to himself. One of those droning Western tunes with no nuance.

'I've got some letters over there.' He pointed to the small table. 'But come and have a look at this,' he said with boyish enthusiasm. He was looking at a map and still humming to himself. 'Guess where I've been?'

Rubena did not know how to deal with this approach. It was very familiar but somehow she realised that he was merely letting his enthusiasm overcome the correctness that he would normally show to her.

'I heard that you were going to look at the pipeline survey that Mr. Line was working on.'

'Dead right,' he confirmed succinctly. 'And do you know what? I found out that the surveyor, Abra Huda his name is, had left some of his work to a student and that was why it was all wrong.'

'Have you told Mr. Havering?'

'No. I'm going along in a minute, but look at this.' He tapped his finger on the map.

Rubena looked at it. It meant nothing to her and she could not afford herself a closer inspection without standing indecently close. He did not seem to notice.

'What is it?'

'Well this is the pipeline, here. The Dhaka-Sylhet line not the Chittagong extension,' he explained. 'And these spots here, here and here for example are the valve stations.'

'What is walve stations?'

'Well they are...'

Rubena felt his eyes upon her face. Her blank, uncomprehending Bengali face. She could not understand his enthusiasm. He was obviously glowing with pride at some achievement of his and Rubena knew that she was as unable to share it as he was to explain it. He straightened up and with a dismissive gesture of his hand he said,

'Oh it's just that something needs amending on the map, that's all.'

She now knew that she had let him down. He had begun to treat her as a real colleague, to share his pleasures and disappointments on the same level as his Western colleagues and she had not come up to the mark. She rapidly scanned the map, standing far closer to him than she knew that she should. As she leaned across to point, their shoulders brushed casually.

'Was it at this place? She put her finger on the pencil mark.

'Yes. Do you know it?'

'Baderpur?'

'Yup.'

Baderpur. Constituency seat of Major Abdul Haq M.P. She had never been to Baderpur. Major Abdul Haq M.P. She saw her husband's adjutant sitting, twisting his fingers, unwilling to talk in front of the child. Her father's old eyes boring into him, skewering him to the seat with the one croaked question, 'And where were *you*?' The man's stumbling apology of an explanation. His tears. They were always ready to weep. Weep whilst you can, if you can weep you are still alive. The photograph in the paper. Her husband's blood-stained body stopped in the staircase, head lolling, sub-machine gun lying incriminatingly across his chest, fingers draped around the trigger guard. And Major Abdul Haq in the background. Completely absolved from any malicious involvement in the attempted coup. Now he was M.P. and working in the Ministry. And his district was Baderpur.

'No, I have never been there. I am hearing of it, of course.'

She moved back to her side of the desk.

'You can do the letters in here if you like. I have to pop along the corridor so it will be quite peaceful.'

'Thank you.' She pulled out a stool from under the table. He had made the offer, it would be unkind to refuse it and in any case, Leila would probably be at work somewhere else in the building and Mrs. Rosario also. Returning to her cubby hole would afford her no company of any sort except her own. She might as well stay where she were.

'Mrs. Chowdhry, please, use my desk. I am not using it for a while. You will be far more comfortable there.'

'Oh but I cannot Mr. Wrighton.'

'Nonsense! It's the sensible thing to do. I'll take this chart with me and you can have all that space.'

Before Rubena could stop him he had gathered up the bundle of letters and deposited them in an untidy pile on his desk.

'In!' Havering's voice rattled the door.

Wrighton found him seated behind his desk, studying a technical journal, pen in one hand, underlining occasional sentences. He did not look up at the intrusion. Wrighton waited, wryly grinning at his *'Assume that I have said Good Morning'* notice.

'Well?'

Wrighton was tempted to reply facetiously, 'Yes thank, you and yourself?' And then almost shivered with fright at the thought of the possible outcome had he done so.

'I've just come back from up country,' he began importantly.

'Did you get the shits?'

'No.'

'You will do. So what was wrong with the survey? Did you find out?'

'Yes.' Wrighton waited, but Havering had looked down at his journal again.

'I'm listening, Wrighton.'

'Abra Huda, the surveyor had subbed the work, or some of it, to a student or some other unqualified personage who had simply messed up the fixes about twenty miles from Mirasharai.'

'The bastard! Bastard Banglas!'

Wrighton stiffened at the bad language.

'Is it retrievable?'

'We will have to re-survey the last twenty miles. I told Abra Huda that we would not use him again.'

'You told him that?'

'And that we would probably extract costs of a re-survey from his fee,' Wrighton finished proudly.

'Ah ha,' Havering muttered obscurely and made a note on a pad by his hand. 'Right I'll organise another survey.'

'There was one other thing.' Wrighton brought up the map to the table. Havering frowned at it. 'On the way back to Dhaka I popped across to look at a couple of valve stations on the Dhaka-Sylhet line–'

'What the hell for? It's nothing to do with you.'

Wrighton was at a loss for words. The scenario that he had carved for himself; of the gradual unfolding of his discovery, of Havering's surprise turning to grudging admiration and then effusive thanks did not, in his mind, start off with Havering demanding what the hell he was doing.

'Well I was... I was going past and I just wanted to have a look for... well I don't have much opportunity to see things in the field...'

'O.K. So you had a look at the line. What of it?'

'Well, I think that there is a mistake on the map.'

'Quite likely.'

'Oh. It's quite normal is it?' Wrighton felt foolishly deflated.

'Is what quite normal? You're not making a lot of sense Wrighton. I'm busy.' He flicked his cigarette ash onto the floor.

'Its... it's this valve station here.' Wrighton pointed to the pencil mark on his map. 'It doesn't appear on the map but it does on the ground. Here at Baderpur.'

Havering looked up. He leaned slowly over and creased the map flat.

'Did you say Baderpur? What the hell were you doing poking your nose around there?'

'I wasn't poking my nose around. I just wanted to look at a valve station and Oggi took me to this one. That's all.'

'Alright Wrighton, keep your hair on. So we've missed a valve station off the map.'

'Quite an important one.'

'Why, is it important?' Havering remarked casually.

'Well it looked it. It was quite large. Had a pig trap and that.'

'What number was it?'

'It didn't have a number. I think the plate had been stolen.'

Havering made another note on his pad.

'O.K. I'll send someone out to do it.' Havering drew the map across to his side of the desk and carefully rolled it up.

'Well I could do it if you want me to.'

Havering paused and then smiled.

'You're too valuable to waste wandering around up country. I've got something that you can do though, right up your street and I'm relying upon you for this.'

'Oh well, er... right.' Wrighton was taken aback by Havering's sudden change of temperament. 'What do you want me to do?'

'Well, it's the financial predictions for the project. You've had a bit of experience in that line I understand.'

'That's true.'

It was not a discipline that he enjoyed but if Havering wanted him to do it then he felt that he ought to apply himself as best he could.

'We've got all the data, or rather, Mac Macleod can call it up. There's the skeleton file.' He slid a cardboard file across the desk. 'Have a glance at it now and then get together with Macleod and see what you can do.'

'Of course you'll have to sit on your left hand,' Bell said knowledgeably. Wrighton looked up from the floor where he was lacing up his shoes. 'Sit on my left hand? Why?'

'So that you don't use it.' Bell spoke as if talking to a child of three years of age.

Ever since Wrighton had returned one afternoon and remarked casually that he had been invited to dinner by a Bengali, the other two had been teasing him with pieces of pseudo important information on social graces. He had been warned that there would be no alcohol for him, that he would be introduced to all members of the family from great grand father to mewling babe and that he would have to eat with his fingers.

He suspected that Bell's latest piece of information was related to the eating habits. He took all this teasing in good heart, not in the least disconcerted by the lurid picture of eating with the natives that the other two had tried to paint for him. Mrs. Chowdhry was, he felt sure, a very Westernised Bengali and was well aware of the niceties of Western style behaviour and how they impinged upon the life of the practising Muslim.

He had been surprised when, upon returning to his office, Mrs. Chowdhry had rather obliquely announced that they were going to have a dinner and would like him to come. His immediate gut-feeling had been to refuse, or to find an excuse and to this end he had enquired when she had intended to entertain, hoping to be able to excuse himself on the grounds of a prior engagement, fabricated if necessary. He was rather thrown off balance by her reply. 'When would you like to come?' There was no way that he could choose the date himself and then declare himself unable to attend. And then, in an instant, he had felt very small and ungrateful, mean in the extreme. Here was this lady, trying to be kind to him, and it could not be easy for her to ask him to come to dinner and yet his first response had been viciously Home-Counties opportunistic hypocrisy. Why shouldn't he go? If you never tried these things you never learned anything. He didn't have any black or brown friends back in Wembley but out here, well, such a lack was inexcusable and yet... he knew few whites who entertained Bengalis.

'Next Thursday would be convenient for me. Is that alright for you?'

'Next Thursday. It's good. I will give you our address.' She had written in a careful, clear, schoolgirl hand, the house number and street number. 'It is new number nine, old number thirty three. The street numbers have been changed.'

So there it was.

'Go on then, why mustn't I use my left hand?'

'It's very impolite,' Tuppin said tritely.

Bell continued, 'They use the right hand for eating with. O.K.? And the left hand, well that's what you wipe your arse with. So you must never eat with your left hand. That's why you sit on it.'

Wrighton combed his hair as he said,

'Listen you two. Mrs. Chowdhry may be a Bangladeshi and she may dress in the traditional style, but she's very Western in her attitudes and behaviour. You can try to frighten me as much as you like,' he smirked at them, 'but I shall be home tonight to tell you that we sat on proper chairs, around a proper table and ate proper food with a knife and fork and talked about Shakespeare and the price of papaya.'

'Oh, that's another thing, and this is genuine, you realise of course, that they will all want to go to bed at half past ten so for heaven's sake don't stay any longer than ten.' Then as an afterthought Bell added, 'And how are you going to get home? I said that I would drop you off on my way down to the Sonargaon, it's not too far off my track, but I'm buggered if I'm picking you up.'

'Don't worry about that, there will be plenty of people there coming back this way, I'll come back with one of them.'

If Wrighton had not seen Rubena Chowdhry standing on the outside steps of the house he would probably have spent another fifteen minutes searching for the residence. Bell had left him on the Mirpur Road and had grimaced when he had seen the sparsely lighted street down which Wrighton intended entering the residential ghetto. He had offered to take him on to the Sonargaon instead but Wrighton had committed himself by climbing from the car and banging on the roof with the palm of his hand to signal Bell to pull away. It was not until the yellow headlamp had flickered around the corner that Wrighton had realised exactly how gloomy the road was. Few of the houses had lights at their gates, unlike the well-tended, even ostentatious residences of the Europeans in Banani. His next pool of light he could see was a street lamp at an intersection situated about one hundred yards down the road.

He had taken a deep breath and started off, walking slowly down the middle of the road so as to be clear of the shadows of the trees. Peering at the gate posts as he walked he had reached the intersection and concluded that he had not yet arrived at Mrs. Chowdhry's house. This deduction he had based upon the information gleaned from accosting two chowkidhars, neither of whom spoke English and from observing that some of the houses were numbered with their old numbers, some with their new numbers, some with the plot number, some with both old and new numbers, and some, not numbered at all. He had been frightened twice by unlighted rickshaws suddenly rattling past him in the dark and he had asked himself the question that would be asked until eternity: 'Why was it that when a rickshaw went past you it always made a tremendous rattle and yet you never heard it creeping up on you?' They seemed to suddenly surge from the gates of hell and hurtle past to disappear into the murk ahead.

Then a snuffling around the ankles had warned him that a friendly pi-dog was giving him some attention. He growled at it and it backed off and slunk away.

When Mrs. Chowdhry had called to him, 'Oh, Mr. Wrighton!' and had waved from the lighted porch, he had been surprised for there were no signs that a dinner party was in progress. He paused at the top of the steps and peered casually over the garden wall into the road by which he had arrived. There were no cars parked outside. He must be the first to arrive.

'Oh Mr. Wrighton, are you having trouble finding our house?'

'Not too much, Mrs. Chowdhry. Your directions were excellent.'

'Please to come inside Mr. Wrighton.' She held aside the mosquito screen door and he entered the porch. Two or three moths flapped unenthusiastically around the lamp, like bored dance hostesses in a tawdry night club.

The incongruity of their dialogue suddenly struck Wrighton.

'You know, you can't keep calling me "Mr. Wrighton". It doesn't sound correct. Here I am, a guest in your house and you call me "Mr. Wrighton"! You must call me Stewart.'

'Fine ...Stewart, and so you must call me Rubena.'

'Thank you Rubena.'

She smiled a happy, unambiguous smile which nevertheless only tipped up the extreme corners of her somewhat stern mouth. She was wearing a dark red sari in what Wrighton guessed was a rather expensive pressed silk design. He supposed that this was the equivalent of a Western woman's evening dress. He felt a little drab in his open-necked shirt and light trousers but was thankful that he had dressed thus because their air conditioning was not switched on. Perhaps they would switch it on later.

As Rubena opened the door to the inner room, Wrighton remarked at the silence within.

'Am I the first to arrive?'

'Oh no Stewart, all the others are here. We are all here now.'

She opened the door and motioned him to enter. It was an average sized room with the typical high ceiling which tended to make all the rooms appear as a cube and which made voices echo and indistinct, lost in the airiness. In the middle of the room hung an ornate antique electric fan which threw searchlight-like shadows into one corner as it swished monotonously overhead. Underneath it sat a small table. What Wrighton would have called a coffee table. It was stranded in a desert of sand yellow carpet which stretched almost to the walls. Against the walls were placed a heterogeneous fresco of chairs, stools, sofas and large stuffed cushions, To Wrighton's anxious gaze, they all appeared to be occupied. And they were all occupied by Bengalis.

Rubena began the introductions.

'Please Stewart, you must meet my father.' She turned to a wizened, grey-haired man who was sitting on a straight-backed chair. 'Father, this is Mr. Wrighton from the office at work.'

'How do you do, Mr. Wrighton.' The man's voice undulated between firmness and frailty, distorting the sentence.

'I'm very pleased to meet you sir,' Wrighton announced gravely. He thought that was appropriate.

'Tell me Mr. Wrighton, is my daughter always well-behaved at the office? Does she do her work well?'

'She sometimes runs in the corridor and I have heard that she smokes cigarettes behind the bicycle sheds!' he declared scandalously.

'Oh Mr. Wrighton!' Rubena exclaimed, horrified and embarrassed.

The old man chuckled.

'That is a public school joke, is it not Mr. Wrighton? Tell me, did you go to a public school?'

Wrighton felt viciously humbled by the good humour with which the patriarch had received Wrighton's facetious reply to what, he now realised, had been a serious enquiry. This man actually wanted to know how his daughter was working and whether she was behaving.

'Oh no sir, I just went to an ordinary grammar school.'

'And then to University, my daughter tells me.'

Wrighton glanced at Rubena in surprise.

'Yes, to... well, to become an engineer.'

'Now, Mr. Wrighton, in your opinion, was the British Government correct to agree to the partitioning of India in the manner in which it did, in nineteen forty seven?'

Rubena came to his rescue.

'Now father you must not keep Mr. Wrighton all to yourself, you can talk to him later. Stewart, I would like you to meet my mother. Mother, this is Mr. Wrighton.'

'I'm very pleased to meet you Mr. Wrighton. Rubena has told us such a lot about you.'

'I am astounded,' Wrighton admitted frankly. 'I did not realise that she was such a fan of mine.'

'Oh Rubena is always talking about the people at work,' she divulged with an innocent candour. 'Your Mr. Havering, we hear about.' She made a face. 'And Mr. Line.'

'No, mother, Mr. Line has gone now. Stewart is here to replace him.'

'I see... Stewart is your first name then?'

'That's right.'

'Like the Kings and Queens of Scotland.'

'Well... er... yes.' Wrighton scratched his head. 'But let me think, they were... er... that was their surname wasn't it? Their family name as it were.'

'Ah yes.'

'Momma can we start to eat? I am hungry.'

Wrighton was now thoroughly confused, for a strapping young lady in a yellow shalvar kamiz had addressed Rubena. Rubena put her arm around the girl's shoulders.

'And this is my daughter, Alice.'

'Your...?'

'My daughter, Alice. She is at the university.'

Wrighton held out his hand to the young lady, not knowing whether or not it was the right thing to do. The girl took it lightly and dipped a short curtsey, stealing a glance at him through long black eyelashes.

And so they progressed around the room. Her brother in law and elder sister and their children. A cousin who had come up from Chittagong on the train, an uncle who had a learned employment at the Ministry of Justice; each was introduced so that by the time that Wrighton had made a complete circle and arrived at the door again his head was swimming with names, faces and relationships. Each one wanted to ask him questions but not mundane questions about his way of life in England but deep-meaning questions about what he wanted his children to become when they grew up, or whether Russia would reach the Indian ocean through Pakistan or what were the chances of India building a barrage on the Ganges to reduce flooding in Bangladesh. He would just get the drift of one discussion when somebody else would butt in and the discussion would fly off at a tangent with the main seam talking their idiosyncratic English and splinter groups on the periphery arguing in Bengali.

He wondered when they intended to eat, they seemed to be waiting for a signal of some sort or a decision. As for him, he had not eaten properly at lunchtime and he could now feel the anticipation of the food bubbling and gurgling the enzymes in his digestive tracts.

'Are you liking Bengali food Stewart?' Rubena enquired.

'To be honest, I don't know. I don't think that I have ever eaten Bengali food.'

'Would you like to try some?'

'Yes, I would.'

'Come and have something to eat then. Come everybody. We are eating now,' Rubena announced to the room.

The children skipped through into the other room where the servant cuffed them around the ears to calm them down. Wrighton waited for Rubena's parents to go through first but they insisted that he sit down and start. He wanted to make sure that he sat in the correct place but, to his slight chagrin, nobody took any notice of either him or where he sat. He found himself sandwiched between Rubena's sister and one of the children who kept putting a finger on a mole on the back of Wrighton's hand. Wrighton felt out of his depth. Nobody had shown him how to eat or what food to eat first. The plates of gaily coloured rice and drab-looking vegetables were absolutely unrecognisable to him. Timidly he tried some indefinable meat. It was stringy. Then some vegetables, they were cold and bitter. Rubena was moving about the table, not sitting down, and eating from food that she had put in her hand and which she replenished at various points around the table. What was he to do? How was he supposed to cope? And then he realised that... it did not matter. Nobody was affording any attention to what he was eating or how he was eating and it was only when he exclaimed in dismay when some juice ran up his arm to his elbow that everyone laughed and Rubena explained,

'Stewart. You must not pick up the wet food like that. This is what you do. Now watch. You take some rice and put it on the wet meat or vegetables and then you press it like this.' She made a doughy ball of rice and meat. 'Then you put it in your mouth.'

'Do you like our food Mr. Wrighton?' Rubena's mother asked.

'I am not certain.' They all laughed at this. 'It's very different from what I am used to.' He had to be careful of what he said. He did not want to upset anybody. 'I like these.'

'Those are ladies fingers. A very delicate vegetable.'

'It's a bit like a bean. A runner bean.'

'Like a green bean? Yes.'

The dessert was a choice of thin yogurt or sickly, sticky rice cake. Wrighton diplomatically had a little of both, organising the consumption so that he finished on the thin yogurt and not the stodgy cake. He was beginning to feel uncomfortably hot from the calories gained through eating, from the proximity of so many people in one enclosed room and from the realisation that the house was not air conditioned at all.

'Shall we have tea in here?' Rubena stood in the doorway. 'Didi, bring the tea in to us.'

Wrighton watched her as she walked through the double doorway, straight body, head level, perfect poise.

'Did you used to carry things on your head when you were a child?' he asked her. 'You walk in... such an upright manner.'

'I still do.'

She scooped up a basket of wooden blocks that the children had been squabbling over, swung it up to her black hair and carried it from the room with no more difficulty than if she had been wearing a hat.

Rubena's father tottered up to Wrighton where he stood in the arc of influence of the electric fan. In his curiously wavering voice he said,

'I have enjoyed meeting you Mr. Wrighton. I am going to bed now. I am an old man. I am ninety six.'

'You are eighty two father,' Rubena interrupted as she followed the servant back into the room.

'I hope that your children are not as insolent as mine sometimes are,' he warbled.

Wrighton bade him goodnight and surreptitiously looked at his watch. He remembered the warning about not staying too late. It was very easy to overstay your welcome in a Bengali house because they were always too polite to throw you out. Rubena poured out the tea and sat on the chair next to him. For the moment they were alone in the room so Wrighton decided to try to clear up a query that had arisen in his mind during all the introductions and which, he felt, involved a potentially sensitive area. He was certain that Rubena would understand his confusion but he was nonetheless embarrassed by it.

'Rubena. All the family that I have met of yours... I get a little confused with the names and relationships....'

Rubena handed him his cup of tea and then repeated the genealogy of those present, although they had, for some reason, not returned to the sitting room after the meal, leaving Rubena and Wrighton together.

He wondered whether this was a polite way of telling him that it was time to go. Wrighton listened carefully to her exposition and then said,

'So I haven't actually met your husband tonight?'

Even as he said it he sensed that he should not have done. Rubena looked at him and smiled. She returned her cup to the table and crossed her hands in her lap as she said,

'I am sorry, Stewart, of course you are not knowing. I am widow.'

'Excuse me, that was very insensitive of me, I should have realised.' Why hadn't he kept his mouth shut? Why had he not thought just a little before speaking?

'It is not your fault, Stewart. He was in the army and was killed. But I have a fine daughter.'

'You have indeed.'

'I want her to become a lawyer.'

'Can women do that?'

'Oh yes, women can become lawyers but nobody will employ them.'

'So, what is the point then? What will she live on?'

'I will find her work. There is much work in this city. You know that women are having no rights under Muslim law?'

'Are you saying that your religion is wrong?' Wrighton had suspected all along that the greater part of Bangladesh's troubles could be laid at the feet of Mohammed.

'It is not the religion that is being wrong. It is the people who are interpreting the religion and the laws. The women should be having rights to property and their children and a career if they are wanting it. This country will always be at the bottom of the pile if you are always pushing the women down. It is the women who are making a nation great, not the men. What are the men doing? All they can do is make war to show how clever they are, isn't it?'

'Do you mean that you want to see women in government in Bangladesh?'

'Yes. Why not? But we have to educate the women first. That is the first problem to solve.'

'Is Rubena preaching again?' Rubena's sister remarked almost tartly as she waddled into the room. 'You see Mr. Wrighton, Rubena is a clever girl. She had education.'

Rubena turned her head sharply away from Wrighton and snapped out a short retort in Bengali. Wrighton was dismayed. He did not want to get involved in a family dispute about who was the most favoured child. He did not want to be ensnared in any quarrels. He already felt sufficiently uncomfortable by his mere presence amongst these obviously intelligent Bengalis. He was humbled when he thought of the range of knowledge that they possessed. They talked about the world, about politics, about England with such firm yet discreet authority. If he had approached somebody in Wembley and asked them to talk about Bangladesh they would have not known where to begin. They would probably have found it difficult to say anything about Ealing, let alone Bangladesh. And these were the Bengalis that Bell and Havering and Tuppin and hundreds of other smug Europeans were calling 'bogwits'.

'Gracious me'!' he exclaimed, overtly noticing his watch. It was a gross, unrefined manoeuvre but he realised with a savage bitterness that he had no refinements in etiquette. 'I really ought to be going.'

Rubena acceded with a gentle inclination of the head.

'I did not see your car.'

'I have a lift,' Wrighton lied glibly, wondering how he was to get home since there were no other guests from whom he could ask assistance. 'He will be waiting for me at the end of the road. Where he dropped me off.'

If Rubena had not believed him, Wrighton could not tell. He arose stiffly from the low chair, his shirt sticking to his back in the muggy room. Rubena glided coolly before him to the door and the other members of the family appeared in the background and twittered amongst themselves but Wrighton derived very much the impression that this was Rubena's show, as it were, and the others were present as tolerated audience. He was not certain that he really liked the feeling of being a point of interest. At the screen door he turned to Rubena standing there in her dark red sari like a rich flame frozen on a candle and, on an impulse, took her hand and shook it politely.

'Thank you very much for a lovely evening, Rubena. I have enjoyed it immensely. And I was interested to meet your family.'

She accompanied him to the front gate.

'You must come again one day. We will enjoy it.' She looked up the street. 'Is your friend waiting? I cannot see his car.'

'Yes, he will be up on the Mirpur road, just around the corner.'

'I will send the chowkidhar to light the road.'

'No, please don't bother. I'm not afraid of the dark. I know the way.' And to strand any argument he stepped out boldly up the street.

15

The evening had not worked out as Mary Havering had planned it. She had easily deceived Alan into believing that she was going to one of her meetings. He had hardly looked up from the bundle of files on his lap when she had flounced through the lounge to the porch and the car.

As she had approached the Sonargaon Hotel her stomach had started to turn itself into knots. She had tried to convince herself that she was nervous because she was driving around the city alone at night but she knew that that was not the reason at all. It was the anticipation that was churning around in her belly.

He was so unpredictable. She never knew what he was going to do next but it was always outrageous. Outrageous and exciting. Once he had put his hand up her skirt in the lift and made her shriek. The other occupants had turned to look at her in surprise in her confused, excited state and as she had cast about her mumbled apologies she had realised that he too had looked just as surprised as the others so that nobody had been able to guess what had happened. He was a real expert. A hot, angry tear oozed out from the corner of her eye as she brutally wrenched the gear lever across the box. A real expert.

Even as she had crossed the foyer she should have realised from the startled expression of the hotel receptionist but, innocent and blinded by the excitement, she had pulled the key from her handbag and walked into the empty lift. As the door had closed she had seen the girl tapping out a number on the hotel telephone and still looking at her across the foyer. Alone in the empty lift she had saucily mouthed an empty shriek into the mirror, thrilling at the memory of the unexpected caress of her private parts in a public place.

The eighth floor. The pink carpet stretching off down the corridor with the hotel's motif marching in single file into woven infinity. The girl at the desk had picked up the phone as she had walked into the lift. The detail flooded back to her now with ironic clarity. As she had put the key in the lock she had heard the phone ringing in the room. It was still ringing when she had opened the door and seen the strange green jacket with the decorative wings embroidered on it, draped across the chair and had smelt the warmth and perfume of the close proximity of bodies. It was still ringing when she had noticed the bare young legs, the bare young European legs. They had to be European, pulsing rhythmically, one sandal jerking and swinging on the tips of the toes like a lantern on a pole. In the grunting and panting she had seen herself, she had heard her own voice. It was her lungs that were expelling the air in ecstatic pulses. It was her hands that were kneading the brown back. It was her head thrown back across the mattress to glimpse through slit eyes the tantalising view of the floodlit roof of the National Assembly building through the full length window. Her full length window.

With all her force she had thrown the key across the room, hoping perhaps to break that screen of her first, thundering immorality. The sharp crack of the key smacking into the glass had produced the effect that the opening of the door and the ringing of the telephone had been unable to do. The girl had squealed but had been too close to the climax and it had bubbled into a gulping, shrieking spasm. As he had straightened his back on a thrust, Abdul Haq had twisted his neck and given her a queer look which she had realised afterwards had been a flash of genuine, triumphant gratitude.

Sobbing with rage, she had hurtled back down the corridor to the lift which in its cold, mechanical, analytical way had knowingly waited for her, closing its doors automatically as soon as she had reached the inside. In the mirror she had seen a distraught unkempt woman. Two floors to regain her control, two floors to regain her composure, two floors for major rearrangement, two floors for fine grooming. She had stepped out of the lift, smiling a little fixedly, but smiling all the same. The reception girl's mouth had fallen open foolishly and she had slowly replaced the unanswered phone receiver, unashamedly staring at her. Head held high, if a little stiffly, eyes straight ahead, if a little moist, she had sailed through the enormous marble reception to the car park and there in the darkness of her car she had howled, uncaring of the ring of white-eyed bogwits staring at her through the screen.

And now she was lost. She searched the crossroads for some familiar sign or landfall and found none. With a creeping anxiety she realised that there was very little motor traffic at all. The sounds were the rattles of rickshaw hoods and the swishes of their tyres. She must have come out of the wrong side of the hotel car park and instead of running back towards Bari Dhara she had been driving headlong into the native old town and in her fury had not noticed. The angry tear had reached the corner of her mouth. She really needed to find a road that she knew, something like the

Great Elephant Road or the Stadium Road but in this quarter, all the road signs were in Bengali script. No English subtitles. She spoke no Bengali so she could not ask; they spoke no English so they could not tell.

A bloody air hostess! Some jumped up jet-setting tart who had been laid in every city from Washington to Tokyo. How dare she muscle in on her man! She performed a savage U-turn in the crossroads causing several rickshaws to arrange themselves slowly but gracefully into a tangle of Meccano. She remembered the room. The discarded uniform jacket, the drooping, draped blouse, the rucked up skirt. Had he taken her by surprise? Had he taken her so utterly by surprise? No, she must have known the score, a tart like that. An air hostess. She was probably on stopover. What was her uniform? Green? Thursday night... Which airline flew out on Friday mornings? Green uniform. Saudi? No. Gulf Air? No, they were Wednesdays. An air hostess on stopover! She probably only lived across the corridor, he could have got rid of her in time had he wanted to. He could have, had he wanted to... Had he wanted to. She recalled the wild, surprised eyes of the girl and she imagined that it was herself, not the girl, spread across the bed, skirt around her hips, nipples pointing at the ceiling. What would she have done? Lying there with a man between her legs and somebody walking into the room? She knew what she would have done. Just the same as the girl. With a scouring envy she recalled the heaving and the writhing as the girl had begun to climax, had been shocked by the intrusion and this had magnified the pleasure beyond all bearing. God! It must have been like a volcano for her. A young tart like that. She had probably never had it like that before. And it need not have happened. She angrily pushed a fist into her lap as she drove with one hand. Of course there had been no need for it to happen. No need. But Major Abdul Haq M.P. had known exactly what time she would arrive at his room. He had set her up. It was part of his kinky game. He had known that he was going to be discovered and the telephone call had warned him of its imminence. The girl had been in ignorance. It had all been a game.

And that chilling, desperate moaning that she could hear was herself.

The two chowkidhars of whom Wrighton had enquired directions earlier in the evening both wished him 'Good evening Saheb' as he ambled thoughtfully back towards the Mirpur Road.

He would take a baby taxi when he got to the main road. A four mile journey, or perhaps five miles, that would be about fifty taka. The driver would ask for two hundred, probably, but Wrighton was certain of his ability to negotiate a price of only one hundred percent above the going rate. A loaded rickshaw went by him in a waft of petrol fumes. Wrighton warily watched the hurricane lamp swinging from the back axle by a piece of bent wire.

So, Rubena was a feminine activist! What a viper they had been nurturing in their bosom! She had never appeared as such at the office. She was always discreet and courteous. Subservient as expected, indeed he had on occasion seen her correcting Leila Rose, or pulling her back into line when she had overstepped the mark of respectful behaviour. It just goes to show that you cannot judge people by their appearances. Fighting for the rights of women in a Moslem society? She must have guts.

The Mirpur road was busy, surprisingly so and to Wrighton's chagrin, all the baby taxis were bundled full of Bengalis. He stood for a moment expecting at least one baby taxi to stop but to no avail. He grinned ironically at the similarity with London. Never a taxi when you want it. Oh well, he would just have to walk home. He felt in his pocket for his compass and took a reading by the light of a fluorescent strip tube serving as a street lamp. From Dhanmondi he really needed to travel north east which was... that way. Up Green Road. Perhaps there would be a baby taxi at the other end.

Ten minutes later he found that his progress was seriously hampered by the press of the crowds. From all sides Bengalis were walking up and down the street, on the sidewalks, in the road, insouciant of the occasional, plaintive shout from a rickshaw puller as he tried to edge his fare through the throng. Up ahead he could see the cause of the crowd. The cinema. Just my luck, he thought. It must be the end of the film, he had never seen so many people congregated at night. For every rickshaw there seemed to be fifty prospective fares and two hundred bystanders watching the bargaining and still the patrons were pouring slowly out of the cinema like a tide of molasses oozing from a split can. They clogged all the street, they blocked the alleyways but there was no bad feeling, there was no rowdiness.

Wrighton felt himself jostled along with the crowd and kept his hand in his pocket on his roll of taka notes. He never carried much money on him because, he never needed much. It was difficult stuff to spend. You could give it away, but to actually find a desirable purchase was difficult. Not nearly as difficult, of course, as finding a necessary purchase. He looked up at the billboard, the giant painted advertisement for the film which was floodlit on the facade above the steps. It seemed that a green-faced man with a dagger in his mouth was involved somehow with a black-haired woman with a red face and a yellow car with no wheels. Whether this latter characteristic was germane to the plot or an omission on the part of the artist was not clear but the hoarding was undeniably attractive in a primitive manner.

Before the cinema was a large road junction which served as a public square. Up one side squeezed some motor cars but down the middle in the alignment of Green Road up which he had walked, crawled the rickshaws, their hoods folded flat, their pullers sinuously edging them through the crowd.

Wrighton had picked a landfall across the square, a bedding shop, and was about to weave and to tack his way across to it when he first heard the car. It was hooting imperiously and to Wrighton's mind it was travelling too fast. Over the sea of black heads he could see the white roof of a small saloon as it swerved around rickshaws and hooted and flashed its way through the crowds. He pulled himself sharply back onto the sidewalk and caught a glimpse of a red-haired white woman shouting through the windscreen as she hauled the wheel to the left and right, forcing the car through the crowd. It was a little Ford like Bell's except that it was in much better condition.

He shook his head disgustedly as he noticed the black and yellow 'Aid' licence plates on the car then in an instant he was cowering with the crowd as the rickshaw exploded in a graceful filigree of flaming screams. Panic stricken, the crowd opened out and then struck with horror it recoiled homogeneously as one of the passengers staggered towards it, enveloped in burning petrol. The petrol had spread to the road and was burning the tar, the plastic hood of the rickshaw was melting in hideous black fumes, burning bundles were crawling pleadingly towards a receding crowd.

Wrighton felt his legs and arms shaking with horror and fright. Those were people in the road. People. He started forwards, slowly; without reflection, the pool of burning tar singeing his ankles as he skipped through it. One wail pierced the moaning and the dying. Fascinated, Wrighton stopped as the red-haired woman staggered from the door of the car and shrieked.

'They're burning! Burn, Banglas Burn!' Her face was witch-like in the hideous illumination. 'Burn!' she shrieked, waving her arms hysterically. 'Burn! Ha ha ha!'

The moaning of the crowd changed perceptibly to a rumbling. Wrighton looked rapidly around the faces. They were looking at the woman with hate in their eyes. He ran across.

'Get in the car!' he shouted. 'GET IN THE CAR!' He grabbed her by the shoulder.

'I'll burn the lot of you, stupid, bloody, Banglas! Stupid, cheating, bloody Banglas!'

The burning lumps had stopped moving, the crowd perimeter was reducing by the second, the rumbling was interspersed with shouts.

'Get in the car you silly bitch! They'll kill you if they catch you.'

I'll burn them... I'll–'

He slapped her hard across the face, left, right, left, the red hair stinging his eyes. 'Get in the car!'

Her eyes blazed with fury now. She struck out with a fist, hitting him smartly on the cheek. He grabbed her hand and they struggled, stupidly, wastefully. She was all arms and legs trying to scratch him, kick him and all the while the crowd crept closer, and more frighteningly, they were now chanting in unison. The circle was almost complete. Wrighton wrenched his wrist free and swung his fist straight into her gut, a lot harder than he had intended. He winced as her tongue burst from her mouth with the air, her eyes bulged and she folded up. He roughly pushed the crown of her head down and she collapsed onto the driver's seat blocking their only escape. He now knew that their two destinies were inextricably linked, they lived or died together.

In a mad frenzy he pushed and shoved, bent and twisted, desperately trying to recall his first aid knowledge. Which way do legs bend? What should he do with this arm? Two thirds of the seat cushion was uncovered when he slid in, left foot straight onto the clutch, lever into gear amongst the jumble of limbs. The crowd had got to his door, he tried to pull it closed, they hung on... Thank goodness the engine was still running. He revved it to breaking point and then let in the clutch, sending the car slithering from side to side in a squealing, smoking wriggle. At the same time someone had opened the passenger door. The woman was half dragged out of the car before he had realised. She had not been able to scream, she had no wind. One hand on the wheel, he grabbed her by the neck. Her blouse ripped, he hung on and aimed the jiving car at the thinnest part of the crowd. The open doors swung wildly about as they zig-zagged through the howling mob. An anonymous bare foot kicked his door shut, bruising his shoulder, he felt the lunge on his arm as the woman was thrown towards her open door. He swung the wheel to the other lock and the crowd at the back roared, the ones in the front squealed as they jumped back from the swaying, thumping car. Her door slammed and then a stone smacked a star in the laminated screen as he burst screaming in first gear out into Airport Road and safety.

He drove mechanically up the road towards Gulshan and Banani. Not knowing what the woman was doing. She was forgotten. He could see the burning bundles on the tarmac and then suddenly he began to quiver and soon he was shaking. He stopped the car by the old Airport Terminal, letting it run to a rest in the dark shadow. They sat there for five minutes or more, the traffic passing normally on the road a few feet away. Not speaking, nursing their wounds, mental and physical. Finally, when the last of his shivers had passed, he turned to his passenger,

'Are you alright?'

She was crouched on her seat, holding her forearm primly across her torn blouse. She looked up at him and nodded, dumbly, the tears coursing silently down her face.

'I had to hit you,' he explained. 'I had to. You were hysterical.'

She bit her top lip and nodded again. He was excused.

'Did I hurt you?' She smiled thinly. 'I'm sorry, but I had to do it. I did.' She swallowed and licked her lips to say something but said nothing. 'I think you are suffering from shock,' He looked around the car. On the back seat lay a thin linen evening coat. He pulled it over. 'Perhaps you should put this on.'

She put the cloth around her shoulders and mumbled.

'Thank you.'

She began to cry again. Wrighton automatically moved to comfort her but then pulled back, afraid of her possible reaction. He sat and looked glumly through the windscreen, seeing the crowds, seeing the explosion.

'Did you hit the rickshaw?'

'I didn't think that I had. It went up after I had gone past. I couldn't get away. Too many people.'

It was the most that she had said so far.

'It's an Aid car isn't it?'

'Yes, my husband is... It's because of my husband's work.'

'They can replace the windscreen if needs be. It's not too difficult. There will be a few dents in the bodywork. I'm sorry.'

'That's alright. You did your best.'

She straightened up in her seat, gingerly and rubbed her stomach.

'Stomach hurt?'

'A bit.' She winced slightly. 'But it's not so tender.'

'I didn't mean to hit you so hard.'

They sat quietly for a few more minutes. Just watching life go by.

'Where do you live?'

'Baridhara.'

'I'll drive you home.'

'No please.' She was suddenly animated. 'Don't put yourself out.'

'I already have. You haven't got much choice. I'm at the wheel.' He started up and drove off.

'I would rather you did not see me all the way home thank you.' She was picking her words carefully. 'I very much appreciate what you have done for me–'

'I didn't want to get lynched either,' Wrighton admitted ungallantly.

'But you must not come home with me. My husband... my husband would not understand.'

'Well I don't know–'

'Please! Please believe me.' The plea was from the depths of desperation and it cut straight through his rising petulance.

'Have it your way.'

'And you mustn't tell anybody what happened.'

'I mustn't... ?' He glanced at his passenger as they crossed the short bridge into Baridhara. 'I won't.'

'Promise.' He reflected. A promise was not something that he gave lightly. 'Promise!' she insisted.

'I promise.'

'Let me drive now please.'

'Are you sure that you are alright?'

'I am sure.'

He stopped the car and got out. She slid across the seat and opened the passenger door for him.

'Let me take you home to show you that I am alright driving. Where do you live?'

Wrighton had things that he wanted to think about before going home.

'Not far away. I'll... walk.' He had nearly said that he would take a rickshaw.

'Now don't be silly.' she chided, the warmth coming into her voice.

'I'm not, honestly, I like walking. I need some air. It's not far.'

She shrugged. 'I shan't forget what you did,' she assured him as she pulled the coat around her shoulders further.

'Mrs... ?' He suddenly realised that he did not know her name.

'Sorry,' she shook her head. 'It has to be like this.'

He watched the car drive slowly away.

16

The task that Havering had set Wrighton kept him in the office much more than before. Not that he had previously wasted his time gadding about the town but there had been occasional justifiable errands that he had not been able to safely entrust to a peon. Now, however, he found that he spent most of his time either in his office, poring over dockets for stores or down at Mac Macleod's end of the building pleading with him to find the record of some expenditure on the computer database. It was just the luck of the draw of course – that he was always indoors. At least he had the satisfaction of knowing that Havering needed him to do the job. He had actually chosen him and told him that it was very important.

'Shingara saheb?' The peon poked his head around the door and swung a plastic bag full of savouries at him. Wrighton looked at his watch in surprise. This was the third morning running that he had lost track of time, being so involved in surveyor's man-hours or quotes for shuttering.

'Dui,' he replied and held up two fingers to cover both possibilities that the peon could not understand his Bengali or could not count. Wrighton bit into the shingara and stood up, straightened his back and then ambled aimlessly around his office as the searing spices scoured the inside of his mouth. I'm now as hot inside as I am out, he thought to himself.

His perambulations brought him back to his desk and he gazed down at the file of loose papers and sighed. It may be important work but it was becoming a bit of a drudge. A docket for twenty taka of photocopying would lie next to another to the value of thousands of dollars for the repair of some piece of machinery. The file was chaos. It was wicked the neglect that had been shown to some of the records. How could you provide any financial analysis when you had things like this? He pulled out a sheet at random. '*Twelve-inch steel pipe, to run ten kilometres...*' I mean, how often did you...? He looked at the paper again. Ten kilometres of twelve-inch pipe? What was that doing there? They did not use twelve-inch pipe, he was certain. It was all fourteen-inch. Who had bought a run of twelve-inch pipe? Where was it? Had they used it? He picked up the stock file and then put it down heavily. No, there was no point in searching amongst these records. He picked up the phone.

'Mac? Have you got a minute, or more like half an hour? I've got a bit of a problem and I think you might be able to help me with your number cruncher... Thanks, I'll come down.'

Mac was sitting with his feet propped up on his desk, flicking through a magazine, when Wrighton entered.

'Not disturbing you I hope?' Wrighton enquired with mock solicitude.

'Come in old boy. Take a pew.' Mac waved at the chair. 'Actually I'm working jolly hard at the moment but I'm too modest to let anybody know.' He nodded to his machine in the corner that was spewing out a roll of paper. 'The trouble is, he can't keep up with me so I have to wait for him every now and then.'

'I'd take your job any day. With or without the French dictionary.'

'You can have it old boy, any time you like. Now what's your cock up?'

'Who said it was a cock up?'

'When anybody from your section comes to me, it's a cock up.'

Wrighton stuck out his tongue and slipped the purchase docket across to Macleod.

'What do you make of that?'

Mac studied it briefly.

'Well I don't see many of these things, you understand, but it looks to me as if somebody has bought some pipe. Not an unexpected transaction considering the aim of the Project. Now was there anything else? I have the crossword to finish.'

'Now Mac, be serious. Have you got the outline spec. for the Sylhet-Dhaka pipeline on disc?'

'You mean the one where they have just had the trouble with the piers?'

'Yes.'

'I can find it. Do you want it?'

'Yes. Can you put it on the screen?'

'Just a minute. Pest!'

He unlocked a cupboard and selected a disc. He turned around the v.d.u. on his desk so that Wrighton could see it and then started working on the keyboard, running through passwords and menus till he found what they needed.

'Ah, here we are. Draft specification...'

'What about the final spec?'

'Just a minute.... There. Will that do you?'

Wrighton frowned at the screen as he concentrated.

'Just as I thought,' he remarked. 'Correct me if I'm wrong but they only used fourteen-inch pipe didn't they?'

Mac swept the screen rapidly with a practised eye.

'There was only fourteen-inch in the spec. The final spec.'

'What about if they changed it in the field. Would that show on here?'

'Should do. Let's see in the amendments... Deviation at Ashuganj... Revision of river bed clearance... No, there are no amendments to the pipe size. Happy?'

Wrighton pushed the purchase docket back to Macleod.

'Look at the size of pipe on that.'

'Hm...Twelve inch. Must be a mistake.' He looked at Wrighton's face. 'But you're not convinced are you?'

'To be frank, I would say from my experience of the way this project is run that it is more likely that somebody bought the wrong size of pipe, than that the mills filled out the wrong docket.'

'Well we can check the docket entry. Hang on.' He returned to his cupboard and brought back the box of discs. 'Right, well we can find the entry for that purchase on the journal.' He glanced at the date on the docket. 'Let's see.' The screen flickered and flashed through columns and charts. 'Ah, we're getting nearer....' They both peered at the screen as the text moved up five entries at a time.

'There it is,' Wrighton put his finger on the screen.

'Please keep your grubby mitts off my nice clean screen.'

'Sorry. But it is definitely twelve-inch pipe.'

'So it would seem.'

'Well what did they use it for?'

'Search me. You're the engineer.'

'But I wasn't here then. You were.'

'Ah, you can't pin this one on me. I'm fireproof. I don't actually bury pipes I just tap keyboards.'

'Now come on Mac, think. How can we find out where it went?'

'Why do you want to know? Is it important?'

'I don't really know. I'd never really thought about its importance. I just want to know what has happened to it. Curiosity.'

'Oh well, that's alright then. If it's just intellectual satisfaction you are looking for then that's O.K. I mistakenly thought that it had something to do with your task.'

'Oh don't be such an ass. You can be infuriating sometimes Mac.'

'Just pay attention. Note down that number there.'

Wrighton scrawled a pencil number on the top of the desk. Mac frowned.

'We use paper in this section. I find I can't get the desk tops into the envelope.'

'Get on with it.'

'Yes sir.   Now if I search for that number which is unique to that transaction, it will tell me its outcome.'

'Magic.   I'll believe that when I see it.'

'Oh you Philistine.   There it is. *Disposed of, $2,000*'

'Are you sure?'

'Look for yourself. '

'Does that mean that it was sold for two thousand dollars?'

'Yes, that's right.   Is that all you wanted?'   Mac enquired and then he sensed that something was amiss.   'Just a minute, how much pipe was there?'

'To run ten kilometres...'

Macleod whistled.

'Somebody made a boo boo.   Bought the wrong pipe and had to get rid of it.'

'That's two hundred dollars a kilometre.'

'It doesn't seem very much does it?'

'Who was it sold to?'

'It doesn't say.'

'Wouldn't it normally?'

'I suppose it would...'   Macleod said slowly.   'Do you think something fishy has gone on?'

'I don't know.   I was just accused of satisfying my intellectual curiosity.'   Wrighton retorted pointedly.

'Touché old bean.   But now they have me to contend with.   Now I'm curious.'

'A lot of people have said that.'

'Disposals... disposals... disposals... Here we are.   Beginning of the year. We shall have to run down until we find a sum of two thousand dollars.'

His eyes scanned the rolling figures.

'I don't know how you can look at that screen when it does that,' Wrighton complained, but Macleod was not listening.

'Here it is.   The number matches up.   Two thousand dollars and the payee was 'A.H.T. Company Ltd.'   Do you know them?'

'It rings a bell,' Wrighton admitted slowly, but he could not for the life of him think why.

Wrighton frowned in concentration as he strode back up the corridor towards his section.   He had been anxious about his meetings with Havering ever since Havering had blown his top about the chap in the

MFA finding out about the problem on the piers. That row had simmered for days and the work that Wrighton had achieved up-country had not, apparently, done anything towards healing the wound. Except that, of course, Havering had now given him this assignment which was important. He could not duck the responsibility. He had been given the job of sorting out the record of the finances and he had discovered this irregularity. It was his duty to tell Havering, he would be failing by not doing so. All the same... Havering was sure to turn nasty and to shout and swear and humiliate and frighten him.

His steps faltered to a halt and he looked at the docket again. Perhaps if he put the docket inside the computer print-out, like so, then he could see what Havering's mood was, before plunging in. If he was open and relaxed he could perhaps approach him along the lines of...'Did we ever to your knowledge use anything other than fourteen-inch pipe on the Dhaka Sylhet pipeline? Just asking from interest, you understand.' That might work. If he was in a foul temper then he could... um... he could ask about whether they had done anything about updating the map to include the valve station at Baderpur. Yes, that was the best way.

'Good morning Stewart. How are you today?'

'Hello Rubena. I am very well thank you. How is your father?'

'He has caught a cold and is a little indisposed.'

'I'm sorry to hear that,' he said with real concern. Whatever the disputed age of Rubena's father, he was not of a vintage that could shrug off a cold lightly. 'Give him my regards and tell him to get better soon.'

'Between you and me, Stewart,' she moved closer to convey the conspiratorial nature of what she was about to divulge, and he could smell that peculiar fragrance of Eastern women, of warm hair and musk, 'I think that he is being a bit of a baby, isn't it?'

'I don't think that you ought to tell him that.'

She smiled a full grin of white teeth.

'Did you get home all right after visiting us the other night?'

'Gosh yes, I haven't seen you since. Thank you very much for inviting me, I enjoyed myself, it was very kind of you. Yes... I got a lift home all right.' He smiled. 'No problem, as you say.'

His face betrayed nothing of the turmoil of emotion within him as her innocent and quite justified enquiry raked over the embers of that traumatic journey home. He was surprised that he could be so cool and detached about it all. He supposed that it was the conditioning of the pace of life in Bangladesh. Death was more present, if that were possible. It was more to the forefront of society. The population did not expire conveniently out of the way in discreet rest homes, their lives were wrenched brutally from them in hideous, stupid, nonsensical accidents or inexorably sucked from them by debilitating disease and starvation and all this happened in the shop window, every day, before your very eyes. For your entertainment.

'Well you must come again.'

'Yes I would like to, but I will have to swat up on my English history so that I can talk on even terms with your father.' She laughed again. 'Tell me,' he said, changing the subject, 'is old bossy boots in a good mood or a bad one today?'

He nodded towards Havering's office door as Rubena's eyes opened in fright and a hand flew to her mouth in a reflex of anxiety.

'You must not call him that,' she hissed, 'he will be very angry when he is finding out. I do not know if he is happy or sad today.'

Wrighton sighed heavily.

'I suppose I shall have to find out by myself.'

Happy or sad. Happy or sad. That was a funny way of looking at it. Havering was a brutal, domineering, rude, intimidating bully. Wrighton had never considered that he might feel happy or sad like anybody else. What a funny way of looking at it. His trepidation made him knock on the door more loudly than he had intended.

'In! Don't knock the bloody door down!'

He felt that he would rather run away but he went in.

'Well?' Havering's cigarette jived in his lips, broadcasting ash onto the desk top. He swept it away with a brawny forearm.

'I think that there is something that you ought–' he began but Havering was paying him scant attention.

'Oh Wrighton–' he interrupted, 'I expect you want to know about that valve station that you found.' He almost sneered the suggestion. 'We've checked up on it. It was number DS 12.'

'Oh but–' Wrighton began but checked himself. He was going to say that that was not possible because he had seen DS 12 and he had seen DS 13 and this station was unnumbered and between the two but something in Havering's manner stopped him. Havering was almost jovial. He was cheery. He wanted Wrighton to be at his ease. He was trying to convince Wrighton. He was wanting him to believe something. '...Yes obviously some bogwit decided that the number plate was of use and filched it.' Wrighton nodded and casually put his hands behind his back, taking the docket and print-out from Havering's line of sight. Just in case. 'So you'll be relieved to know that there is no great rewriting of maps necessary.'

Havering grinned at him and looked him in the eye, challengingly, just as Bell had done when he had told Wrighton that he had given him Line's room.

Wrighton swallowed. Havering was lying. He did not know why but he was convinced of it.

'Oh good,' he said thickly. 'That was what I was coming in about. I was just going past, as it were...'

'Well you can carry on then. I'm relying on you to do a bit of financial analytical wizardry. O.K.? It's very important.'

Is it heck! He just wants me confined to barracks for as long as possible.

'I'll get on then.'

Wrighton left the office. Havering watched the door close behind him and then smirked and shook his head.

Something is going on and Havering is involved in it or at least knows about it. Why had he lied about the valve station? It was not a mistake on Havering's part, it was downright lying. Wrighton had never told him that he had bracketed the valve station at Baderpur; that he knew that it could not be either DS13 or DS12 so Havering had not known that Wrighton could tell that what he said was untrue. Perhaps somebody was tricking Havering? Perhaps Havering had believed the explanation that had been given him? Wrighton tried to be charitable but was certain that Havering was lying.

He closed his office door and switched off the a.c. so that he could think in the five minutes of cool peace before the room started to heat up again. Who else was involved in this? Mac? No, not Mac. He was too straight and in any case he had obviously known nothing about it for if he had, he would never have agreed to help him. He would easily have put stumbling blocks in his way. Mac...

He grabbed the phone and hurriedly stamped out the number.

'Mac?'

'The very same.'

'It's Wrighton. Stewart.'

'Oh not another–'

'Shut up Mac and listen. Are you alone?'

'Well I like that–'

'Can I be overheard?'

A silence ensued then Mac's normal, serious and slightly concerned voice said, 'What's going on Stewart?'

'Listen Mac, that check that you did for me....'

'What on the–'

'Yes, yes..' Wrighton interrupted. 'You know the one. Keep it under your hat O.K.? Don't tell anybody that I asked you to do it and don't tell anybody the result.'

'Are you in trouble Stewart?'

'I don't think so. When I can tell you something definite I will. Trust me. But keep our little business a secret. Just you and me.'

'Mum's the word old boy. Not a smatter.'

'Thanks, you won't regret it.'

'I expect I will!' he laughed and then added seriously, 'And if you need my services again, don't hesitate to call upon them. I couldn't care less. They can't touch Mac Macleod. He's inviolate.'

'Thanks Mac. I hope you're right.'

Sandra Hardwicke lazily turned her twizzle stick in the long glass, stirring up the bubbles like the methane from the bottom of a pond. A few shouts from the pool pierced the gloomy interior of the club but she paid them no heed nor interest. She sighed and lifted her feet to the chair opposite. What a drab place! If this was supposed to be the social centre of the British community in Bangladesh it was a poor reflection of that community. Or perhaps it was a true reflection of a community barren of interest or intellect. She gazed languidly around the room. That old soak, Harry, was occupying his usual stool at the bar and entertaining a dark-haired man with a beard and lugubrious eyes. He is something to do with the accountancy section of the BHC, isn't he? Whatever he is, he is drinking as though his boots were on fire. Perhaps it is the influence of Harry.

'Now you see...' Harry was declaiming to the eager moon of a face that the accountant had turned to him... 'all this work study stuff is all right you know, all this time and notion business–'

'Motion.'

'Eh?'

'Time and motion. It's time and motion.'

'Yeah, that's what I'm saying. All this time and notion stuff is all right as long as you know how to interpret it. That's the important bit. It's no good if you can't interpret it.' He poked the man in the stomach with his finger and pushed back a few strands of white hair onto his sunburned crown. 'I'll give you a frinstance. Now what country, generally speaking, has got the reputation of being ahead with business methods?'

'Well, Japan.'

'No.' Harry scolded him as if he were a mischievous schoolboy purposefully quoting the wrong answer.

'It must be Korea then, they've done wonders–'

'The States. Harvard Business School. And all that. No, it's the States. People always talk about the USA as having it's head screwed on right when it comes to business methods don't they?'

'Oh right.'

'Well, back in the war, the second world war, the Yanks used to run it like a business.'

'I suppose that was all it was for them really, wasn't it?'

'You know we had Motor Torpedo Boats and Motor Gun Boats and that?'

'Yeah.'

'Well these MTB's and MGB's were a good idea and so the Yanks copied us, only they called theirs "PT"s'. God knows why.' He took another swig from his glass. 'Anyhow, they wanted to do it better than us so they sorted out the best crews that they had got, I mean, they identified the crews that had been the most successful and they analysed them and they discovered that many of them were football players and strong swimmers. What do you make of that then?'

Well I can't follow what he is talking about and I am sober so what the devil does the other chap make of it? Sandra mused. Perhaps I need another drink. Perhaps if I were as drunk as they are, I would understand them perfectly. But do I want to?

'So what they did was, they recruited in the navy and the army and that for all the good swimmers and footballers to join the PT boats, and what do you think happened?'

'Well, I expect they ended up with some really good crews.'

'Ah!' Harry exclaimed triumphantly, 'that's where you are wrong. Cos you see, they hadn't calculated how important luck and providence was in the success of the other crews you see, so they didn't get any particularly noticeable increase in efficiency but there was one very important effect directly attributable to their time and notion rubbish. Do you know what that was?'

The accountant shook his head slowly, his eyes following half a phase behind each oscillation. Sandra expected him to fall off the stool. She was disappointed.

'When they got to the end of the war, the States had lost nearly all their champion swimmers and footballers, Ha Ha! That's what their business ideas cost them.'

Sandra turned away and listlessly picked up a magazine which she had read several months earlier.

'Telephone madam.'

The bearer was holding the phone on a tray with the plug in his hand, motioning to the socket on the wall and stealing glances at her legs. Bloody natives! Anyone would think that their women didn't have any legs the way they keep looking at ours. Well you can jolly well step over them.

'Plug it in there. It'll only be my husband apologising for being delayed at the office and saying that I should go on to Newmarket and get the cloth by myself, which is what he suggested in the first place.'

'Madam?'

'Just plug it in, thank you.'

Wrighton sent away the Land Rover at the gates and nodded at the chowkidhar as he walked up the drive to the British Club, through the pools of shadow cast by the flaccid-leaved trees. A nice cool lime and soda at the deserted afternoon bar was just what he needed to help him marshal his thoughts.

'Mr. Wrighton!' a voice hailed him as soon as he entered and he gloomily dismissed any hope that he might spend a quiet time in reflection. 'What are you drinking sir?'

'Hello Harry.' He looked at Harry's companion.

'This is... um... this is....' Harry turned to the accountant in bemused despair. 'I want you to meet Mr. Wrighton. He works for Consolidated on a World Bank project and he is a pipeline engineer.'

The man proffered a wet fish which Wrighton shook whilst reminding himself that Harry had a formidable memory when drunk. But then, wasn't he always?

'Landlord!' Harry addressed the Bengali bar man. 'Give this man a drink.'

Oh who cares? Wrighton thought. It will take my mind off things, talking to these two for a while. At least they are harmless.

'Lime and soda please.'

'Mr. Wrighton,' Harry explained, 'believes fully in my theory of the Piltdown table, don't you sir?'

Wrighton racked his memory as he ran through the content of their previous meeting.

'Oh yes,' he agreed. 'I think we concurred on the major points at issue.'

'So what are you doing here at this time of day? You should be slaving under that demon Havering.'

'Well to tell you the truth, I came down here for a quiet drink and time to think.'

'No point in thinking. Action is what counts. I never got anywhere, thinking.'

'I never got anywhere,' the accountant said.

This is a bit depressing, Wrighton thought. 'Now, here is something you can help me on, Harry, you've been here some time. Is there anywhere that has a good English library? Has the High Commission got one? Somewhere I could browse through some books?'

'The British Council is what you need. Down on Fuller Road. Turn left at the big tree.'

'The British–?'

'British Council. Where all the women talk like men and the men talk like women. 'S'true,' he affirmed. 'Mind you, the women aren't much to look at. About the only palatable one is Plain Jane. She'd be alright face down in a bowl of sherbet. That's the place you want. British Council.'

'British Council,' the accountant echoed helpfully.

'And this is down on–'

'Fuller Road,' a clear voice prompted him. He swung around in surprise. 'I'll make a pact with you Stewart.'

'Hello Sandra, I'm sorry I didn't see you there.'

You weren't looking, you were too busy wasting your time with those two drunks. 'I'll take you down to the British Council if you will come with me to Newmarket to buy some cloth.'

'Well that's very kind of you, that would suit me but I don't want to impose myself on you.'

Hell's bells what a wimp!

'Do you always drive this fast, Sandra?'

'When are you going to call me Sandy like everybody else?'

'If you want me to call you Sandy then I will, but I've told you why I don't like it. Do you want me to call you Sandy?'

I don't think I do, somehow. It makes it a little different to be called Sandra and to have the car door held open for me when I get in and out. It makes me feel a little special.

'No, you can keep calling me Sandra. Hang on! This is a tight corner!'

I'll show him how I can drive. Look at him sitting there, gripping the window ledge in terror.

'Why does everybody drive so fast here? It doesn't seem to get them anywhere more quickly. I can't understand it.'

O.K. Clever Dick, but I don't meet a bullock cart at this junction every day. 'I suppose it's boredom. It makes life exciting. Don't you want your life to be exciting?' You boring engineer.

'No I don't thank you very much. My life has more than enough excitement for me at the present.'

'Wow! I bet it's really exciting being an engineer.'

'Well if you must know. Only the other day, on this very road...'

'Go on...'

'No. It's nothing.'

'You can't stop there. What were you saying? On this very road... Well?'

'No it's nothing. I made a mistake.'

Come on tell me. What happened? What set your pulse a-racing? What made your hair stand on end? Something did, I know it did. I can tell by the way you have suddenly clammed up as if you had realised that you had said too much. What was it that made your life suddenly exciting? I wish I knew. It wouldn't be anything ordinary, that is for sure.

'How far down Airport Road is the Newmarket?'

'You're not going to tell me are you?'

'Mmm?'

'Oh, you are infuriating Stewart Wrighton!'

And when you teach me to dance you infuriate me more. You turn my leg into position, you twist my ankles into angles and you tell me that I have done it wrongly and you make me do it again and again and again until I get it exactly right. I tell you that it is only dancing and you snap back at me that if it was 'only dancing' that I had wanted to learn then I could do that myself and you bend again to the brushing together of the heel on the impetus turn and the 'finishing diagonally to centre' and all the while you are touching me, holding me, bending me to your will and I am complying as hard as I can and still it is not enough for you but you don't see it. You don't see me as a woman, just as an article to bend into form and lines, to agitate to music, to ply to rhythms. I want to scream at you, 'Look at me, I am a woman with a woman's body and a woman's mind, can't you see what you are doing to me with your tranquil brown eyes and your firm arms?' But I know that your only reaction would be to say something like 'Let's try the open chassé one more time but this time remember, toe, heel, toe, heel,' God how I hate you Stewart Wrighton!

'Oh that must be the place there, it looks like a miniature version of Wembley stadium.'

'Does it? I'll park her in the shade.'

'Don't you lock it?'

'Sometimes I do, sometimes I don't. As the whim takes me. This kid will look after it for a couple of taka.'

'Is that safe?'

'Who cares?'

'Oh...'

'Come on, this way in. Give me your arm. Don't shy away I'm not going to bite you!'

Crikey, he's shaking like a jelly. Ha ha ha! You're not dancing now are you? You know I'm a woman. Perhaps I should squeeze a little too close to you as we go through this crowd, hmm? What do you think of that then? Like it?

'Are you feeling hot, Stewart? You are sweating quite a bit.'

'I don't usually feel the heat this much. It must be the crowd. The press of... the people.'

'Quite. That's where we've got to go. Over in the corner. It whiffs a bit, with these open drains but they have the best range of cloth.'

'What do you want cloth for?'

'A ball gown.'

'A ball gown?'

'Yes a ball gown. For the New Year's Eve dance. You are going aren't you?'

'Well I hadn't really thought about it.'

'It's only a few weeks away.'

'I suppose it is.'

'Oh you must come. We're getting a table up. I'll put you on our table. Leave it to me, I'll get the tickets.'

'Oh well, thank you. That's settled then. Let me know how much I owe you when it all comes through.'

'Oh Geoff will do that, he's the brains with the money. I just help him spend it. Now what do you think of this cloth for a gown?'

'Well...'

'You do look funny when you wrinkle up your nose like that. It makes your glasses go all wonky. I can tell that you don't like it.'

'I don't think that it really suits you. It's a bit girlish.'

'Well thank you very much. Always first in with the compliments.' Why do I let him insult me like this? 'Couldn't you have put it a nicer way?'

'Sorry, that was my nice way of putting it.'

'You beast! What about this chiffony stuff?'

'For a gown?'

'Yup.'

'What are you wearing underneath?'

'Stewart, how dare you!'

'I mean it will–'

'I was thinking of wearing nothing underneath.'

That's made him uncomfortable. Ha! That's brought the colour to his cheeks. Look at him struggling now. He's trying not to imagine me swirling around the floor in a diaphanous billowing gown and nothing underneath!

'W...what I was trying to say was that it will need to have a proper underskirt with it. If you could get some net it would probably be best.'

'But not without?'

'Not if you want me to dance with you.'

'I did not say that I did.'

'Very true and I hope that you will be able to reward Geoff for his trust and confidence by fulfilling your role as his perfect dancing partner.'

'Sometimes, Stewart, you are unbearably pompous. Hamid! Seven yards of this one. Snip! snip!' Now where is he wandering off to? 'Don't get lost!'

'No I'm just going to look at those bricks.'

A pile of bricks. A pile of bloody bricks. He is down at the market with me and he is more interested in a pile of bricks than my party dress.

'Now that's an interesting thing. What do you think that is?'

'It's a brick, Stewart. Even I know that.'

'What kind of brick?'

'A brick is a brick is a brick.'

'Wrong.'

'I suppose I had to be. But does it matter? It is a particularly nondescript, rather grey-looking brick.'

'Exactly.'

'What do you mean, "exactly"?'

'You have hit on the exact point that I was trying to bring to your attention. The brick is grey-blue.'

'What colour should it be for Christ's sake?' Oh my God! There he goes, wincing at my blasphemy.

'What colour are all the other bricks in Dhaka?'

'Now I come to think of it, they're a sort of orangey pink.'

'That's right. But this brick is an overburn. It's an engineering brick.
That's why it is that colour.'

'What is an engineering brick?'

'It has to be much harder than a house brick, to last longer and take
greater compression stress.'

Now he thinks he is at the bloody office.

'You mean that it is a stronger brick, that's all. What's so special about
that?' That's got him thinking. That's slowed him down a bit.

'It's just that I didn't know that anybody made engineering bricks in
Bangladesh, they haven't got the heat in the ovens for it. They are only
wood-fired you know.'

'Of course.' Of course I know what they burn in the brick ovens. I
spend all my days down at the brickfields don't I? Where do you pick up
all this boring piffle-paffle? 'What are you looking at now?'

'It's just the name on the brick, that's all.'

'What, A.H.T.? Do you know them?'

'I've come across them before, quite recently.'

But you won't tell me about them will you because you have clammed
up again? I can tell, you are already miles away in thought.

'Come on then, I've got my stuff. I had better take you to the British
Council before they shut. Stewart....'

'Yes?'

'You're not bringing that brick in the car.'

A.H.T. Twice in one day. Within hours one of the other. First it is
buying ten kilometres of pipe at ridiculous knock-down prices and now it
is producing engineering bricks. And it was the same trademark on the
brick as was on that building board at the shopping precinct. A.H.T. was
the name of the company which had used our aggregate and substituted
crushed brick in those piers that failed. When something went wrong...
A.H.T. was there, benefiting, profiting.

Wrighton discovered that in order to withdraw a book from the British
Council Library he had to enrol, so he paid his taka and filled in the card
whilst the white-shirted clerk sweated over the card index and register of
numbers. He was not holding out much hope of finding what he wanted
but he nevertheless made his way to the appropriate shelf and was
surprised to find that they had one copy of the British Ballroom Dancing
Society Yearbook. It was a good fifteen years old but the instruction for
the steps that he needed would be in there, they didn't change.

As he was making his way back to the counter he had another surprise. Rubena Chowdhry was standing in the queue before him, a heavy tome tucked under her arm.

'Well, well well, Rubena, we mustn't keep meeting like this.'

'Oh Mr... Stewart. Hello. Are you taking a book as well?'

'Yes, I've just joined. Are you a member? I didn't realise that the British Council was for–'

'You didn't realise that the British Council was for Bengalis as well?' She laughed off his wounding ignorance. 'Well I didn't realise that Europeans were allowed to use it. I am so rarely seeing them here.' She showed him her volume of British Indian history. 'For my father, you know. He is always taking a great interest in this question. I think that he would have made a great statesman.' She peered with interest at his book which he held rather tightly to his chest. 'And what are you reading?'

'Oh it's just something I needed for a friend.' He tried to dismiss it.

'What is it about?' She put her hand on the cover. 'Let me see. It is not saucy is it? I know you Europeans are reading books like that.'

'No it is not!' Wrighton quickly released the book to her.

She flicked through the pages of club details and competition results and the diagrams of the latest steps and the advertisements for dancing shoes and gowns and then she stopped at a photograph of a couple demonstrating the quickstep. She pursed her lips slightly, suppressing an impish smile.

'Ah, this is the dancing that we are seeing on the Western film and on Western television. When the man and woman are dancing this you are very close to each other isn't it?'

'That's the way it has to be done.' He took the book from her and handed it to the clerk for stamping.

'Is that the way you are doing it?' The tips of her mouth were curling up again but Wrighton did not notice.

'For Pete's sake Rubena, it is no more licentious than the dancing that some of the dancing girls do in classical Hindu studies that I have seen. Some of their poses are very ero... suggestive.'

'Ah...' she said with complete composure, '...of course, the Hindus...'

They passed out of the cool bungalow full of books and into the blinding car park.

'Oh, it's Mrs. Hardwicke! Is that the friend that you are borrowing the book for?' she asked mischievously and before Wrighton could regain himself she had hobbled across to the car. 'Hello Mrs. Hardwicke! I met Mr. Wrighton in the library. He said that he was getting books for you so

I thought that I would come and say hello to you.'

Sandra Hardwicke was momentarily overcome by the assailing Bengali woman in a sari with a big book tucked under her arm. She had never met her before in her life.

'I'm awfully sorry, I don't know–'

'Of course you are not knowing me, Mrs. Hardwicke, but I am knowing you. I saw you in *"An Inspector Calls"* at the Dhaka Stage. You were playing the girl.'

'Good Heavens, but that was–'

'Three years ago. I remember it. It was a very good play by your Mr. J.B. Priestley. I thought you were excellent.'

'Well thank you.' Sandra Hardwicke glowed in the praise, all the more fragrant for its three year's maturing. 'Miss...?'

'Mrs. Chowdhry. I work with Stewart at the office.'

'Can we drop you anywhere Rubena? We are going back up to Gulshan.'

'Very kind I'm sure. But I have my rickshaw waiting just over there. Very pleased to have met you. Are you doing another play soon?'

'We are still looking for one. I'll tell Stewart when we do so that you don't miss it.'

'Very kind of you. Goodbye Mrs. Hardwicke, Goodbye Stewart.'

As they drove away, waving to the upright figure of Mrs. Chowdhry perched on the swaying rickshaw, Sandra Hardwicke said confusedly,

'She said you were getting some books for me?'

'Oh she misunderstood. Although I have got a book, I got it because of you but not necessarily for you.'

'You'd better let me see it then.'

Wrighton put the yearbook on the back seat.

'It won't mean an awful lot to you. It is a dancing textbook.'

'They have things like that in there?'

'They had. One copy. I have got it now.'

'What do you need it for?'

'To teach you to dance.'

'But I thought you knew how to dance.'

'I learned to dance a long long time ago.'

'You poor old man. How old are you Stewart?'

'A lot older than you and I need the book to remind me of some of the intricacies of the steps. Don't forget, I spent my time learning the man's steps. The lady's steps are somewhat different.'

'Oh yes, I never thought of that.'

'Actually,' Wrighton tried to sound casual, 'you might as well look after the book, you know, keep it at your place because I will only need it at your house. I won't need it at Banani house.'

'And your two macho house pets might think you were a bit of a pansy if they saw you reading it, is that it?'

'Something like that.'

'Who was the Bengali lady, Mrs. Chowdhry?'

'Just someone I work with. An interpreter. A very good interpreter, actually. And a very intelligent lady.'

'She's got a lot going for her then,' Sandra remarked shortly but Wrighton did not notice. 'We could have given her a lift.'

'No point. She only lived around the corner.'

'Oh did she?' Sandra stated stonily but to annoy her, the bloody engineer was now feigning a consuming interest in a patch of burned tar outside the cinema.

17

'Come on Wrighton, show a leg! It's nine o'clock!'

Wrighton turned over and tucked the bedclothes around his ears as he would have done in Wembley but the thin sheet provided no insulation against the pounding of the fists on his door.

'All right,' he grumbled. 'I'm awake.'

He pulled his alarm clock nearer to his unspectacled eyes and squinted at the dial. It was indeed nine of the clock. He sunk back onto the pillows, his head muggy with sleep and the heat.

Of late, he had been so tired in the mornings. Once or twice at the office he had caught himself yawning and day dreaming in the torpor-inducing warmth. The columns of figures would march up the page like soldier ants and then disperse into the undergrowth as his eyes went out of focus; the dockets, the bills, the invoices would merge into a pastel patchwork across his desk. He would become befuddled by irrelevant detail, entering into calculations of gigantic complexity and monumental uselessness whilst striving to keep his eyes open and his brain functioning as efficiently as he could. Just keep going till the end of the week and then, Friday morning... he could sleep...

The thumping thundered around his room. He awoke with a start.

'I'm coming!' he shouted. He was angry at having fallen back into sleep. He hauled himself from the bed and stumbled, dumbly into the bathroom where he splashed some water on his face.

At the breakfast table, Bell was drumming the palms of his hands on the table top to accompany the percussion of the music which was thumping out from the cassette recorder. The cutlery bounced and jangled on the table top.

'Yeh, yeh, yeh, babe, swing it!' he exhorted Wrighton.

'Do you have to have it so loud?'

Bell grinned at him and deliberately turned the volume up.

'Can't you take it, old man? Life getting on top of you?'

'I shouldn't think anybody else is getting on top of him,' Tuppin commented obliquely from the corner by the bookcase.

Wrighton slumped in the chair in despair. It was pointless trying to fight these two so he just succumbed. If they wanted to be noisy and crude and brutal then he would not stop them. It was just too much effort for too little effect. He crunched through his toast in a miserable interior silence and thought of other things.

'Hey, did I tell you we minced up a Bangla the other day?' Bell yelled.

Tuppin leaned over and turned the music down.

'What was that?'

'We minced up a bogwit down at the pad. Kerpow! Legs and arms everywhere. Now you see me, now you don't.'

'Is it in the paper?' Tuppin enquired. 'What happened?'

'We were doing static tests of the engines and some bogwit was up on the top of the craft. Christ knows what he was doing up there, probably looking for his goat or something. Captain says to me, "Rotate" You know the props are on pylons that we can rotate through twenty degrees to steer the craft?' Tuppin nodded. 'Well I rotated twenty degrees to starboard like he said and then suddenly there was this rattling on the cabin windows as bits of minced bogwit whistled past into the wide blue yonder. Everyone yelling and waving things on the ground, then they start running in all directions looking for bits.'

'Who was it, one of the Bangla engineers?'

'Don't know. We never found out. Took all day to change the sodding prop and we had to sluice down the cabin ourselves 'cos none of the Banglas would come on top in case they got minced as well.'

'Perhaps this is the true purpose of the Hovercraft project – population control.'

'I can think of cheaper ways of doing it.'

'Not so much fun though.'

'For Pete's sake you two, give it a rest will you? I'm trying to eat my breakfast.'

'His Lordship is trying to eat his breakfast,' Tuppin mimicked. 'How is his Lordship's dancing class progressing?'

'Satisfactorily,' Wrighton answered carefully.

'I bet! Is Sandy as randy as they say?'

'I don't know how randy "they" say she is and I am not interested in learning,' Wrighton replied coldly.

'Ah, get on with yer, Tuppin, you're just jealous!' Bell accused him. 'Just 'cos you've never got anywhere with her.'

'I've never tried,' Tuppin retorted.

'When are you two going to get into your thick skulls that men and women can have relationships other than those requiring them to jump in and out of each other's beds?'

'You're a bit touchy this morning Wrighton. 'Feeling alright?'

'Oh... I didn't sleep very well that's all.'

'Are you lunching here?'

He considered the question. If he ate at Banani House he would be tied to the house in the middle of the day.

'No, I think I'll go down to the club.'

'Madam come,' Moussi announced from the doorway and Mina the masseuse swung into the room.

'You go first,' Bell suggested.

Mina closed the bedroom door and locked it as she always did whilst Wrighton crossed to the bed and switched off the a.c.. She found it uncomfortable to work with it on.

'How are you Mr. Wrighton?' she asked in her sing-song Indian voice.

'Oh, I'm not so bad.'

'You are looking very tired.'

'I am very tired, Mina. I have been getting very tired lately. I don't know why.' He was surprised how despairing he sounded. 'How is your baby?'

'She is getting stronger and very noisy.'

'Ah, they do that.'

He lay down on the bed in his boxer shorts. He was aware of Mina standing looking at him, hesitating. Then she said,

'If you are feeling very tired Mr. Wrighton I think I will give you a special Indian massage. You will like it. It is with incense as well.' From her voluminous bag she brought a small cedar wood box and extracted a stick of incense. 'It must stand in something.'

Wrighton looked around the room.

'What about my pencil tin? It could stand in that.'

'That will do.'

She lit the stick and placed the tin on the table near to his pillow. It was a heavy perfume which hung persistently around the barely glowing stick as if a particularly pungent bouquet of flowers had been placed there.

'You must relax now. Stay on your back.'

Wrighton tried to concentrate upon the sensations. I can feel fingers on the front of my neck and now around the back as if she were going to strangle me, he thought calmly. Now she is moving my backbone about just behind my neck, I can feel the vertebrae moving I can hear the gristle grating. I shall just let my head flop, I'm too tired to hold it still. Now I can feel her pulse in her fingers as she holds the back of my head, I am in a cradle, floating away on a cloud, drifting. Now she is stroking my temples, gently. That incense is a bit strong it makes me feel quite groggy.

'This will take away your tension. Now breathe deeply and slowly. In.... and out. In .... and out.'

The deeper I breathe the more I can smell that perfume. It is quite overpowering or perhaps it is the massage on my temples that is making me feel so detached. Yes it must be that. It is draining away my tension. It must be the massage. The front of my shoulders, then the back of my shoulders, gently kneading, not like her normal pummelling, this is smooth. I can feel the tingling at the backs of my eyes before I go off to sleep. It would be a pity to sleep and miss the massage.

Ah, now she has started on my legs, I like this bit. I can feel her moving down to the foot of the bed. I expect she is removing her sari as usual. I don't know why she ever starts with it on, she knows that she cannot massage me properly when she is restrained by that tube of cotton.

The knees, and down to the ankles and up to the knees and back down to the ankles and this time out to the toes and up under the sole of the foot, around the achilles tendon up the calf. Up the thigh to the top. I remember the first massage she gave me. 'Mr. Wrighton' she said, 'You have very long legs'. Well they certainly make her stretch. Oh dear! That was a mistake. Her fingers slipped up the leg of my pants but I shan't say anything, it doesn't matter, I don't want to embarrass her and I'm feeling warm and soft and oh! she has done it again. Down to my knees and up the front of my thigh and oh, actually it is quite nice. I suppose I ought to tell her. Where is she now? I can feel her hands. It is very gloomy in here, I hadn't realised how dark it was. Perhaps the sun has gone in. Don't be silly, the sun doesn't go in at ten o'clock in the morning! If I could get my head off the pillow... there she is, lurching towards me and drawing back again, like the waves on the beach. It's funny how she keeps changing the shape of her face like that. It must be a trick that they can do. Her fingers are touching me now every time, I'm sure they are. A little further up each time, a little longer each time. It's making me grow big, I know it is. I suppose she is not embarrassed, I suppose this kind of thing happens sooner or later to everyone and she is a married woman so she knows what it is all about. It is not my fault that I am straining at my pants, she must know that. When I peek out from below my eyelids, gosh how heavy my eyelids are, when I peek out from below my eyelids I can almost imagine that she is not wearing a blouse anymore and those great breasts of hers are swinging freely below her. I think they are swinging freely below her. I'm sure they are. I can see the great brown nipples and now they are stroking up the front and my sex is giving a little kick just like it did that day at chapel...

'How old are you now Stewart?'

'Twelve sir.'

'And do you like singing in the chapel choir?'

'Very much sir.'

'Good, good. You have a fine voice, Stewart and you must try to develop it.'

'Yes sir.'

'I expect you know that at your age your body changes in quite a few ways and some of these can affect your singing voice.'

'Sir?'

'Just come into the chapter room for a minute. It won't take long.'

'Yes sir.'

'Shut the door. Do you like singing God's word, my boy?'

'Yes sir.'

'Good. Well, we will have to see how you are developing. Have your testicles dropped yet?'

'I don't know what you mean sir.'

'No, I suppose you don't. This is a job I have to do with some boys. It is all part of the Lord's ministrations. Just lift up your surplice and undo your trousers.'

'Sir?'

'Just the fly buttons so that I can get my hand in. Don't worry it's quite warm. That's right. Now what have we here? Now these are your testicles, Stewart. I expect you boys call them "balls" or something don't you? Hmm? No need to be ashamed, we have all been boys you know.'

'Yes sir.'

'Ah, now don't worry about that, it is quite a natural reaction, indeed it is a healthy reaction and letting it grow like that will give you a fine strong voice. Let's see how big it will become. Perhaps I can make it bigger by stroking it. Yes that's very good. Now you can exercise this, you know, the more you let it grow like this the purer your voice will become. Is it a pleasant sensation?'

'Sir?'

'Does it feel nice Stewart?'

'Sort of sir.'

'Well this is one of the Lord's rewards to you. You must exercise yourself regularly and you will find it quite pleasurable. The Lord has made it
like that to encourage you. You know that you can rub it like this don't
you? Yes, that's a good healthy kick.'

'Sir... Have–?'

'What is it Stewart?'

'Have you finished in there sir?'

'Oh yes, I'm sorry, I get distracted. That is not the first time that you
have grown big like that is it Stewart?'

'No sir.'

'You have probably found that other things can make it grow big
haven't you?'

'Some.'

'Well you should concentrate on those. When I see you next week I
want you to tell me some of the things that you have found that made you
grow big.'

I am certain that this room is getting darker and smaller. It's closing in
on me. I can just see Mina rocking back and forth, I must be seeing
things, she appears to be stark naked...

Wrighton lay still and listened to the rickshaw bells tinkling outside his
window. He must have dropped off to sleep and had a queer dream. It
was such a queer dream, disturbing – snatches of childhood interwoven
with his life in Dhaka. He opened his eyes and gazed drowsily around the
room. That incense that Mina had used was powerful stuff, his room
reeked of the stale after-odour. He looked into his pencil tin but the stub
of the incense had been removed. He could not find his alarm clock but
his watch told him that he had slept till almost midday. Well, he had
obviously needed it. He sat up and his head cleared a little. What on
earth had Mina thought of him, drifting off to sleep like that in the middle
of the massage? It was a good job that she knew nothing about his dream.
He winced at the thought of it. He threw open his windows to air his room
and rid it of the lingering perfume, carefully closing and locking the
mosquito screens on the inside.

After a tepid shower he discovered that he had a hunger so he grabbed
his swimming bag, slipped on some clothes and took a rickshaw down to
the club. The other two had obviously left hours ago for the house was in
silence.

As he climbed out of the rickshaw he realised that he had made a mistake in thinking that he could get an easy lunch. It was Friday and the place was bulging with children racing around demanding food from their parents who were, in the greater part, either lounging around in the sun or playing tennis or squash.

He wandered along the edge of the pool and recognised the woman with the long black hair and dark eyes who had nearly drowned him that day. She was standing on the spring board from which she caught his eye momentarily and then executed a neat jack knife dive into the pool. Wrighton gazed miserably at the ever-increasing ripple of water. He would never learn to swim like that, never. He was still gazing when, unnoticed by Wrighton, she pulled herself from the pool, snatched up her towel and walked past him to the changing rooms. As she passed she remarked casually,

'It's easy when you know how.'

Wrighton started from his day dreaming. That was what she had said to him when he had nearly drowned in the pool. Why was she taunting him? Why pick on him or was she like that with everyone? He swung around but a retort never came to his mind and in any case, he knew deep down that he would not have had the guts to deliver it had it materialised. He watched the retreating figure in the swimsuit, as if the tightly drawn costume held the key to the mystery of their non-communicative yet provocative relationship. It was almost as if she were bullying him.

He dismissed her from his mind. He just had to accept that there were some things that he would never understand and perhaps some occurrences that truly had no explanation.

He went into the bar. As soon as he entered he automatically glanced at Harry's corner to reassure himself that the world was still turning on its axis. Unfortunately, Harry had chosen that moment to look across at the door.

'Mr. Wrighton!' he boomed. 'Come here! I want to talk to you.'

Wrighton's heart sank but he applied his bravest and purest face as he strolled over to the bar. Harry was sitting, quite primly, on his stool, with a paper serviette tucked into his open necked shirt. He looked like an artichoke heart.

'Hello Harry.'

'Do you like scampi?'

'Well... yes.'

'Eat that!' Harry slid a plate across to him. 'I've got two plates.'

'Well I–

'You haven't had lunch have you?' Harry demanded and Wrighton somehow felt that Harry knew the answer. He had a shrewdness about him that Wrighton had not noticed before. It could not be that he was sober could it?

'No I haven't,' Wrighton admitted, his mouth watering at the sight of the fish. He argued to himself that he would never get anything from the club kitchens before the end of the afternoon.

'Well eat that then. It's worth its weight in gold, that is. A club meal with no parents. An orphan of a meal. I've got a proposition to make to you while you are eating.'

'Oh yes.' Wrighton tried to sound neutral. He did not like the way that the conversation was turning.

'What are you doing this afternoon?'

Wrighton looked placidly at Harry's egg head, its few hairs glistening on the sweat, whilst his mind raced on, trying to guess what this was all about. Should he say that he was terribly busy? But then he might miss an opportunity that he had waited all his life for. He could not conjure up in his mind any opportunity that he had waited half his life for. However, if he said that he was free he might find himself enmeshed in some degrading exercise involving carting Harry from bar to bar until the early hours of the morning.

'You're a canny bastard, Wrighton,' Harry remarked at his silence.

'No... ' Wrighton was embarrassed. 'I was just thinking what I was doing this afternoon and ... erm–'

'Good! You're obviously free.' Harry shovelled another forkful of scampi into his mouth and yelled, 'Lime and soda for my mate here.' He turned to Wrighton. 'We're going sailing so eat up!'

'Sailing!'

'Didn't you notice the wind?'

'The wind?'

'The stuff that wrestles with the tops of the eucalyptus trees not the type that makes you blush.'

'But where do you go sailing? Have you got a boat?'

Harry stopped chewing for a moment and looked at him. He carefully put down his knife and fork and drained his glass of beer.

'I've got a five metre catamaran, glass fibre, at the potato starch factory on the Meghna. I imported it as a kit and built it.' He spoke evenly and exactly and Wrighton gained the impression that he was recounting something that he had never told anybody before. A secret revealed. 'It goes like shit off a shovel.'

'Do you normally sail it alone then?'

'Finish yer grub. You're in my crew now so you obey orders.'
'Aye aye captain.'

Wrighton had only ever seen Harry being transported, usually drunk, in a rickshaw, so it surprised him somewhat to be taken out to a smart jeep. Even more surprising was Harry's driving. He drove carefully, quietly, with a modicum of consideration but a busy efficiency. Wrighton watched him as he threaded the jeep between the rickshaws and around tollygaris, menacing the baby-taxis just sufficiently for them to give him the road without it being a statement of bravado or a declamation of virility. He made no disparaging remarks about the natives. He called nobody a 'bogwit' or a 'birdbrain' but he passed through the traffic like sand through a sieve.

'How long have you been in Bangladesh, Harry?'

Harry glanced across at him, as if unaccustomed to the distraction of having a passenger. He effortlessly spun the wheel and the jeep veered down a dark alley beside a peeling, leaning mosque.

'Short cut,' he announced. 'Saves time. Over twenty years.' This reply puzzled Wrighton till he recalled his initial enquiry. 'I know what you're thinking. Why don't I drive like a maniac?'

'It wasn't that–' Wrighton began.

'Liar! It was written all over your face. I used to drive like that. When I first came out here but I never got anywhere any faster than anybody else so I sat down one day and decided to work out a philosophy of driving that would leave me relaxed and save my brake linings.'

'Well it seems to work.'

'I know it works.'

Wrighton stared apprehensively at the stone steps which disappeared into the turgid brown waters of the Meghna which ran swirling past the miniature quayside of the potato starch factory. He felt incongruous in his swimming trunks and tee shirt, surrounded by a score of natives and he wondered whether he was being wise. He turned back to call to Harry who was just emerging from the paymaster's office which they had used as a changing room, laying their belongings on piles of sweet smelling hessian sacks.

'Are you sure that we can carry the boat down those steps?'

'We are not going to carry the boat anywhere, these gentlemen will.' Harry designated the surrounding natives with a sweep of his hand. 'Now what do you know about sailing?'

'Nothing.'

'That's what I like. A man with an overblown and conceited opinion of his own capabilities. No matter. Pay attention. This is the boat.' He pointed to a small white catamaran sitting on a patch of bare grass. 'That tall aluminium thing sticking up is the mast. Now we try to keep the mast sticking upwards so that the sail can catch the wind. If the mast does go in the water we will probably have to unbolt it to set the boat upright.'

'J... Just a minute...' Wrighton did not care whether this was a joke or not, he still needed to settle in his own mind what risks were involved in this venture. 'Why should the mast touch the water?'

'Well if we capsize –'

'But you said that the boat was unsinkable.'

'Unsinkable, yes. But that does not mean that it cannot capsize. You'll see what I mean when we get going, the boat tips over a bit.'

'Oh. Carry on.'

'We sit on this bit of canvas here and stick our toes under here. These things are the twin rudders. Made 'em myself after I smashed the other ones. I'll steer with the tiller-bar and hold the sheet with this rope here.'

'It doesn't sound very nautical. Are you sure that you can sail this thing?'

'A Pathan might not be able to say "Lee Enfield" but he could still shoot you with one.'

'Right, so you sit there and hold that rope and steer with that bar... what do I do?'

'I'm coming to that. Give me a hand up with this cool box.'

They lashed the coolbox to the bottom of the mast with strong cord.

'Now your job is to sit here and hold onto this rope.'

'Is that all?' It sounded rather easy. 'Why do I have to hold this rope? It goes to the top of the mast but doesn't seem to do anything.'

'You hold the rope so that you don't fall over the side when you lean out.'

'Lean out?'

'Yes, you know. You've seen it on telly. The boat tips one way and you lean the other.'

Wrighton grinned thinly but said nothing. Since Harry had explained the whole system in such a matter of fact manner then it must be safe.

Harry moved amongst the boys and men, tapping selected ones on the head. They followed him to the boat, chattering noisily.

'They like this boat,' he explained confidentially, 'because it goes faster than the river boats and it doesn't have an engine. They think it is magic.'

He leaned over the hull and threw two mildew covered lifejackets back into the office doorway. 'We won't be needing those.'

'No lifejackets?' Wrighton remarked coolly.

'River's no deeper than twenty feet at the most. You can't drown in that.'

Wrighton remembered childhood warnings of how you could drown in two inches of water if it covered all your respiratory orifices, but in the face of Harry's scorn he did not protest.

Harry called out an order and the men picked the boat up and wiggled it inexpertly down the steps.

'Our job is to keep the tiller off the stone steps. That was how I buggered up the other one. So keep this end up.'

They waddled and shuffled like a Chinese carnival dragon, down the hot stone steps into the river. Wrighton could feel the mud under his feet. Surely they should get on board soon? When the water reached his thighs Harry at last instructed him to 'jump on'. Wrighton took a leap, slipped on the mud river bed and fell under the hull. He floundered out from underneath to the jeering and shrieking of the Bangladeshis. He sheepishly clambered on board, aware of his sodden shirt.

'Inspecting the hull for barnacles?'

'Something like that.'

The boat was wallowing lifelessly out into the Meghna whilst Harry adjusted ropes and cords and tested the tiller.

'We'll just have to drift for a while till we come around that bluff of trees, then we'll catch the wind.'

They hauled up the sail and made fast and then sat and watched a lumbering country boat of rough-hewn timber and patched jute sails crawl down the middle of the river. Wrighton had not realised that the Meghna was so wide. He could not see the other bank. He surreptitiously held his rope a little tighter as they drifted towards the bend in the river. Harry was watching the ripples on the water surface.

'Another ten yards,' he warned, as if leaving the lea of the bluff was going to rocket them up to mach 2. 'Five yards, hold tight.'

Wrighton smiled to himself, Harry was quite sweet really.

Suddenly something made a resounding 'crack' above his head and simultaneously the boat lurched over to one side, lifting him inboard.

'Lean out!' Harry yelled furiously as he adjusted ropes and suddenly they were off, chasing down the river, the wind cracking in the sail and two plumes of water rising behind them from the rudders. Wrighton was petrified.

'Lean out further, I'm not letting in the sheet. I want to enjoy this wind.'

Wrighton leaned out until his head and shoulders were well down below the level of the gunwales. The Meghna was flashing at him, twelve inches below his left ear, hissing and thudding and above him, the sail was strapping to the thrumming mast, singing vibrations down the rope that he was now seriously and with great application, hanging on to. Thirty seconds later they whisked past the country boat, sluicing it with water from their rudders. The Bangladeshi sailors stood wide-eyed and mute, staring at this impish invader from another century. On and on they tore, the pace not slowing even when they reached the confluence with the Burra Ganga.

They hurtled into the main stream, over the wake of a diesel powered river boat, rusty iron and hundreds of passengers whooping and whistling. Wrighton swallowed about a pint of water when Harry changed course suddenly to avoid a boat load of tomatoes and he was ducked below the surface of the river, green water tearing over his head, drumming on his ears, just his hand visible for a split second above water, still grasping the cord. Then he was out in the hot air again spluttering and laughing and cheering with the others, exhilarated. Round another country boat, lumbering along with a load of bricks, the water level washing over the freeboard where two brown bodies were monotonously baling it out again.

Wrighton twisted himself to look back at Harry. He was sitting in the stern, one hand tugging on the sheet, the other hanging on the tiller and a broad, happy grin carved across his face. He nodded and indicated something of interest forrard. Wrighton turned and was shaken by the sight of the biggest ship he had ever seen. And they were hurtling towards it. It looked enormous. Although it was probably only about five hundred tons, when you are lying with your head on the surface of the river, everything assumed impressive proportions. Harry was aiming at a point two thirds of the way down its side which would give them the space to pass astern of the ship but something was not computing in the calculation, they were getting closer and still the boat was before them. Frantically, Wrighton yelled out to Harry,

'Look out, it's going backwards!'

Harry peered past the clapping sail and then yanked over the tiller. Suddenly Wrighton was airborne. The water dropped away from under his left ear and he was hoisted six feet into the air as the catamaran lifted onto one hull.

'Hold on!' Harry yelled, adding optimistically, 'Lean out further!'

Wrighton pulled on the rope till his shoulder ached and braced his feet against the canvas strap. Still higher he went and further over leaned the mast. Harry at the stern was juggling ropes and the tiller, unwilling to relinquish the speed, balancing the catamaran on one hull and steering by bringing in the sheet and letting it out again. When it seemed that all was lost and they would plough into the rust-scoured stern of the tramp, Harry twitched the tiller and the hull came down with a crash, pushing Wrighton under the water again till he managed to pull himself clear. They zipped behind the ship with ten feet leeway. Wrighton could feel the threshing of the propeller as it churned the muddy water in his ears. They immediately ran into the lea of the vessel and the wind was sucked from the sheet. The catamaran ploughed cascades of greeny-brown water over the bows, threatening to break the cool box loose from its lashings. Wrighton sat up, spitting out mouthfuls of river water. A hundred yards away lay the far bank, they coasted gently towards it, not speaking. The water slapped indolently between the double hulls. Wrighton looked across at Harry. Harry searched his face anxiously for some reaction.

'Let's go back and do it again!' Wrighton smiled.

'That's ma boy!' Harry slapped him on the shoulder and began to instruct him in the manoeuvre of tacking.

Twice more they tacked back up the river and with bated breath, turned and hurtled back across it and each time the exhilaration and excitement were just as great, not diminished by one scruple. Wrighton could not remember when he had enjoyed or experienced anything to such a depth before. It left him bright-eyed and eager.

After the third crossing, Harry turned the catamaran southwards a little way and after a few minutes he nudged the bows onto a low, grass covered shoreline.

'All ashore!' he called. 'Grab the line!'

Between them they pulled the boat up out of the water and Harry lowered the sail to make doubly sure that the boat did not blow away. Then he lovingly unlashed the cool box and hauled it ashore. Wrighton helped him carry it.

'I like this place.' Harry surveyed the featureless scrubby grass mound upon which they were seated.

'You've been here before have you?'

'Yeah, once or twice. It's nice and quiet.'

'That's a point. By now we should have twenty or thirty Bengalis parading around goggling at us. Where are they?'

'Walk up to the top of that mound and you'll see.' He waved a can of beer in the direction. 'Go on.'

Intrigued, Wrighton stood up and wandered up the ten feet to the top of the mound. He was not prepared for what he saw from the top. This was why they were not being pestered. From the top of the mound the ground fell away gently for about twenty feet at which point it slipped unobtrusively back into the Meghna. They were on an island about thirty feet wide and a hundred yards long. He trotted back down the slope.

'How did you find this place?'

'Just came across it. Pattie?' Harry pushed a bag of savouries towards him. 'Vegetable, no meat. They won't kill you. The missus made them.' Wrighton took one gingerly. 'Yes, you've got to enjoy these places whilst you can. This island for example, probably won't be here next year. It's only been here two seasons.'

'What happens?'

'Floods, monsoon. All the water and silt comes down and the river just wanders about where it likes and wherever it happens to be when the water level falls again is where it stays. A sort of riparian musical chairs.'

'These are nice.'

'Have another, help yourself.'

'I didn't realise how hungry I was.'

'It always makes you hungry, sailing. Even if you've just had tiffin, always the same.' He wiped the back of his hand across his mouth and then delved into the cool box. 'Of course...' he coughed apologetically, 'I always drink beer myself, but I have got a couple of Pepsis if you want one.'

'Yes please.'

Harry threw a bottle over to him.

'Bottle opener's on the string on the cool box.'

Wrighton stretched out his legs in the afternoon sun and gazed down at them as if he had only just discovered them. He had, in fact, only just realised how brown they were. His frequent floundering in the club pool and wandering around Banani in shorts had ensured that they had quickly disguised his recent arrival. His arms too were brown. He lay back on the earth and closed his eyes, allowing the sun to toast his eyelids and create yellow and pink patterns in his mind.

'This is the life!' he murmured.

'You would soon tire of this all day long. When I came out as a lad I used to spend as much time out in the sun as I could but now, somehow I don't need to. It's not that the sun bothers me it's just that...' Harry paused and scratched the underneath of his chin thoughtfully, rippling the folds of tan flesh. 'It's so banal. It's the same every day. Drove the missus potty. That and the filth.'

'I thought you said that your wife was out here. She made these.' Wrighton sat up and took another pattie out of the box.

Harry looked at him and then he fiddled with his sandal buckle.

'I'm talking about twenty years ago, my first wife. She came out with me as a company wife, You know...' he listed an ironic inventory, 'Company house, company jeep, company wife. She couldn't stand it. I don't know what she had really expected to find out here...' He stopped and fixed his eyes on a point somewhere in the air. 'I don't think I really understood her. I was young, I was ambitious, this job was a career marker for me. May, my wife, came out after I had been here a month, getting the house ready. She drove from the airport with a handkerchief soaked in cologne cramped over her nose and her eyes tightly shut, convinced that when she got to the house it would all be different. 'Course it wasn't.' He grunted harshly. 'She stayed in the house for three weeks. Wouldn't go out. Wouldn't entertain. I had to pay for her ticket home. She never came back. Not even for a visit. I stayed on. I had a job to do. I suppose I tried to convince myself that it would all be all right. I dunno. You don't always do the right thing. I suppose I should have gone back to the U.K. but damnit, it was my career and... thinking about it I could have been more understanding. It just seemed to me that she was out to stop me from getting on in the world.' He grinned sadly at Wrighton. 'Which of course, she did. No company wife? – no prospects, no career.'

'Where is she now then?'

'Windsor. I see her from time to time. Not very often actually. Last time was about three years ago. I still send her money, it costs me nothing to live out here and she's got a bit from her parents to live on. We never got divorced you see so she still lives on as Mrs. Harry Dudgeon, and all face is saved. Her neighbours think she's a widow.

'After she had gone I pretty soon took up with a Bangla girl. You know what it's like, when you're young, you've got needs. I found the European wives easy meat but somehow insipid. So I picked this girl up in a village one day. Bought her from her father, took her back to Dhaka. What fun we had teaching her to run a house! She had never been inside a pukka house before, never been to school. She was a good girl though. Gave me a son, Nurul. He's fifteen now. I paid for him to go to college but he wanted to go back to the village after his mum died.'

'She died?'

'Yeah. When he was about twelve. Pretty girls these village girls but they're not very strong. She caught diarrhoea one year and that was that. She just wasted away. I was up-country at the time, she was dead by the time I got back. They just waste away,' he said softly. 'They've got no strength you see. Not like you or I. We have been properly nourished from the day we were born, but they need closely looking after. You think you've built them up a bit, they put on a bit of weight but somehow they just buckle under when they are ill.'

Wrighton cleared his throat which had become dry.

'So who made these patties?'

'Ah that's my new girl. Had her about three years. We've got a baby girl eighteen months old and she's going to be a strong one. I'm making sure she is fed properly from day one. None of this watery fish soup lark.'

'Good idea,' was all Wrighton could think to say.

He slowly drained his Pepsi which had become tepid in the sun and amused himself by gazing at various scenes through the rippled glass of the bottle, turning it occasionally to distort the image further. Harry was unusually quiet and it was to break this almost brooding tranquillity that Wrighton asked.

'Do you know of a company called 'A.H.T.'?'

'A.H.T.? What do they make?'

'Well bricks at least.'

'There's hundreds of brickworks along the Meghna. Could be any one of them. Could be them.' He pointed out to the midstream where two country boats were waddling along like floating fortresses, the pig-pink bricks stacked up almost to the level of the thatched cabins.

'No, it's not them.' Harry raised a surprised eyebrow at Wrighton's certainty. 'This company makes engineering bricks, high grade blues.'

'Not in Bangladesh it doesn't,' Harry retorted with equal certainty. 'They can't get the heat. All the engineering stock have to be imported.'

'Perhaps they were imported then, the bricks that I saw.'

'Must have been. What made you think they were Bangla bricks?'

'Well...' Wrighton began slowly, trying in his mind to decide what had, indeed convinced him that these bricks were native to Bangladesh. 'I suppose it's because I had just come across this company, A.H.T., a couple of times in our paperwork at the office and then when I saw these bricks down in Newmarket and they had 'A.H.T.' on them I assumed that it was the same company.'

'Coincidence.' Harry looked up at the sun. 'We must push off to get back before dark.'

'Aye aye capt'n.' Wrighton stood up smartly.

They tacked doggedly back and forth up the river, happy with the exertion, not speaking. Wrighton was thinking about a man who had come out to a strange country with his wife to launch his career and had obstinately refused to admit that it would not work out. He was imagining the pleadings and the weepings, the recriminations and the accusations and he searched occasionally, the archaeology of Harry's face for evidence of their having occurred. He was seeing a man, knowing that his career would never develop, becoming gradually alienated from his wife, seeking comfort in the country of his fortune to an extent where he had no reason to return to the land of his birth. A man drawing his solace from alcohol because his chosen mode of life obstructed the expression of his intellect. Harry could speak Bengali in the imperative tense but Wrighton doubted that he could have expounded upon the Piltdown Table with his girl, no matter how close they were. Wasn't it strange that when he talked about his Bengali girls, neither of them appeared to have had a name yet his wife whom he rarely saw, the living monument to his failed romance, was called 'May'?

A man with a legal wife in Windsor, a dead mother of his son in Bangladesh, a teenage son who had returned to the village, a new woman and a baby daughter and apparently, no European friends.

18

When Wrighton arrived at the Hardwicke's, Sandra was lounging on the sofa, ostentatiously studying the Ballroom Dancing Yearbook that he had borrowed from the British Council library. She pulled down the hem of her skirt primly.

'I was filling in the time doing a little homework.' She turned the page with exaggerated interest.

'I'm sorry I'm late, Sandra.'

'You forgot me.'

'No I didn't, I didn't!' Wrighton protested, feeling powerless as he was dragged into the vortex of one of her silly games.

'I sometimes wish I could,' Geoff remarked. 'You must tell me how you do it.'

'You beast!' She threw a shoe at her husband who caught it with an infuriating ease.

'I was out sailing and then when we got back there was a bit of a problem at the house.'

'Sailing!' they exclaimed together.

'Where on earth did you go sailing?' Geoff added.

'On the Meghna and the Burra Ganga. Where they meet.'

'What did you sail on? I mean, how were you...? I didn't know that you were a sailor.'

'Nor did I until today.'

'Who did you go with?'

'Harry...' Wrighton searched his memory for the surname, knowing that he had heard it recently. '...Harry Dudgeon.'

'Not Harry from the British Club?' Sandra was horrified.

Wrighton nodded.

'That drunk!' Geoff remarked 'And was that your first time? You're either mad or very brave.'

'Probably a bit of both.' Wrighton replied and he hated himself for not defending Harry. 'I was also late because when I got back to Banani House, Bell and Tuppin were holding a sort of kangaroo court on the staff. They had got the cook-bearer, the day chowkidhar and the night chowkidhar lined up against the wall and they were throwing all kinds of threats and menaces at them.'

'What on earth for? Did they burn the toast?'

'Bell has had his stereo stolen and Tuppin has lost his watch.'

'What about you?'

'I can't seem to find my alarm clock. But that is probably just careless-ness. No one would bother to steal an alarm clock would they?'

'Banglas will steal anything,' Sandra observed bitterly.

'When did all this stuff go missing?'

'Well that is what I can't understand.' Wrighton had to be wary about what he said. 'This morning when I left after my massage–'

'Your massage?' Sandra repeated.

Wrighton looked at her and said clearly, 'My massage.' And then began to blush. 'We all have one, every Friday. An Indian woman comes to the house–'

'An Indian woman?'

Wrighton blushed more.

'Take no notice, Stewart, she is just teasing you. Many of the Europeans have visiting masseuses.'

'Spoilsport!' Sandra pouted.

Wrighton took a breath and started again.

'After my massage, I left for the club. I couldn't hear anybody in the house so I assumed that Bell and Tuppin had both left as well, after their massages.'

'Would you not have seen them?' Sandra was puzzled. 'I mean, as it is you practically live in each others' pockets.'

Wrighton thought painfully back to the morning's massage and formed his explanation carefully.

'Well Mina did me first and then went on to do the other two. I... er stayed in my room afterwards... for a while. You know, enjoying the peace and quiet, writing letters and things and so I didn't really know what they were doing. Apparently, after their massages, they both, unusually fell asleep. And when they woke up they noticed their things were missing.'

'Well what did the chowkidhar say?'

'What do you expect? He swears blind that nobody came into the house and that the only person to leave was Mina, the masseuse.'

'Where was cook?'

'Marketing.'

'It must have been your masseuse then. She didn't use joss sticks did she?'

'I think they did mention something about incense.' He squirmed inwardly as he recalled Mina asking for a container to put the incense in. 'Why?'

With a callous detachment Geoff explained, 'She drugged them. Probably used a mild form of hashish. A well known trick. I'm surprised they fell for it.'

'Oh I can't believe that Mina would do such a thing.' Wrighton was shocked. But he knew that he was shocked because he was now sure that the befuddled stupor of his waking had not been due to his tiredness and, worse still, he feared the rising strength of a doubt that had been laying siege to his hastily erected defence all day long; had he dreamed the naked body of Mina moving over him or had it really happened...? He shuddered.

'You'll soon find out. If she doesn't turn up next Friday...'

'Yes, I suppose so.' Wrighton acceded.

'Oh we've got the tickets for the New Year's Eve dance.' Geoff waved a wad of pasteboard in the air.

'Thanks, how much do I owe you?'

'Four hundred taka, but don't bother with it now. I presume you'll come here first and go down with us.'

'If it's no trouble.' Wrighton paused, 'You know, it's very kind of you to look after me like this. I'm not accustomed to people bothering with me.'

'Ah, poor little Stewart!' Sandra mocked.

'No, I didn't mean it like that. I meant... well just thank you, that's all.'

'As far as I'm concerned it's a pure business proposition. You teach my wife to dance and you keep her out of my hair as a bonus.'

'I hadn't thought of it like that.'

'And I hope you won't!' Sandra warned him. 'Go on Geoff, clear off and let Stewart teach me some dancing with the bit of time that he has got.'

'Before you retire, Geoff. Tell me. Have you, in the course of your work in the Commercial Section, ever come across a company called A.H.T.?'

'Do they owe you money?' Geoff laughed.

'No, it's not that, at least, I don't think that they owe us money. I was just wondering whether you had ever heard of them.'

'Doesn't ring any bells. Do you want me to keep an eye open for them?'

'I should be interested to hear anything about them if you should discover it in the course of your work but for heaven's sake, don't go treading on people's toes.'

'Do you mind! I am a career diplomat. I don't even admit that people have toes.'

After he had gone Sandra and Wrighton half heartedly moved some of the furniture but the immensity of the task only became apparent to them when they tried to move the potted plants and so Wrighton suggested that they perfect some of the body positions in the small area that they had cleared. Ever since his gaffe about Sandra's trousers he had punctiliously avoided any references to her attire or any utterances that could be interpreted as a comment upon the suitability of her dress and Sandra, for her side, had never worn trousers again for a dance lesson. It was a sort of a pact that bound them in a mute mutuality.

'Why do I have to use the inside edge of the foot here?' Sandra complained. 'It's far easier with the foot flat.'

'Well that's the step.' Wrighton could not think of any other way of explaining it. 'It would not be right in any other way. It would look silly.'

'It looks pretty silly as it is. Are you sure that you are right?'

Wrighton stared at her for an instant. The thought that he could be in the wrong had not occurred to him. That was how to do the step, he knew it was. He did not question why or how he knew, it just happened to be. But a short, mocking smile was curling around Sandra's lips and bubbling in her eyes. Wrighton sighed. She wanted confrontation and obviously did not feel much like dancing.

'Look it up in the book,' she challenged him, slipping out of his arms and scooping up the Ballroom Dancing Yearbook that she had been pretending to study, when he came in. She held the book at face level before him. 'Go on! Have a look. Start where the piece of paper sticks out.'

Wrighton sensed a prickly change in her attitude. Something had upset her, he did not know what. Surely it was not his insistence on attention to detail, on repeating the steps until at last they were one hundred per cent right? Surely that had not upset her? She must know that this is the only way to dance? Any fool could shuffle around a floor in time to music, but she had said that she wanted to learn to dance.

Fearfully, he looked at her eyes. They were resolute and challenging. He looked away again. Why could he never cope with situations like this? His heart began to beat in his chest and his throat became tacky. She was waving the book in his face. He took it and opened it at the marked page and even as he opened it the mystery resolved itself. What a fool he had been! Why had he not checked? The black and white photograph was of the mediocre resolution characteristic of cheaply-printed volumes but the caption was bold, glaring, uncompromising and unambiguous in its revelation. *'Miss Phyllis Dunbar and Mr. Stewart Wrighton (Home Counties, North) dancing to victory in the All England Tango Competition at the Lyceum.'*

'Well?' she demanded.

Wrighton cleared his throat. He had no idea what to say.

'It's a long time since I've seen one of these books,' he said weakly. 'I didn't know it was in there, I honestly didn't.'

'Oh I know you didn't!'

Wrighton began to wonder whether he had misinterpreted the whole situation. He had assumed that she had thought that the real reason that he had obtained the book was to show her how clever he was and not in order to check on some dance steps, but now, somehow, he was not so sure that this was the case.'

'"Miss Phyllis Dunbar and Mr. Stewart Wrighton (Home Counties North) dancing to victory in the All England Tango Competition at the Lyceum," she read. 'You're only a bloody champion dancer! she accused him, 'and all you said was that you had "done a bit of dancing".'

'Well not... er... not really. I'm not really a champion–'

'Stewart!' she spat out at him, sternly pushing him down onto the sofa. He collapsed like a clothes horse. 'How can you say that? You were presumably Home Counties champions before you went in for the competition? Am I right?' He nodded. 'And to get to that position you presumably danced against the others and were judged to be the best in your region. Is that how these things work?'

'More or less.'

'So you were Home Counties Champion, which meant that you were the best tango dancer in the Home Counties.' Wrighton wanted to interrupt but she silenced him with an irritated wave of the hand. 'You went in for the competition and you won it which meant that you were the best tango dancer in all of England. Can you argue with that?'

'Not on the facts. The interpretation–'

'Sod the interpretation! Oh Stewart, why didn't you tell me?'

'I didn't think it was important.'

'Why do you have to be so bloody self-effacing? If you're a champion you tell everyone, there's no point in being the best otherwise. Why do you always have to hide your light under a bushel? You idiot! You'll never get anywhere in life if you never tell people how good you are. You can't wait for them to find out. They won't bother to look. You have to go out and tell them. Don't you want to get on in the world?'

'Not like that.'

'It's the only way.' She slumped down onto the sofa at the side of him and put her hand gently on his arm. 'Sorry, I didn't mean to shout at you–'

'Or swear–'

'Or swear. But you do make me so bloody mad sometimes. Who was Miss Phyllis Dunbar? Looks quite pretty.'

Wrighton realised that this was a convention of speech. Phyllis could have had three noses and they still would have been indistinguishable amongst the amorphous tones of the photograph.

'She was my dancing partner.'

'Your girlfriend?'

'My dancing partner. She had a boy-friend. Big chap called Walter. He worked on the buses but he didn't like dancing. He sometimes picked her up from the dance school by making his bus wait for her at the end of the road but some old gal complained and he got reprimanded and so after that I had to walk her to the station and wait with her.'

'Was she frightened of trains or something?'

'I suppose she must have been...' Wrighton replied distractedly. He was seeing Phyllis' bright eyes twinkling up at him as she waited shivering on the frost-covered platform for the ageing train to lumber up the gradient. He could still feel the pressure of her arm linked in his, pulling their bodies unnecessarily closely together, her sparkling, chattering conversation covering inadequately her nervous excitement. He would open the carriage door for her, a little touch of chivalry that he knew always pleased her disproportionately to the effort expended. He would stand and wave foolishly at her little furry hat until she was out of sight and then walk back through the night streets, feeling smugly chivalrous and detached.

One day, Walter had turned up at the school, waiting outside in a big Ford with the engine running noisily. Phyllis had come out of the door on Wrighton's arm as usual and had jumped when she had seen Walter. Big, hairy Walter. Wrighton had felt her trembling through her coat and it almost seemed as if she had wanted to shelter herself behind him.

'Brought the motor along, give yer a lift 'ome doll.' He stood over her, dwarfing her, oppressing her. Then he turned and looked at Wrighton.

'This is Stewart, Walter,' Phyllis' tiny voice had said. 'You remember, I told you I danced with him.'

'Oh yeah, Stewart.' From beneath ragged, bushy eyebrows, his eyes glowered an unconcealed contempt for the pansy dancer. 'Git in doll!'

He had left her to walk around the car and open the door for herself.

Several weeks after that she had begun to talk occasionally about getting married to Walter. She had seemed to mention it only when she and Wrighton were alone. It was not ecstasy, it was not euphoria it was an intangible indecision. As if she had wanted Wrighton to tell her whether or not it was a good idea. As if, she had wanted, Wrighton had laughed at the thought, as if she had almost wanted Wrighton to propose himself as an alternative evil. Laughable. She already had a boyfriend. Wrighton would have to look for a girl without a boyfriend.

Sandra's quiet voice said, 'Where is she now, do you still see her? Did she marry her Walter on the buses?'

'Now that's a funny thing. I don't believe she did. It was all to be fixed up and then she emigrated to Canada to be a nurse.'

'Didn't she warn you?'

'Oh I had met Marion by then. I wasn't dancing anymore. Marion didn't approve of it. She's very strict church.'

Sandra opened her mouth to speak and then slowly shut it. Looking at Wrighton's face she realised that she had made him see for the first time in his life that Phyllis had been in love with him, that if he had proposed she would have accepted with joy and they could have danced through their married life together.

And she hated herself for that.

'I'm sorry Mary I shan't be able to come this week either... Yes I've missed a few but I just don't have so much free time as I used to, before Stewart left.' Marion idly twisted the telephone cord around her fingers and made a grimace at her reflection in the hall mirror. Mary Gonzales said something about 'all the girls at the knitting circle missing her' but Marion was not really listening and the conversation petered out to an awkward silence.

'So... we might see you next week then dear?' Mary prompted.

'Yes, perhaps next week.'

As she replaced the receiver a letter fluttered through the letter box and dropped to the tiled floor. She could see that it bore a Bangladeshi stamp. A letter from Stewart. She picked it up and opened it as she walked back into the kitchen. The letter from Stewart. 'Why doesn't he phone?' her mother had asked.

'Boys! Time for school!' Marion called up the stairs.

'Oh mum, can't we–'

'Richard?'

'Yes mum.'

'Charles?'

'Yes mum.' The two boys' heads appeared at the top of the stairs.

'What did I just say?'

'Time for school,' Richard repeated dully.

'Right then.' Marion resumed her walk into the kitchen whilst the boys thumped down the stairs and then began to argue over their satchels on the hall stand. She picked up her coffee cup and looked at them from the doorway. They saw her standing there and stopped squabbling. 'Good,' she said and then came and pecked them on the cheeks. 'Straight home after school,' she reminded them.

'Yes mum,' Richard called dutifully and as soon as the front door had shut behind him, he punched Charles in the back.

She dropped each page to the table top as she read it and when she had finished she left them there like the dead leaves on the garden path.

He has got to come home. Parties, dancing, swimming, going out in sailing boats. Where would it end? She could do nothing from such a distance. If he didn't come home soon it would be too late. He would be changed. He would not be her Stewart.

'Bachelor Status' the company had called it. It was unchristian to send a married man like Stewart out there amongst those... those people. He doesn't realise how people react to him, he just does not realise. And she had never told him. The whole situation was wrong. It was dangerous. 'Don't forget you're a Brandon. Brandon women have always been strong.' Well he would just have to come home, that's all. They will just have to send him back.

'Impossible, Mrs. Wrighton, impossible.'

Marion stared at Cockcroft's head and it seemed to shrink as she felt her strength draining away from her. Whilst waiting in the ante-room and watching his secretary type, Marion had been so certain, so sure and so confident. In the train coming up, she had run through all the arguments, justifying them to herself, but she had not seen them as the company would.

'The job is not finished yet you see, and that is what we are paying him for.'

'Yes but...'

What could she say? 'Yes but I want him back?' 'Yes but I want him away from those subversive influences?'

'I can understand the situation, Mrs. Wrighton, but it is not unusual in this industry. Surely you know that? We can't go making exceptions.'

'I just thought–'

'I'll be straight with you. I'm not calling him back.' Marion nodded dumbly, not trusting herself to speak. Brandon women have always been strong.

'Have you thought about eventually joining him?'

Marion shivered involuntarily.

'Oh I couldn't do that. No, I couldn't go out there.'

'But what will you do if we have to keep him out there? You know Mrs. Wrighton, being married to a Consolidated engineer involves responsibilities on the behalf of the spouse as well. If he proves his worth we might find a position for him in the Far East.'

Marion watched Cockcroft scratch his nose. She could feel the blood beginning to pound in her temples. She must have misunderstood what he had just said.

'Have you had lunch?' he asked.

Have I had lunch? Nothing was making sense anymore.

'Not yet,' she replied mechanically.

Cockcroft pressed the switch on his intercom. 'Sam, book me a table at the Grill.'

'Yes Mr. Cockcroft.'

'I think you and I should discuss this somewhere more comfortable.'

19

Ever since Mary had returned home from her meeting with the car dented and the windscreen cracked, Alan Havering had detected a difference in her. She was more ironic, more demanding and somehow, more secretive. She had dismissed the damage to the car with a glib explanation of being caught in the fringes of a demonstration. It was probably true.

Havering stubbed out his cigarette. Probably true but he had no way of checking. Why did he have to check for Christ's sake, she was his wife wasn't she? What could she be possibly doing that he did not know about? What did she not want him to know? Why was he doubting her? He must put his mind back on the work.

He fingered the tatty letter lying before him and gritted his teeth. It was a good job that Mrs. Chowdhry had not suspected anything when she had translated it. 'I am not finding it on the map Mr. Havering.' was all she had said. He would have to see Abdul Haq and get this settled once and for all. He snatched up the telephone receiver from its cradle.

'Havering,' he announced. 'Get my car out.' He redialled a number and then tapped his fingers impatiently whilst the crochet of telephone wires considered his request for connection. 'This is Alan Havering at Consolidated. I need to see Abdul Haq this morning, I'm coming round now.' He took a measured breath and then snapped over the polite Bengali procrastinatory protestations, 'Don't give me that shit! Just tell Major Abdul Haq M.P. that it is in our mutual interest.' He slammed the receiver down.

'Mr. Havering, it is a pleasure to see you after such a long time.' Abdul Haq's unctuous voice raised the hairs on the back of his neck 'Won't you sit down?'

Havering made a conscious and successful effort to control himself, realising that reaction would do no good in the long run. 'And how is Mrs. Havering?' Abdul Haq enquired with a pellucid innocence that set boulders of suspicion rumbling through the caverns of Havering's mind.

'How is Mrs. Havering?' he thought. Why should he want to know? Why did he ask? Just a minute, just a minute, he steadied himself, you are being stupid. Remember, he always asks doesn't he? Yes but... Listen, Mary would never go with a Bangla even a greasy charmer like Haq. She never would, she never would. And then he realised that it was his wife's fidelity that he was putting into doubt.

Haq placed the tips of the fingers of both hands together to make a tent, imitating a gesture that he had seen a diplomat do in a British film years ago in Oxford.

'Now, I understand that you have something to discuss...'

Havering checked that the door was closed and then drew the soiled letter from his shirt pocket and laid it with deliberation on Abdul Haq's desk. Haq read it carefully.

It seemed that a Forhad Miah was claiming compensation for damage to his land which had occurred when the gas pipeline had been run through it. It was identical to hundreds of letters that Havering had thankfully unloaded onto the shoulders of that fool Wrighton to keep him out of mischief. Only in one detail was it different. Abdul Haq noticed.

'Mmm.... Baderpur,' he said quietly. 'That's a pity!'

'A pity!' Havering choked. 'Is that all you can say? A pity! You told me that you had Baderpur all sewn up. That you had settled with all the residents, the farmers, the mud scratchers, peasants and lay-abouts and that you guaranteed me, you guaranteed me....' He emphasised the point by stabbing the surface of the desk with his forefinger, '...that we would get no claims from there. "None at all" you said.'

'How embarrassing,' Haq replied . He wondered whether his secretary was standing with his ear wedged to the crack of the door, collecting information, spying for Haq's enemies. Like Haq, the man was a Sylheti, born to corruption and treacherous with the truth. Sylhetis had been learning to cheat the British for generations – the jute harvest, the tea levy, the rice seed grant. And all this time the British, who had claimed distinction from the natives by virtue of their superior intellect, had learned nothing. Havering was just a present-day representative of this ignorant and conceited race. And if he believed that his threats and bullying would confound a Sylheti, then he really knew nothing of the country or the people. Haq smiled comfortingly at him. 'Who else has seen this?'

'The woman who translated it. She made some remark about "never having had one from there before,"' Havering recalled, inaccurately, 'but I managed to convince her that it was on my patch and was part of another village and luckily, she accepted that explanation. She's not very bright. Do you realise what would have happened if that had gone to Wrighton?

The whole thing would have been blown sky high.'

'My dear Mr. Havering. I am sure that you told me some time ago that your Mr. Wrighton was a little stupid and not very good at this job.   I cannot see why he should suddenly become a threat to us.'

Havering could not either.   He just had this feeling that if Wrighton had got hold of that letter he would not have rested until he had found out everything that there was to know about it.   He had that frightening tenacity of mean intelligence.   He was not clever he was just a drudge, but Havering did not know how he could explain that to Haq without making it appear that he had miscalculated his opponent.

'Well luckily he didn't see it.   But I don't want any repetition of this.' Then he added as an uncharitable but quite feasible doubt crept into the back of his mind, 'I suppose you did settle with them all?'

'My dear Mr. Havering, of course I did.'

You lying bastard, Havering thought, you kept some of that money to one side for yourself and now your typical Bengali, egotistical greed has threatened to wreck this entire project.

Abdul Haq put the palm of his hand on the letter to restrain Havering from removing it from the desk.

'Leave this with me, Mr. Havering, you have my word of honour that you will hear no more from Forhad Miah or any like him.'

'I hope so.'

'Before you go, Mr. Havering, would you and your charming wife agree to grace my table at the British High Commission New Year's Eve Ball?   I would be most honoured.'

Havering thought quickly.   It would do him no harm to be seen dining in public with an influential government minister.

'I would be delighted.'

'You know it is soon being the festival of Christmas?' Leila Rose said incongruously.   Rubena and Mrs. Rosario looked at each other and then at Leila.   Receiving no explanation, they bent to their work again.   'And then after that it is the Christian New Year and you know what they are doing then, isn't it?'

Rubena laid down her pen, warily and wearily.   Mrs. Rosario stoically continued writing.

'Are you going to tell me what they do then Leila?   You are obviously not wanting to do any work.'

'Well, I have heard that all the men are taking their wives to the Hotel Sonargaon and they are having a big party every year.   And they drink alcohol and their wives drink alcohol and then they dance with each other's wives. Are you realising? They take other people's wives and hold them and dance with them... in the Western way,' she added with heavy meaning.

'Is that all you are wanting to say? Have you no work that you can do?' Rubena chided her gently. She had not the strength of interest to be more forceful upon this particular subject.

Leila did not recognise the rebuke but continued dreamily,

'I think I would like to see the dancing.'

'You are a shameless girl.' Mrs. Rosario looked up from her work and pushed her spectacles up her nose with the end of her ball-point pen.

Undeterred, Leila continued dangerously,

'I would like to see just once, what it is like to be dancing in the Western way.'

'Are you not seeing on television? Is that not sufficient?'

'I wonder what it is feeling like, to be dancing with–'

'Leila!' Mrs. Rosario exclaimed. She was shocked at the indulgence of the conversation.

'–with Mr. Wrighton!' Leila continued mischievously. 'What do you think Rubena? What would it be like to be dancing with Mr. Wrighton?'

'Leila Rose, you are a dishonourable girl with no conscience. You must apologise to Mrs. Chowdhry,' Mrs. Rosario ordered her in a scandalised voice but it trailed away in puzzlement at Rubena's smiling reaction.

'It is a dishonourable thing for a girl to be listening at a door. To be listening to the private conversations of other people. She should have the courage to be asking outright for what she is wanting to know,' Rubena observed obscurely.

Mrs. Rosario pushed her spectacles back up her nose, more fiercely this time, concentrating her mind on what she must have missed in the conversation. She had the strange feeling that they were talking in a different language. Rubena turned to her at last.

'Mrs. Rosario you are looking lost.'

'I am feeling it also.'

'That is because you are polite and well behaved and you are not the girl who creeps around to listen to private conversations.'

Mrs. Rosario's mouth opened and closed.

'Well what did you say to him then Rubena ?' Leila demanded

'So you were not hearing the entire conversation then, little girl?'

'Well, that fool of a peon came up the corridor and...' Leila shrugged the remainder of the explanation.

Rubena turned to Mrs. Rosario and explained,

'Leila did a shameful thing. She listened to a private conversation between me and Stewart er... Stewart Wrighton.' Mrs. Rosario nodded blankly. Leila chewed her shawl in anticipation. 'Mr. Wrighton was asking me if I would go to the New Year Dance with him.'

Mrs. Rosario gazed at Rubena Chowdhry in perplexed astonishment. She wanted to ask 'And did you say yes?' although she knew that Rubena, being a devout Muslim, would not have appraised such a proposal as having the remotest chance of success but she was so surprised by the enormity of the occurrence, that she found her voice stranded somewhere in her throat.

'And what did you say? What did you say?' Leila bounced up and down on her stool, catapulting a pen across the table.

Rubena looked at her in mock astonishment.

'Why, I thanked him for his offer and explained to him that it was impossible but that he should be asking you and you would be certain to be saying "yes".'

'Oh Rubena!' Leila Rose shrieked in horror, 'You are not telling him this!'

'It would be serving you right if I was.' Rubena wagged a finger at her.

'Quite.' Mrs. Rosario found her voice at last.

'Oh Rubena.' Leila Rose expired sadly.

Wrighton winced as the tune that he had already heard six times in a row began its seventh recital. Enough is enough. He swung his legs off his bed and stood up, noticing with surprise that he felt absolutely no compunction whatsoever about walking around the house clad only in his underpants.

Rubena had been very sweet. It was a stupid thing to do, he realised, looking back on it, but it had come to him on an impulse. She had been there in his office, he had just discovered his dance ticket in his case and he had looked up and thought, 'well why not?' She is a friend. I have eaten in her house. She is of the right sex. There will be certainly other Bengali women there. Why not? As soon as he had begun to ask her he had seen the obstacles rising before him but she had been sweet and not made fun of him. She had been very correct and had smiled that funny smile that only tipped up the corners of her mouth. She had explained that she felt it an honour that she would always remember but that he should now realise that it was impossible and so forth....

Wrighton clenched his teeth and grasped the door handle with great determination. That confounded tune!

He found Bell hunched over the cassette recorder almost in a position of supplication to an idol.

'For Pete's sake Bell, can't we change the music a bit? I could sing that one backwards now.'

He thought at first that Bell had not heard him, then the stocky neck wrinkled as the head turned slowly up to him. Wrighton gasped slightly at the red-rimmed eyes and the tear-stained face and dumbly took the damp letter from Bell's fist.

'*Dear Gerry,*' it began, '*You knew what the situation was when you took that silly job. We had it all out before you went. I told you ....*' Wrighton found his eyes skimming the page, '*...some good times together... been moving apart now for some time, you know we have... somehow easier with you being away... cleared my mind....*'

Wrighton looked at the broad back stretched in grief. The great, boasting, braggart. The lying money cadger. The great tough nut. The jilted. He lay the letter gently down on the arm of the chair and put his hand on the brawny shoulder. Mechanically, Bell's other arm flipped the buttons on the cassette player.

'That's alright old man,' Wrighton said softly. 'You play it as much as you like. As much as you like.'

He turned as Tuppin surged into the room, wet from the shower.

'Can't you turn that bloody–' Tuppin stopped. He had never seen that look in Wrighton's eyes before.

'Go and finish your shower. Leave him alone.'

The last weeks of December were difficult for Wrighton. At Banani House, Bell was morose and inconsolable but became aggressive and rude whenever he or Tuppin tried to help in any way.

The tough man was going to fight this on his own. Wrighton feared that he was sliding towards a fall that would shock him more than the rupture with his wife. He seemed to want to vent his anger and frustration on every female.

As if to corroborate the collective perfidy of women, Mina had never returned to give them their Friday massage, giving substance to the supposition that she was the thief. To be tricked by a Bengali was bad enough; to be tricked by a Bengali woman was devastating to Bell's machismo. Tuppin tried to pretend that it had not happened and neither Bell nor Tuppin would believe Wrighton's protestations that he had lost only his alarm clock, true though it was.

And then there was the problem of the New Year's Eve Dance. Wrighton had got a ticket and an invitation to sit at Hardwicke's table. Tuppin had wheedled himself onto the table of a jute factory manager whose wife he had designs on but Bell... he steadfastly refused to purchase a ticket or accept any invitations. He spent most of his spare time propped up at the bar of the British Club, glowering across at Harry Dudgeon and blaspheming loudly about the entire philosophy of entertainment, whilst sinking cans of luke warm beer.

At the office, Wrighton wrestled with the problems of the audit and financial analysis but always at the back of his mind was the tension of not knowing why Havering had lied to him on purpose about the valve station at Baderpur. Of course, Havering did not know that Wrighton was aware of his attempted deception but equally, Wrighton did not know what the deception was intended to conceal.

From underneath this uncertainty, Wrighton was about to dislodge, quite innocently and in complete ignorance, the first pebble of the land-slide which would bring his world crashing down around his ears. And it started at the New Year's Eve Ball.

20

'How are you getting down to the Sonargaon then?' Tuppin asked.

Wrighton self consciously adjusted his bow tie in the mirror and called over his shoulder,

'The Hardwickes are taking me down.'

'How are you getting to the Hardwickes?'

'Rickshaw.'

'In that get up!'

Wrighton stopped and pondered for a moment.

'Yes,' he insisted, 'in this "get up". In any case, no one will see me. It'll be dark in about twenty minutes.'

'Just as well.'

'What do you mean by that?'

'Well... haven't you got any proper evening dress?'

For an instant Wrighton was back in the tailor's shop in London, with the haughty assistant wrinkling up his nose at the suggestion that his light-weight jacket could also serve as an evening jacket.

'This was all I could find.'

'You look like an ice-cream salesman.'

'It's been said before. If it's any consolation to you I feel like one.'

'Rather you than me.'

'Quite.' Wrighton nodded towards Bell's room, 'What's he doing?'

Tuppin lowered his voice. 'Says he's going down the club.'

'There won't be anybody there! What is he going to do for Pete's sake?'

'Search me. Get drunk I suppose.'

'That'll make a change. I will readily admit that pouring his royal highness into bed at three o' clock in the morning has lost its appeal for me. Well, I must go and polish my sandals.'

'You're not wearing–'

'Just joking.'

Wrighton paid off the rickshaw puller who, despite Wrighton's noises of discouragement, decided to wait for the return journey. The Hardwicke's chowkidhar saluted him and opened the gate, the bearer had the door open already.

'Evening saheb.'

'Good evening. Is master in?'

'Come straight in!' Geoff Hardwicke's voice called from the interior. 'Lime and soda on the table. Take a seat.' Wrighton took the glass prepared for him and sat down. 'Whilst I remember... you asked me to find out something about a company called A.H.T.?'

'Yes, that's right. Have you?'

'Well yes and no.'

'That's a good diplomatic answer. Thanks a lot!'

'I asked amongst the Section and they know it as a sort of umbrella construction and building company such as they have in Bangladesh, but we have never dealt with it. It's owned by Abdul Haq. "A.H.T." – Abdul Haq Trading Company.'

'What!' Wrighton jumped in his chair.

'Oh dear, have I hit a raw nerve?'

'No... no. I was just surprised that was all.'

'Obviously,' Hardwicke observed drily. 'You have had dealings with Major Abdul Haq have you?'

'This is the one in the Foreign Ministry, the MFA, that we are talking about?'

'The very same.'

'No, I haven't had any direct dealings with him. Alan Havering, my boss, has had to negotiate with him upon occasions, but not me. I don't even know what he looks like.'

'I'll point him out to you. He'll be there tonight.'

'What is he like as a politician?'

'What do you mean?'

'Is he honest?'

'Stewart! You are asking a representative of Her Majesty's Government to pass comment upon the honesty of a politician of the host country! I didn't think you were so naive.'

'Sorry.'

'What can I say about him? He is a Bangladeshi politician. He appeared like a primrose after the rain except that in his case it was as a loyal army officer after an attempted military coup of about ten years ago. The coup failed and Abdul Haq was instrumental in suppressing the uprising. A drop or two of blood was shed somewhere in downtown Dhaka and it was all over. And Abdul Haq was a good boy and put in a ministry.'

'Oh come along boys you are surely not talking politics tonight!'

Sandra swished elegantly into the room, intuitively aware of the effect of her ball-gown. She held out the skirt in a fan and remarked casually to Wrighton, 'That cloth made up nicely didn't it?'

'It takes my breath away,' Wrighton admitted. 'It's very er... you're er–'

'Oh yawn, yawn!' Hardwicke interrupted. 'Don't tell her she's pretty because that is exactly what she wants to hear.' He turned to his wife who was pulling a face at him. 'You'll do,' he said and added a warning, 'But wait till you see what the competition is like. I hope for God's sake you don't outshine the Old Man's wife. It'll torpedo my career if you do.'

'That's all you think–'

'The Old Man?' Wrighton queried.

'The High Commissioner.'

'Ah'

'Come on, let's get going now that madam is ready, we'll miss the first course otherwise.'

As they walked up to the entrance of the hotel, Wrighton was inescapably reminded of the spotlight-drenched arrivals at Hollywood first nights, where unending limousines disgorge tiaras and tuxedos before a goggling gaggle of humanity, crowding on the sidewalk, boggling at the spectacle.

Here, the cars were gliding up to the entrance to allow their occupants to alight onto the marble apron. It was true that some of the vehicles were four-wheel drive utilities but then others were pennant-bearing limousines and these reinforced the illusion. And around it all, where the yellow light faded into the thick shadows, wavered the brown, mute crowd of Bengalis, watching without understanding, watching from simple curiosity, watching without envy. They completed the illusion.

Inside, the crowds of couples swirled and intermingled, chatting bright-eyed and eager to enjoy themselves; a gorgeous tapestry of interwoven colours, bare shoulders and smiling teeth.

They were swept along and into the ballroom where the tables had been set out around the dance floor, many already filled with laughing groups, calling to nearby tables, introducing each other, reforging acquaintanceships.

'That's the British Airways table over there,' Hardwicke nodded. 'We always save them one on the basis that there is sure to be a crew here on stopover... and they usually manage it.'

Wrighton glanced at the table which was populated with healthy sun-tanned Europeans, presided over by a silver-haired captain.

'Do they have to keep rank even on their days off?' he remarked but Sandra and Geoff had disappeared around a group of partygoers and he had to squeeze through to catch them up.

They reached the table that Geoff Hardwicke had reserved and people began greeting each other with back slaps, hand shakes and kisses. Wrighton was pulled in warmly to the group and made to sit next to Sandra and opposite an unattached lady from the clinic with whom he surprised himself by undertaking a long and, to him, seemingly pointless conversation but which seemed to entertain her faultlessly.

Everybody talked, everybody had something to say, everybody ate and everybody drank. Wrighton managed to obtain a jug of water which served his needs fully, as for the rest, he had never seen such a heterogeneous assembly of multicoloured drinks which the revellers kept producing from the battery of cool boxes arranged around their feet. Some of them had brought their own ice cubes, one had even procured a jar of olives.

He looked at Geoff who was expanding a story of some sort by stretching his arms to their fullest extent and wagging the beard on his chin; at Sandra whose coiffure was bobbing up and down as she emphasised some aspect of an animated conversation that she was having with the man at the side of her; at the lady from the clinic who was inclining her head and cupping her hand to her ear to endeavour to catch what her neighbour was trying to explain and he just felt very warm and contented that he could be amongst so many happy people.

They were swallowing their dessert when the band performed a roll of drums, the lights dimmed in the room and a pair of spotlights converged upon the dance floor like a bikini-top.

'This'll be good,' Geoff hissed down the table to him. 'The cabaret! Always a good laugh.'

As he finished talking, the double doors at one side of the room swung open and in a burst of laughter a rickshaw lurched into the room, pedalled furiously by a white man dressed in a lunghi.

Wrighton stared open mouthed at the man as he began his comic patter. Then, perplexed he glanced down the table to an empty seat. Sandra caught his eye.

'Shut your mouth dear, you'll catch flies in it.'

'But that's...' Wrighton pointed at the rickshaw comedian who until ten minutes previously had been making polite conversation, seated a few chairs down the table from him.

'Shhh! He's good isn't he?' Sandra whispered into his ear and he could smell the wine, sharp on her breath.

The comedian finished his turn and departed via the other set of double doors amidst shouting and stamping of feet. At the same time a pair of tramps wandered on and sang a couple of plagiarised tunes in the style of Flanagan and Allan about the price of pineapples and the market at DIT 1 and other related subjects. And so it continued. At the end of the twenty minutes, when the players took their bow, Wrighton found that he was wiping the tears of laughter from his eyes.

'It was good wasn't it?' a thick set man at the side of him nudged him with his elbow.

'It was very good, very funny. Quite a talented bunch aren't they?'

'All from the BHC. I suppose diplomats are like that,' the man declared vaguely and Wrighton remembered that he was something to do with the British Council. What was it that Harry had said about the British Council? 'Where the men all talk like women and the women talk like men.' That was it! He was not far from the truth. Wrighton wondered whether Harry was here tonight.

The floor cleared and the band struck up a raucous interpretation of a modern popular tune. A few couples leapt out of their chairs to throw themselves into a frenzy but most were content just to tap their feet and digest a while.

Wrighton gazed across the room where the lights were strewn with streamers and where the occasional menu card fashioned into a paper aeroplane would launch forth from the British Airways table and be frozen momentarily in mid air by the flashgun of a camera.

'Stop dreaming, you're here to dance.' Sandra stood before him and began pulling at his hands.

Wrighton was horror-struck. This was not dance music. Surely he had not spent all that time and effort teaching this woman to dance proper ballroom dancing to have her confuse it with this... hideous, senseless, meaningless cacophony?

'I can't dance to this!'

'Come on, stop arguing!' Sandra was a little loud, he thought.

'I can't!' he insisted, 'I'm sorry, but I can't dance to this music.'

'Can't dance, won't dance!' she accused. 'Come on Michael.' She pulled the man from the British Council willingly from his seat and they took to the floor to perform uncouth and uncoordinated gyrations whilst shouting conversations alternately into each other's ears.

Wrighton blinked in disbelief. What a waste! He felt devastated.

Sandra had just completely and comprehensively denied the fundamental reason why he had taught her to dance and what was worse, what hurt him more, was that she did not appear to have realised it.

Geoff Hardwicke was listening with apparent distraction to the conversation of his neighbour and tapping his hand to the music on the white table cloth which now bore a litter of bottles and glasses. He caught Wrighton's eye.

'Another drink?' he shouted. 'Beer? Gin? .Oh sorry! I forgot. How about a lemonade?'

'Thanks.'

Just then, through a providential marrying up of gaps in the jiving humanity, Wrighton caught sight of a familiar face. With his glass in his hand he squeezed and excused his way across the ballroom, between the tables.

'Happy New Year Don!' He held out his hand. Don Finkelstein looked at him for a split second and then his face cracked into a lopsided grin.

'Stooart me ol' buddie. How y'a doin'?' He pumped his hand up and down. 'Say, where ya bin? I ain't seen yer around.'

'I've been busy Don. You know, work?'

Don Finkelstein sucked his lip in mock contemplation.

'Work... Sounds kinda familiar but I can't quite place the meanin' of the word.'

Wrighton laughed and took a swig from his lemonade.

'How did your cricket match go?'

'Well, we finally got a team together, no thanks to you. There wasn't many of us Yanks in it of course, but some of the Aussies played and the Canadians and a Dutch guy. Yeah we had a good afternoon.'

'What did the spectators think of it?'

'Frankly Stooart, I don't think they understood a darn thing that was going on. Frankly, neither did I. I jus' ran when they hollered "run" but I can go back to the jolly old U S of A and tell everyone that I've played cricket, yessir!'

'Are you going back soon then?'

'Three months.'

'Then where? After the USA?'

'I got plenty o' time to think about that... What's that honey?' He spoke to the platinum blonde girl who was tugging at his arm. 'Stooart, you're gonna have to excuse me, I got my duty to do.' He nodded at the woman.

'You go ahead Don. It's been nice knowing you.'

Wrighton gazed vaguely across the ballroom, trying to locate his table, a task complicated by the habit of the revellers who often abandoned their own table to sit with a friend elsewhere and as one table resembled another when no one was sitting at it, identification was not the instant process one would have liked or expected. He had almost walked into Havering before he had noticed him but before he could retreat he had been grudgingly acknowledged.

'Ah Wrighton!' he grunted in a matter of fact manner but Wrighton was not listening. He was gazing thunderstruck at the ginger-haired woman hanging on to Havering's arm. The woman in the car. The one who hit the rickshaw which burned. The woman who would not tell him who she was and suddenly he felt intensely angry at the deceit. No wonder she would not tell him. She had known all along who he was.

Havering looked at his wife pointedly and then at Wrighton. He sighed and turned dismissively to his wife, not seeing through his half-closed eyes, the anxiety twisted across her face. 'Mary this is er...' He paused for a moment, obviously unable to remember Wrighton's Christian name. 'Er... Stewart Wrighton. One of the people at work. Wrighton, I don't think you've met my wife Mary.'

'Oh but I–' Wrighton began with a force powered by a raging vindictiveness and then he caught sight of the woman's pleading, begging, eyes. The fear, the dreaded terror.

'What?' Havering sensed something amiss.

'How do you do, Mrs. Havering.' She took his hand limply. Her hand was shaking.

'Pleased to meet you Mr. Wrighton,' she mumbled and stumbled.

'I was going to say....' Wrighton explained as he cocked a discreet ear to the band, 'that I was going to ask your wife for a dance.'

Havering looked at him. His eyes were open now. Wrighton returned the shrewd gaze, his heart fluttering. Havering frowned and shot a glance at his wife. Then his eyes flicked back to Wrighton.

'Please yourself,' he said flatly. 'I'll be over there!' He pointed at a distant table with the whisky bottle that Wrighton had only just noticed clenched in his fist. He lurched away.

'This is impossible... I....'

Wrighton took her hand firmly and led her onto the dance floor.

'Can you dance?'

'Yes, a bit.'

'Good. Then dance.' He took her in his arms and began easing her gently around the room to the now moderated tones of the band.

'I think it would look better if you smiled,' Wrighton suggested.

'You must not cross Alan like that, he will kill you. He is very jealous.' She forced a smile onto her face.

'Cross him like what? I only asked for a dance.'

'But he could see that something was going on. He's got a terrible temper. He'll kill you.'

'I doubt it. I've survived his temper before. It's not very nice but in this case you've only got yourself to blame. Why didn't you tell me who you were at the time? You knew who I was didn't you?'

She shook her head hard.

'I swear I didn't Mr. Wrighton. I honestly didn't.'

'I think under the circumstances, you can call me "Stewart".'

'Believe me Stewart, I did not know who you were. I had never seen you before. I knew you existed. Alan must have mentioned you from time to time.'

'No doubt.'

'But tonight was the first time that I learned who you were, honest.' Wrighton could feel her body trembling in his arms and he knew that she was speaking the truth.

The music stopped as Wrighton asked,

'So why didn't you tell me who you were?'

They began to walk back to Havering's table.

'I can't say why,' she said fiercely, 'I can't. I can't.' She began to shake again and Wrighton sensed that he was skimming the brink of something which he would rather not know.

'Alright, alright. Forget it. It's not important. I can't return you to your husband in a state of nervous debility, he would wonder what on earth I had done to you.'

'He wouldn't notice a thing,' she observed sourly as they reached the table. 'Thank you for the dance Mr. Wrighton.'

'Ah! Is this your Mr. Wrighton that I have heard so much about?' A stoutish Bengali man dressed in immaculate evening dress rose and turned to Wrighton. He held out his hand. 'I am Major Abdul Haq M.P.' He paused to allow Wrighton sufficient time to feel honoured. 'Your Mr. Havering has spoken of you often.'

'You... er... you surprise me.' Wrighton admitted before he could think of anything else to say. He looked across at Havering who shrugged his shoulders, apparently baffled. 'I didn't realise that I was the subject of your negotiations.'

'Ah not the subject, Mr. Wrighton but you appear on the periphery. Tell me, how do you like Bangladesh?'

Wrighton looked at Haq. He could see the stocky figure of a soldier tailored into the evening dress, worn like an extra uniform. He could see the glinting teeth smiling at him from under the moustache. Was the military man fully tamed? How did he come to be running a construction-cum-building company? Why was he being so pleasant to Wrighton? What did he want from him?

'Well it's a lot different from where I come from,' Wrighton remarked lamely.

'Where do you come from Mr. Wrighton?'

'Well I don't suppose you know it, it's a part of Greater London really, called Wembley.'

'Oh yes, I know it Mr. Wrighton. I have been to a football match at the Empire Stadium there.'

'Oh really?' Wrighton was astonished.

'When I was at Oxford.' Haq smiled back in explanation.

'Oxford.' Wrighton nodded in confirmation. He should have guessed.

'Whilst I think of it Wrighton, I'll need your figures in a couple of weeks to make a progress report for the board. You'll have to get them done by then.' Havering laughed nastily. 'More overtime.'

Wrighton's smile was thin. Havering knew very well that Wrighton's conditions of service did not admit the existence of overtime.

'There you are Stewart!' Sandra's voice accused loudly as she grabbed him by the arm. 'Come and dance with me Stewart. Michael's gone and left me. He had to go for a wee-wee.' She giggled.

Wrighton felt himself blushing with embarrassment tinged with anger.

'Sandra please!' he hissed, 'I think you have had a little too much to drink.' He turned to the table. 'Please excuse me I must assist er... I....'

'We understand Mr. Wrighton. It's been a pleasure to meet you.' Abdul Haq confided in the syrupy tone of a professional politician.

Wrighton glanced briefly around the table. At Abdul Haq examining Sandra Hardwicke with ill-concealed interest; at Havering, blowing the ash from his cigarette and playing with the whisky in the bottom of his glass; at Mary Havering sitting stonily apart from either of them, her hands hidden below the table.

'You haven't introduced me to your friends,' Sandra complained loudly as Wrighton took her firmly by the arm. He winced as several people looked at them.

'Come on, keep your voice down. Everyone is looking at you. I'll take you back to the table.'

'Spoilsport!' She pouted like a little girl as he threaded her around the dance floor.

As soon as they had returned to their seats she suggested that they have a drink. Wrighton was still distracted by the memory of the shaking body of Mary Havering in his arms; of the hunched, haunted, scowling Havering, crab-like over his whisky glass; of the self assured, oily Haq.

'Yes please. Something long,' he said.

'I'll get you one of ours.'

So that was Abdul Haq? Abdul Haq of the Ministry of Foreign Affairs and Abdul Haq of the AHT Company Limited. He had been the only one who had appeared at ease at Havering's table. Perhaps this was a skill that he had cultivated to further his ministerial ambitions. But which of his skills did he use to run the building and construction side? His military training? Wrighton had no answer.

He absently watched the whirling couples on the floor. Every now and then he would catch sight of Geoff Hardwicke turning in the maelstrom, or some other person whom he knew by sight before they were eclipsed.

'Here you are.'

Sandra sat down next to him at the table rather heavily. They had turned their chairs outwards. She giggled again.

'Almost missed it!' She pulled a mock serious face at him. 'I'm sorry Mr. Wrighton.' She leaned on his shoulder. 'I will be a good girl now.'

'That's all right,' he said a little too stiffly and took a grateful sip from the tall glass that she had given him. 'Oh, this is nice. What is it? I don't think I've had it before.'

Sandra Hardwicke looked at him carefully and then said in a dismissive manner.

'Oh it's called a Pimms. Don't you know what a Pimms is?'

'Wrighton shook his head. 'Never heard of it.'

'Well it's just a sort of blend of herbs and things that you put into a tonic. It's quite well known in the tropics.'

'The tonic is presumably what gives it the bitter after-taste?'

'I suppose it must be,' she observed with a studied detachment that Wrighton was later to recall. 'Who was the red-haired lady I saw you dancing with?'

'My boss's wife.'

'A good dancer is she?' She leaned over him and brought her face searchingly near his. He could see her breasts rising and falling in her bodice. He looked away quickly and drained his drink.

'Not particularly. We weren't really dancing, just moving around the floor socially as it were.'

'I thought you only did proper dancing,' Sandra remarked tartly and laced her arms around his neck pulling him towards her.

'I could hardly refuse to dance with the boss's wife could I?' He gently disentangled her fingers and brought her hands down to her lap and held them there, trying to ignore the excited beating of his heart.

'You refused to dance with me. Why don't you want to dance with little Sandy?'

She tried to put her arms around his neck again which aroused an unsettling mixture of excitement and disgust. She was an attractive woman but she was tipsy and did not really know what she was doing. He caught her hands again and thrust them down into her lap.

'It was not–' he began but was interrupted by the jovial voice of Geoff as he returned to the table.

'Ho Ho! Groping my wife eh? Well carry on, carry on! What's mine is yours.' Wrighton tried to protest but the shock of the accusation had taken away his speech. 'Pull your frock down dear, everyone's gloating.' Hardwicke pulled down her ball gown which had ridden into her lap.

At last Wrighton found his tongue.

'Geoff, You don't think... I would never... It had never crossed my mind... I...' he stopped. Hardwicke was laughing at him which made him angry.

'I was only joking Stewart, for Heaven's sake, and anyway, as for it never crossing your mind, I take that as an insult. She's an absolute cracker.'

'No but I mean–'

'Stewart I know exactly what is going on. She is becoming tipsy that's all. Don't be so sensitive!'

'I'm not sensitive.'

'There you go again. If that isn't being sensitive then I don't know what is.' He turned to Sandra who was lolling in the chair. 'Darling get me a drink please and give Stewart something... like a neat lemonade or–'

'I'm not used to it that's all,' Wrighton muttered. 'Back in Wembley–'

'You are not in Wembley, Stewart, that is the whole point about it. You are in Bangladesh and out here we enjoy ourselves. O.K.? Sandra has had perhaps a little too much to drink and you don't approve of drinking but that's no reason to be miserable and censorious. Here, drink this.'

Wrighton sat angrily silent and drew short sips from his glass. It was grossly unfair of Hardwicke to tease him like that and to criticise him. He had a wife at home who did not behave like that. She had never been vetted by the Foreign Office but she knew how to behave. She would never have done anything resembling what Sandra had done. He took a gulp from the glass. It was more bitter than he had remembered from last time. And that putting her arms around his neck and thrusting her bosom... her nicely rounded, firm breasts up at him, invitingly, heaving... He gulped another mouthful from the glass. The hussy! Imagine it! He had been teaching her to dance thinking that she wanted to learn and all the time she had been making a pass at him. He glanced across at her, sitting playing with a spoon, and felt his heart thumping and was annoyed even more that his baser animal instincts responded to her exuding sexuality despite his cerebral attempt to remain uninvolved. And where was Hardwicke for Pete's sake? Where had he gone now? What was he supposed to do if she threw herself at him again? Enveloping him in the filmy material of her ball gown, dragging him down into the abyss of licentiousness between the warmth of those thighs that he had felt. Yes, he had felt them, but he had not been feeling for them. He had just been aware of them. He could hardly have been otherwise with his hands pushed into her lap, trying to prevent her from draping herself like a liana vine around his neck. He turned away, seething with outrage and looked, without seeing, at the dancers.

Poor little man! Look at him sitting there, red with embarrassment. How narrow-minded could you be? And his eyes...! Nearly bursting out of their sockets when I stuck my tits out at him and then the way that he tried to look away and pretend that he hadn't seen them! He was so funny! And he hadn't even noticed me drag up my skirt when he had pushed my hands down... and the way that he had sat like a ram-rod when I had put my arms around his neck, trying to pull back but finding that the movement only pulled my bosom against his! Ha! He has a lot to learn. He is a schoolboy! My God, his wife must have him just where she wants him. Sobriety! Church! And here he is swigging gin and Pimms as if it was going to be rationed and all the while thinking it is a kind of lemonade! Hello! What has he seen now? He's stiffened like a cat spying a dog through the park railings.

'Who is that woman with the long dark hair sitting over there?'

'Which one?'

'Over there look, where I'm pointing. Next to the man with the grey hair.'

'It's a bit rude to point Stewart.'

'I don't care. Who is she?'

'Let me have a look. Oh that's the old man's wife. Quite well preserved isn't she for a forty year old?'

'I'm going to dance with her.'

'Pardon.'

'I'm going to ask her to dance.'

Oh my God! Do something Sandra. 'Stewart, she is the British High Commissioner's wife. That is Melissa Fox-Crowe. Sitting next to her is Godfrey Fox-Crowe, the High Commissioner! You can't just ask her like that. You don't even know her.'

'I have met her already.'

'You have? When?'

'At the pool at the British Club. She showed me how to swim and now I am going to show her how to dance.'

'Stewart sit down and don't be a bloody fool. Look, you don't know it, but that Pimms you've been drinking–'

'She nearly drowned me. Dived over and under me and nearly drowned me. Frightened the life out of me and then said sweetly, "It's easy when you know how".'

Oh, Geoff, Geoff. Where are you? For God's sake do something. Why are you never here when I need you?

'Stewart come back... don't be a fool, come back!'

'Hello darling, where's the mad methodist run off to?'

'Oh Geoff! I've done a dreadful thing.'

'What's the matter? Hey! Stop that crying, come on, come on, I know you were only messing about I've never doubted you, you know that.'

'Geoff it's not that. Listen to me. Those drinks... the Pimms. I've been feeding Stewart Pimms and gin and he has been drinking it like lemonade.'

'Probably do him a world of good!'

'I just wanted to show him. He was so snooty about the dancing and then I thought it was so funny that he couldn't recognise the taste of alcohol. I thought it would be funny to get him drunk to see what he would do.'

'Where is he?'

'Oh Geoff, he's gone to ask Melissa Foxe-Crowe for a dance. Something about getting even with her for splashing him at the pool. You've got to stop him Geoff. Oh I'm sorry, I'm a fool. I shouldn't have done it. He's got a pint of Pimms and gin in him. He's not used to alcohol. He's going to make a terrible scene. You must stop him.'

'It's too late. Look.'

Stewart eased his shirt collar nervously with his finger. He had proudly put on his new tie but now he realised that he had tied the knot a little too tightly. He looked across the room again. Above the girl's head the frosted glass window dimmed and brightened as the occasional passer-by in the street blocked out the light. She sat below, demurely waiting to be asked. He looked at the parquet floor and fiddled with his collar again. He would have to do it! He could not sit here all day. She had lovely golden curls and green eyes and she was Martin Miller's girl. Everybody knew that she was Martin Miller's girl. They had been seen on the top deck of the bus, Martin was smoking and she was holding herself slightly aloof but was still with him.

Stewart looked down at his fingers and pinched at a hang-nail. Martin Miller was a brute and a swaggering bully. He would bash up anybody who went near his girl. He had given Jim Craven a black eye last term. Everybody knew that it was him although Jim Craven had not told anyone. If he found Stewart dancing with his girl he would bash him up too. But... but Martin Miller did not come to the dance school. Dancing was for cissies. His girl came though, and Stewart Wrighton wanted to ask her for a dance.

The record had played out nearly a third of its track now, Stewart knew them all off by heart. If he sat here a little longer then he would hardly have enough time to dance one circuit of the room and then it would not be worth asking her after all. He would leave it to the next record... or perhaps next week. She was looking at her watch. Oh no! Surely she was not going yet? Didn't she catch the bus up by the cinema? The bus that went at a quarter to? She would be going and then he would not be able to ask her. Perhaps if he danced with her and she missed the bus she would let him walk with her up to the bus stop and wait until the quarter past bus came. But Martin Miller might see him there. He could always pretend that it was just coincidence.

Stewart stood up and she immediately looked across the room at him and smiled. She smiled! She smiled! He gave a little smile back and started across the floor. There was no going back now. The curly golden hair and green eyes were still there as he felt the soap shavings crackle under his dance shoes. Half way across. Now everybody knew what he was going to do, they could all see him, he could not back out now. He couldn't suddenly disappear into the cloakroom. He could feel himself isolated on a sea of wood-block flooring, despite the mis-matched couples gyrating around him. He was two thirds of the way across now, three quarters, her long black hair framing the dark eyes which were surveying him in a quizzical and mystified manner and now the grey-haired man at her side, realising that she was not listening to him, was also turning and was looking at him approaching. He was there, at the table, bowing correctly

'May I have the pleasure of this dance please?'

Good God! It is that wimp from the swimming pool! The cheeky so and so. Just because I spoke to him he thinks he can come and ask me for a dance. What does he think he can do? I was taught to dance properly at finishing school. I was groomed for this life. Who does he think he is standing there looking like a cheap croupier at a run-down casino? Dance? Madame Marie-Claire taught me to dance at *L'Ecole Sainte Mathilde* in Grenoble. I shall make mincemeat of you, you inconsequential little squirt. I had better pacify Godfrey, his eyes are nearly standing out of his head.

'It is alright Godfrey. We have already met have we not?'

'That is correct, at the swimming pool.'

'Oh yes, I'm afraid I don't quite remember...'

'Stewart, Stewart Wrighton. You may call me Stewart.'

The cheek of the fellow. Well at least he knows which arm to offer me.

'May I call you Melissa?'

No you may not! 'Why yes, of course you must... Stewart.' I'll play him along for a while. 'This is a waltz is it not?'

'Yes that is correct. You can dance the waltz I hope?'

Oh the gall of the man! 'You can dance the waltz I hope?' Patronising sod! The first dance that you ever learn and he wonders whether I can dance it or not. Well, we'll soon see who can dance the waltz. I'll make him look like a drunken giraffe. I expect his waltz will be like shunting wagons on the railway, bang! gap! bang! gap! Ha! Let's see if he even knows how to hold me properly.

Oh! That's a bit of a surprise he... er... can. Must be beginner's luck. Now we're off and... natural turn, closed change, whisk. He's smooth, he's smooth, he's very smooth but after all, this is very basic stuff, anybody can... what is he going to do at the corner? A natural turn or an impetus...?

'It's quite a nice band isn't it?' Wrighton attempted to make pleasant conversation but for some unknown reason his head was feeling a little fuzzy. 'They keep strict tempo quite well don't they?'

Melissa Fox-Crowe smiled the inscrutable smile of a diplomat's wife.

'Yes... even the Hollywood Bowl Orchestra I found a little wanting in that respect a few years back.'

'Oh really? I didn't realise that they played dance music.'

'Oh this was just at a party, a private function, you know.' She eyed the corner warily. He was leaving it too late, he wasn't paying attention. She grinned and prepared to brace herself for the shock of colliding bodies as three novice couples ambled towards the angle.

'Well just look at that!' he said in a detached, insolent manner.

'What?' she began to enquire but rapidly brought her mind back to the job in hand as he quickly led her through a succession of steps leaving her mind whirling with disorder.

'A big open space,' he replied innocently. 'I could have sworn there were half a dozen people here a second ago.' Melissa Fox Crowe had followed his lead automatically whilst she had tried to analyse the last three steps but it had all happened so quickly and with such maddening ease. 'You can't beat a jolly old double reverse spin into reverse corte and hesitation to clear the field and baffle the opposition, what?'

Of course that was what he had done. She could see now. Now that he told her. Clever, very clever. Never done that before. Bit risky but it had worked.

'You seemed a little tense before we negotiated that corner?'

'Oh no–'

'Oh but I could feel it, in your shoulders. You must relax more, it really is quite fun.'

The bastard! The patronising working class bastard!

But Melissa Fox Crowe began to experience a niggling unease. He swept her around the room, passing between couples using gaps that were not there before and which closed behind him. He could read the floor as a London taxi driver reads traffic. He was using unusual, innovative combinations of steps, ignoring the mould of traditional teaching in which Melissa had perforce been schooled. She had to pay attention all the while, she could no longer predict which steps were coming next, she had to rely on the lead he gave her and he always gave it to her faultlessly and unambiguously.

She realised that, over the years, she had become lazy in her dancing. She always knew which variation of step her partner would use next. They had been taught that way. She knew deep down of course that she should rely on the man's lead but when had she last danced with a man who, not only knew what he wanted to do next, but was capable of communicating it to her? And all the while this man was passing inane comments and observations which only served to emphasise his complete mastery of the dance, of his body and of her. The band was beginning the last eight bars when he asked nonchalantly.

'Finish with a flourish?' But whilst she was congratulating herself on having followed his every lead, on not having failed at any point, he suddenly remarked, 'Oh, where did they come from?'

It was enough to distract her just sufficiently for her to put one foot wrong. He stubbed his toe on her shoe, retained his balance despite his stride having been brutally truncated, aborted the step and magnificently converted it into a drag hesitation leading directly into a backward lock. He smiled at her and the couple that he had been trying to avoid whisked past their left elbow with inches to spare. She was livid with herself.

'My fault.' She gave the conventional apology which always triggers the gallant denial from the partner and the assumption by him of the blame.

'Quite!' he observed succinctly.

Her eyes blazed with a mixture of anger and mortification as the music ended and he led her into a spin curtsey and bowed politely to her as he smiled with triumph in his eyes.

Geoff Hardwicke and Sandra had been perched on the edge of their chairs, teetering between anxiety and frustration. Anxious for what might happen and afraid that they would be unable to prevent it. As Melissa Fox-Crowe performed her curtsey they both, quite unconsciously, sighed away their tension.

'He's one hell of a dancer you've got to hand it to him,' Geoff observed.

Sandra was looking at the couple as they came together again and Wrighton began to lead Melissa from the floor. The concentration that Sandra had lent to the dancing had served to sober her up remarkably.

'He's upset Melissa, look at her eyes! I don't know what he's said to the silly bitch but she's smouldering like a volcano.'

'Thank God it's over anyway. He got through it alright.'

'I wasn't worried for him. You had better go and get him, just in case.'

The band struck up for the next dance as Hardwicke unfolded himself from the chair.

'Oh no Geoff! No!' Sandra grabbed his arm in alarm, her eyes fixed on Wrighton and Melissa, standing stock still on the floor.

The band was playing a tango.

'You dance quite well,' Wrighton had said to Melissa as if to appease her as he walked her back to her table.

'Thank you Mr. Wrighton,' she said shortly, allowing her anger to show through.

'But you must learn to relax a little more,' he advised pleasantly, too pleasantly, aware that his every word was grating on her conscience. He could still remember the water closing over his head and the panic of disorientation and he knew that he had allowed her to escape lightly with one discreet stumble in the waltz.

'I'll try to remember your advice,' she said through teeth clenched in a professional smile.

'After all, it was pretty elementary stuff wasn't it?' He gave a dismissive laugh. 'A waltz... ha!'

That was it. That was too much. Melissa Fox-Crowe turned on his arm to face him.

'You patronising little suburban dancer!' she spat at him, her chest heaving with emotion. 'Just because you–'

'Ah now that's what I call a real dance,' Wrighton interrupted her and cocked his ear to the band. 'A tango.'

He looked her directly in the face. His two warm hazelnuts gazing with a placid challenge into the searing jet black of her eyes.

'I dare you,' he said quietly, and pushed his spectacles up his nose.

She flicked back her hair with a toss of her head and moved into his arms, assuming perfectly the slightly crouched, and daringly suggestive stance of the tango.

'Could we have the finalists for the All England Tango Competition on the floor please?'

'Please, please don't fuss so!' Stewart pleaded with gentle insistence to Genevieve, his dance tutor, who was trying to flick fluff from his jacket and simultaneously arrange the bow on Phyllis' dress. 'You'll only make us nervous!'

Phyllis laughed a short laugh.

'Make us nervous,' she said. 'I'm petrified already.'

Stewart looked around the ballroom. The Lyceum was big. Bigger than anything that he had ever danced in. It was glowing with thousands of watts of spotlight and surrounded by tier upon tier of spectators, the women brightly clothed, the men all in evening dress, row upon row of penguins and parakeets. He was not nervous, there was no cause to be. He and Phyllis had worked at the sequence that Genevieve had devised for them until they were quite simply perfect at it. It could not be faulted, so as far as Stewart could see, the judges would really be judging Genevieve's artistic acumen in assembling such a display rather than their talent at performing it. It was out of their hands. They had become tools.

They had dropped one step from the sequence. It was to have been the finale, a sequence of spin turns culminating in Stewart supporting Phyllis merely on the crook of his right arm for a final lunge, reverse spin and flourish. They had tried this many times but were neither of them satisfied with it. To keep balance, timing and position on such a sequence was just too difficult for them yet they comforted themselves with the thought that if it was too difficult for them then it would almost certainly be too difficult for their competitors since they were all very much of the same level of expertise.

'...And representing the Home Counties, Phyllis Dunbar and Stewart Wrighton from Perivale...'

'Go on!' Genevieve hissed and gave them an excited shove in the small of the back.

Stewart took Phyllis' hand and led her to the floor, smiling encourage-ment at her. He looked around. It was immense. It felt as if it were a football pitch. He scanned the borders rapidly as he took up position towards the middle of the floor, the optimum position for them to start their carefully rehearsed sequence.

'Three judges in front of the band, two down the left side,' he hissed to Phyllis from the side of his mouth and then turned to smile up at the supporting members of the dance school who were applauding them madly.

The final few couples were individually announced and took their places and the band struck up.

'Alright Phylly, this is it. Take it like a rehearsal. You can do this with your eyes shut.'

He had become expert at talking without moving his lips. His partner squeezed his hand to show that she had heard and then they were off.

They insinuated themselves between the other dancers, creeping and twisting in the idiosyncratic method of the tango, suggestively, as if they were secretly doing something else far more naughty but leaving only the dancing visible. Melissa Fox-Crowe found that she followed lithely and easily Wrighton's lead as they zig-zagged around the room, cunningly dancing rings around the other couples. She glanced down at them with the innate contempt of the dance, relieved as she was, that Wrighton was apparently an accurate but unimaginative dancer of the tango. Often the case, she smiled to herself, thinking of the dare and how easy it had been for her to call his bluff. She would show him if he thought that he could get the better of her!

'Well that has warmed us up a bit, Melissa.' Wrighton's quiet, steady voice interrupted her musings. 'How about some variations? If you can handle them from a suburban dancer.'

'Anything you like,' she replied sweetly, hiding any slight misgivings with the satisfaction of knowing that her jibe at him had made a mark.

'Right,' he said calmly. 'This little selection I call the "Bex Bissel" because it sweeps the floor clear for proper dancing.'

Instantly, she felt the pressure of Wrighton's thigh inside hers as he lengthened their stride to increase the speed. Somewhere at the base of her spine she felt a vertebra crack into place as her leg stretched out far behind her and still he was there, leading her on, impetuously.

'Let's get rid of these two,' he suggested in a matter of fact manner. 'They've had a good run for their money.' And he bore down upon a vacillating couple, wedged them into a corner and then lunged Melissa at them, crowding them against a table. She felt her eyeballs roll from the surge and wanted to apologise to the startled dancers but he wrenched her away and in a half-beat running promenade crossed the floor and frightened another couple into retirement.

'You're mad,' she hissed. 'Stop it at once.'

'Oh look,' he ignored her, 'that table is far too close to the edge of the floor. It really is most inconsiderate of them. They ought to give us dancing room.'

The world spun around in a blur of lights and colour and she heard an exclamation behind her and the crash of tinkling glass as her swirling gown swept the end of the table.

'This has gone far enough!' she warned through her teeth. 'Take me back to my table!' She tried to withdraw her hand but found that it was held vice-like despite the apparently delicate grip.

'Surely you're not trying to chicken out?' he asked in mock surprise as they shunted another couple up against the band. 'Is my suburban dancing too mundane for you? If you go back to your table now, Melissa my dear, you go back alone. How would that look? Wife of the British High Commissioner abandoned on the dance floor.'

'You bast–'

'Tch tch tch! Manners. Didn't they teach you anything at school? The thing is Melissa my dear... you've got to learn what it is like to be out of your depth and friendless, just like I did, when I was in the pool.'

'That was just a bit of fun–'

'So is this.' He gripped her hard, his hand cutting momentarily below her shoulder blade. 'Now we've got the floor to ourselves let's show them how to really dance the tango.'

Terrified, Melissa Fox-Crowe hung on as they veered and swerved across the floor, pausing on mountain peaks to ski down the other side, skidding across glaciers. She was thrown across his knee, her long black hair sweeping the floor in an orgy of abandon that she had not known since adolescence. The world lunged and plunged at her, upside down and sideways. Vaguely she sensed that they were alone on the floor, the parquet slipping beneath her sequin-showered shoes, the enthralling syncopated tango rhythm possessing her body and always guided by the pressure against her thigh and his hand at her back. They turned, they swirled, they rocked, they promenaded, she didn't know the steps, she could only follow his lead, he could have been making them up for all she knew but whatever she did, it seemed to feel right. Yes, that was it. It seemed to feel right. She knew that her breath was coming in excited gasps, a flush was stealing up her neck, she smelt hot, he smelt hot, they were the embodiment of the tango. To hell with it! This was exactly the kind of dancing that had been frowned upon at finishing school. This was the dancing they had secretly aspired to. She kicked out her foot on the spin, flicking her ball gown waist-high, she flung her head into the turns, her hair smacking against the side of his head, she softened, she moulded herself, she married her body into his and now there was just one body moving sensuously, erotically.

'Last four bars,' he grunted, 'what about the finale Phyllis?'

She stole a rapid glance at him. The perspiration was dripping down his temples. She did not know what he meant. He seemed to be some-where else and yet, he was there, spinning with her, round and round, pivoting first around his thigh and then hers. She could feel a draft across her buttocks and realised that her gown was right up but, what the devil! she didn't care. This was dancing! Round and round, the last two bars, a flying check into a reverse spin, the world, the lights, the white plate-faces froze and then sheered off in the opposite direction and suddenly, madly, she was free, free of his arms, thrown down savagely to the floor in a curtsey, her head bowed, hair in tumbling disarray across her shoulders, the back of her hand smacking the parquet exactly on the final beat.

She remained there, her legs crumpled under her, spittle dripping from her lips, her shoulders heaving, staring at the wood grain of the floor and then into her radius of vision crept the toe of his shoe. She looked up, throwing her hair from her face like a gypsy. He was standing there, swaying slightly, slowly regaining his breath and proffering her his hand. And then she became aware of the noise as she stood up. Cheering, stamping, yelling, crashing of bottle openers on empty bottles. Her mouth dropped open. The band had floored their instruments and were applauding; the leader, wiping perspiration from his eyes with his sleeve and grinning like a Cheshire cat.

She took Wrighton's hand and together they walked slowly from the floor. Everybody seemed to be standing, cheering. At the back, several men and women were wobbling on a table where they had climbed to obtain a better view and now as Wrighton and Melissa threaded their way to the top table, she was being patted on the back, 'Well done!' and 'Fantastic!' 'What a show!' she could hear from right and from left. Then she remembered Godfrey and who she was and how she was supposed to behave. Fearfully she turned her eyes to her husband. He was standing by the table, as the others were, flushed in the face and clapping madly. This was unreal.

'I say, Melissa my dear, I didn't know you could dance like that!' Was all he could find to say as he gazed at her with a mixture of astonishment and admiration.

'Neither did I,' she admitted as she slumped thankfully into the chair.

'Good evening sir.' Geoff Hardwicke had sidled into the group and gently taken hold of Wrighton's arm. 'Can we have Mr. Wrighton back now please sir?' He laughed easily but Wrighton could feel the insistence in his grasp. 'We've got some lemonade for him.'

'Well I er...' The Old Man was lost for words. First his wife shows her knickers to everyone and now his Commercial Attache filches guests from his table. What was the world coming to? Perhaps he was getting old.

'One minute Geoff,' Wrighton said, and turned to Melissa Fox-Crowe who was mopping her entire face with a napkin. 'Thank you for the dance Melissa,' he said correctly.

Her face appeared from the fringes of white cloth like a sunrise over the Himalayas.

'Oh...' she swallowed hard, 'it was my pleasure,' she replied a little breathlessly.

'You see, it's easy when you know how,' Wrighton threw at her. He saw her wince as the arrow hit the target. 'Right then Geoff, anything left in the cool-box? I'm parched.'

21

Wrighton tried to ignore the perspiration dripping down his temples and studied the column of figures again. The numbers were wavering. He closed his eyes for a few moments' respite.

And when he shut his eyes he could see Melissa and himself swirling around the dance floor. The shame and mortification welled up inside him still, despite several weeks having passed since the Ball. And now he despised himself. He despised himself for being naive enough not to recognise alcohol; he despised himself for lacking the courage to go and apologise to Melissa Fox-Crowe for the embarrassment that he had doubtless caused her. As for Sandra, he felt no annoyance with her, it had just been a bit of fun. She did not know any better.

Havering had been walking around the pool with Abdul Haq and had missed the entire spectacle. Wrighton was thankful for that but he still had to endure remarks made to him by complete strangers, people in the queue at the bank or down at the market. Even Tuppin had regaled a morose Bell with substantially fantastic accounts of the performance. Wrighton's conscience was in no way enervated to know that by his own atrocious behaviour, he had earned the respect of Tuppin, an incorrigible philanderer. He didn't need that sort of recognition.

He toted up the figures again and pencilled a line across the next segment of the graph. Havering was busy and had been occupied now for a couple of days, preparing for a trip to Bangkok. He was due to fly out that very afternoon. He grunted. So be it! Let Havering enjoy himself in the fleshpots; his preoccupation suited Wrighton's purpose. Whilst Havering was running around booking hotels and organising visits to frozen food warehouses, he found little time to squeeze Wrighton.

From his desk drawer he drew out a cardboard file and perused the papers within. He had a photocopy of the purchase order for the twelve inch pipe and the disposal docket, showing it to have been sold to the company owned by Abdul Haq. He had tracked down the route by which the aggregate for the pipeline piers had been delivered to the site near where AHT had built the commercial centre. How it had been switched was not difficult to imagine. It would have been merely a matter of a few taka to the lorry driver. Someone would have signed for it of course, but miscellaneous delivery notes were not kept after the completion of the site, so no proof could ever be forthcoming. But he had copies of the damning documentary evidence which he had been able to find. Havering's idea to keep Wrighton in Dhaka by giving him the financial analysis responsibility had backfired. Wrighton was in a far better position to discover any irregularities in Dhaka, with all the data at his disposal, than wandering about fields with a theodolite.

His mind slipped back to those fields near Baderpur, to the valve station amongst the scrubby trees; to Havering's bluff insistence that the station had been numbered correctly, not knowing that Wrighton knew that he was lying. The more Wrighton thought about his discoveries the more he found himself recognising an unproven conviction that the Baderpur valve station held the key to the mystery.

The phone buzzed. It was Havering, abrupt as usual.

'Wrighton, come into my office.'

He carefully folded up the file and slipped it into a bundle of miscellaneous papers in his drawer. Feeling rather conspiratorial, he looked around his office before he closed the door behind him.

Havering was slouched comfortably in his chair behind his desk. There was something in his manner that set the warning bells ringing. He was even more self-assured than he had been lately. He was gloating. Wrighton could feel the old fear returning.

'Wrighton what are you doing here?'

'Well, you asked me... correction, you ordered me into your office.' Wrighton tried to put some spirit into his response. He did not see why Havering's rudeness should always be accepted and ignored.

'Don't try to be funny Wrighton.'

'Nothing was further from my mind.'

'Wrighton you are here, because you were sent here. I didn't ask for you, I got stuck with you. Since you have been here your work has been mediocre and your social graces zero and now...' he moved aside a sheet of paper on his desk, 'you start meddling in things which don't concern you and breaking the security regulations of the company.'

Wrighton looked down. From the desk glared up at him the delivery note for the twelve inch pipe, the purchase order for the aggregate and all the other documents that he had just been looking at in the file in his office. He closed his eyes momentarily, thinking hard. How the deuce had Havering found out?

'If you're going to play at being James Bond,' Havering sneered, 'remember to put the stuff back when you have finished copying it.

Don't leave it lying by the photocopier.'

Wrighton could have kicked himself.

'What's wrong with photocopying documents?' He tried to gain time to think up a workable riposte. 'You gave me the task of financial analysis.'

'You know damn well these have nothing to do with your responsibility. Who are you working for?'

'What do you mean, "who am I working for?"'

'You're obviously trying to spy for someone. Who's paying you?'

'Consolidated are paying me, just like you. Not paying me enough, either.' Wrighton was thinking of the parsimonious overseas allowance that they had grudgingly given him.

'So you thought you'd make money selling industrial secrets?'

'What! You don't believe that!' Wrighton was amazed. The idea was preposterous.

Havering stood up and moved slowly and menacingly around the desk to Wrighton. Wrighton could feel the strength draining out of him as he stared at Havering's finger pointing at him. He could smell the nicotine on it.

'You're in trouble Wrighton, big trouble. Think carefully before you say anything. Go and get the copies that you made of these papers and bring them straight back.'

Without a word Wrighton turned and walked back to his office. He vaguely heard somebody speak to him in the corridor but he did not know whether he replied or not. He emptied the photocopies from the cardboard file and laughed ironically at himself. Oh yes, he had carefully concealed the photocopies from prying eyes, very clever. And he had left the originals on the photocopier. What an idiot! At that moment Havering swaggered in.

'I don't suppose I can trust you to give me all the copies.' He took the file from Wrighton and leafed through the papers. Then he pushed Wrighton rudely aside and opened the other drawers. 'Back in my office, and bring your residence permit.' He strode out, leaving the door open.

Wrighton fumbled in his jacket and dumbly followed Havering back to his office. It was all going wrong. It was all going so terribly wrong. Why did it always go wrong? Why did he always make a mess of things?

Havering was looking at his watch.

'I'm off to the airport in ten minutes.' Wrighton noticed for the first time the bag slumped in the corner of the office. 'But I'll be back. I shall break you Wrighton. You won't have a career worth talking about when I have finished with you. Not only do you contravene security regulations but you assault the native staff employed on the project. We take a very dim view of that.'

Wrighton felt beaten and bludgeoned almost comatose. Things were not making sense anymore. What Havering was saying just could not refer to him.

'I do what?'

Triumphantly, Havering pulled from his desk a sheaf of papers and thrust them at Wrighton.

'That's a writ from one Abra Huda, surveyor, alleging that you physically assaulted him before the undersigned witnesses,' he said in a falsely offhand manner. 'You really can't go around hitting Banglas and expecting to get away with it.'

'I... I...'

Havering took Wrighton's residence permit from his loose fingers and flung it into a steel safe which squatted by the wall.

'The MFA have insisted upon the suspension of your residence permit until the case comes to court.' He swung the heavy door and withdrew the key, smiling. 'And I, of course, have to comply with their instructions.'

Wrighton gazed down unseeingly at the writ in his hand, the mixture of modern intaglio printing and Islamic script as ancient as Allah. It began to ripple before his eyes as tears of frustration and rage brimmed.

'I never hit the man,' he said quietly, almost to himself. 'What is he talking about? Why has he done this?'

'Peon!' Havering yelled at the door and then turned to Wrighton. 'You are confined to Dhaka until I get back. Then we will decide what is to be done with you.' He kicked the bag across the floor to the peon. 'In the car for the airport!' he ordered and then turned to Wrighton. 'You're finished Wrighton. Finished.'

Wrighton collapsed in his office, his head in his hands. Whichever way he looked at it he was suspected of industrial espionage and accused of assault. He could not believe it. It was so unreal but he could only blame himself. Of course, Havering was right. If he wanted to play at spies then he ought to be better at it. Imagine leaving those photocopies there! They must have been there for nearly ten days. No that can't be right. They would not lie there for ten days. The photocopier was in daily use. Where had they been in the interval? Had someone given them to Havering recently or had he found them himself and hung on to them? If Havering had had the photocopies for ten days, what was the point of delaying the admonition? This question brought Wrighton up with a start. Something did not fit in the scenario that he had just been subjected to. Why had Havering chosen today to confront him? What was going on? What was it Havering had threatened him with? 'I shall break you' he had said hadn't he? And then something about being confined to Dhaka until 'we decide what is to be done with you'. We decide. We. Who was coming back with Havering? He would have to find out. 'When the cat's away....'

He picked up the phone.

'Yasmin could you get me the London office on the phone please? I want to speak to Mr–'

Wrighton stopped because Yasmin was already speaking over him. For a telephonist she had a remarkably poor understanding of the functioning of the telephone.

'–sorry Mr. Wrighton.' she was saying, 'but before he was going away Mr. Havering was saying to me that I was not to make any connections with London without his authority.... and he is not here.'

'That's alright Yasmin, forget it. No problem.'

'Thank you Mr. Wrighton.'

He dropped the receiver to the cradle and nodded his head sagely. Havering had certainly tried to isolate him.

'When the cat's away...'. When the cat's away. Of course. The cat, in this case had a telephone in his office upon which you could speak to London, by-passing the switchboard. Wrighton jumped from his chair and made his way to Havering's office. Three fifteen in the afternoon in Dhaka, that would be... nine fifteen in the morning in London. Just right.

'Consolidated,' a woman's voice announced from the receiver.

'Put me through to the drawing office please.'

'Trying to connect you.'

'Drawing office.'

'This is Stewart Wrighton. Who is that?'

A silence ensued, then,

'Our Stewart Wrighton? The one who went to India?'

'No, the one who went to Bangladesh. Is that you Chard?'

'Yeah. Where are you?'

'Dhaka. Look can you do something for me Chard?'

Chard turned away from the phone and he could hear him saying to the office, 'It's that old bugger Wrighton, he's calling from Bangladesh. What's the weather like out there? It's bloody raining here!'

'Oh it's about, I don't know, twenty, twenty five degrees. Sunshine.'

'Did you hear that? He says its...' Chard's voice faded away again.

'Look Chard,' Wrighton called him back impatiently, 'Can you tell me something?'

'I'll try old fruit, I'll try. What do you want to know?'

'Have we got any operations in Bangkok?'

'Blimey I don't know, ask the Gaffer when you see him. He's on his way there now.'

'Cockcroft's coming to Bangkok?'

'Yeah. On his way to Dhaka.'

He put down the receiver. Havering was bringing Cockcroft back to Dhaka and together they would tear him to pieces.

Suddenly he thought about Mac Macleod. He ought to be warned because Havering would almost certainly go for him as soon as he had realised his complicity. He picked up the phone and then replaced it on the cradle. It would be better to do this face to face.

Mac's office door was locked. He cross-examined the secretary in the adjacent room.

'I'm looking for Mr. Macleod.'

'Mr. Macleod not there!' the man replied stolidly.

Wrighton puffed out his cheeks.

'I can see that he is not there,' he said, trying to remain calm. 'Where is he?'

'Mr. Macleod gone.'

'Yes, I can see that too. His office is empty. Now that we have established that he is not there and that he has gone can we find out where he is? Is he downstairs? Is it his day off?'

The man looked at him with his mouth hanging loosely open then he screwed up his eyes and seemed to make a decision.

'You Wrighton Saheb?' he asked as if confirming some suspicion that he had nurtured from childhood.

Wrighton took a breath and let it out slowly. Patience was all that was needed. Patience.

'Yes I am Wrighton Saheb and I am looking for Macleod Saheb. Do you know where he is?'

The man picked up a cast-iron stapling machine of extravagant proportions and pulled an envelope out from under its base. He handed it to Wrighton.

'Chitty from Mr. Macleod.'

Wrighton frowned at the anonymous envelope and then pulled it open, intrigued. But his intrigue soon turned to anger and shame as his eyes skimmed down the short page.

'Stew, just a quick line. By the time you get this I shall probably be back in London. Havering has found out about your enquiries somehow and has blown his top. He went straight to my boss and had me sent back to London, 24 hours' notice for 'security breaches' or some such thing. I can't say that I'm shedding bitter tears at the thought of a flight back to UK! Sorry I couldn't help more, you're on your own now. Good luck and be careful.– Mac.'

The letter was undated and obviously written in a hurry. Wrighton could imagine Mac calmly collecting his affairs whilst Havering ranted and raved up and down the office, unheeded.

'When did Mr. Macleod go?' Wrighton shot at the man, hoping perhaps that he could catch him at home.

The Bengali showed the whites of his eyes, startled by the sudden question then he wobbled his head infuriatingly and flapped his hand about vaguely.

'Last week.'

'Last week!' Wrighton shouted. The man flinched. 'Last week?'

He studied the letter again. Poor old Mac! Wrighton had even let him down, although Mac had not blamed him in any way. He felt very humble as he stumbled back to his office. And in his office he was met by the writ, glaring facetiously up at him from his desk.

'Bagpipe music' That is what Havering always called the Bengali script. 'Bagpipe music'. He pressed the buzzer to summon an interpreter. He might as well have an English translation of it. It was odd that Havering had not needed one. Almost as if he had known what was in it.

There was a discreet knock at the door and in response to his invitation, Rubena glided around the door and Wrighton was surprised to find himself reflecting that she was quite a magnificent woman in a sedate style. Rather like a trainee Queen Victoria. He handed her the writ.

'Could you translate that for me please Rubena? Err...Do it here. Just let me know what it is all about please. No need to write anything down.'

She drew up a chair and surveyed the paper professionally.

'Well Stewart, it is a legal declaration of wrongdoing and a writ, declared by...' she searched the text, 'Abra Huda, a surveyor, that he was bodily insulted, struck with the hand and fist and abused in the company of the undermentioned witnesses who are also attesting.' She turned the sheet over and tapped the bottom of the sheet with her forefinger. 'Yes, those two there, they have signed with their thumbmark... and that the person who had done the wrong doing was–' She looked up sharply. Wrighton looked at her boldly.

'Yes?'

'Stewart it...' she looked back at the paper in confusion.

'Nothing to worry about Rubena, I rather suspect that it mentions me doesn't it?'

'Yes, but it must be making a mistake isn't it?'

'Havering doesn't think so. He's had me confined to barracks. Not to leave Dhaka. He's confiscated my residence permit.'

'But why are...Is it true?' She waved the paper angrily.

'Do you believe it Rubena? Do you believe that I struck with the hand and fist one of your countrymen?'

'No I am not believing this lies!' she retorted.

Wrighton was amused in a detached manner to see that even though her skin was brown, he could tell that she was blushing.

'Well Havering believes it and that is what matters. He has gone off to Bangkok to meet Cockcroft.'

'Mr. Cockcroft the Director of company?'

'The very same, and after he has spent three days in Havering's company, he will believe it also and then they will come back here and tear me to pieces.' Wrighton grinned weakly. 'And then I suppose I shall get sent home like Mac Macleod.'

'Mr. Macleod has gone?' Rubena remarked in surprise.

'About a week ago apparently, and it was all my fault.'

'Why is it being your fault?'

'I asked him to do something for me which he should not have done and Havering found out and made a fuss about it.'

'But that is not your fault. Mr. Macleod was knowing what he was doing. He is not a silly man.'

Wrighton looked at the Bengali woman, wrapping her simple beliefs about her with her sari.

'No he was not a silly man, just unlucky.' He looked at his watch. 'I suppose that I can do what I damn well please now,' he said recklessly and then it was his turn to blush for using such strong language before a woman. 'What do you think I ought to do about that?' He nodded at the writ.

Rubena seemed to be thinking deeply about it.

'I will take it with me and translate it for you, at home. The case will not be heard for many months yet.' Without waiting for his assent she folded the writ and slipped it somewhere inside her sari.

'Now you see it, now you don't!' Wrighton observed a little too jovially. 'I think I'll go home. I'm not doing any good here.'

He stood up and held the door open for Rubena. It had taken him several weeks to convince Rubena and the other interpreters that they should go through the doorway before him and not follow behind. As she drew level with him she said,

'I can help you Stewart. You must not be despairing. You are a good man and I am thinking that Mr. Havering is not a good man. The good man is always winning.'

He gave her an indulgent smile. Everybody cherished illusions of some sort.

Wrighton acknowledged Mohammed's salute as the gate swung open and he plunged into the shade of the porch. Before opening the door he could hear the music beating out and he groaned.

'Tea please Moussi and two toast.'

The cook-bearer popped back into the kitchen and as Wrighton dropped his bag onto the floor and sagged into a vacant easy chair, Tuppin remarked loudly to Bell,

'Well if it isn't Fred Astaire!'

'Oh very funny, ha ha!'

Bell made a told-you-so face at Tuppin who pouted back at him. Wrighton ignored them and stared vacantly at the opposite wall up which a gecko was spasmodically crawling. At length he leaned over to the tape recorder and turned down the volume and said,

'Either of you know a chap called Mac Macleod?'

'Irish feller,' Bell said with authority. 'Got busted for embezzlement about a week ago. Used to drink at the Golf club. Why?'

'I just wondered. One of the projects he was assisting with was related to ours,' Wrighton said vaguely, hoping that they would not detect the disgust that he felt for himself for failing to defend Mac's character. So, that was the story that they were putting about – embezzlement. And of course Mac was not here to defend himself. He wondered what story they would put out about him once that he had gone. Inefficiency? Nervous breakdown? Fraternising with the natives? Persona non grata?

'Here, listen to this,' Tuppin commanded, the *Dhaka Times* spread out on the table. "Fire kills man", he read. "Because of failing cooking pot or faulty stove in a gutcha house in Baderpur a man was burned to death. Forhad Miah was found by his wife lying on the floor, well aflame. The house burned with him. A case has been registered in this regard.' Well, what do you make of that?'

'Bit gruesome,' Wrighton remarked. He had become accustomed to Tuppin's unhealthy appetite for newspaper stories.

'Who do you reckon killed him? Tuppin demanded.

'Killed him?' Bell looked up.

'Well it was obviously not an accident was it?'

'Wasn't it? He was cooking. The stove blew up. Happens all the time.'

'When did you last see a Bengali man cooking?'

'This morning, at breakfast. Moussi is a Bengali in case you hadn't noticed.'

'All right then,' Tuppin insisted, 'when did you last see a Bengali village man cooking?'

'Well–'

'They don't cook, do they? The women run the house. The men sit around outside. The last thing that a village man would do, would be to cook. It's always the women who are burned alive at these stoves for infidelity.'

'Just a minute,' Wrighton interrupted, 'are you saying that this is a form of institutionalised execution, burning people at the stove?'

'Of course it is. That is why it is reported in the paper. But for a bloke to be burned at the stove, that really is an insult. Do you reckon it was his wife's lover that killed him?'

'Christ knows!' Bell grunted.

'And what was the poor man's name?' Wrighton asked.

'Forhad Miah. Do you know him?' Tuppin enquired facetiously.

'And he lived in Baderpur?'

'Yup.'

'Don't think so.'

With a convulsive thrust of his legs, Wrighton turned and kicked off back up the pool, angrily thrashing through the water, gouging out great troughs with his arms, fighting his way through a football crowd. The other end. He turned, grabbed a lungful of air and then kicked again, gliding under the surface, feeling the water rippling down his spine just as he broke through and then picking up his mad cadence of shoulder-stretching haulage.

Accused of industrial espionage! Confined to Dhaka. His residence permit confiscated. Served with a writ. Threatened with dismissal from the project and return in disgrace. Mac Macleod sent home for helping him. Twelve-inch pipeline sold to Abdul Haq's company at a knockdown price. All his documentary proof confiscated by Havering. A Bengali burned in Baderpur. Same name as the one demanding compensation that Rubena had told him Havering had taken a personal interest in.

Coincidence. Must be hundreds of Forhad Miahs. Thousands.

His fingers crashed painfully into the coping stone at the edge of the pool and he stood up in surprise. Few people used the pool in the winter months of January and February. It was too cold, they claimed. Twenty degrees centigrade air temperature was too cold. He pulled himself out and went to the men's changing rooms.

'Ah ha! How's my crew then? Been working off some frustrations?'

Harry Dudgeon was propped up at the bar. Since the day's sailing on the Meghna, Wrighton had felt himself able to give a little more time to Harry than he would have done before. But Harry could be infuriatingly obtuse when he was drunk and this caused the same annoyance to Wrighton as it would to the parent of a promising child who disobediently stamps in a puddle.

'Hello Harry,' he greeted him, mentally checking his canvas deck shoes for puddle splashes.

'How do you know...' Harry began grandly, '...that you are walking on the floor? How do you know that you are not actually walking on the wall and that gravity works at ninety degrees to the way that we think it does?' He scratched his belly through his shirt and turned to the shadow of the barman. 'Lime and soda for the crew.'

'Surely if gravity worked at ninety degrees to the direction in which we thought it worked then we would not know. We cannot walk on the walls because the denomination "floor" is dictated by the direction in which gravity works.'

'Possibly,' Harry conceded, swallowing a mouthful of beer, 'but how do you know that what we see as the floor, someone else is not seeing as the wall?'

'I don't. I am merely saying that our floor can easily be some other being's wall or ceiling. The only reason that we call it a floor is because that is where gravity pulls us to.'

'Yes. Bit of a dark horse aren't you Wrighton?'

'Eh?'

'Not seen you for a few weeks. Not since the New Year's Eve Ball.'

'Ah. I would rather not talk about that. I do not consider it to be the peak of my achievements in Bangladesh. I am awaiting a curt summons to the BHC Residence for a dressing down. Among other things.'

'I don't see why,' Harry said. 'She enjoyed every minute of it. They are always the same these Foreign Office wives. A bit tartish behind the haitches.'

But Wrighton was not listening. He was watching a man walking up the path with a rolling sailor's gait. He called down the verandah, 'Sandy!'

The man stopped and shielded his eyes with his brawny forearm.

'I remember,' he called back, 'feller who couldn't see the swimming pool under his nose. Remind me of your name.'

'Wrighton.'

'That's it.' He swayed into the bar through the screen door. 'Work for pipeline people don't yer.'

'That's right. This is Harry Dudgeon.'

'Oh I know Harry. I've still got the hangover.'

'So have I. Glorious isn't it?' Harry responded. 'When's your plane? Time for a quick one?'

'Aye.'

'Where are you going?' Wrighton asked.

'Home. I've finished. I've done me job and done it well.'

'There's one more job you could do for me,' Harry said. 'A friend of mine is in trouble and needs a bit of help.'

Sandy looked at his watch. 'Fire away!'

Harry's watery eyes met Wrighton's over the beer glass.

'Get it off your chest then Wrighton. Tell us all about it.'

'I... don't know what you mean.'

'Do as he says, lad. A trouble shared...'

Wrighton looked from one to the other. Harry was nobody's fool. Wrighton gave way and was soon pouring out the sordid, complicated story in a jumble of half-formed accusations and shaky deductions.

When he got to the end, Harry and Sandy sat silently. The electric fan swished interminably around as if lunging at them and then retiring like a mechanical rapier. Wrighton fiddled with his glass on the bar.

At length Harry said, 'Never liked Havering. Always trying to fart higher than his arse. Of course you know that he's mad don't you? Ever noticed the way he greets people?' Wrighton shook his head. 'He lowers his eye-brows. Any anthropologist will tell you that throughout the world the sign of greeting is raised eyebrows. Whatever the race. Even monkeys do it. But he brings his down in a threatening gesture. It's the dominance of the reptile brain. The man's mad.'

Sandy rubbed the stubble on his chin,

'Well I don't know anything about monkeys and eyebrows but one thing stands out a mile. This man Havering is petrified of you.'

'What!'

'I think you're right, Sandy.' Harry waggled his glass at him.

'But I find him so difficult to deal with. He... he frightens me,' Wrighton admitted.

'You frighten him,' Harry snorted. 'Why do you think he wants to keep you in Dhaka? He's terrified that if you are left to your own devices, you might discover something embarrassing.'

Sandy nodded slowly and said, 'I reckon you're getting too close to unearthing whatever is going on.'

'And don't worry about your village man, whatever his name was, being burned,' Harry reassured him.

'Forhad Miah?'

'Yes. It's a very common name and what your pimpish colleague gleans about Bangladesh from reading the *Dhaka Times* is as valuable as a broken fingernail. What you have got to consider, me old sailor, me old dancing sailor.... is what are you going to do now?'

'How do you mean? What can I do?'

'Well...' Sandy apologised, 'I've got a plane to catch. I'm not too good on all the theory stuff. I'm much better on me own, up a pole with me cutters and some wire but if I've understood you correctly, yer boss has gone away?' Wrighton nodded. 'Well then, that gives you three days. Don't let us down.'

Wrighton slept badly, tossing and turning, mulling the problem over in his mind. When morning came and with it Moussi and his morning tea, he felt that he had not benefited in any way from the hours abed. He had neither slept peacefully nor solved the problem of what to do.

During the drive into the office, he hardly spoke to his driver at all and when he smelt the biscuit factory it made him ask himself for how many more mornings he would be inhaling the caramel smell of baking biscuits and wincing at the jarring jangling of rickshaw bells.

He sat in his office with Sandy's words ringing sonorously inside his head. 'Don't let us down'. Sandy, the uncomplicated self-contained electrician who willingly gave of his time to help sort out the problems of a virtual stranger when he should have been racing to the airport. He must not let that effort go to waste but what could he do? What could he do?

And then, it all seemed to fall into place with a serenity that was almost supernatural. He realised that he could do whatever he liked. All the staff would obey him and Havering was not there to stop him.

He set to his financial analysis and worked for a hectic three hours, taking no breaks at all. He intended to make it as difficult as possible for Havering to blacken his name. He would show him.

He scooped up his sheaf of papers and slipped downstairs to the typist's room.

'Jill, could you do me an enormous favour please?' Jill was a European woman. The wife of a Dutch diplomat.

'I rather suspect young man, that you want me to type a memo the size of the Bible and you want it yesterday.'

'Um... That's about the level of it. Look, it's this.' He laid the sheets on the desk and turned them as he was explaining. 'It's my financial analysis report. These are the graphs and diagrams, they fit in where I have put the arrows so if you can leave space in the text, do so.'

'And when do you want it Mr. Wrighton?' He looked at the shamble of papers in her tray and the stack of files on the table behind her. 'Well?' she taunted him.

'Umm... I'd rather hoped that I could have it for correction before Mr. Cockcroft arrived from Bangkok.'

'Ah ha... Were you? And when does this Mr. Cockcroft arrive? Before Easter is it?'

'Er... Three days' time actually.' Wrighton gave a little embarrassed laugh.

'Mr. Wrighton! Have you any idea how often Mr. Havering comes down here to see me and ask me to hurry up with his typing?'

'No I don't.'

'And how often,' she demanded, the sternness rising in her voice, 'do you come down to me and demand that your work be done in priority? Well? How often?'

'Well... I'm not sure–'

'I will tell you how often. This is the first time that you have ever asked me for a favour!' She returned to her normal sweet voice. 'I'll have it done in two days.'

'You'll ... er–'

'I will have it finished in two days. How many copies do you want?'

'Five please.'

'Stewart!' she called as he began to leave, 'I always put Havering's work to the bottom of the pile when he asks for it to be done first. Such a rude little man!'

Wrighton skipped up the stairs towards his office. He was certain that keeping his work up to date and up to standard would count in his favour whatever happened. As he rounded the corner of the stairs he nearly knocked over the rotund form of Mrs. Rosario.

'Whoops! Sorry Mrs. Rosario. Didn't see you there.'

Mrs. Rosario recovered her composure and, inevitably, pushed her spectacles back up her nose.

'And yet, Mr. Wrighton, I am thinking that I am big enough to be seen.' She laughed at him as he opened the door for her.

'Good Morning Stewart,' Rubena's voice came from inside.

He poked his head around the door post.

'Good morning Rubena, good morning Leila Rose.'

'Good morning Mr. Wrighton.' Leila Rose discreetly took her feet from the stool and slipped them back inside her sandals.

'Could I see you for a minute Rubena please? I need your advice.' Wrighton could feel the seed of a plan germinating.

'I will come to your office now.' She put down her paper. Leila Rose pouted.

'Now, now, Leila Rose!' Wrighton wagged his finger at her. 'You are thinking bad thoughts, I can tell by your face.'

Her jaw fell open in surprise and Mrs. Rosario remarked,

'There, you see Leila Rose! Even Mr. Wrighton is seeing that you are a bad girl!' She snorted into her work.

'If you are worrying about your writ–' Rubena began but Wrighton waved away her apologies.

'No, it's not that Rubena. I am in no hurry to know the content and if what you say is true–'

'I am always telling the truth.'

'I'm sorry. I meant... that you said that the case will not come to court for many months and if that is so, then it becomes merely academic since I shall certainly not be in Bangladesh in two or three or four months time.'

'You are not knowing the will of Allah,' Rubena replied mysteriously.

Wrighton looked at her for an instant and then continued.

'I really want your advice on how to get to Baderpur.'

Rubena was puzzled by the importance that he appeared to place upon a simple question.

'You are going by jeep?' she nodded.

'Without a residence permit' Wrighton added. 'Mr. Havering took it away.'

'The problem is at the Demra Junction police post outside Dhaka, on the Sylhet road isn't it? They will be stopping you and asking for your papers.'

'They don't stop everyone surely?'

Rubena frowned as she thought hard.

'Not everyone.'

'Well how would they know to stop me?'

'You are not Bengali. You are a white man.' She smiled ironically. 'They always stop white men.'

'Is there any way out of Dhaka to Baderpur which does not go past the police station?'

'You are really wanting to go?'

'Yes.'

'I think we can find one. Why are you wanting to go to Baderpur?'

Wrighton wondered how much he should tell her.

'I want to look at a valve station that we built there.'

'And Mr. Havering is not wanting you to go?'

'That's about it.'

'No problem. We can get there and back in a day. I can leave my work till later in the week.'

'Just a minute....' Wrighton was horrified, 'I can't take you, Rubena. I'm going on my own.'

She seemed not to hear him.

'I think I shall be going with you.'

'Rubena, I said–'

'You are not speaking Bengali, Stewart. I must go with you. Have you told the driver? He needs to prepare the truck.'

'Rubena! I... What does he need to prepare?'

'He will need to fill up with petrol,' she said seriously. 'Which truck are you taking? We must go down and see them.'

The drivers refused as a body to take Wrighton and Rubena to Baderpur. Havering had left instructions before his departure that Wrighton was not to be taken anywhere other than from home to work and back again.

Rubena flew into a rage and shouted at them, thrusting her chin at them aggressively, hunting them down in all corners of the cool, shady garage. She attacked their courage, she attacked their loyalty. 'Are you calling yourselves men? Has Mr. Wrighton ever been unkind to you?' Eventually Wrighton had to take her by the arm and lead her away. He could feel her shaking with anger.

'Leave them, leave them Rubena. It's not their fault.'

'There is not one driver who will take us. Men have no courage!'

'It is something simpler than that, Rubena. You are not as frightening as Mr Havering. As long as they are more scared of Mr Havering than they are of either you or me, then they will do what he says. Its simple power politics.'

'They are making me very angry.'

'You don't say!'

'Yes they are,' she insisted, not understanding the nuance.

'Don't worry, Rubena, we'll find another way. I know a man at the British Club who I'm sure would lend me his truck if I asked him.'

They walked back up the stairs to the offices.

'But I am coming with you!' Rubena decreed finally. 'I am.'

Wrighton stopped in the corridor and leaned against the cool wall whilst he thought. She could do no harm. She knew that what they were doing was against Havering's instruction. She would certainly be more at home up country than he would. She could interpret for him.

'All right,' he agreed, 'I will pick you up at your house.'

'Why not at the office?'

'I think that the fewer people who know about it the better.'

'But you have no enemies here Stewart. Not now.'

'We do not know what other orders Mr Havering has left behind him. If I don't tell anyone, then they are not put in a position of having to deny me something.'

'We will have to leave early.'

'Five o'clock? Your house?'

'I will be there Stewart.'

'Fine.'

22

Wrighton sat planning and plotting in the rickshaw as it gently wobbled him back towards Banani House from the club. The Harry of yesterday was the one that Wrighton would want to remember, not the Harry of today. For today he was the vapid, drunken slob with vague, unfocussed eyes and jelly for a brain. It would have been pointless to broach the question of Wrighton borrowing his jeep; apart from not being able to stand up, Harry was totally incapable of understanding any persuasion which did not come with a froth on top of it.

Wrighton remembered Sandy's exhortation from yesterday. 'Don't let us down'. Well, he was not going to give up now. Somehow, tomorrow morning, he and Rubena would go up country and solve this mystery once and for all. He would need transport and a means of bringing back incontrovertible proof should he find any. He must be capable of arranging that.

He paid the rickshaw puller at the gate and frowned for a minute at Bell's decrepit Ford saloon. Mohammed patiently held open the gate and when finally, his favourite master condescended to turn towards him, he snapped into a smart salute.

'Bell can you lend me your car?'

'What's wrong with your Land Rover?'

'Nothing, but it's needed at work.' Wrighton was shocked to realise how easy it was to lie.

'How long do you want it for?'

'A day. All tomorrow. I want to go up country.'

'What? Nothing doing, Sunshine! I thought you wanted to nip down to the club or something, not go on an expedition. What do you want to go up country for?'

'Lend me your camera then.' Bell looked at him sideways as if trying to decide what was different about him. 'Go on,' Wrighton ordered him. 'Go and get your camera.'

'Well you can look at it if you like...' Bell disappeared across the corridor into his room. 'Haven't you got a camera?'

'No.'

'Well why do you suddenly need one?'

'Because I need to take some photographs, dunderhead!' he parried as Bell returned carrying an expensive-looking leather bag.

'Jolly good camera this. I know it's small but the lens is fantastic. Zeiss. The proper Zeiss not the pretend one.'

It was indeed a neat camera complete with a separate flash unit and a wide angle and telephoto lens daintily packed into a sort of leather cosmetic case. It was not the sort of camera that Wrighton would have expected a brutish flight engineer to possess. It was somehow, effeminate.

As if in explanation Bell said, 'Of course it is not the camera I would have liked but... but it was given to me by a... local big shot in our village. He's got pots of money and I helped him take down his greenhouse and move it across the garden. He had had this greenhouse built out of aircraft grade aluminium alloy 'cos he was a director of Handley Page at the time. He got the apprentices to build it as an exercise you know. When it came to move it I knew a bit about the locknuts they use on airframes so he suggested I help him.' Bell looked Wrighton straight in the eyes as he always did when he was making up a story. 'Old Sir Arthur just said to me...' Bell dried up. Wrighton's cool brown eyes were on him. He tried to go on. 'Er... said to me–'

'Just show me how it works, Bell.'

'Right... Right... That's your shutter release–'

'What does that mean?'

'It's the lever that releases the shutter. The shutter is cocked when you wind on the film.'

'Do you mean that it is the lever that I press to take a picture?'

Bell took a deep breath. He seemed to be on the point of saying something but Wrighton forestalled him.

'Well is it?'

'Yes.'

'Right! Now I assume that I look through here and press this lever. Is there a film in it?'

'No.'

'Press this lever here to take a photo, right?'

'Yeah.'

'Then what do I do? Wind on the film I suppose?'

'You push that lever all the way around and let it flip back.'

'Like this?' Wrighton operated the lever. Bell nodded. 'O.K. Well that's fairly simple. Do I need to focus it?'

'When you look through the view-finder... got it?'

'Yes.'

'Turn this ring here...'

'Oh I see, it comes into and out of focus. And that is what I will take the picture of, is it?'

'Yeah.'

'What's this?'

'Aperture.'

'This?'

'Shutter speed.'

'This?'

'Film speed.'

'And are they all important?'

'Wrighton have you ever used a camera before because I'm blowed if I'm going to lend–?'

'I asked if they were important.'

'Of course they're bloody important.'

'Wouldn't it be possible for you to set most of them for me so that I can leave them as they are?'

'I suppose so,' Bell admitted reluctantly. He was upset by Wrighton's ability to dig the sand out from under his tottering anger. 'What speed film are you using?'

'Well what speed have you got?'

'What speed have I got?'

'You surely don't expect me to possess any film do you? I haven't got a camera. If I had, I wouldn't be borrowing yours.'

'You've got a cheek–'

'I'll take it off the housekeeping money that you owe me shall I Bell? You go and get a film and I'll practise with the camera empty for a while then you can put the film in and set it up for me. How many pictures can I take on one film?'

'Twenty four or thirty six.'

'Put a thirty six in and then that should be sufficient for the whole day. I can't think that I would want to take any more than that many photos.'

With a lot of apparent bad humour Bell grumbled across to his room. When he came back he showed Wrighton how to change the lenses, what the wide-angle lens was for and how to use the telephoto and then he put the film in and set the camera up so that all Wrighton had to do was to point it, focus and press the lever. Wrighton carried it carefully into his bedroom.

'Don't worry Bell I'll look after it.'

'You'd better.'

Wrighton grinned at him. He was not at all intimidated by Bell. Not now. Just as he settled on his bed to consider the problem of transport for the morrow, Moussi announced through the warped bedroom door,

'Memsaheb come.'

Memsaheb? He wasn't expecting any Memsahebs. It was probably one of Tuppin's love entanglements.

'O.K. Mohammed. Show her into the dining room. I'll be out in a minute. *Tik hay?*'

'*Tik hay!*' Mohammed replied, gratified that Wrighton had used his native Urdu and not the Bengali '*Tikka say*'.

As Wrighton approached the dining room door he could already hear Bell in full flood.

'...and the Duke, of course, the Duke of Edinburgh that is, he is quite a nice chap really. Not stuck up at all. He came over to me, he left his group on the lawn and came over to me where I was talking with my boss and he said er... well I mean somebody had obviously told him about how I had managed to get the craft back upstream on only one engine and he said to me... er...'

'Oh dear!' Wrighton thought, 'if I leave him any longer he will be explaining how the Queen spilt the marmalade at breakfast.' He went in.

Bell was perched on the edge of an easy chair in a pose of intense supplication. Opposite him sat a discreetly bored, very diplomatic, smartly turned out Sandra Hardwicke.

'Oh hello Sandra!' Wrighton was both pleased and surprised.

'Hi Stewart!'

'I was just telling Sandy about the time that the Queen and Prince Philip came out to Dhaka,' Bell explained.

Whilst he was turned towards Wrighton, Sandra pulled a hideously comical face behind his back. Wrighton sat down casually.

'Oh, do you want a drink? Tea? No coffee I'm afraid. Got gin and vodka.'

'Tea would be very nice.' She smiled.

Wrighton turned to Bell.

'Ask Moussi for some tea would you?'

Bell opened his mouth to shout and then shut it when he noticed Wrighton's meaningful nod towards the door. He was flabbergasted.

'I'll... I'll get some tea.' He stood up and walked towards the door almost as if discovering the route for the first time in his life. As the door shut Sandra said,

'We've only just got back from Nepal actually.'

'Oh yes? How was it?'

'Heavenly. Mountains, snow, a bit cold but the people are so much nicer. Not Muslims you see. Mostly Hindus and Buddhists.'

'Did you go trekking?'

Sandra laughed and rocked back in her chair, hugging her knees.

'You do say the funniest things.' Then she became serious. 'Stewart, I haven't really seen you since the Ball–'

'Ah yes.' Stewart felt a weight descend upon him. 'I can only say that I am dreadfully sorry and I hope that I haven't got you or Geoff into trouble.'

Sandra looked at him queerly.

'You are serious aren't you?' she said in amazement. 'I came here to apologise to you. You know that I got you drunk on Pimms don't you?'

'I realised on the following morning... and for the rest of the day,' Wrighton said sourly.

'It was a stupid, wicked and nasty thing to do. I hate myself for doing it. I don't know why I did. It was horrible. Please don't think badly of me. Can we still be friends?' She leaned forwards and took Wrighton's hand pleadingly in hers.

The door swung open and in bounced Bell.

'Moussi is going to get the chocolate digestives out of the fridge, you are honoured...' He faltered as he noticed Sandra's hand in Wrighton's.

'Yes that's O.K. Sandra,' Wrighton agreed in a business-like manner. 'As far as I was concerned it had never changed.' Sandra blushed and withdrew her hand. Bell looked away pointedly. 'Now tell me a bit more about Kathmandu.'

Sandra Hardwicke settled herself back in the chair as Moussi swept gracefully in, proudly bearing the tea tray upon which he had arranged the best china and their chocolate digestive biscuits. Just as he settled it down onto the table a commotion erupted in the hallway as Mohammed's voice echoed around the bare walls.

'Burra Memsaheb aya hay!' he said.

Wrighton looked at Moussi who straightened up and explained mysteriously. 'Big madam come,' and went out.

The three of them looked at each other and then burst out laughing.

'A touch of Osbert Sitwell,' a cultured voice observed from the hallway. 'Laughter in the Next Room.'

Sandra put her hand to her mouth, Wrighton knitted his eyebrows in perplexity. Where had he heard that voice before?

'May I come in?' Melissa Fox-Crowe asked from the doorway. It was clearly quite an effort for her to enter such a humble abode.

Wrighton and Bell stood up like jacks-in-the-box.

'I was just passing,' Melissa Fox-Crowe explained and looked pointedly at Sandra.

'Good afternoon Mrs. Fox-Crowe,' she said.

Wrighton, whose head was spinning with questions decided that he could only play it by ear and Melissa for the moment seemed to be in control so he said,

'We are just having tea er...'

'Melissa,' she prompted.

Wrighton smiled gratefully. He was unsure where he stood but he was certain that he knew why she was there. She had not been 'just passing', she had come for an explanation and apology and to make matters worse she had come to him and not, as it should have been, he to her.

'Oh that would be lovely.' She glanced at the table. 'And chocolate digestives! Where on earth did you get those from? They have run out in the Commissariat.' She glanced across at Sandra.

Wrighton picked up the implication immediately.

'Oh there has been no double-dealing, Melissa, Sandra has not been supplying us with goods from your Commissariat.' He looked across at Bell who was standing with his mouth still open but was waving his hands frantically in a gesture of warning. 'One of my house mates here, Gerry Bell, got them for us didn't you Gerry?'

Melissa flicked her head around and the long dark hair swished across her shoulders. She fixed Bell with her dark eyes. 'And what do you do Mr. Bell?'

'Ho...' his voice squeaked. He cleared his throat discreetly. 'Hovercraft Project.'

'How interesting.'

'I'll... order some more tea.' He left hurriedly.

'Please sit down.' Wrighton said.

She sat down opposite Sandra. The contrast was obvious. Sandra was nicely turned out, neat, pretty. Melissa was expensive, immaculate, poised, stunning. Wrighton looked from one to the other.

'Sandra was just telling us about their trip to Nepal weren't you Sandra?'

'Did you drop in on the Mallinson-Bentleys whilst you were there?' Melissa enquired sweetly.

'No Mrs. Fox-Crowe we went up to Pokhara and stayed in one of the mountain guesthouses.'

'How charming.' She took a sip of tea and grimaced. 'Oh it's sugared.'

'Oh that'll be Bell's tea. Sorry.' Wrighton explained as she disdainfully replaced her cup on the tray. Wrighton was racking his brain, wondering what the deuce he was supposed to do with these two women when Fate wrenched the tiller from his hands. The outside door banged and to the characteristic sound of a sports bag sliding across the hall floor and fetching up against the far wall, Tuppin yelled out,

'Hey someone down our road's getting a bollocking! The gaffer's car is outsi–' He stopped at the doorway.

It had not occurred to Wrighton to wonder how Melissa Fox-Crowe had arrived at their house. Had he done so he would certainly have concluded that she had used the car from the High Commission but the sudden revelation to him that the beflagged limousine was parked outside their house, shook him somewhat, but not as much as the sight of the High Commissioner's wife sitting in the dining room drinking tea, shook Tuppin. He choked on his sentence and immediately turned as red as one of his traffic lights. Wrighton grasped the situation by its spiky bits.

'Ah, Melissa, do you know Arthur Tuppin?' He turned to Tuppin and with some relish said, 'Arty let me introduce you to Mrs. Fox-Crowe, the wife of the British High Commissioner.'

'Pleased to meet you.' Tuppin's voice came out in a mechanical whisper. 'Please excuse me, I must go and get changed.' He bowed out backwards in a comically subservient manner and narrowly avoided impaling himself on the tea cup and saucer that Bell was trying to introduce through the same doorway.

'Watch it Tuppin!' Bell growled, forgetting himself but was pulled back into the corridor with his cup and saucer where Tuppin engaged him in a frantic whispered conversation.

Melissa asked, 'Do you share the house with anybody else?'

'I don't think there should be any more surprises. Please excuse my house companions, we don't entertain much at home. We are honoured today.'

'I have got something I would like to mention to you...' Wrighton's heart sunk, '...but it can wait.' Melissa looked pointedly across at Sandra.

'Well I was just going.' Sandra took up the cue. 'Thanks for the tea. I'll see myself out.' She left.

Wrighton turned back from the door and took a deep breath.

'Melissa–' he began.

'I believe that you are teaching Mrs. Hardwicke to dance. Is that so?'

'I did give her some lessons,' he admitted, 'but I haven't since Christmas. I've been too busy and they have been away. Have I done wrong?'

'Where did you give the lessons? Here?'

'Oh no!' Wrighton laughed. 'And have those two apes gawping at us?' He nodded towards the door. 'I taught her in her house. It's bigger than this one.'

'Not difficult. Are there really three of you living here?'

'There should be four but we don't use the other bedroom. It got flooded.'

'We have a very large room in the Residence...' Melissa began.

'Yes?' Wrighton was not seeing the point.

'I would like you to come and teach me dancing, Mr. Wrighton.' She rushed the sentence out like a blushing schoolgirl. 'Any time that's convenient to you. I am free quite often.' She flushed a little.

Good Heavens, Wrighton thought, she is embarrassed.

'To be truthful, Melissa. I really think that I ought to apologise for my behaviour at the New Year's Eve Ball. You see, I had had some alcoholic drink. I don't drink alcohol.'

'Apologise?' She was clearly puzzled. 'What on earth for? It was the most intensely enjoyable experience that I have had for years.' She added in a low voice, 'Don't apologise my dear.'

'Oh.'

'Now when can you come and give me some lessons?'

Wrighton smiled grimly at the humour of it all.

'The trouble is, I am not certain that I will be here much longer.'

'Oh I see. That's a pity. When does your contract end?'

'I don't know. They can terminate it when they like.'

'That's a little unsettling isn't it?'

'Just a little,' he admitted drily.

There was a knock at the door.

'Come in!' Wrighton called.

Bell appeared in the doorway, still clutching a tea cup, a queer grin of bemusement across his face.

'Er... sorry to interrupt Wrighton... er ma'am... There's a lady to see you Wrighton.'

Much to Bell's apparent satisfaction, Wrighton was lost for words. Melissa Fox-Crowe retrieved the situation.

'I must go, I was just passing by.' She uncrossed her model's legs and stood up in a swish of silk skirts. At the doorway she said, 'Can you come up for tea next... Wednesday afternoon?'

'For tea?'

'At the Residence. I'll send the car for you and we can continue our conversation, if you wish.'

'Thank you. I shall look forward to that.'

'Don't bother to see me out I'm sure Mr. Bell can accompany me to my car.'

'Yes ma'am.' Bell grovelled whilst staring in wide-eyed disbelief at Wrighton.

Melissa Fox-Crowe haughtily inspected Wrighton's third visitor from top to toe as only a woman can. Wrighton wordlessly showed her into the dining room. It was Mary Havering.

'Mr. Wrighton–' she began as soon as he had closed the door.

He interrupted her. 'I understood after our last meeting that we were on Christian name terms, Mary.' This was the wife of the man who was out to destroy him.

She sunk into an armchair.

'Have you got anything to drink?' Her voice was loud.

'You mean alcoholic?'

'Oh I forgot, you don't drink do you?'

'Gin or Vodka?'

'Vodka.'

'Moussi!' The door opened and Tuppin's head appeared His eyebrows shot up at the sight of yet another woman.

'Moussi is marketing,' Tuppin explained.

'Have we got any vodka?'

'Well...yes.. do you want some?' He looked appreciatively across at Mary Havering who was sitting with her head back and eyes closed, her heavy breasts prominent through the thin blouse.

'Yes please, Tuppin. You might as well bring the bottle.'

'And a glass?'

'Yes and a glass.'

He nodded and glanced again at Mary Havering then made a face at Wrighton.

'I haven't been able to see you since the dance,' she explained as she refilled her glass. 'But I wanted to... to explain.'

'I am listening.'

'God! You don't make this any easier do you?'

'It seems to me...' Wrighton said quietly, 'that I am the innocent party

in all this. I saved you from a lynching at the hands of a mob and you
would not deign to reveal your identity. I accept that, at that time you did
not know who I was and that you merely wanted to remain anonymous for
your own reasons. Then at the ball I, quite intuitively, I feel, sensed that
you didn't want me to admit to your husband, my boss, that we had met
and so I went along with that deceit. I have not asked for any explanation
but if any is forthcoming I don't see how I can make it easy for you.'

'That night–'

'That night?'

'You know bloody well which night. That bloody night. That bloody
night when the Banglas were burned,' she shrieked.

'All right, all right. Calm down.'

'That bloody night I had been out. Alan thought that I was at one of
my women's meetings–'

'Look, I am sure this does not concern me,' Wrighton protested. 'You
don't have to tell me.'

'You wanted an explanation. This is the explanation. Do you know
where I had been? Do you?'

'I don't think I need to know.'

'I had been to see a man who's got lead in his pencil. A real man. The
only trouble was...' she hiccoughed morosely, 'when I got there his bloody
pencil was in some other tart's pocket.' She shook with anger and spilled
her glass down the front of her blouse.

'Mrs. Havering, I think you should–'

'S'not Mary anymore then?' she lisped. 'Silly. Spilt my drink. All wet.
Mr. Bloody Clever Wrighton. Not clever enough for my Alan though are
you? He may not have a prick but he's got brains! Blouse all wet. Have
to take it off.' She began to fumble with the buttons of her blouse.

'Oh my giddy aunt! You're going home. Tuppin!' he shouted.

'You rang milud?' Tuppin appeared in the doorway. He had obviously
been listening outside.

'Take Mary Havering home please. Her car is outside.'

'You want me to take her home?' he confirmed as he watched the great
orbs of Mary Havering's breasts appear through the ever widening gap at
the front of her blouse.

'Yes, do you know where they live?'

'I do as a matter of fact.'

'I thought you might.'

'How do I get back?'

'I'll leave you to work that out but I shan't wait up for you.'

Wrighton rubbed his face in relief as Mary Havering's car drew slowly away from the house. Through the windscreen he could see Tuppin's face fixed in the incredulous expression of a pyromaniac who had just been given a timberyard and a box of matches.

What an afternoon! Wrighton could hardly believe it. Then his eyes lighted on the angular black shadow which projected beyond the back of the house and he almost hugged himself with joy. Lines' Land Rover! Why hadn't he thought of it before?

'Mohammed!' he called.

Mohammed came slap-tapping across the hot concrete in his bare feet.

'Saheb?' he saluted even more smartly than before. The Burra Memsaheb had visited his master. That made him important.

'Have you got the keys to the Land Rover?'

Mohammed nodded and shuffled across to the truck. He wrenched open the door and took the keys from the ignition lock. Wrighton realised of course that this was the safest place to keep them since the garden was always guarded so the truck could go nowhere.

As he walked around the truck, inspecting it, he was followed suspiciously by Mohammed. A large steel fender had been bolted across the front of the radiator grill. This had apparently taken all the shock of the impact with the rickshaw for it was bent and in several places, flakes of red paint still adhered to it. However, the damage overall was slight and nothing was obstructing the wheels. Most of the side panels appeared to have been pummelled by fists. He looked in through the open door. The passenger side of the windscreen had been smashed almost clean away but the driver's screen was untouched. The glass still lay on the floor and the seats were white with mildew.

'Does the engine work?'

'Garry herab hay. Very bad truck,' he replied discouragingly.

'I know its history, Mohammed, I only want to know if the engine works.'

'Saheb?'

'Never mind. Give me the keys.'

He grabbed a rag from the back and rubbed down the seat to remove the bloom then he slid into position. He put his hands on the wheel and wriggled about to settle himself in. It seemed a decade since he had driven a vehicle He looked around the controls. Obviously a petrol-engined model. He turned the key and checked the fuel gauge. It was half full. That surprised him. He had expected the petrol to have been siphoned out by now. The engine fired at the fourth or fifth groan but it picked up quickly to the noisy roar that could be heard anywhere in Bangladesh. The noise brought Bell yelling into the garden.

'Hey! Mohammed! What the hell–?' Then he saw Wrighton. 'Sorry Wrighton I didn't see you there. Thought Mohammed was mucking about with the truck.'

Wrighton revved the engine, flicked off the key and listened. It cut off sweetly. It suddenly occurred to Bell what Wrighton was intending.

'For Pete's sake Bell, shut your mouth. Every time I've looked at you this afternoon you've had your gob stuck open!'

'You're not thinking of going up country in this are you?'

'Haven't got much choice have I? No-one will lend me a car.'

'You're mad.'

'It works.'

'You won't get two hundred yards in that. You'll be mobbed. Everyone will recognise it. They'll lynch you.'

'I'll go down Airport Road. I've no need to go anywhere near D.I.T. 2.'

'No, I can't allow it,' Bell declared with final officiousness.

'You can't stop it,' Wrighton pointed out. 'It's the vehicle issued to Raymond Line. I took over his job, it's my vehicle. It's nothing to do with you.' He stepped down from the driving seat. 'Mohammed. I want you to clean this van, inside.' Mohammed rolled his eyes.

'Very bad truck, saheb.'

'I'm only asking you to clean it. Sweep up that glass and get any glass out of the seats, here and here. I don't want a lacerated bum. Clean the mildew off the seats and get those brown stains off the inside of the roof.'

'That's blood,' Bell called over his shoulder as he stomped away. 'It's where the baby ended up. Are you in for dinner?'

'Yes.'

'What about Tuppin? Where is he for God's sake?'

'He won't be back for dinner. He's taken Mary Havering home.'

Bell turned to say something and then shrugged his shoulders. He had not understood anything that had happened that afternoon.

23

Rubena Chowdhry sat in her porch and watched through the mosquito screen as the torpid mist writhed in the dark street like a ghostly sleeper disturbed in his slumbers. Nearby, her chowkidhar coughed and then hawked bitterly. She could hear the chair creaking and she knew that he was meticulously wrapping himself in his blanket in a futile attempt to keep out the coolness of the winter morning.

Futile, because he was so thin that he would always feel cold. They should have got rid of him a long time ago. He was too old to be any good as a chowkidhar. He slept all night to rest his bones instead of staying awake to guard the house. Not unsurprisingly for such an old and frail man, his valour was tempered with a generous measure of self-preservation. When, one night last year, some dacoits had vaulted over the wall in order to burgle the house, the chowkidhar had displayed a prodigious feat of physical effort in climbing over the wall into the next garden in order to escape them. There, he had fallen foul of their neighbour's chowkidhar who was doing his job properly and after some hurried, gasped explanations, the alarum was raised in the quarter and the dacoits were hounded out and sent on their way empty handed.

The man coughed again, a racking, rasping cough. They could keep him on still, Rubena decided. He would not last another winter. He might as well die in security.

She pulled her anorak more closely around her and snuggled her head into the hood. She had put on a plain cotton sari which would keep her warm in the morning but she had discarded her sandals for a pair of Western-style tennis shoes that her uncle had brought back from a visit to London. They would be sensible for wandering around up country; she had no qualms about mixing her traditional dress with modern Western dress if it suited her. The anorak, which was a treasured object, she had bought from one of the returning diplomats who had been skiing in his holidays and could find no use for it in Bangladesh. She supposed that Europeans did not feel the cold in her country.

Outside the garden wall the pi-dogs were scratching at the pile of refuse, snuffling and growling at each other. Down on the Murree road she could hear a killer-truck bucketing along, its tailgate rattling and clattering. She heard it whistle a few times and then the noise faded.

Slowly she became aware of a low whining drone of a Land Rover grinding along in bottom gear and then she saw the two headlights materialising through the mist. This must be Stewart, she thought and gathering up her bundle, she slipped out of the porch and noiselessly opened the gate. She turned and glanced without emotion at the chowkidhar who stirred not a jot in his cocoon of blankets.

With a squeak, the Land Rover stopped outside and the door fell open and Stewart appeared.

'I wasn't sure in this mist if I had got the right house,' he whispered in greeting.

'Good morning,' she whispered back as she climbed into the passenger seat. 'Oh!' she exclaimed, seeing the windscreen.

'Oh yes, sorry about that. It'll be a bit draughty.' He took her bundle and dropped it over the back of the front seat into the van. 'All set?'

She carefully zipped up her anorak.

'I am ready.'

He let in the clutch and they lurched forwards.

'Sorry! I'm still getting used to it.'

'It is no matter. Why is there no glass?'

'It had an accident and nobody has repaired it.'

'With all the dentings on the outside and the no glass it is looking like a killer truck.'

'In a sense it is.' She looked blank-faced across at him. 'Now, down the Murree Road and round by the stadium, is that right?'

'It is good road.'

He did not speak again for nearly fifteen minutes and then it was only to check that he was taking the correct turning. She lurched and banged and bumped with the truck and wrapped her arms around herself for warmth as the mist rolled in through the broken window and soaked her face. Why was the windscreen broken on her side? Where had he got the Land Rover from? What were they doing at this time of the morning, stealing out of Dhaka like a pair of love-match youngsters. She smiled safely in the darkness of the truck. A pair of love-match youngsters. She liked that analogy, it was so preposterous.

She envied him his hardiness as he drove without a coat but with a thin woollen jumper draped around his shoulders. But then he had glass in his windscreen.

Grey formless shapes moved by on both sides. Sometimes they resolved themselves into recognisable objects but more often they dissipated before any sort of identification was possible.

'Turn left, here, Stewart, we do not want to go to the Saddarghat.'

'I should think not,' he said. 'In this mist we'd probably end up in the Ganga.'

On the whole, he knew his way about surprisingly well for someone who had only been in Bangladesh how many months...? Four? Five? Not many Europeans ventured outside Gulshan.

He had changed during those months. Perhaps he had not noticed it, but she had. She glanced at him, grey silhouetted in the gloomy cab as he screwed his eyes up, peering at the fog and then frantically wrenched the wheel around and back again to avoid a small boy herding three cows and a calf. He seemed to take everything in his stride. Even the volcanic Mr. Havering and his temper did not seem to disturb him. She had thought him weak at first meeting but perhaps it was merely that he had not been put adequately to the test.

'Are you alright there Rubena? Warm enough?' She raised a non-committal hand. There was no point in complaining if he could not see that she was shivering. In any case, he could do little to alleviate the situation. 'I wish this confounded fog would clear. I feel worn out already. It's not the easiest way to drive. Shouldn't the sun be up by now?'

'It would be good if the fog was lasting a little longer Stewart.'

'What?'

'The police post is at the end of this avenue, in about another mile. I don't think they will be watching much in this cold.'

'Hmm. Good point. I had forgotten about that. What do we do if he stops us?'

'We can turn around and then be going around the little streets or I can shout at him.'

'Baksheesh?'

'Baksheesh might be difficult. How much to give? If you are offering too little he is insulted and calls his chief. If you are offering too much then he is worried that you are doing something wrong.'

'You know, I'm glad I brought you along Rubena, you really cheer me up!'

'I am answering your question.'

'I was only teasing you.'

But I do not understand why you are teasing me. To what purpose? I am not thinking that it is funny. I am cold and damp and I do not know why I am bumping along in this truck with you. Perhaps we are being fellow travellers. You are looking for one truth and I for another. Perhaps we are looking for the same truth. We will find it, *Inshallah*, we will find it.

We are coming up to the police post now but you do not know. You have not even noticed, you are too busy making a fuss about how difficult it is to drive in this fog. You are not noticing what is going on around you, you are only looking forwards. I can see the sentry. He is asleep in his doorway, squatting, wrapped around in his grey rug like a dacoit, his useless rifle growing from the crook in his arm. We are driving straight past him and he is ignoring us, no, he has stirred. He is lifting his stupid, dopey head but we have already gone past him into the fog before he has even focussed his eyes.

'Where did you say the police post was?'

'We have just passed it.'

'What! You could have told me!'

'It is no matter. No problem.'

'But you said that all kinds of nasty things could happen.'

'He was sleeping. Did you want me to wake him up?'

'No, Rubena, no I didn't.'

'That is good then.'

They reached the first ferry ghat before the sun had managed to break through. Although the fog was becoming lighter and silvery, it was still all-enveloping. The first notification that they had reached the ghat was when Wrighton nearly collided with a killer bus which had stopped in the road. As he pulled out to drive around it, a bus came the other way, followed by a stream of trucks and buses and other native conveyances. This was the traffic which was unloading from the ferry.

The beggars materialised from the fog and began to clamour at the windows, tapping with their fingers and grinning obsequiously with their heads on one side. Then two small boys carrying on their heads, broad shallow baskets, squabbled over the truck in an attempt to sell their bananas. Wrighton bought four green fruit knowing that by the end of the day they would be ripe enough to eat. Then a stunted Bengali in a filthy loin cloth beckoned to them in the peculiar palm downwards manner of the Far East. Wrighton knew what was expected of him.

They grumbled and roared down the loose gravel and sand ramp to the rusty jaws of the waiting ferry. The man had hung onto the back of the truck for the ride and now he jumped off and vigorously invited them to drive onto the ramp. Gesticulating madly, he placed them at the front of the empty ferry in the middle. Wrighton switched on the headlights.

Now that the only obstacle to loading the ferry had been overcome, the queue surged forward, hooting and revving, scrabbling and slipping onto the ferry. One baby-taxi raced down the outside of the queue to the front but there his luck deserted him as did his brakes, for he careered off down the side of the ghat into the river. The crowd jeered as the little motor coughed and spluttered valiantly in the water before slowly sinking out of sight. The driver and his fare, a portly merchant, floundered ashore. They were already shivering in the misty air as they immediately began an acrimonious dispute.

'Well at least the argument should warm them up a bit,' Wrighton remarked, having observed the plunge with a frighteningly singular detachment.

With a clanging of obscure bells and a rumbling below the plate steel deck, the ferry slid sideways from the ghat and into the river. It whooped a siren and they began the gentle rocking journey down the river. A few minutes later they met the yellow mournful eyes of a truck planted at the bows of the other ferry and the two boats slid quietly past each other in mid stream.

By the time that they had reached the second ferry crossing the sun was high in the sky, shining with that half-hearted commitment of an over-worked sun enjoying its slack season. They journeyed along, Wrighton apparently ignorant of Rubena's existence, not speaking, immersed in his thoughts. He had thrown off his sweater which had been draped around his shoulders to keep out the early morning dampness and already she could see the sweat beginning to trickle down his spine. She had wrapped her shawl around her face to protect herself from the bombardment of dust and grit. Wrighton seemed to feel no compassion, seeing her swathed so.

'You look as if you are in purdah,' he shouted across and laughed. Her eyes met his without expression. 'That is something that I have never understood,' he continued now that the train of thought had been set in motion, 'I have never understood why Muslim women wrap up like that.' Just at that moment they passed a rickshaw providentially bearing two be-burkhaed women. 'Look! Like that. They must be terribly hot. Why do they do it?'

'It is religious custom.'

'Yes, but they must be cooking in that outfit.'

'It is not fit for women to show more. It is wrong.'

Wrighton shrugged.

How can he understand? He is not Bengali. He is not a Muslim. He is not a woman. Deep within her, her sense of justice clamoured out that the system was wrong, that women should not be downtrodden but her religious indoctrination told her that this was the way it should be and that she was wicked to think otherwise. She could not imagine herself otherwise'. True, she had seen Bengali women who had 'gone Western', who dressed always in Western clothes, who smoked, who drove cars. In fact she knew one or two and in knowing them she had realised that they had not changed. It was the outside that had changed. Inside they were still Bengali Muslims so what was the purpose of changing just for show? They did not believe themselves to be European. Indeed, they were proud to be Bengali so what was the point in wearing the baubles of the West?

And this man here at the side of her. This Christian. Why was he passing comment upon her religion? She had not criticised his beliefs. His women went with other women's husbands, they drank intoxicating drinks, they talked loudly and kissed people in the street. Some of them dressed like men and rode motor bicycles, sitting astride them in the masculine way. They showed their bodies off to every stranger.

Yet still the horribly persistent question nagged at her and teasingly refused to be answered. What was she doing here? Why was she being shaken and plastered in a noisy Land Rover? Was it the morbid attraction of Baderpur, Abdul Haq's upazilla? Abdul Haq who had found her husband dead in the presidential palace, grotesquely sprawled on the stairs and implicated in the doomed coup from which Haq himself had emerged shining with innocence and loyalty. Was it the mystical attraction of being in this man's territory? Or was it the attraction of the man, Wrighton?

'What is your wife thinking of you working out here?' she asked suddenly, boldly, as if to exorcise the preposterous suspicion that Rubena herself might be attracted to Wrighton.

'Does that look like a tea stall over there?' he nodded at a wattle shack by the road side. 'I'm parched. Do you want a drink?'

'I think it is tea stall.'

In one easy movement he swung the Land Rover off the road and swept across the dusty verge to park in the meagre shade. A handful of hens scuttled, protesting into the shelter of the stall. Wrighton climbed down stiffly from the truck and straightened his back.

'You all right? Not too stiff?' he enquired with unusual brusqueness.

'I am all right,' Rubena declared as she unwound her shawl.

Wrighton laughed at her and she was discountenanced by such an unfriendly and insensitive reaction.

'You look like a panda,' he said. 'Look at your face.'

How rude! How coarse! She glanced quickly at her face in the wing mirror and hastily dusted the white grime from around her eyes with the tail of her shawl, flicking at it with little angry flicks. The men sitting in the tea stall were laughing but they stopped when Wrighton turned towards them.

'Do you want tea or a pepsi or something?'

'Yes please.'

'Well which? Pepsi...?'

'Pepsi.'

They sat together on a rickety wooden form under the palm-thatched porch and watched the ceaseless movement of traffic churning up and down the road. The man brought Wrighton tea in dirty crockery and a bottle of Pepsi-Cola which he set onto the table. Holding the point of a six-inch nail onto the crown cork of the bottle, he brought down a stone sharply onto its head, plunging the nail two inches into the bottle. Then he withdrew it and inserted a straw. Wrighton watched the procedure with interest.

'Never seen that done before.' He wiped his thumb around the outside of his tea cup to remove most of the grime. 'Oh here comes the audience.' A collection of loafers and children began to collect in front of the tea stall to stare at the newcomers. Rubena made a movement to disperse them but Wrighton stopped her. 'They're not doing any harm.'

Not doing any harm. Not doing any harm. I don't like being stared at, Rubena reminded herself bitterly. I am not a film star. I am not a dancer. I do not need a crowd of people following me. It's alright for you, you are used to it. Wherever you go, you have a crowd of people watching you, following you. You Westerners must love it.

'Go away! Get on with your business!' she snapped at the crowd, knowing that she could address them such from the protection of Wrighton's side. The men at the front showed the whites of their eyes and turned away slightly but could not move for the press of people behind.

'You'll only excite them Rubena, it's best to leave them. You can't make them go away.'

'You are used to it. You like it,' she found herself accusing him.

'No, I don't like it. In England it would be considered very rude to stand and stare like that but I am not in England and in any case, I can do nothing about it. If they want to stand there then they can do so, just as much as I can sit here.'

Suddenly with a terrifying shriek, a lorry lunged from the road, scattering the crowd in terror and foundered to a halt by the stand. A man built like a monkey with skin burned black and dressed only in a loincloth and dirty cotton vest, jumped from the cab and ambled over to the stand. He stood talking to the owner who was poking minute hewn logs into the baked earth oven upon which rested the steel plate bearing the bubbling teapot.

A little anxious at being left alone, Rubena watched Wrighton as he got up and casually sauntered over to the lorry and inspected the load. Presently he was back, sliding along the form to sit close to her, a little too close. She edged away.

'I want to talk to the driver of that lorry.'

She looked at the man. He was very black and very dirty. She did not want to talk to him.

'Why are you wanting to talk to him?'

'I want to know where his bricks came from.' He beckoned the man over to him. The driver hesitated, looking from the smiling European face to the scowling Bengali woman's face, then he made up his mind and stood before Wrighton and saluted.

'*Boshen!*' Wrighton said, and the man sat down uncertainly. Wrighton turned to Rubena. 'I'm getting the hang of this language now.'

The driver was looking with an innocent frankness at Wrighton.

'Ask him please where he collected his bricks from.'

What was driving this man? Why was he sitting there, hunched over the table, eyes bright with anticipation? He was as if drugged with some mysterious quest. Rubena swirled her shawl testily around her shoulders and snapped out the question.

'Baderpur,' the man replied.

And then they were off, Wrighton not giving Rubena time to finish her pepsi, urging her on, chivvying her. They had to go to Baderpur because that was where the bricks came from. Nothing made sense any more. The bricks were grey-blue; they should have been orange. Rubena did not understand. Only that they had to go to Baderpur.

With the overhead sun flattening the already flat countryside with its wafer shadows, they went skittering through villages, stones rattling in the wheel arches, bumping through towns on tar-humped roads, onward,

onward, buffeted by the dust and heat blowing through the windscreen, senses drummed by the thundering of the engine, the whining of the gears and when she glanced across at him for companionship, for recognition of her existence even, his eyes never left the road, his hands gripped the wheel as he willed the van to get nearer and nearer to Baderpur.

When she finally distracted his attention from the road for long enough to convince him that they should stop and eat, he stopped there and then and pulled out a pack of sandwiches whilst Rubena occupied herself with the contents of her lunch tin. He sat at the wheel, glaring in the direction of Baderpur as if afraid that it would hide if he averted his watch. She purposefully took a leisurely time over her meal whilst he tore and ripped at his bread and swallowed great gulps of water from his bottle and then, having finished and seeing that Rubena was still eating, he started off up the road for a way, walking briskly as if he intended to continue on foot. When he had walked a hundred yards he suddenly swung around and marched back to the truck to find that she was still eating so he stretched the map out on the bonnet and studied it, his eyes searing the paper with their regard.

Forty five minutes later they were in Baderpur but there was still no respite for, paradoxically, he now appeared uninterested in the town itself. He drove down the main street muttering to himself.

'What are you looking for Stewart?'

'It's got to be here. It's got to be–'

'What is it?'

'Should be able to see the chimneys.'

'What are you looking for? What chimneys?'

And then he turned to her and looked at her with such amazement on his face, as if it was inconceivable that she should not know.

'The brickworks of course. They've got to be here somewhere.'

I am not in your head. I do not know what you are thinking. Why don't you ask someone instead of driving around madly? And then she saw some chimneys in a dip to their right and she found herself jumping up and down like a school girl on sports day.

'Over there Stewart! Over there!'

But he had seen them and soon they were bounding through the scrub to park on a small promontory overlooking the brickfields. There he drew his bag from the back seat and quietly sat sketching for a few minutes. Rubena watched him, feeling the hurt of exclusion.

Knowing that what he was doing was important to him and that he was still unwilling to share it with her, only exacerbated the wound. He used to tell her what he was doing. She was his colleague, he consulted her, asked for her advice. What had happened since yesterday? Now he was treating her as if she were merely an interpreter. She watched him working with the compass and annotating his sketch then he drew out a camera and began to photograph the stacks of reddish bricks turning slowly to that unusual grey blue as they cooled.

Then he drove down to the gate and, through the good offices of Rubena, the foreman in charge allowed them to wander about like tourists. Wrighton seemed particularly interested in the ovens and then abruptly he announced that he had seen enough and they drove back out of town.

'We are not going back to Dhaka then?' Rubena enquired as he turned the van onto the main road.

'No I need to find one more thing.'

'But it will be dark soon.'

'We can find it in the morning. I thought we could stay overnight at Fraser's,' he said casually. 'You know, Fraser's Resthouse, on the tea garden. O.K. by you?'

She heard herself concurring although every fibre of her body was stiffening with suspicion and fear. What was this Rest House? Why did he want to stay away for a night? With a little shiver of what could have been either fear or excitement she realised that perhaps he had intended all along to stay away overnight and that he had meant her to be with him. She glanced at him at the wheel. He was relaxed now, he was even humming something to himself. That must be it! He was sure of himself now. Well! He would see! She could still fight for her honour!

At Fraser's they were given two suites on the east wing opening directly onto the swimming pool. They ate a cold meal alone in the dining room. They were the only guests. As they finished Rubena could feel her heart beginning to thump with anticipation. She had seen it on the Western films. The man always made a move after dinner.

'Had enough to eat?' Wrighton asked.

'I am having sufficient thank you.'

'Right, well I am going to bed. We need to start early tomorrow. Sleep well.' And picking up his bag, he tottered down the corridor to his room.

Rubena sat, staring down the gloomy corridor. She waited for a moment and then slowly followed him.

As she unwound her sari she could hear him moving about the

adjacent room, even to the thud as he dropped a shoe and the creaking of the bed as he climbed onto it. She slipped below the mosquito net and lay on her own bed. Her eyes strayed to the communicating door. That would be the way that he would come in. The traditional communicating door, the Victorian innovation designed to keep adultery from the eyes of the servants. She wondered for how long she should resist him since he was sure to be stronger than her. A minute? Five minutes? And should she make a noisy protest or would this bring assistance? She realised that she did not want assistance. Her eyes returned to the door handle, watching for it to turn.

From Wrighton's room came the discreet but unmistakable sound of sleep.

For a few seconds she watched the sun dappling through the rattan screen. Where was she? Then as she remembered, she heard the sound of a body plunging into the pool outside. She stole from her bed and sidled over to the window. By pulling the screen slightly away from the frame she could just see Wrighton forging up the pool in an adequate, if rather wasteful, crawl. He reached the far end and hauled himself out. Rubena pulled the screen aside and watched the water sluicing down his tanned body. As far as she was concerned she was peeping at a practically nude man. She held her breath as he stretched his arms and twisted his torso in a series of unrefined and grotesque movements doubtless intended to loosen up his body for the day.

Little blue swimming shorts. He was wearing blue swimming shorts. She found her eyes drawn slowly down his chest, further down across his flat belly, down towards that part of a man's body that she had almost forgotten. Her eyes flitted butterfly-like across this place and then, realising that no punishment could be forthcoming, she allowed them to steal slowly back.

Suddenly, he dived into the pool again and thrashed his way back up towards the building. Catching sight of her he called out,

'Come on in, it's lovely!'

Why shouldn't she swim? Why shouldn't she swim? Why should she remain earthbound by her religion and customs? When she was a child, living in the village, they all used to swim naked in the tank. They used to tumble in together, shrieking and yelling and falling over each other in the brown water. She tried to recall the caress of water sliding over her thighs, swirling around her body, lifting her hair and then sticking it harshly to her back when she jumped up. Why shouldn't she swim?

Nobody would see her. She could swim in her underclothes like the Western women did, she only had to slip off her sari... Her daydreaming was suddenly shattered when she realised that she was not wearing her sari yet but was standing in full view of Stewart Wrighton in her sleep-crumpled underthings. With a backward shock she let the screen drop hurriedly and stepped away from the window.

'Are you not coming in then Rubena?' Wrighton's voice called from outside.

As if terrified that he would follow his voice into the room, she snatched up her sari and began to frantically wind it around her. She saw his shadow pass across the window and heard his screen door bang as he returned to his room. She looked down at her knees. They were trembling.

At breakfast, she wanted to explain to Wrighton that Muslim women could not just strip off and dive into a pool when they felt like it but she was angry that he would see this as a failing in her own way of life. She was also acutely embarrassed, like a little girl, because he had seen her partly dressed and yet, within her she felt the tumult of hypocrisy churning over the accusation that not a few moments earlier she had been standing there, brazenly thinking of his body as she had not thought of a body for some years. She ate, her face downturned and her eyes averted. He did not mention the subject and so she felt peculiarly unachieved.

Then they were back on the road. Wrighton pushing relentlessly on in his obscure search, engrossed, silent, obsessed. Rubena slouched in her seat, grit grinding in her teeth, dust in her eyes, buffeted and pummelled by the wind. She understood little of his activities that day. Not because she was incapable of understanding them but because she did not try. He had excluded her, by design or default, and so she was no longer interested.

She had wondered whether by coming out to Baderpur she had hoped to find what she had been subconsciously searching for all these years. Her Holy Grail. Coming with Wrighton, a man driven by a mysterious, invincible dynamo, she perhaps had thought that somehow the two forces would combine to produce a power of such proportions that the craggy crust of lies and deceit which had enrobed the truth would be shattered and cast asunder and the truth would shine through, all the truth, the twin truths, his and hers; startlingly, glitteringly, scorching the doubting eyeballs of the non-believers.

But as she now sat there, brutalised by the truck, oppressed by the heat and ignored by Wrighton, her eyes gently closed in a fine gesture of resignation; the small, dry tear creeping from the corner of one eye would have revealed to an onlooker, had there been one, that she now knew that she had ceased to care.

Let him drive over paddy fields! Let him make his sketches! Let him take his photographs! She, Rubena Chowdhry, just did not care anymore.

But the admission tore her up inside and she blamed him for the pain. Baderpur was Abdul Haq's upazilla, the man who had found her husband's body. The truth had to lie hereabouts. Wrighton had looked for his truth in little bits and in little bits he had found it. Oh! he kept his own counsel but she could tell by his mannerisms. You don't work close to a man for that long without learning a little of how he behaves, how he reveals himself. His frenetic scribbling in the sketchbook, the discreet nods of confirmation that he had occasionally addressed to himself, all indicated that he was content in his fixation.

And now, as they drove back into Dhaka, he had started again that dreadful humming.

And she? All she could see was the newspaper photograph of her husband's blood-drenched body, obscenely cast head downwards in the stairwell of the palace; gunned down as he had allegedly tried to assassinate the General, the sub machine gun still clutched across his chest, his guilty finger on the trigger and his torso corkscrewed in a wringing agony of disbelief, an arm twisted through the stair rail as he had fallen.

'Nearly home, Rubena.'

She closed her eyes but could still see his mouth silently shouting his innocence. She screwed her eyes tighter, tighter still to erase the picture but she knew that it was forever graven in her mind. In an attempt to expunge it, she tried to conjure up the other photographs that she possessed of her husband in uniform. One, marching at the head of his platoon, another, him proudly receiving his commendation from the General and yet another, taken illicitly by a fellow officer during an exercise, ironically, of him firing at a target. Yes! He was a crack shot! He had always been in demand for the competitions.

'This is your road, Rubena.'

This was the picture that she liked the best. There was depicted within it the camaraderie that had kept him in the Army. He was happy, surrounded by his smiling men, rifle tucked neatly into his left shoulder as he squinted at the target on the range. Rubena frowned. His left shoulder. His left shoulder.... With a gun he was left-handed. He was left-handed. He was left-handed! He supported the barrel with his right and squeezed the trigger with his left. That was what he was doing in the snapshot. She could see it in her mind's eye. But the newspaper photograph showed him holding the gun by its grip in his right hand with his right forefinger in the trigger guard. His left hand was twisted through the rails, but his left hand should have been holding the grip and trigger. If he had been coming down the staircase toting a gun and had thrown out a hand to check his flight, it would have been his right hand, not his left. He would not have transferred the gun clumsily across his body into a position of unfamiliarity and impotency. He had come down that staircase without a gun! He had never had the gun! It had been put on him afterwards by the person finding the body... or shooting it. Abdul Haq had found the body.

She realised that she had known all along. She had not been searching to uncover her truth, she had been hoping to bury it. She had allowed herself to be influenced by the same insidious corruption that had impregnated her husband's death. But now, having recognised this, she knew that all she required was the strength to crack the kernel of this depravity. She could now see the road that she must take.

'Rubena, this is your road. Rubena...?'

She turned to Wrighton, the end of her shawl pressed into her mouth and saw him gasp. 'Rubena, are you alright? Rubena?'

Here was a man concerned with her well-being. A strong man although he did not know it. She wanted a strong man to put his arms around her and shield her from life's woes, to protect her; a man to stroke her hair comfortingly, to listen to her troubles and sweep away her problems.

She put her hand to cover her eyes but sensed that Wrighton had turned towards her. Her thoughts, her feelings her protestations were bubbling out in Bengali. Wrighton could decipher neither word nor meaning.

'Rubena, dear, I can't understand you. I'm sorry.'

He called me 'dear'. His arm is coming towards me now. I'm going to give in. I'm going to submit. I want to surrender.

'It must have been a very tiring job for you, Rubena, I'm sorry if I've worn you out.'

His arm has stopped on the back of the seat. He won't come any closer. I want him to. He won't touch me because I once told him it was wrong. His whole being is urging him to hug me and comfort me but because I told him it was wrong, Stewart Wrighton has controlled himself. He has remained within the stupid, idiotic, fabricated bounds of decency that we have both recognised. I cannot explain to him that I need his strength just now, for myself. He will not know why I am crying. It will be... because I'm tired.

'I am sorry Stewart. I am not sleeping very well this night.'

Poor old Rubena, she must have been exhausted. Hardly surprising really, considering what she had to do for me. A good night's sleep would soon put that to right. She was a real tower of strength, I would never have been able to do it without her. And I've got my result, oh yes.

Mary Havering thought that her husband was cleverer than Wrighton! Ha! She would see. They would all see.

Violently he rammed the Land Rover alongside a killer bus, the steering wheel began to kick and snatch as the wheels rimmed the storm drain. But Wrighton did not care. He was reckless in his exaltation.

'You WANT to go don't you?' Marion had accused him. 'You want to go!'

He ground the lever roughly into third gear and the truck pulled ahead of the lurching bus. Well, he had wanted to go, there was no denying it now. He had needed to test himself and he had so nearly failed. So nearly... but not this time.

'You're nothing but a baby! Go and have a paddle, Stewart, there's a good boy,' his mother had cajoled.

Well he could bloody swim now and dive in as well.

He was approaching the biscuit factory and the traffic was congealing by the Tejgaon traffic lights. Tuppin's traffic lights. What was Tuppin doing now? At this very moment? Probably jumping up and down on Mary Havering! He grinned in wicked indulgence, shocking himself with his ability to conjure up such an image. Dhaka looked different to him now. The defeated army, stumbling out, dragging its broken weaponry would always see the town differently from the sprightly victorious liberators entering in their wake. Same town, different morale.

He slipped Bell's camera and the sketch-pad into the top of his bag and zipped it up whilst he waited for the lights to change. He patted the bag reassuringly. 'Soon be home.'

The truck's tyres thrummed on the tarmac of Airport Road and squealed slightly as he veered across the lanes and turned into the Mohakali Road towards DIT 1.

'Don't be so bloody self-effacing!' Sandra Hardwicke had said.

'Careful Mr. Wrighton,' he addressed himself mockingly, 'pride comes before a fall. Or in this case, before a tollygari.' He skidded the van to a stop as one of the typically overladen and uncontrollable specimens of the genus, oozed across the road. He pummelled his horn as the half ton of cement in paper sacks, wobbled and flounced its capricious route before him.

At the sound of the horn one of the pushers glanced at the truck and then with a shout, dropped his end of the cart and stood before the bonnet of the truck. Wrighton looked at him, slightly irritated and then blew his horn again and indicated to the man that he would be more gainfully employed in pushing the tollygari which was now completely blocking the road, but the man was taken with a sudden madness and continued shouting excitedly at Wrighton. Then he stepped forward and smote the bonnet a resounding slap. Wrighton revved the engine and looked around uneasily as a muttering crowd of vacant-eyed loafers assembled and stared, listening to the man's exhortations without apparent emotion. Wrighton was not deceived by their docility. He knew the power of the orator on an ignorant crowd of unoccupied men and he did not like what he saw. He knew that he had to make a move to get away from whatever was upsetting them.

'Come on, clear out of the way you bogwit!' But the man had been joined imperceptibly by the crowd who began to shout and point at Wrighton.

'Shit!' Wrighton exclaimed. 'They think I am Line!'

Of course, any European looks like another in the eyes of a Bengali. He'd forgotten all about the van with its bent bumper bars and smashed windscreen and dented bodywork. But the crowd had recognised it. Why had he turned down this way? What had made him do it? It wasn't even the most direct route home!

He had no time to pursue these questions for at that moment, half a brick smashed through the remaining pane of the windscreen and hit his forearm which he had instinctively thrust up before his face. The glass fragmented and ricocheted around the inside of the van like shrapnel. Then they were banging the van, rocking it, climbing on it. The noise was terrifying. He had locked the doors but they would get in eventually. Fear gripped him right down in the pit of the stomach. Good old original fear. It was the swirling water over his head, it was the bullies in the ice cream queue, it was the sinister silver nose of the airplane pointing at him over the fence.

'Aaah!'

He screamed and the sound of his voice shocked him with its pure expression of distilled terror. Arms were coming through the window on his door, he slid the pane shut, trapping a wrist and then pushed it hard enough to cut skin and still the banging, thundering on the bodywork and the truck rocking from side to side. He scrambled over the back of his seat towards the back door. He hit his head on the roof, his wrist was stingingly numb, he barked his knees on the floor as he toppled over. He tried to steady himself against the fearful lurching.

Grab the bag! Gotta get the bag! Everything depended now upon that bag. He crawled back up to the front. Brown hands were already tugging the bag through the windscreen. He bit hard till he felt bones crunch and heard screaming pain. He skittered down the steel platform to the back door, dragging the bag with him. Outside, one of the Banglas was lighting a piece of rag.

Curling his legs before him he lay on his back and with both feet he kicked the back door with all his strength. It crashed open into the crowd and bounced back. He kicked again and then followed out. Petrol fumes were heavy in the air, the rag was at the filler pipe. He had to run. Head down, he charged into the crowd.

'You stupid buggers!' he shouted. 'You'll kill the lot of us!'

Then he ran.

For Sandra Hardwicke who wanted him to be more positive.

He ran.

For his father who wanted him to be better than he.

He ran.

The crowd yelled as it aimed blows at his head and his body.

For Melissa Fox-Crowe who insisted that, 'It's easy when you know how.'

His feet pounded the hot tarmac.

For Phyllis Dunbar who would have married him had he asked.

Get away from the van.

For Alan Havering who wanted to destroy him.

Get away from the van it's going to blow up and take all these stupid bogwit Banglas with it.

A fist punched his ear knocking him stupid.

He ran.

For Mac Macleod whom he had let down so badly.

And above all for–

Then the tank blew up.

24

As Saudi Arabia slid slowly towards the rear of the plane, Arthur Cockcroft picked up the morning's copy of *The Times* again but failed to find any interest in the print. He abhorred these long flights but what he was doing was in Consolidated's interest; he could not have declined the invitation to attend the official opening of the Chittagong Extension Gas Pipeline. So there he was. He would just have to grin and bear it. And upon reflection, he conceded that the Chittagong Extension was an achievement to be proud of. It had been planned, laid and brought on stream with the minimum of fuss and in a record time. It had only taken two years after that trouble with Havering and Wrighton.

He twisted his ankles and eased off his shoes. There was one other passenger in the first-class section, a very affluent-looking Bengali so Cockcroft had no qualms about offending him. He wriggled his toes on the carpet, yawned, loosened his collar and reclined his seat.

This time, of course, he was flying direct to Dhaka, not stopping via Bangkok as he had last time. He closed his eyes as he recalled those hectic days in Bangkok, in and out of the bars in the daytime and the clubs at night. Havering worrying himself to death in case the supermarket should fail to deliver his frozen food order in time for their flight back to Dhaka. Cockcroft hadn't gone to Bangkok to buy meat and had been irritated by Havering's preoccupation with his own well-being.

He opened his eyes as he sensed the warm, scent-laden passage of the hostess wafting down the aisle to the front. Even the hostesses were not so young as they used to be, he reflected morosely, this one was nearly forty and no chicken. He watched her as she fiddled with a locker at floor level on the bulkhead, squatting primly, regulation position, hand lazily lying at the hem to maintain modesty.

He glanced out of the window at the sky. They were chasing the sunset to Dhaka. Scheduled arrival at six in the evening should give him time to shower and change for the dinner-dance at the Sonargaon. Tomorrow he would visit the pipeline, hoping to God that the nearest portion was within a couple of hours' drive and then, duty done, he would get the hell out of the country and fly home.

He could still see Havering slouched in that dingy office, explaining in short, angry phrases how the whole scheme had been put in jeopardy by the incompetence of Wrighton and why Wrighton had to be got rid of and how Wrighton had been leaking information to some other interest. Wrighton, Wrighton, Wrighton! At every turn Havering had butted against him.

And so they had called in Wrighton and for a moment Cockcroft had thought that there had been some mistake for the sunburned figure that had strided into the room had nothing of Wembley about it, nothing of the drawing office. It was the paradigm of the colonial civil engineer: healthy, bright-eyed, alert. The contrast with the testy, bag-eyed, chain-smoking Havering was marked. Cockcroft liked a man to be a man. Nothing wrong with booze, fags and women – except that you ended up looking like Havering.

But however tawdry and dissipated Havering had looked, he had lost nothing of the aggression and sense of purpose that had got him the assignment in the first place. Cockcroft had known what the man was capable of. He had grunted with satisfaction as Havering had weighed straight in.

'Where have you been Wrighton?'

'Good morning Mr. Cockcroft, do you mind if I sit down?' A nice little touch, he had thought, recognising the real authority in the room. A trifle facetious in the circumstances and guaranteed to rile Havering. Perhaps he was in for a show after all. 'I understand that you wish to see me sir?'

'I want to see you Wrighton. Didn't I tell you that you were not to leave Dhaka whilst I was away?'

'Yes and you also said that I was finished and that you were going to break me.'

And Cockcroft had sat back and left them to duel. It had promised an interesting contest even though he had no doubt as to the result. Havering with his cunning would make mincemeat of Wrighton. Granted, Wrighton had a sharp tongue but he was far too honest to be clever.

'Why did you disobey me, Wrighton?'

'Because I knew that I could and get away with it.'

Cockcroft suppressed a smile.

'You're a disgrace to the profession.'

'I am wearing a tie, you are not.'

That barb had tickled Cockcroft and enraged Havering. It was obvious that Wrighton was going to make his dismissal as enjoyable as he could.

'Who drove you? I'll have him fired. I gave strict instructions.'

'Oh don't worry, you can't terrify the driving pool any further. They all refused to a man. I drove myself.'

'Whose truck? They had no right to let you have a truck.'

'My truck.'

'Your truck?'

'Well, Raymond Lines' old truck. I reckoned that it was due to me as I took over his job.'

'I see. And where is it now?'

'Burned out in Gulshan by DIT 1. You may have seen the report in this morning's paper. *"Driver is absconding."* That was me. I was attacked by the mob. That was how I got this bruise on my cheek.'

'So you just left it there?'

'Thank you for enquiring about my health. I managed to get away thank you and apart from some bruises and a nasty graze on my leg when I was blown ten yards down the road by the explosion, I am on top form.'

'And you left the truck there?'

'Yes, I had no further use for it.'

'I see.' And Havering had made a note on a piece of paper. 'And what about your residence permit? How did you manage that?

'Oh I didn't bother about that. I just didn't stop at the police post. The man was asleep and I missed him in the fog. It's easily done you know. Did you enjoy your visit to Bangkok?'

'Don't try to be funny Wrighton, you are in deep trouble.'

'Well someone has to be.'

'Who were you copying documents for?'

At this point Cockcroft, although loathe to interrupt the performance, had requested a clarification and Havering had outlined how he had found Wrighton and Mac Macleod abstracting documents from the files and copying them for some other organisation yet to be discovered. It sounded a little fantastic but Havering probably knew what he was doing. Old Wrighton wasn't going without a fight though. Cockcroft could still remember back to the London office and Wrighton's angrily pointing finger that had been levelled at his chest when Cockcroft had told him that he was being posted out to Bangladesh. Wrighton had been close to losing his temper then but now... Cockcroft looked at his eyes. There was something there. Something indefinable but full of unuttered menace.

'Well Wrighton? What have you got to say to that? Who were you copying the documents for?'

'Which documents?'

'The ones you were copying, damn you!'

'Which ones?'

'You know damn well which ones.'

'Show me.'

And then Havering had stubbed out his cigarette and turned to Cockcroft in a slightly ingratiating manner and explained again about the documents but all that Cockcroft had retained of the explanation was the image of Havering's hand, fidgeting with the ashtray. It was irritating. Cockcroft had asked, quite gently,

'And where are the documents? Can I see them?'

Havering prevaricating, more ashtray fiddling and then they had been interrupted by a peon who had insisted on giving Wrighton an envelope; an achievement that merited the Victoria Cross in the face of Havering's vein-pulsing fury but he had been rewarded by a kind word in Bengali from Wrighton which he had worn as his medal.

'And this writ!' Havering had exclaimed . 'Striking one of the Bengali surveyors! Our colleagues on this project! How can you ever justify that? It's monstrous! I tell you sir, it has taken all my effort to keep Wrighton out of trouble and this project running since he has been "assisting" me.'

Cockcroft had looked at the writ from curiosity. Fiscal stamp and squiggly writing. It was quite attractive in a garish way. Of course it made no sense to him at all. He had glanced up from it to cast an eye over the alleged aggressor. He was sitting comfortably in the back of his chair in a relaxed attitude, his hands crossed across the envelope in his lap. Havering was leaning forward to the desk, fiddling with a cigarette in the runnel of the ash tray. Fiddling, always fiddling. 'Tell me about the concrete pier failure, Havering,' he had suggested. 'That was a masterly telex that you sent me on the subject. Did Wrighton have any hand in that?'

'Oh yes, did he have a hand in it! Within two days of me discovering the fault, Abdul Haq was on the blower about it to me from the MFA. That is the kind of assistance I got from Wrighton! Shooting his mouth off at some arty farty party no doubt.'

'Oh dear, we don't really like our secrets to be broadcast around the ministries Mr. Wrighton.'

'I understand that sir.'

'Tell me Havering, how was the consistency of the suspect concrete tested?'

'Well I put it all in the telex.'

'Yes but just remind me.'

'I don't remember now sir, I can look it up.'

'Mr. Wrighton, wasn't reinforced concrete structures one of your specialities?'

'Yes sir.'

'And did you blab to Abdul Haq about it?'

'No sir.'

'Who did?'

'I hesitate to say sir.'

'It was that bloody woman interpreter wasn't it? Mrs. Clam Chowder or whatever, wasn't it?'

'I believe that it was probably a woman. Since I told nobody and Rubena Chowdhry, the interpreter, told nobody, that only really leaves–'

'What are you saying Wrighton?' Havering was black with menace.

'Yes can you explain yourself Wrighton?'

'I was merely saying that since it was not me and it was not Mrs. Chowdhry then the information must have come from someone that Mr. Havering had told.'

'I told no-one, Wrighton, no-one! Do you hear?'

'Except–'

'What do you mean "except"?'

'Well I expect that you told Mrs. Havering, It's only natural.'

'Mary doesn't talk about my work to anybody.'

'Are you saying,' Cockcroft had enquired, 'that she knows about your work but doesn't tell anybody?'

'Exactly. My wife knows her place.'

'Well it's not what she said to me,' Wrighton had announced calmly.

'You what?' Havering had shouted and Wrighton had continued, unimpressed by Havering's intimidation.

'What she said to me indicated that it was she who had told Abdul Haq.'

'Mary said that to you? My wife, said that to you?'

'As good as.'

'As good as!' Havering was sneering in disbelief now. 'She hardly knows Abdul Haq. Only met him once or twice.'

'She gave me the impression that she knew him very well.'

'I don't believe you!'

'Well I suggest that you ask her.'

'I bloody well will. I bloody well will!' And then a slight shadow had passed across Havering's mind, rattling odd doubts perhaps, reviving old suspicions. Wrighton was playing very cleverly, he was shaking Havering almost to the foundations and yet, he had provided no tangible denial of the charges that Havering had laid against him. As far as Cockcroft was concerned, they still stood and Wrighton, however smart he was being, was still under suspicion.

But Cockcroft had had enough, his patience was wearing thin, enjoyable as the game was it was time that they came to the judge's decision. He hadn't at that time realised just how far away he was from the final score.

'Right then, so what's the decision Havering? What do you think ought to be done with Wrighton? You're in charge out here.'

A thinly veiled look of satisfaction trailed across Havering's face.

'I don't want him on the project.'

'What have you got against him?'

'Well... well... all that we have just been through. His incompetence, his disobedience... his... his–'

'What do you say to that Wrighton?'

'I am sure everything can be explained to your satisfaction.'

'All right then, explain that!' Havering had snapped, tapping the writ on the desk and sitting back for the first time with a certain smugness.

'Well, it is a writ but then we should not take these things too seriously in Bangladesh.'

'Assault is fairly serious, Wrighton.'

'Yes, but I didn't actually do it.'

'The writ says you did.'

'Oh I agree that the writ says that I did. It would not be of any use to you if it didn't. But then if I put money in the right place I could get an affidavit swearing that I was the King of England, no problem. What I have done, in fact, is to have the writ invalidated since it was obvious to any sane person that I was incapable of assaulting anybody and its continued validity was liable to cause hindrance to the project.'

'You've done what?' Havering exploded.

Wrighton had drawn a sheet of paper from his pocket.

'It's a little creased, I'm afraid but as you can see this is a letter from the Ministry of Justice annulling the writ since it was patently dishonest. You can keep that copy. I have another at home. Safely at home.'

Cockcroft was not sure of the legality of the scenario which was developing before him.

'Wrighton do I understand you to say that this writ is now completely invalid?'

'That is correct, sir.'

'He's bluffing! He wrote this letter himself.'

'Phone up the Ministry of Justice if you don't believe me... you can speak to Rubena's uncle.'

'You mean that some jumped-up Bangla in Mrs. Chowdhry's family has done this for you?'

'I wouldn't put it in those terms but I would suggest that his word carried more weight within the judiciary than that of Abra Huda, the alleged plaintiff.'

'But that's corrupt!'

'Yes, isn't it? It took me a long time to work out that the important thing was to make the corruption work for you. I trust, sir, that we can dispose of the writ?'

Cockcroft had nodded without shifting his gaze from Havering and Wrighton had casually tossed the writ into the bin.

'Ah, what about the truck?' Havering had bounced back to the attack. 'You steal a World Bank truck and set light to it. What will they think of that?'

'Well Mr. Wrighton, what do you say to that? And it had better be good.' Cockcroft had added that rider for dramatic effect for he was certain now that he had no need to threaten Wrighton. He appeared to know exactly where he wanted to go.

'On the way up I took the liberty of leafing through some of the accounts records. I know Mr. Havering does not like me doing it, but I have taken a photocopy of a couple that you might find interesting. If you look at item fourteen just here, you will see that it relates to the writing-off as a total loss of the Land Rover which had been assigned to Raymond Line, and this is the World Bank acceptance of this action which was audited and agreed under "miscellaneous business" at the last meeting of the sub-finance working party. So you see, as far as the World Bank is concerned, they wrote off that Land Rover. It no longer existed and as it did not belong to Consolidated, you could not deny me the use of it. I could do what I liked with it. It belonged to nobody. It concerned nobody. I could even allow it to be burned to a wreck without causing anybody the slightest distress.'

'Yeah but–'

'No Havering, I think we must accept this. Have you got anything else against Wrighton?

Before the sweating Havering could mouth a reply, Wrighton had remarked quietly, as he idly looked through some snapshots which he had taken from the envelope in his lap, 'I think now is time for me to take the initiative Mr. Cockcroft; you two have had it for long enough.'

Cockcroft had found himself dumbfounded for once in his life.

'Well I–'

'Just look at these photographs, they are rather interesting.'

And apparently, it had all started with a brick that Wrighton had seen in a market somewhere which had no doubt been a stolen load and this brick was the wrong colour but it had the same letters on it as the company that had appropriated Consolidated's aggregate for the piers and then when he had been out checking some survey points or other, up country he had come across a valve station that was not marked on the map and Havering had lied about it, which had made him think that something was going on and then he had found that a load of twelve-inch pipe had been ordered and flogged off for peanuts to the same company whose proprietor, he had discovered, was no lesser a personage than Major Abdul Haq M.P. and when Havering had confiscated Wrighton's proof and confined him to Dhaka he had felt strongly enough about it to disobey him and go up country where he had visited the constituency of this Major Abdul Haq M.P. There, he had found a brickworks producing bricks in gas-fired ovens which was funny because the pipeline didn't go within seven miles of it and yet when you visited the valve station whose existence no-one acknowledged, and looked through the telephoto lens you could see that pressure reducers had been fixed to the Christmas tree and that a pipeline obviously led off due east to Baderpur and you could even distinguish, on this photo here sir, that the drop in pressure as recorded upon the gauges was from nine hundred p.s.i. to eight hundred and fifty p.s.i. which was exactly the difference required to run a twelve-inch pipe from a fourteen-inch pipe and...

It had been a masterly piece of detection completed in the face of determined obstruction and presented with the precision of a man who now knew what he wanted.

Wrighton had gently nudged Cockcroft into some important observations by his simple, ingenuous clarifications; 'Bell lent me his camera.... Rubena volunteered to come as interpreter... Geoff Hardwicke made some enquiries for me.' – Havering had been unable to call anybody to his aid except Major Abdul Haq M.P. yet the type of people who had willingly helped Wrighton, although not powerful individually, had proven themselves stronger than such a treacherous liaison.

There must be some quality in Wrighton's character that makes people want him to succeed. This same quality must be tragically lacking in Havering's. Havering must have upset a lot of people.

Cockcroft fished for his shoes and began to pull them on. And to think, if only Abdul Haq had waited for a couple or three years, he could have had gas from the Chittagong extension whose opening Cockcroft was now having to celebrate. But of course, Haq would have had to pay for that gas, unlike the unmetered supply that he had arranged to have installed at his brickworks.

He pulled on his other shoe and threw his *Times* onto the empty seat at the side of him. The seat-belt warning had just come on and through the window he could see the twinkling of lights as with a thud the undercarriage locked down and the airliner began its descent to Dhaka.

'Let's hope they've cleared all the bloody goats off the runway this time,' he muttered to himself.

Even at six o'clock in the evening the heat in Dhaka was like stepping into an oven. He gasped in dismay. He was getting too old for this type of caper.

Confusion reigned in the baggage hall where the Bengali travellers noisily clambered over the moving carpet, dragging bundles and bags back from the jaws of oblivion.

'Mr. Cockcroft, sir,' a voice called, 'your baggage is over here.'

He turned.

'Thank God for that!'

Wrighton had loaded his suitcase onto a baggage trolley.

'Did you have a good flight sir?'

'So so. Look, Wrighton, I don't want to bugger about in here–'

'No problem sir, follow me.' He led the trolley straight up to a customs bench. 'Hello Abdul Malik.'

The Bengali customs man grinned at him.

'Ah, Mr. Wrighton. How do you do?'

They shook hands.

'Abdul, this gentleman is big boss. My big boss. He's coming as a guest of the Government for the pipeline celebrations. He's got nothing to declare, O.K.?'

'Nothing to declare?'

'No camera, no video, no stereo.'

'No camera?'

'Sorry, we're in a hurry, Abdul.' He thrust a bundle of taka into the man's hands and indicated to Cockcroft that they should leave. The customs man made as if to oppose their departure but thought again and pocketed the bundle of notes. Outside, the Land Rover was waiting, attended by a driver in khaki trousers.

'If you sit in the back sir, I'll get your cases put in.'

Cockcroft sat in the air-conditioned van and sighed thankfully. His move from the airport to the vehicle had only been a few yards but already his shirt was wringing wet. Wrighton climbed in beside him.

'We'll go to my house sir. You can have a shit, shower and shave, and then I'm afraid we'll have to leave at about half seven to go to the dinner.'

Cockcroft nodded whilst Wrighton turned and gave orders to the driver. It appeared that the driver's name was 'Shithead'.

The dinner had been good. Cockcroft realised that he had been expecting something uneatably native but the cook was Australian and every dish had been recognisable and edible. The speeches had been made and he was now content to sit wearily watching the expatriates revelling in yet another excuse to dance with each other's wives.

Wrighton, tanned and healthy, looked distinguished in a dinner jacket. He had turned out to be quite an ambassador for Consolidated. He had tackled the tangle of problems left by Havering's departure with diplomacy but also with the right degree of astute practicality that had ensured success with the minimum of fuss.

But what had astonished Cockcroft more was the appearance of Marion. Thinking back to their lunch together at the Grill he had retained the vague image of a rather inconsequential, mousey woman who had wanted, for reasons of her own, to not let her husband out of her sight, but here she was, laughing and gay and creating quite an impression. She was resplendent in an emerald evening dress and displaying a very neat pair of shoulders.

Suddenly, a lanky man with a beard broke through the dancers and, towing a blonde woman in his wake, made straight for their table.

'Well if it isn't old Stewart!' he shouted in enthusiastic greeting.

Wrighton bounced up.

'Geoff! Sandra! Where did you spring from? Kathmandu too cold for you?'

'We were just flying through. We're staying with the Bennets.' He nodded at a couple at a distant table. 'They brought us out for the evening. So, how are you? Long time no see.'

'Come and sit down. Let me introduce you to everyone. This is Mr. Cockcroft, my director from London.'

Cockcroft rose heavily and shook hands. The blonde woman gave him quite a pert smile. He looked thoughtfully at Hardwicke.

'I have heard of you Mr. Hardwicke. What do you do in Nepal?'

Sandra sat and looked at Marion. Marion looked back.

'I'm in the Commercial Section.'

'That means he's spying on the Chinese,' Wrighton said mischievously.

'Take no notice. Stewart is wildly inaccurate as usual,' Hardwicke remonstrated.

Wrighton continued, 'And this is Marion, my wife.– Sandra and Geoff Hardwicke late of the British High Commission, Dhaka, now of the British Embassy, Nepal.'

Marion leaned forwards to shake hands. It was not only a nice pair of shoulders that she possessed, Cockcroft observed.

'How do you do.'

Cockcroft watched Wrighton as he continued around the table.

'And Major Abdul Haq...'

'Ah yes.' Hardwicke became professional for an instant. 'I must congratulate you sir. If the *Kathmandu Times* is reliable I understand that you have a new ministry.'

Cockcroft did not openly acknowledge the fact, but he admired the way Haq operated. Here was a man he could do business with.

Major Abdul Haq M.P. graciously inclined his head towards Hardwicke.

'In view of the successful inauguration of the Chittagong Extension Pipeline, largely due to Mr. Wrighton here,' he smiled smoothly, 'the President saw fit to make me Minister for Power.' He indicated the clerk sitting at the side of him. 'I even have a personal assistant!'

'Oh yes, of course!' Wrighton added, 'And this is Rubena Chowdhry, the Minister's personal assistant.'

'By your appointment you have achieved a lot, Mrs. Chowdhry. I hope you will not consider me undiplomatic if I congratulate you as well.'

'Thank you Mr. Hardwicke. You are most kind. But I am still having a lot more to do.'

'Rubena is a very determined woman,' Wrighton laughed.

She sounds as if she eats rickshaws for breakfast, Cockcroft thought. No wonder Haq looks uneasy.

The band straggled into a slow waltz. Sandra Hardwicke jumped up and clapped her hands.

'Oh come on Stewart. Come and dance with me.'

As Wrighton opened his mouth to speak, Cockcroft saw a glittering sparkle of anticipation suddenly spring into his eyes, almost as if it had caught him unawares, but even as Cockcroft watched, Wrighton looked across at his wife and his eyes, those strangely hazel eyes of his, dimmed and the light just faded away.

'I am sorry, Mrs. Hardwicke,' she said. 'My husband does not dance.'

Turn over for details of more books
by Martin Lloyd.

Every Picture

'... a tender and engaging love story...'

When the son of an earl meets the daughter of
a coal miner in the doorway of the art college he
does not tell her that he is a viscount.

Why should he?

How was he to know that their paths would cross
and recross and that he would fall in
love with her?

And once that has happened, he finds it impossible to
tell her the truth for fear of losing her. At the very
moment that they finally admit their feelings for one
another, the relationship is wrenched asunder as their
lives take a violent and unpredictable turn, casting their
two destinies onto divergent courses.

Will they ever meet again?

Published by Queen Anne's Fan ISBN: 9780 9547 1505 2

The
Chinese
Transfer

Martin Lloyd

The

Chinese Transfer

a thriller romance that you will
not want to put down

'...this is storytelling as it used to be...'

Paris in the 1970s – student demonstrations, union strikes and
oppressive heat. Coach driver Simon Laperche is sent to Orly
Airport to pick up a Chinese group and take them to their
hotel in the city. A run of the mill job. He could do it with his
eyes shut. It was a pity about the guide, but then, he could
not expect to please everybody.

Abruptly, things go wrong. The plane is diverted to Lyon and
Laperche is ordered to drive his coach south to meet it... and he
has to take that infuriating guide with him. Unknown to them
both, a terrorist unit has targeted their group and
is intent upon its destruction.

Stalked by the terrorists, the driver and guide continue to bicker
as they struggle to bring their group safely to Paris. Will the
mutual respect which eventually begins to grow between
them prove strong enough when the test comes?

Published by Queen Anne's Fan ISBN: 9780 9547 15021

Rue Amélie

Rue Amélie

Martin Lloyd

another fast-paced thriller from Martin Lloyd.

Following the success of *The Chinese Transfer,* Martin Lloyd takes us back to the seedy side of Paris in the 1970s. Joel LeBatard, a driver for a small-time crook, loses his boss's car and his position. With no job and soon to be thrown out of his bedsit, he accepts a commission from a woman he meets at a funeral, to find out where her father had invested his secret pension.

LeBatard discovers that others are on the same trail – a ruthless big-time gangster whom he has already been stupid enough to upset, and an ex-colleague from his army days who now heads an undercover squad in the Ministry of Defence. They will stop at nothing to get their hands on the very thing that he is looking for, but nobody can tell him what it is.

The hectic action takes them to the four corners of Paris. Whilst pursuing his relentless search, LeBatard struggles with two difficulties: is his new employer telling him the truth and how, in the face of such energy and charm, can he uphold his vow never to get mixed up with another woman?

Published by Queen Anne's Fan ISBN: 9780 9547 1507 6

No Harm
in Looking

A beautifully bound hardback with
nine colour plates.

being a collection of

TALES OF EROTIC FANTASY

for the delectation of

LADIES AND GENTLEMEN ALIKE

*especially illustrated
and published in this edition
for the author's friends.*

K. T. Yalta

Published by Queen Anne's Fan ISBN: 9780 9547 1508 3

Hunting the Golden Lion

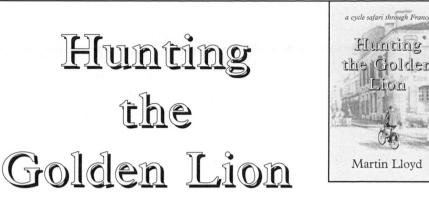

a cycle safari through France

Having recklessly declared in a previous book that it must be possible to cross all of France staying only in hotels called the HOTEL DU LION D'OR, Martin Lloyd is challenged by his critics to prove his assertion in the only way possible – by doing it.

Surely it will be a straightforward and leisurely ride through France? As long as the hotels are no more than a day's cycle ride apart, of course. And if your bicycle has been constructed this century, and if you remember to take with you all that you need... and if your name isn't Martin Lloyd.

Is this why, on the the first day of his safari, he is standing in his pyjamas on a pavement a thousand miles from home, clutching a broken bicycle with a bleeding hand?

Published by Queen Anne's Fan ISBN: 9780 9547 1506 9

MARTIN LLOYD

The Trouble with France

Martin Lloyd's new international
number one blockbusting
bestseller

"...makes Baedeker's look like a guidebook..."

When Martin Lloyd set out on his holiday to Suffolk why did he
end up in Boulogne? What caused Max the Mad Alsatian to steal
his map and what did the knitted grandma really think of his
display of hot plate juggling? The answers to these and many
more mysteries are to be found in THE TROUBLE WITH FRANCE.

THE TROUBLE WITH FRANCE contains no recipes and no hand
drawn maps. It docs not recount how somebody richer than you
went to a part of France that you have never heard of, bought a
stone ruin for a song and converted it into a luxurious retreat
which they expect you to finance by buying their book.

Nor is it the self satisfied account of another ultra fit expedition
cyclist abseiling down Everest on a penny farthing but Martin
Lloyd attempting an uneventful ride on a mundane bicycle
through an uninteresting part of France... and failing
with outstanding success.

THE TROUBLE WITH FRANCE is destined to be a worldwide
success now that Margaret's Mum has been down the
road and told her friend Pat about it.

Published by Queen Anne's Fan ISBN: 9780 9547 15007

The Trouble with Spain

MARTIN LLOYD

FROM THE BESTSELLING AUTHOR OF
THE TROUBLE WITH FRANCE *COMES*
THIS EAGERLY AWAITED SEQUEL

'...makes Munchausen look like a liar...'

Still smarting from his brutal encounter with Gaul as detailed in his much acclaimed book, THE TROUBLE WITH FRANCE, Martin Lloyd drags his bicycle over the Pyrenees to pursue the twin delights of sun and breakfast.

What factor will defeat his proposed headlong plunge into raw hedonism? Will it be his profound and extensive ignorance of Spanish history or perhaps his coarse insensitivity to the culture of the peninsula? Or would it be the damning condemnation that he is just too lazy to learn the language?

Read THE TROUBLE WITH SPAIN and you will discover nothing about bull fights and enjoy no colourful descriptions of sensual flamenco dancing but you will learn why you cannot train goldfish to be guard dogs and you will clearly understand why even Martin Lloyd's trousers ran away from him.

CAUTION

This book contains moderate use of humour, some expressions in foreign language and a short but ultimately frustrating scene in a lady's bedroom.

Published by Queen Anne's Fan ISBN: 9780 9547 15014

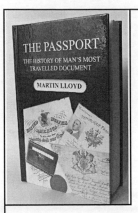

THE PASSPORT

The History of Man's Most
Travelled Document
by Martin Lloyd
THIRD EDITON
Hardback 294 pp. 83 b&w illustrations

The passport is a document familiar to many, used and recognised worldwide and yet it has no basis in law: one country cannot oblige another to admit its subjects simply by issuing a document. But the state, by insisting on the requirement to hold a passport, provides for itself a neat, self-financing data collection and surveillance system. This well illustrated book tells for the first time the story of the passport from its earliest origins to its latest high-tech developments. Handwritten documents adorned with wax seals, modern versions in plastic covers, diplomatic passports and wartime safe conducts, all drawn from the author's collection, complement the exciting exploits of spies and criminals and the tragic real life experiences of refugees. Whether recounting the birth of the British blue passport of the 1920s or divulging the secrets of today's machine readable passport, Martin Lloyd has written an informative and engrossing history book which is accessible to everyone.

'*...a lively and thoughtful book...*'
SUNDAY TELEGRAPH

Published by Queen Anne's Fan ISBN: 9780 9573 6392 2

Neither Civil nor Servant

Twenty-four years in the Immigration Service

Paperback 442 pp. sixty b&w illustrations.

Neither
Civil
nor
Servant

Twenty-four years in the
Immigration Service.

Martin Lloyd.

When Britain joined the Common Market, Martin Lloyd joined the UK Immigration Service.
For the next twenty-four years he rubbed shoulders with royalty and rascals while stamping passports in the company of scholars, schemers and scatterbrains.

This colourful narrative traces Martin Lloyd's progress from Heathrow's Terminal Three, when Concorde was a novelty, through the first waves of political asylum refugees to the complexities of manning the United Kingdom's first real international land border – the Channel tunnel.

His dealings with the dangerous, the illegal, the lunatic and the famous are recounted within the framework of the politics and the social issues of the time. This is no high treatise on the international right of the movement of labour; it is a down-to-earth account of how the Immigration Service functioned at the human level and of the challenges faced by those employed to police the borders of the United Kingdom.

Martin Lloyd is an amusing and entertaining public speaker and brings to this work the wit, humour and sharply focused observation for which he is well known.

Published by Queen Anne's Fan ISBN: 9780 9573 6390 8

Fire, Smoke and Iron
Fuego, Humo y Hierro
Spanish artists and the
Bilbao iron industry

Martin Lloyd

Fire Smoke and Iron

Fuego, Humo y Hierro

Spanish artists and the Bilbao iron industry.

Paperback 66 pages,
95 full colour illustrations and 35 black & white.

Bilbao in Spain has been producing iron for centuries, drawing
in workers from all over the country. Its rapid industrialisation in
the nineteenth century was helped in no little measure by British
capital and entrepreneurship. Ships carried Welsh coal to Spain
and brought back Spanish pig-iron for the steelworks of South
Wales. By 1985, it was all over. But the rise, heyday and demise
of the Bilbaoan iron industry has been forever fixed in oils,
water colours and bronze.

This book shows how iron is made into steel; illustrating the
machinery involved and explaining the processes used.
It then illustrates the evocative paintings which have recorded
this industry in its various stages and explains and
interprets the activity depicted.

Published by Queen Anne's Fan ISBN: 9780 9573 639-3-9